Praise for the Mundy's Landing series

"Take one part Brothers Grimm, one part James Patterson, one part magic, and you've got Wendy Corsi Staub's remarkable new *Blue Moon*. You never know who's around the next corner or coming at you from out of the past."

Reed Farrel Coleman, *New York Times* bestselling author of *Where It Hurts*

"Staub is at it again, offering up a new and terrifying series that will have readers wanting more. This book has a terrific plotline that keeps readers guessing up until the last page . . ."

Suspense Magazine on *Blood Red*

"I loved *Blood Red* . . . it's suspenseful and scary. This is a serious winner!"

Alison Gaylin, author of *What Remains of Me*

"A quiet town's dark past and a serial killer's quest for his ideal victim create a perfect storm in Staub's . . . new thriller."

Kirkus Reviews on *Blood Red*

"A fast-paced, thrilling ride of suspense and terror that will keep readers guessing till the end."

Fresh Fiction on *Blood Red*

By Wendy Corsi Staub

Mundy's Landing Series

BONE WHITE
BLUE MOON
BLOOD RED

And

THE BLACK WIDOW
THE PERFECT STRANGER
THE GOOD SISTER
SHADOWKILLER
SLEEPWALKER
NIGHTWATCHER
HELL TO PAY
SCARED TO DEATH
LIVE TO TELL

WENDY CORSI STAUB

BONE WHITE

Mundy's Landing
Book Three

WM

WILLIAM MORROW
An Imprint of HarperCollins*Publishers*

Map courtesy of Brody Staub.

BONE WHITE. Copyright © 2017 by Wendy Corsi Staub. All rights reserved. Printed in the United States of America. No part of this book may be used or reproduced in any manner whatsoever without written permission except in the case of brief quotations embodied in critical articles and reviews. For information, address HarperCollins Publishers, 195 Broadway, New York, NY 10007.

First William Morrow mass market printing: April 2017

ISBN 978-0-06-234977-4

William Morrow® and HarperCollins® are registered trademarks of HarperCollins Publishers.

17 18 19 20 21 QGM 10 9 8 7 6 5 4 3 2 1

FOR MY COUSINS BILL AND KAREN CORSI—
Always there for me,
Always upbeat,
Always loving and dearly loved.

For my husband Mark,
And for our March birthday boys, Morgan and Brody.

Acknowledgments

I express my gratitude to booksellers, librarians, and readers everywhere; to Megan Rutter and Stacy Amico Ruvio for patiently answering my questions about forensics and genetics; to Heather Graham Pozzessere for the title; to my editor, Lucia Macro; her assistant, Carolyn Coons; Liate Stehlik, Maria Silva, Shawn Nicholls, and countless others at HarperCollins who played a role in bringing this book to print; to my literary agent, Laura Blake Peterson, and my film agent, Holly Frederick, at Curtis Brown, Limited; to Carol Fitzgerald and the gang at Bookreporter; to Cissy, Degan, Celeste, and Susan at Writerspace; to Alison Gaylin and Greg Herren; to John Valeri; to Peter Meluso; to Mark Staub and Morgan Staub for the manuscript feedback and marketing support; to Brody Staub for putting Mundy's Landing on the map again.

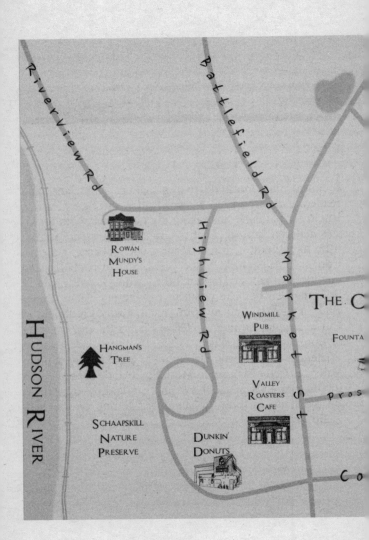

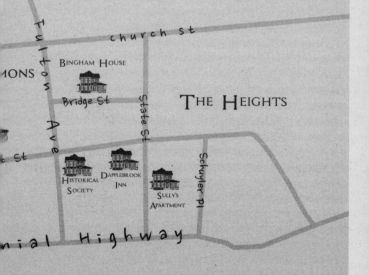

MUNDY'S LANDING

N

Church St

Bingham House

Bridge St

THE HEIGHTS

Fulton Ave

State St

MONS

St

Historical Society

Dapplebrook Inn

Sully's Apartment

Schuyler Pl

nial Highway

Prologue

July 1666
Hudson Valley, New York

The crowd jeers, and Jeremiah Mundy grips his younger sisters' hands, steeling himself for the unthinkable tragedy about to unfold.

Thou art a man now, he reminds himself, echoing the last words his father, James, said to him weeks ago, before he and Mother were taken away.

At fourteen, Jeremiah felt in that moment, and feels in this one, like a mere child. Yet he promised his parents that he would accept his manly obligation, taking charge of his sisters and the household in their absence. He just never dreamed the absence would endure for weeks, let alone . . . forever.

But forever it shall be.

James and Elizabeth Mundy are sentenced to die today at the hands of the black-clad, hooded hangman who, like the others present, recently arrived in this year-old colony perched on the Hudson River's western bank. They were due last fall, having traveled from England with sorely needed supplies. But a harsh winter froze the river before the reinforcements could make their way north from the port of Manhattan. The Mundy family and their fellow settlers were left to fend for themselves for nearly five months.

Day in and out, Jeremiah trudged with his father through a swirling white maelstrom to chop wood and feed a fire that did little to stave off the bitter cold. They could not hunt, nor could they forage. For a long time, there was no way to feed the relentless hunger. The family nearly starved to death.

But they did not. They were the lucky ones. They found the means to salvation—horrific means, and yet, as Jeremiah overheard his parents saying, what choice did they have?

Starvation does peculiar things to a person. The hunger is unbearable, a living, breathing monster growing within your gut, its ferocious growls drowning out the voice of reason. You will do anything, anything within reason—and eventually, anything well beyond the realm of reason—to feed the beast. And when you have—when you've done the unthinkable, and the agony has abated—you'll fear not just for your life, but for your sanity.

There will be no turning back.

When at last the supplies and reinforcements arrived in May, only the Mundys remained of the three dozen original English settlers.

"Look there! Satan himself blazes in the Goody Mundy's eyes!" a man proclaims from the crowd behind Jeremiah.

"Ay, and peculiar eyes they be," comes the reply, and he recognizes the rasping voice of the Goodwife Barker, whose brother was among the first of the winter's casualties.

Peculiar . . .

Jeremiah closes his own eyes: one a piercing shade of blue, the other a chalky gray.

Years ago, back in England, he caught a glimpse of

himself in his grandmother's looking glass and was startled to see that he, like his mother, had one pale iris and one fully pigmented.

"'Tis a rare gift," his beloved grandmother told him, and he believed it . . .

Until now.

Rare, yes. Not a gift, but a curse.

The subject of his mother's "peculiar" eyes came up at the trial—offered as additional evidence of Elizabeth Mundy's guilt, lest there be any claim that her initial confession had been coerced through bodily torture.

A stalwart Jeremiah had witnessed that torture, a public spectacle that unfolded on the riverbank on a gray spring day. The entire colony turned out to watch, bristling with anticipation like an amusement-deprived London audience flocking to post-Restoration theater.

His father was first to be strapped to the ducking stool as Jeremiah, helpless, stood apart from the gawkers and gossipers. Their voices and the chirping chatter of woodland creatures were drowned out by violent splashing as James Mundy was repeatedly submerged in the murky current. Each time he sputtered to the surface, he defiantly proclaimed his innocence, determined to let them drown him—until the moment they assured him that his wife would be spared the same punishment if he confessed.

And so he did.

Jeremiah's fists clenched as he listened to the confession. Either way, his father would die: drowned in the river, or sentenced to death for murder. At least James Mundy had preserved his wife's dignity and her life . . . or so he believed.

They had lied.

Jeremiah's mother had her own turn on the ducking stool. A pair of burly men—the same men who escort her to her doom this morning—held Jeremiah back when he tried to rush to her side. She endured nearly three hours before confessing to the heinous crimes of which she and her husband had been accused.

The trial, now a mere formality, was swift; the verdict unanimous; the sentence so inevitable that the platform was being built beneath the sturdy branches of an oak tree even before the trial had concluded.

The crowd assembled at sunrise, as eager to know that the devil had been banished from the settlement as they are thirsty for diversion from daily drudgery.

Eyes squeezed shut to block out the horrific sight of the crude wooden structure, Jeremiah scours his memory for the image of his mother's face as it once was—serene, affectionate, exhilarated by the promise of life in this New World. But he can envision it only pale with worry, and then—oh, and then contorted in feverish wrath as starvation took hold.

At the telltale pressing of the crowd around him, he opens his eyes to see that it has parted, allowing the procession into the clearing.

Flanked by pairs of the settlement's strongest men, Mother and Father appear even more frail than they were a few days ago, when they were sentenced to death after they confessed to murder—and worse. Far, far worse.

Twelve-year-old Charity, the elder but smaller of Jeremiah's sisters, begins to whimper. Priscilla, eight, remains as silent and stoic as her brother, grasping his hand firmly.

The magistrate reads the charges in a booming voice and orders that the death sentence be carried out immediately.

Jeremiah shifts his gaze toward the forest on the far end of the clearing as an escape fantasy takes shape. His parents shall break away and run toward the trees. They'll disappear into the dense woods and find their way to the water, eluding their captors and the executioner's twin nooses, and—

A gleeful roar disrupts the comforting daydream. Elizabeth Mundy has fainted. The brutes yank her upright again and drag her toward the gallows beneath the oak.

Priscilla remains steadfast at Jeremiah's side, but Charity tugs his hand. "I cannot bear to watch."

"We must."

With a plaintive wail, his sister wrenches herself from his grasp and flees, capturing the crowd's interest.

Jeremiah will comfort her when the ordeal is over.

Someone touches his shoulder, and he turns to see Goody Dowling, whose husband and sons are building a home on land adjacent to the Mundys'.

Her expression is not unkind. "I shall see to the girl."

She hurries away, leaving him dumbfounded.

He's scarcely wondered what might become of him and his sisters after today, but when he does allow himself to speculate, he assumes the other settlers will shun them, forcing them to leave this place.

Where will they even go?

When they fled England a year ago, they were destitute, evicted by their landholder with nowhere to turn in an overpopulated country. Their only hope of salvation lay across the sea. The British had recently wrangled control of the New Netherland colony from the Dutch and renamed it New York, luring settlers like the Mundys with the promise of opportunity, freedom, and abundant land.

Even if Jeremiah and his sisters could afford to pay for passage back to England, they'd be as alone there as they are here. Grandmother was struck by the plague before they left. When she passes on, Aunt Felicity will join them in the New World, perhaps already having begun the journey. They have no other family to speak of.

Here, they may not have relatives or friends, but they do have a home—if home can be defined as land, shelter, and food. The last has finally come in abundance with crops in the fields, fish in the river, game in the forests.

What little Jeremiah knows of the world beyond this settlement is formidable and fraught with danger. Mountains and forests teem with feral creatures and unfriendly natives. Neighboring settlements are few and far between, populated by the Dutch, no ally to the English.

Having glimpsed the teeming port of Manhattan last year and found it rife with strangers and filth, he has no desire to make his way back accompanied by two vulnerable little girls.

Thanks to a stranger's unexpected benevolence toward the imminent orphan and the crowd's murmuring of sympathy as Charity fled, Jeremiah wonders whether he and his sisters may be permitted to stay on in their parents' home. It isn't the ideal scenario, yet it's the only one he can fathom.

Now, however, isn't the time to plan for the future. Somehow, he must find the strength and courage to focus on the present.

Thou art a man now.

His parents stand on the scaffold, side by side, hands bound, facing the crowd.

Father's jaw is set, his gaze fixed straight ahead. Mother searches the crowd as the hangman wraps a length of rope around her skirt, binding her legs.

Her gaze lands on Jeremiah. There is no evidence now of the madness that gripped her last winter in the throes of famine. In his final glimpse of her peculiar eyes, he sees a frantic question.

Then the hangman blindfolds her with a length of cloth and commands the prisoners to bow their heads for the nooses.

Sunlight glints against the gold ring on his mother's hand, and Jeremiah swallows a rush of bile.

Priscilla's grasp tightens on his hand.

The hangman nods, satisfied that the nooses are fixed. An expectant hush falls over the crowd as he descends a rickety ladder creaking under his weight.

The command is given, and in that moment, Jeremiah finds his voice at last. "Fear not!" he calls out, and to his own ears, his voice is shockingly strong and sure. "I shall protect my sisters and we shall make you proud and—"

His final message is lost in a roar of approval from the crowd as the platform drops.

Mercifully, the taut rope snaps Elizabeth Mundy's fragile neck, killing her instantly. But James has the brawny build of a man who has spent his thirty-three years enduring long hours of physical labor. His muscular neck sustains the fall and he is left to strangle at the end of the rope, his body contorting with futile efforts to breathe.

His agonizing gasps render the assemblage mute in collective horror. They had turned out to the promise of entertainment, only to bear witness to a grotesque scene that will forever after haunt their nightmares. They scuttle away until just the hangman and the Mundy siblings remain beside the scaffold, accompanied by a flock of fat gray geese that has alighted nearby like scavengers.

Watching his mother's corpse sway gently beside her husband's agonizing spasms, Jeremiah remembers another death. Brutal as the arctic air on that February day, it left a numbness that has yet to subside. Perhaps it never will.

Priscilla's sturdy little body wracked with silent sobs, she buries her face against Jeremiah's chest, dampening his shirt with her tears. He holds her fast against him, refusing to budge his gaze from their father until at last his struggle has ended.

He watches as the hangman cuts his parents' bodies down from the branch to be hauled away for unceremonious burial.

Priscilla pulls back to look up at him, her blue eyes raw and swollen. "What will happen to us now?"

"We shall return to our home and never speak of this again to anyone but each other and Charity. No matter what happens, for the rest of our lives. Do you understand?"

"I do."

Satisfied, he looks over at the hangman, loading their dead father onto a cart like a sack of grain.

"Wait here for me, Priscilla. I shall return momentarily."

She slumps against the oak's broad, sturdy trunk as he walks over to the man.

"Sir," he says, "may I have a moment with my mother?"

The man regards him for a long moment, then nods.

Jeremiah crouches on the grass and reaches among the folds of his mother's skirt. Her hands are bound with a strip of cloth, fingers clasped as if in prayer. To the man standing above, it may appear that he wishes to touch her hand one last time in farewell.

But Jeremiah's fingers close over the gold gimmal ring she's wearing. He tugs. Her finger is bent, and it fits her snugly, difficult to remove.

I must have it.

He tugs harder, and feels the sickening crack of bone as he removes the ring.

Closing it in his fist, he bends to press his lips against her forehead.

There, he whispers the final message she hadn't heard above the roar of the crowd. Nor, God willing, had anyone else.

"We shall never tell."

Chapter 1

July 20, 2016
Los Angeles, California

We shall never tell.

Strange, the thoughts that go through your head when you're standing at an open grave.

Not that Emerson Mundy knew anything about open graves before today. Her father's funeral is the first she's ever attended, and she's the sole mourner.

Ah, at last, a perk to living a life without many—*any*—loved ones: you don't spend much time grieving, unless you count the pervasive ache for the things you never had.

The minister, who came with the cemetery package and never even met Jerry Mundy, is rambling on about souls and salvation. Emerson hears only *We shall never tell*—the closing line in an old letter she found yesterday in the crawl space of her childhood home. It had been written in 1676 by a young woman named Priscilla Mundy, addressed to her brother, Jeremiah.

The Mundys were among the seventeenth-century English colonists who settled on the eastern bank of the Hudson River, about a hundred miles north of New York City. Their first winter was so harsh that the river froze, stranding their supply ship and additional colonists in the New York harbor. When the ship arrived after the thaw, all but five settlers had starved to death.

Jeremiah; Priscilla; their sister, Charity; and their parents had eaten human flesh to stay alive. James and Elizabeth Mundy swore they'd only cannibalized those who'd already died, but the God-fearing, well-fed newcomers couldn't fathom such wretched butchery. A Puritan justice committee tortured the couple until they confessed to murder, then swiftly tried, convicted, and hanged them.

"Do you think we're related?" Emerson asked her father after learning about the Mundys back in elementary school.

"Nope." Curt answers were typical when she brought up anything Jerry Mundy didn't want to discuss. The past was high on the list.

"That's it? Just *nope*?"

"What else do you want me to say?"

"How about yes?"

"That wouldn't be the truth," he said with a shrug.

"Sometimes the truth isn't very interesting."

"Life is easier when things aren't interesting."

She had no one else to ask about her family history. Dad was an only child, and his parents, Donald and Inez Mundy, had passed away long before she was born. Their headstone is adjacent to the gaping rectangle about to swallow her father's casket. Staring at the inscription, she notices her grandfather's unusual middle initial.

DONALD X. MUNDY, BORN 1900, DIED 1972.

X marks the spot.

Thanks to her passion for history and Robert Louis Stevenson, Emerson's bookworm childhood included a phase when she searched obsessively for buried treasure.

Money was short in their household after two heart attacks left Jerry Mundy on permanent disability.

X marks the spot . . .

No gold doubloon treasure chest buried here. Just dusty old bones of people she never knew.

And now, her father.

The service concludes with a prayer as the coffin is lowered into the ground. The minister clasps her hand and tells her how sorry he is for her loss, then leaves her to sit on a bench and stare at the hillside as the undertakers finish the job.

The sun is beginning to burn through the thick marine layer that swaddles most June and July mornings. Having grown up in Southern California, she knows the sky will be bright blue by mid-afternoon. Tomorrow will be more of the same. By then, she'll be on her way back up the coast, back to her life in Oakland, where the fog rolls in and stays for days, weeks at a time. Funny, but there she welcomes the gray, a soothing shield from real world glare and sharp edges.

Here the seasonal gloom has felt oppressive and depressing.

Emerson watches the undertakers finish the job and load their equipment into a van. After they drive off, she makes her way between neat rows of tombstones to inspect the raked dirt rectangle.

When something is over, you move on, her father told her when she left home nearly two decades ago. She attended Cal State Fullerton with scholarships and maximum financial aid, got her master's at Berkeley, and landed a teaching job in the Bay Area.

But she didn't necessarily move on.

Every holiday, many weekends, and for two whole months every summer, she makes the six-hour drive down to stay with her father. She cooks and cleans for him, and at night they sit together and watch *Wheel of Fortune* reruns.

It used to be because she craved a connection to the only family she had in the world. Lately, though, it was as much because Jerry Mundy needed her.

He pretended that he didn't, that he was taking care of himself and the house, too proud to admit he was failing. He was a shadow of his former self when he died at seventy-six, leaving Emerson alone in the world.

Throughout her motherless childhood, Emerson was obsessed with novels about orphans. *Treasure Island* shared coveted space on her bookshelf with *Anne of Green Gables*, *The Secret Garden*, *The Witch of Blackbird Pond* . . .

She always wondered what would happen to her if her father died. Would she wind up in an orphanage? Would a kindly stranger take her in? Would she live on the streets?

Now that it's happened, he's down there, in the dirt . . . moving on?

She'll never again hear his voice. She'll never see the face so like her own that she can't imagine she inherited any physical characteristic from her mother, Didi—though she can't be certain.

Years ago, she asked her father for a picture—preferably one that showed her mother holding her as a baby, or of her parents together. Maybe she wanted evidence that she and her father had been loved; that the woman who'd abandoned them had once been *normal*—a proud new mother, a happy bride.

Or was it the opposite? Was she hoping to glimpse a hint that Didi Mundy was never normal? Did she expect to confirm that people—normal people—don't just wake up one morning and choose to walk out on a husband and child? That there was always something off about her mother: a telltale gleam in the eye, or a faraway expression—some warning sign her father had overlooked. A sign Emerson herself would be able to recognize, should she ever be tempted to marry.

But there were no images of Didi that she could slip into a frame, or deface with angry black ink, or simply commit to memory.

Exhibit A: Untrustworthy.

Sure, there *had* been plenty of photos, her father admitted unapologetically. He'd gotten rid of everything.

There were plenty of pictures of her and Dad, though.

Exhibit B: Trustworthy.

Dad holding her hand on her first day of kindergarten, Dad leading her in an awkward waltz at a father-daughter middle school dance, Dad posing with her at high school graduation.

"Two peas in a pod," he liked to say. "If I weren't me, I'd think you were."

She has his thick, wavy hair, the same dimple on her right cheek, same angular nose and bristly slashes of brow. Even her wide-set, prominent, upturned eyes are the same as his, with one notable exception.

Jerry Mundy's eyes were a piercing blue.

Only one of Emerson's is that shade; the other, a chalky gray.

Beyond the plate-glass window, midtown Manhattan is moist, dark, and dirty, wriggling with fat-bellied tourists looking up at skyscraper spires, and pissed-off New Yorkers looking down as they scuttle for subway steps.

Rush hour, and the pub is busier than usual. The regulars, mostly Long Island or Jersey-bound Penn Station commuters, are jammed alongside Billy Joel fans heading over to a sold-out show at Madison Square Garden a few blocks away.

NYPD Missing Persons Detective Sullivan Leary and her longtime partner, Detective Stockton Barnes, arrived well ahead of the crowd and grabbed a pair of stools beneath the specials chalkboard. Two-for-one drafts till seven, along with free mini buffet—Swedish meatballs, lentil samosas, and crab rangoon in tinfoil chafing dishes.

After days like this, happy hour is anything but for Sully and Barnes. Yes, they solve the vast majority of their missing persons cases. Some reports are false alarms, filed due to misunderstandings or missed connections. Some people disappear deliberately, despite their families' insistence that there must be foul play. Spouses have affairs, kids run away, deadbeat parents abandon children.

Those things happen every day. The missing either eventually find their way home, or resurface in far-flung locations.

There are abductions and accidents, of course, and a few cases do end tragically. Usually, you can see it coming; steel yourself for the inevitable.

That's how it was today, on the case they just closed with the usual heap of paperwork before adjourning to the bar. It began forty-eight hours ago with a missing, possibly suicidal teenager and was resolved early this morning when someone discovered his body, wrists slit by his own hand, decomposing alongside goat carcasses behind a Chinatown restaurant. Sully anticipated it would end that way, but the kid's parents did not. The note in his pocket was addressed to them—grief-stricken immigrants whom he blamed for a variety of slights, most, according to his siblings, imagined by a troubled young man.

"This isn't like you. Stop dwelling," Barnes tells her when she wonders, not for the first time since they sat down, how the bereaved parents are going to sleep tonight—and for the rest of their lives.

"I'm not dwelling. I'm just speculating."

"Bad idea. Move on, same as always."

Move on. Funny you should say that, Barnes . . .

He's provided her with the perfect opening to say what's on her mind, but even now, she can't quite bring herself to do it.

"Excuse me, is this seat taken?" A statuesque brunette gestures at the vacant stool next to Barnes.

"If it were taken, someone would have been sitting there," Sully mutters to Barnes after he tells the woman that it's open. "Anyway, *I'm* sitting *here*."

"What does that have to do with anything?"

"Never mind."

She watches the woman swivel her stool toward Barnes, ready to start a conversation.

There was a time when Sully was irked by the assumption that she and Barnes are a couple. These days, it's the opposite.

Is it so hard to believe that a drop-dead gorgeous African-American man who can have his pick of nubile beauties might be romantically attached to the scrawny, middle-aged likes of Sully, with her Chee-tos and cream complexion?

Apparently, it is. The brunette asks Barnes, "So, do you come here a lot?"

Lame.

Sully sips her barely touched Jameson, glad she swore off dating fellow cops after she divorced one.

And it's not as if she and Barnes have anything in common beyond the job. He's worldly, gregarious, and charming. She prefers familiar places and faces and is . . . well, not so charming.

"Hey, Sully, you want another drink?"

"I just got this one," she snarls at Barnes.

Unruffled, he orders another for himself, and a chardonnay for the brunette.

To his credit, he curtails the small talk with her and turns back to Sully. "Extra prickly tonight, aren't we?"

"Hell, no. I'm a freakin' marshmallow."

"You? A marshmallow?" He throws back his head and laughs.

Yeah, Sullivan Leary is no marshmallow—not tonight, not ever. Not after more than a decade as an NYPD detective, and not before, either.

Raised in a no-frills, rowdy New York family, she's quick-witted and quick-tempered, with a fierce sense of justice. She likes everything strong: her tea, her Irish whiskey, her men . . .

Ah, but the strongest men in her life have shared her blood and her law enforcement vocation. Others, particularly her ex-husband, proved weak.

Barnes is not weak, and he isn't family, which makes him . . .

"I'm serious," he says. "Something's getting to you. Is it the case?"

"This case? Today? No." She scowls.

"Then what?"

Her cell phone rings before she can say what she'd been about to say when the brunette barged in.

Looking down at her phone, she recognizes the 518 area code and Mundy's Landing exchange, though not the last four digits. Earlier this month, she and Barnes devoted the better part of their Hudson Valley vacation to a missing persons investigation linked to a century-old unsolved murder case.

Sully excuses herself and strides toward the door with her phone. Beyond the air-conditioned pub, cigarette-smoking bar patrons pollute a steamy, neon-lit canyon shadowed by concrete and steel towers. She sidesteps Helga, a neighborhood homeless woman who's sleeping soundly on the sidewalk beside the closed metal gate of a notions and trimmings store. Her blanket is a torn garbage bag, her pillow a cardboard sign crookedly lettered with just two words: Help Me.

Sully tries, often bringing her a sandwich or hand-ing over what little money she herself can spare. It isn't much—loose change, occasionally a dollar or two.

"Good evening, Detective Leary," a familiar voice says in Sully's ear. "This is Miss Ora Abrams, curator of the Mundy's Landing Historical Society."

She smiles, picturing the dainty elderly woman who wears her snow white hair in a Disney princess bun. "Nice to hear from you. How are you?"

"Quite well, my dear. I'm calling with some news. You may recall that the society has offered fifty thousand dollars to the person who solves the Sleeping Beauty murders?"

"You mean the Mundypalooza reward? I mean, for your event?" she amends, aware that Ora isn't a fan of the colloquial term.

Every summer for twenty-five years, the historical so-ciety extends an open invitation to amateur detectives to try their hand at solving the village's century-old Sleep-ing Beauty murders.

"Yes, I've just come from a meeting with the board of directors," Ora goes on, "and we've decided that you deserve the reward."

Sully gasps a lungful of tobacco smoke and rotting Dumpster garbage. "But, Miss Abrams . . . I mean, I didn't *solve* it."

"You were much closer than anyone else over the years, other than that dreadful person."

The dreadful person, of course, is *Holmes*, the Sleep-ing Beauty Killer's twenty-first-century counterpart, who'd unlocked the historic case and then set out to du-plicate the crimes.

"If you'd had one more day," Ora goes on, "you'd have figured it out."

One more day, and more innocent lives would have

been lost. Two local families found a happy ending, but several others weren't as fortunate.

Fifty thousand dollars would buy a whole lot of . . .

Freedom.

But Sully forces herself to say the right thing. "The reward should go to Annabelle Bingham, Miss Abrams. She and her husband can use the money," Sully points out—as if she can't.

But Annabelle and her family live at 46 Bridge Street, one of three Murder Houses targeted by both Holmes and the 1916 Sleeping Beauty Killer. She, too, had pieced together the original crimes and narrowly escaped becoming a copycat victim.

"The Binghams suggested that the reward go to you. We all agree. It's our way of thanking you for all you've done for Mundy's Landing."

"But I didn't do this alone. My partner was—"

"Detective Barnes? A delightful man. Splendid suggestion."

"Suggestion?"

"We'll honor you both with the reward—two names on the check."

"I really think the Binghams deserve it, Miss Abrams. I wouldn't feel comfortable taking all that money, and I know Detective Barnes won't, either."

"In that case, we'll divide it. Half the money will go to the Binghams, and the other half to you two."

"But—"

"That's the end of it. We'll award the money at a ceremony next month. I hope you and Mr. Barnes will be able to join us."

"I'll be there," Sully promises.

And not just for the ceremony.

Hanging up, she puts her phone back into her pocket and takes out a couple of twenty-dollar bills. Bending over

Helga's sleeping form, she tucks the money alongside the woman's withered hands that are clasped as if in prayer.

Back in the bar, Barnes is, predictably, chatting with the brunette on the next stool. Seeing Sully, he breaks off to ask if everything's okay.

"Everything's fine." She reclaims her seat, picks up her drink, and swirls the amber liquid in her glass as the truth sinks in. "Everything's great, actually."

"Excuse me, Stockton?" His new friend touches his arm. "Would you mind watching my wine while I go to the ladies' room? You never know when someone might slip something into it."

"Is it just me, or was that wishful thinking?" Sully mutters as the woman walks away.

"It's just you. Who was on the phone?"

"What would you say if I told you we just won a nice little jackpot?"

"I'd ask if you were talking to the lottery."

"The lottery doesn't call people."

"How would I know?"

"You don't play the lottery?"

He shakes his head. "My money comes the old-fashioned way. I earn it."

"So you're turning down your half of the twenty-five grand?"

"What now?"

She explains the situation quickly, concluding, "I told Ora they should just give the Binghams the entire thing."

"No, come on, Gingersnap, you need that money. You keep telling me you've been in credit card hell. Here's your chance to buy your way out."

"I know."

"I'm spending my half on a real vacation to make up for the one I missed. You can come with me."

She smiles faintly "Where are we going?"

"Cuba. It's not off-limits anymore. I heard commercial airlines are going to start flying there this fall, and I have Cuban blood—my abuela, remember?"

"She was born in the Bronx." You ride around with someone all day, every day for years, you know little details like that.

"Her parents were from Havana. Come on, we'll go before tourism ruins everything. We can lie on an unspoiled beach, smoke cigars, drink rum . . . Think about how nice it would be to get out of here."

Another perfect opening. This time, she won't let it go by.

"I have thought about it, Barnes. And you're right. I do need to get out of here. But not just for a week, and not to Cuba."

His eyes narrow. "What do you mean?"

"You know what I mean. And you knew it was coming. I've had enough. I've got to go. For good."

He sips his drink, staring at the tiered rows of bottles behind the bar.

"Aren't you going to say anything?"

"You said you'd never leave the city."

"No, *you* said that, Barnes."

"About you."

"Well, you were wrong. I've been thinking about it ever since we got back from Mundy's Landing. My lease is up next month. My rent is going to skyrocket."

"So it's because of Sir Douchebag?" His nickname for her pompous landlord. "Or is it Manik Bhandari?"

And there it is.

They say there's one case in every law enforcement career that gets you in the gut, no matter how hardened you are. After almost two decades on the job, Sully confronted hers last year.

She and Stockton were on a routine investigation in a rough neighborhood when a couple of joy-riding junkies spontaneously declared open season on the NYPD and started firing. The bullet that just missed Sully hit the seventeen-year-old honor student. Manik sobbed for his father like a frightened baby and died in her arms before she even realized she'd been struck by the second bullet.

Though her forehead wound is long healed, the scar still sometimes burns, a cruel stigmata of flesh and soul. She plays the scene over and over in her head, imagining a different outcome—one in which she saves Manik. Sometimes she, too, survives. Sometimes she doesn't. But at least she dies a hero.

"It pushed me over the edge," she admits.

Barnes opens his mouth, undoubtedly to remind her she'll get over it.

She curtails him. "Nick Colonomos called yesterday and offered me a job—detective on the Mundy's Landing force."

"You're actually considering it? Listen, you can't—"

"I already said yes."

"You'll be bored out of your mind up there."

"Maybe. But boring sounds like a decent alternative to . . ." She taps the scar on her forehead.

"You can't make a snap decision based on one incident. You need to give this some time. At least wait until the end of the year, or even next summer. By then, if you still—"

"There's a job now. It won't be there in a few months."

"Something else will come up."

"Not there."

"Why do you have to be *there*?"

"Why are you trying to talk me out of this? Are you going to miss me that much?"

She waits for his usual retort, but it doesn't come. He pushes their drinks away and clasps his large black hand over her bony, freckled one.

Looking her in the eye, he says without a hint of irony, "Yeah, Gingersnap. I'll miss you."

Jerry Mundy's obituary was published this morning.

Not in the *Los Angeles Times*, of course. No such prominence for a man who'd lived a solitary, humble life. His obit appeared only in the relatively obscure neighborhood online paper, the one that generates headlines from Girl Scout cookie sales and lost puppies, largely ignoring all crimes more serious than jaywalking or littering, with a front page devoid of politics, wars, global terrorism.

Judging by reader engagement, the obituaries are far more popular than the news, occasionally edged by the weather forecast, depending on the day. The comments section breeds complaints about the Southern California weather or lack thereof, and subsequent complaints about the complainers.

Over on the obituaries page, comments aren't always reverent, or even coherent. A few are written entirely in capital letters that transform condolences into screaming threats: *I'M PRAYING FOR HER SOUL*, or *I WILL COME BY THIS WEEK WITH RIGATONI.*

Someone who goes by SamIAm writes just *RIP* on every obituary, and a person named Maynard—first, or last?—comments on all of SamIAm's comments, accusing him of disrespecting the dead with *stupid drive-by acronims*. Someone else corrects Maynard's spelling: *Its acronym. Learn how to spell, freaking moron.*

No one corrects the *Its*.

Fascinating, this window into other people's lives.

And deaths.

The deceased are depicted in formal portraits or colorful candids, some recent, others courtesy of the prior century. A black and white photo depicts a ninety-year-old man as a handsome young soldier, the accompanying write-up referencing Normandy and a Purple Heart. A septuagenarian is shown in 1950s glam, with dark lipstick and cropped hair, her bangs riding high above heavily penciled brows and at least an inch of forehead. She's survived by a devoted husband and three sprawling generations.

You can learn a lot about a person, reading an obituary.

Unless that person is Jerome Mundy.

No photo. No comments, other than the obligatory *RIP* courtesy of SamIAm.

No frills. No charming anecdotes, no unique facts. Unlike his fellow deceased, he didn't have invention patents. Wasn't appointed to Ronald Reagan's administration. Didn't set a Guinness Book of World Records for humming "Ninety-nine Bottles of Beer on the Wall" all the way through, not once, but one hundred consecutive times.

Surprisingly, the hummer, alphabetically listed right before Jerome Mundy, died of natural causes.

Hard to believe no one strangled that *guy.*

An ironic thought, all things considered.

Jerome Mundy's obituary reads like a short story thrown into an anthology of opuses.

Born in Los Angeles in 1940, survived by one daughter, Emerson Mundy, of Oakland. Died of natural causes.

That's it. The end.

Strange.

Seeing it there in black and white, you can almost believe it.

Even the lie.

To: emerson.mundy@ousd.com
From: nancy@dapplebrookinn.com
Date: June 1, 2017
Re: Your Upcoming Stay

Dear Ms. Mundy:

   As the General Manager of the Dapplebrook Inn, I review upcoming reservations on the first of every month. Your last name caught my eye. Do you have a familial connection to Horace J. Mundy? He was a great American politician, and one of Mundy's Landing's most esteemed native sons. Our inn was built as his private residence in the late nineteenth century.

   I will look forward to your reply, and to welcoming you on the 21st.

   Best,

   Nancy Vandergraaf

Chapter 2

June 21, 2017
Mundy's Landing, New York

The dusky two-lane highway is bordered by woods, rambling cobblestone walls, and spotlit homes. Some are pillared stone mansions, others turreted Victorians, a few transformed into office buildings or apartment houses. All are steeped in bygone grandeur.

Approaching a fork in the road, Emerson notes that the business district lies east; Schaapskill Nature Preserve, west. That's the site of the old riverfront settlement, but it closes at sundown.

She bears east. Schaapskill will have to wait until tomorrow. There, she's hoping . . .

What, Emerson? What are you hoping?

That you'll discover some long-lost treasure or connection to your roots?

That you'll feel something other than this festering longing, loss, frustration, loneliness, anger . . .

Something other than sorry for yourself?

She abruptly turns off the arctic blast from the A.C. vents. Rolling down the window, she sucks warm, woodsy air into her lungs.

The road broadens to four lanes and straightens. Houses and trees give way to a series of interconnected parking lots and painted concrete buildings marked by familiar logos you'd find in any other American town: Dunkin' Donuts, Mobil, Holiday Inn, Home Depot, Wal-Mart, and every fast food chain known to man.

Inhaling fryer grease along with exhaust, she hits every traffic light alongside an adjacent pickup truck reverberating loud bass.

Roy Nowak, her fiancé, drives a similar vehicle, but he only listens to soft rock. He knows all the words to every song, and he sings to her, sometimes *about* her. She should probably find it endearingly romantic, but lately, it grates.

"I'm not tiny, Roy, and I'm not a dancer," she protested just the other day when he lyrically transformed her into the heroine of Elton John's ballad. Seeing the wounded look on his face, she smiled to show that she meant it lightly, adding, "I'm definitely not a seamstress for the band."

Predictably, he stopped singing—and stopped talking—for the remainder of the evening.

She met him last September, on a union picket line during a contract dispute. A torrential downpour hit out of nowhere. Roy had an umbrella. Emerson did not.

He was smart and earnest and had good manners—hardly the most earth-shattering qualities in a romantic prospect. But then, who needs drama?

"I just lost my dad. I'm not in a good place," she told him when he asked her out.

"I'm a great listener, if you want to talk about it."

"I . . . I can't. Not . . ." *Not with a stranger*, she thought, but that wasn't quite it. Not with anyone.

She said only, "Not yet. It's too soon."

"Then we'll go out, and we'll talk about other things, or," he amended, watching her expression, "we won't talk at all. Have you seen *Finding Dory*?"

"What?"

"It's a feel-good movie. Don't you want to feel good?"

"I would *love* to feel good," she relented with a smile.

They went to the movie—an animated film about a forgetful blue fish who knew that she'd somehow become separated from her parents as a child, and longed for a family reunion. Emerson sobbed her way through it, Roy's arm resting around her shoulders.

It was cathartic—both the purge of grief and the companionship.

Roy has been there for her ever since. He'd be here with her now if she hadn't told him that this is something she needs to do alone.

Past the sprawl, a white chamber of commerce signpost reads Welcome to Mundy's Landing.

Brick-paved streets meander beneath a leafy canopy, lined with gabled rooftops and nineteenth-century storefronts. Vintage street lamps illuminate post-prandial pedestrians with leashed dogs or baby strollers. The broad green is dotted with benches and blooming planters, a gazebo, and a fountain featuring a copper statue of Gilded Age financier Horace J. Mundy.

Her Horace J. Mundy.

Leaving the town square, she ascends the steep incline of Prospect Street into The Heights. In this aptly named neighborhood, the 1916 Sleeping Beauty Killer staged a series of grotesque tableaus. Almost a year has passed since the original culprit was identified and the copycat unmasked, making this the first summer in a quarter century that the village isn't hosting a "Mundypalooza."

Tonight, all is quiet at both the historical society's

floodlit mansion and the notorious Murder House across the street, where the first butchered corpse turned up a century ago.

Farther down the block, the Dapplebrook Inn is alive with activity. Every window along the three-story brick façade beams with light. People are dining and sipping cocktails at candlelit tables on the wide veranda. An elegant couple climbs into a waiting car beneath the wisteria-covered portico.

Emerson turns into the driveway and pulls around back, startling a squat, furry creature browsing in a Dumpster at the parking lot's rear. Its masked eyes shoot an accusatory glare into the headlights as if *she's* the interloper.

"Hey, *I'm* the one who belongs here," she tells the raccoon as it scuttles into a tall clump of rhododendron. "I'm a Mundy."

She opens the door, unfolds her legs, and grabs her suitcase from the trunk.

The evening is warm, fragrant with June roses and honeysuckle. Strains of classical music and conversation float through the screens to join the night hum of air conditioners, and cicadas and frogs in a nearby stream.

The brick mansion presides against shadowy foliage and a purple starlit sky. It was built in 1892 as a summer home for the illustrious Horace J. Mundy, who spent Hudson Valley summers hobnobbing with Roosevelts and Vanderbilts. Last summer, Emerson had discovered that he'd been her great-great-uncle, and that her roots do indeed stretch back to Mundy's Landing's earliest settlers.

Emerson's sneakers crunch along the gravel driveway as she makes her way past blooming bushes and lace-curtained windows. Beneath the branches of an enormous tree, a shovel and a couple of gardening rakes are propped against a wheelbarrow that holds burlap-wrapped shrubs waiting to be planted. The patrons on the porch don't give her a second glance, busy eating and drinking, chatting and being served.

A young waiter holds the door open for her on his way out. A tattoo peeks out beneath his white shirt cuff.

"Checking in?" he asks with a smile.

"Yes."

"Enjoy your stay." He steps outside, letting the door swing closed behind her as she steps over the threshold.

She takes in the polished hardwoods, period wallpaper, carved woodwork, and sweeping staircase.

Home at last.

Not really.

Intellectually, she knows that it's not a true homecoming if you've never been here before.

Emotionally, she begs to differ.

"You must be Emerson Mundy," a voice greets her, and she sees a slender, attractive woman in her late forties or early fifties. "I'm Nancy Vandergraaf, the general manager."

Nancy is tall and trim with short, stylish auburn hair. The women's civic club type, Emerson finds herself thinking as they shake hands.

"In your e-mail, you said you're visiting Mundy's Landing to learn more about your ancestors?"

"Yes. I'm new to genealogy. I wanted to see where my family came from."

"I'll be happy to help with your research. I've lived here all my life and I know everyone in town." She grabs an old-fashioned brass key from a desk drawer. "You must be exhausted. I'll show you up to your room."

"Wait, *up?*"

"We have you on the second floor, in the Jekyll Suite. It's our premier accommodation—a complimentary upgrade. I thought Horace's niece should stay in what was once his own bedroom. Here, I'll take your luggage."

"Oh, you don't have to do that. It's heavy."

"I'm stronger than I look," the woman says with a smile.

So is Emerson, but she allows Nancy to swing the bag over her shoulder as if it weighs mere ounces.

"Have you had other descendants visit?"

"No, and I've been managing this inn for years. None of Horace's sons are living, and their families are scattered. There are Mundys who live here in town, though," Nancy adds, leading her toward the graceful wallpapered staircase. "Different branch of the family, but they'd be your distant cousins. You're all descended from Jeremiah Mundy, one of the village's founding fathers."

To Emerson, Jeremiah and his sisters had always seemed like characters in her beloved childhood books. Plucky orphans surrounded by vengeful strangers, the Mundy siblings not only survived, but thrived.

Their saga, like her favorite novels, had a most satisfying ending: by the time the village incorporated nearly a century after their parents were executed, residents named it after Enoch Mundy, a Revolutionary War general.

Jeremiah's grandson was one of many illustrious offspring who redeemed the family name, and made Emerson long for a connection—one her father denied.

"They must have been so upset," she said to him, years ago. "Can you imagine watching your parents die like that? What a horrible ordeal."

"For the kids, yes. But there are worse ways to die."

"Worse than being strangled to death by a noose?"

"It's faster than you'd think. You fall, your neck breaks, and it's over. Better than slowly wasting away."

"You mean like the ones who starved to death?"

"I mean like anyone who wastes away."

Pushing away troubling thoughts of her father, Emerson focuses on a series of framed sepia-toned exterior photographs of the mansion through the years. Some show vehicles parked beneath the portico: horses and surreys, bicycles with enormous front wheels or tandems, roadsters with rumble seats and running boards. Others include people in fashionable clothing from Gibson Girl shirtwaists to flapper fringe to miniskirts and go-go boots.

She thinks of the framed snapshots that filled her own childhood home. They've been sitting in a box in her Oakland apartment for months. She couldn't bear to display them when she returned from her father's funeral. It was too soon. Too late.

Nancy points to a Victorian-era portrait of three young boys. "These are Horace's three sons—Robert H. Mundy, Joseph H. Mundy, and Arthur H. Mundy."

"What are the H's for?"

"Horace, of course." Smiling, she points to another image, of a young man wearing a straw boater and pinstriped suit with a watch chain looped across his buttoned waistcoat. "This is the oldest, Robert, all grown up. He was lost on the *Titanic*, but he died a hero. He saved these children. Here they are after they were rescued at sea."

She points to a grainy photograph of a group of bedraggled ragamuffins posed in ill-fitting winter clothing. The eldest can't be more than six or seven, clutching a well-bundled baby in her arms. In the background, a ship's railing and a dense blur of sea and sky confirm the shipboard setting.

"Taken on board the *Carpathia*," Emerson guesses, familiar with the *Titanic* tragedy.

"How did you know?"

"I'm a history teacher."

"Then you're going to love *this* picture."

From roughly the same era, it shows a pair of young teenage boys wearing vintage baseball uniforms, bats dangling from their hands.

"The one on the left is Congressman Maxwell Mundy Ransom, descended from Jeremiah's sister Priscilla Mundy Ransom. Do you recognize this young man?" Nancy points to the boy on the right.

"Should I?"

"I'll give you a hint. His initials were FDR, and he wound up in Washington alongside Maxwell. Or rather, not quite alongside . . ."

"That's Franklin Roosevelt?"

"It is. They were friends all their lives. See that? Your family had quite an exciting past."

"Tragic, too," Emerson murmurs, thinking of Priscilla, a newlywed pregnant with her only child when she was widowed weeks after she'd written that revealing letter to Jeremiah.

We shall never tell . . .

They reach the wide second-floor hallway lined with white-painted doors, each closed and bearing a brass nameplate: the Lavender Room, the Sarah Suite, the Delano Room . . .

Halfway down the hall, Nancy shows her oval oil portraits of Horace's parents, Aaron and Sarah Mundy. He's dignified but homely in a beard and black topcoat; the woman more handsome than pretty, with a mass of dark curls coiled on her head and a festoon of lace at her fleshy throat. They were painted by Martin Johnson Heade, a prominent nineteenth-century artist linked to the Hudson River School, mostly known for his landscapes.

"Here we are." At the end of the hall, Nancy unlocks a pair of double doors leading to the Jekyll Suite—not, she tells Emerson, as in Dr. Jekyll and Mr. Hyde.

"It's named after the coastal Georgia island where Horace hobnobbed at the turn of the last century with Rockefellers, Astors, Morgans . . . you probably know all about that, as a history teacher."

She does. The elite group of prominent businessmen hunted, fished, and talked politics and finance. Those discussions paved the way for the Federal Reserve and changed the course of history.

Nancy pushes open both doors with a flourish, like a grande dame in a vintage movie, and motions Emerson across the threshold.

The lamplit room has towering ceilings, tall windows, ornate dark wood moldings. Mahogany furniture is well-polished, scrolled and carved, yet not overtly fussy. Hunter green walls color-coordinate with richly patterned upholstery, rug, and draperies. Florals are conspicuously absent; the aesthetic luxuriously masculine.

There's a marble wet bar topped by a backlit glass cabinet filled with cocktail glassware. Above the fireplace, an intricately sculpted stone frieze depicts soldiers in an ancient war. Stacked wood and a maroon leather hearthside chair await the next chilly evening.

This is a room where a gentleman might retire with a snifter of brandy, a good cigar, and a Hemingway novel—or perhaps Hemingway himself. He was rumored to have been a friend of Horace, according to Nancy, who points out a massive gilt-framed portrait of an unsmiling bearded man, posed in top hat and tails in a blooming summer garden.

"Is that Hemingway?"

"No, it's Horace. He commissioned John Singer Sargent to paint it in London in the 1890s, right around the time the house was being built. Sargent was sought after by all the most aristocratic families both here and abroad."

Aristocratic. A far cry from Emerson's own life, especially after two heart attacks left her father on permanent disability from his job as an airline baggage handler.

"Is this what the room looked like back when my family lived here?" she asks Nancy.

"We tried to keep it authentic. Some of the furniture is reproduction, but most are antiques original to the house. A few pieces, like that side table and the mantel clock, are original to the room itself."

"I feel like I'm going to turn around and see Horace standing there."

An odd glimmer flits across Nancy's face, like a fast-moving wisp of summer cloud.

"Have people seen him here?" Emerson asks in surprise. "His ghost, I mean?"

"Do you believe in ghosts?"

"No."

"Neither do I," Nancy says firmly, setting Emerson's bag on a wooden luggage rack with tapestry straps. "Some people assume that all historic places are haunted. They see what they want to see, hear what they want to hear."

"What, exactly, *do* they see and hear . . . *here*?"

"The usual—apparitions in old-fashioned clothing, that kind of thing. And they hear footsteps, creaking, voices . . ."

Unsettled, Emerson clears her throat. "Voices?"

"It's just the wind in that big old maple right outside the window," Nancy assures her. "We tried to get a permit to take it down a few years ago, but it's on a historic tree registry. You have to jump through hoops just to have it trimmed, so we haven't in a while. When the leaves brush against the screen, it sounds like someone whispering. Anyway—I'll show you the bedroom and bathroom."

Through an archway, a four-poster canopy bed awaits, covers turned down.

She'd begged her father for a bed like that when she was a little girl. He responded as he always did when she wanted something they couldn't afford—ice cream, gymnastics lessons, money for new shoes . . .

Rather than say no, he'd prop his beefy elbow on the

table, beckoning her spindly arm for a wrestling match. "Beat me, and you get a yes."

He never let her win.

"You have to get stronger," he'd say with a shrug.

"How am I supposed to do that?"

"Lift some weights. Do some pull-ups."

Now, at last, she has her canopy bed, if only for this brief interlude. The linens are a dark charcoal shade, not quite black, not entirely gray. A plush white robe and spa slippers sit at the foot. In the adjoining marble bathroom, votive candles line a narrow ledge above the claw-foot tub, and apothecary countertop jars are filled with luxury brand toiletries.

Back in the main room, Nancy shows her how to control the television, concealed in a tall cabinet, and points out the placard that has a phone number for the night manager, should she need anything after hours.

"So there's no one on site?"

"Just the guests. And the ghosts," she adds with a grin. "Any other questions before I leave you to unpack?"

"Is there a safe?"

"No. We've never had a problem here, but if you have valuable jewelry or electronics you're worried about, I'd be happy to lock them into my desk downstairs."

"No, that's okay. I was just curious." She wasn't worried about jewelry or electronics, but the far more valuable— to her, anyway—old letter she'd carried from California.

"If you're hungry, the restaurant is open until eleven, and the food is very good."

"That's great. Thanks again, Nancy."

"My pleasure. Good night!"

Emerson closes the door after her, and tilts her head against it. Eyes closed, she takes a deep breath that transforms into a yawn. Some decent food, maybe a little wine, a hot bath, bedtime in this sumptuous suite . . .

When was the last time she got a full night's sleep?

It's been months. Almost a year, really.

Last summer, she packed her dead father's existence into cartons just as generations before her had done. She didn't seal them, just folded the flaps and piled them into her car. Back in her small Oakland apartment, she stacked the boxes in a corner of her bedroom. There was no other space.

Nightmares hidden within that cardboard mountain seemed to seep into her brain as she lay in its shadow every night.

We shall never tell . . .

Other years, she'd slipped back into her Northern California life as comfortably as she did her softest fleece after a hot LA summer. This year, nothing seemed familiar. She felt adrift on a wreckage-strewn foreign sea until Roy appeared on the horizon like a rescue ship.

Now that she's found her way to Mundy's Landing, her engagement ring seems to have transformed from life buoy to anchor. What if she wants to stay? Would he be willing to come with her?

The question is overshadowed by a more important one: Would she want him to?

Roy Nowak left California before dawn Monday morning, the day after his fiancée flew to her history teachers' conference in Washington, D.C. The day after he discovered he'd been right all along.

Last minute cross-country flights were well beyond his budget, so he got into his truck and started driving east, stomach churning along with his thoughts. He was on the road all day and straight through that first night, so tense that he'd bitten his nails until there was nothing left but ragged ridges embedded in swollen flesh.

Late yesterday afternoon, he stopped at a motel on the

outskirts of Columbus and slept in his clothes, intending to rest for only a few hours before getting back on the road to make it to New York before Emerson did.

His wakeup call never came. That's what you get for staying in a dive. That, and bedbugs. It was nearly nine when he finally woke up this morning, itching furiously from little red bites all over his arms.

Ah, the irony. He raked his useless fingertips along his skin in a futile effort to scratch the red bumps before grabbing his phone to text Emerson.

She asked why he was up so early, thinking he was back home in Oakland.

Can't sleep when UR far away, he texted back.

Her only comment was a heart.

He returned the heart, and asked, RU still in DC?

Yes. Morning session starting. TTYL

Talk to you later? Really?

She didn't pick up when he called her from the road, weaving in and out of traffic, doing thirty miles above the speed limit. Instead, she texted that she was with conference colleagues and couldn't talk. The next time he tried her, she picked up but said she was about to get into a cab to the airport.

"Which flight are you on?"

"I'm not sure."

"You don't know your flight?"

"I don't have the number in front of me."

"Well, which airline?"

Again, she claimed she wasn't sure, that her ticket info was buried in her suitcase.

"Then which airport?" He clenched the phone in one hand, steering wheel in the other, itching—literally—to scratch the bug bites.

"Which airport?" she echoed.

"There are two. Dulles, or National?" He propped the phone to his ear with his shoulder, attacking the rash with maddeningly useless fingertips. "You must know which one, if you're on your way!"

"Dulles."

"Where are you landing in New York? JFK? LaGuardia? Newark?"

"Why are you asking me this? Why do you sound so crazy? I feel like you're—"

"Crazy? I'm your fiancé! Don't you think I deserve to know where you are?"

Dammit. He shouldn't have lashed out at her.

Double dammit—he'd just blown past a state trooper hidden in bushes on the median.

"You need to know where I am every minute of every day?" Emerson was saying. "You need to stop—"

He quickly apologized, hearing sirens behind him and spotting the trooper's red lights whirling in his rearview mirror. "Just promise you'll call me when you land. I worry."

She promised.

But she hadn't kept it.

So much for his plan to intercept her in New York. How could he, without a clue which flight she was on, or even where she was landing?

Instead, he navigated the bottleneck at the Lincoln Tunnel into Manhattan and kept going, heading north, toward the Bronx.

She still hasn't answered his texts, and her phone rings into voice mail.

Does she know? Is she avoiding him?

His fingertips have rubbed the bug bites raw and bloody. Still, his skin crawls with itches he can't reach, hot little stabs taunting from deep in his flesh. The bugs must have hitched a ride, burrowed into the folds of his clothing.

He needs to wash these clothes, and everything in his duffel bag, in hot water. He needs a meal, a shower, some ointment. No skeevy motel this time—just a few hours' reprieve before he heads north to Mundy's Landing.

Off Pelham Parkway, he drives around block after block for fifteen minutes before squeezing his pickup truck into a vacant parking spot. He taps the bumpers of the cars parked in front and behind him, barely noticing, not caring.

The streets teem with traffic and people, the warm air thick with sweat and pungent spices and accented voices. Roy backtracks to the address he'd thought to scribble down before he left home, just in case. He grips his phone in his fist, willing it to ring.

Where the hell is she?

Does she know, somehow, that he's on her trail?

But how could she know?

She couldn't—unless, of course, she's having him followed.

He finds himself looking over his shoulder as he approaches the familiar four-story building, searching the crowded sidewalk. So many people, and none of them seem to notice him, but you never know.

He rings the bell for apartment 5B and waits for the familiar "Who is it?" to crackle over the intercom.

It doesn't come.

She, too, is out of reach, or ignoring him.

He sits on the stoop rubbing his knuckles along his arms, pushing fresh pinpricks of blood into smears from wrist to biceps.

"Looking for someone?"

He looks up to see an old woman regarding him from the doorway.

"Yes, Sylvia . . ."

Crap. What *is* her last name?

Schmo. That's what he calls the men who come and

go in her life—Joe Schmo. It's easier than learning a new name every couple of months, though she did marry the latest one.

"She lives in 5B," he tells the woman, standing to extend his hand in a proper greeting. "I'm Roy Nowak."

"Josephine Pikalski."

She's not as old as he thought. Middle-aged, but her face is worn and her hair is gray and straggly. She's had a hard life. Who the hell hasn't?

"Nice to meet you, Josephine," he says, shaking her hand with his blood-streaked one.

"Call me Jo."

Ah, another Jo Schmo. That strikes him as oddly hilarious. A strange, snorting little laugh escapes him. Seeing her expression, he considers explaining that the stress is getting to him—the road weariness, this damned rash, his MIA fiancée . . .

He asks where Sylvia is.

"Out. You just missed them."

"Out for the night?"

"Out of town. Atlantic City."

"On a weeknight?"

She shrugs. "It's payday."

He curses under his breath. Some things never change.

"Do you know when she'll be back?"

"Who knows. I'm feeding her cats."

"Then you have the key. Can you let me in, please?"

"What're you, kidding me? I can't go around letting strangers into her apartment."

"But I told you, I'm Roy Nowak." Seeing her blank look, he adds, "Sylvia's *son*."

"How do I know that?"

"How do I know you're really Jo Pikalski?"

"Ask anyone. I've lived in this building thirty-four years."

Right. And Ma hasn't even lived here for three months.

Roy shakes his head and turns away.

"You're welcome," the woman calls pointedly from the stoop.

He was supposed to thank her? For what?

He ignores her, striding away, eager to get back on the road and head north, to Mundy's Landing.

Miss Savannah Ivers
c/o Anthropology Department
Hadley College
Hadley, NY 12579

June 13, 2017

Dear Miss Ivers:

I am Ora Abrams, curator of the Mundy's Landing Historical Society. I read with interest yesterday's Tribune article featuring this year's most accomplished Hadley College graduates. Congratulations on earning your undergraduate degree in forensic anthropology, and on being awarded the prestigious Sahir Malouf research grant. I knew the late Professor Malouf very well when he was on the faculty, and he often assisted me with museum research over the years.

I understand that you are spending the summer working in the lab, and wonder if you might be interested in discussing a confidential project for which I will compensate you very well.

I have enclosed my business card with this letter. Please call me at the historical society to schedule a meeting for further discussion of this venture.

Sincerely,

Aurora Abrams
Mundy's Landing Historical Society
62 Prospect Street
Mundy's Landing, NY 12573

Chapter 3

At eighty-two, Miss Aurora Abrams shouldn't be driving at all, let alone at night. Not according to her physician, David Duncan III, the man responsible for her growing not-to-do list. At her most recent checkup—almost a year ago now—he said she shouldn't be doing a lot of things that make life worth living, like eating chocolate-covered cherries for breakfast, having a bedtime nip of brandy, or continuing to work at the museum.

"You only go around once, Doctor."

"Yes, but we don't want to fall off the ride before it's over, do we, Ms. Abrams?"

"That's *Miss* Abrams." None of this newfangled women's lib "Ms." stuff for Ora, though she contradicts based on her mood, or whether she likes the speaker.

She doesn't care for Dr. Duncan, who lacks the folksy, relaxed bedside manner of his grandfather, Ora's longtime physician, whom she fondly called Dr. Dave.

David III occupies the late David I's office, on the second floor of a redbrick building on Market Street. Westerly Dry Goods used to be on the first floor, but now it's a clothing shop called Tru Blu. Every time Ora passes the silly sign, she wonders what the new owner has against the letter E.

Everything changes. Not for the better.

"Time to hand over your car keys," Dr. Duncan said.

"Hand them over to *whom*?"

"Figure of speech. At your age, reflexes aren't what they used to be. Neither are your senses, or your memory. You're a danger to yourself and to others on the road."

"Nonsense! I've always been a cautious driver. I've never—"

"Nothing personal. Happens to all of us sooner or later," he cut in, attempting to temper his rudeness with a smile and a pat on her hand. "You'll adapt."

"How do you expect me to get where I need to go?"

"I'm sure plenty of people will be willing to give you rides, and—"

It was Ora's turn to interrupt, tartly. "Have you forgotten that I have no family, Doctor?"

Never married, no children, and her last living relative, Great-Aunt Etta, passed away years ago. It was Dr. Dave who signed Aunt Etta's death certificate, and Papa's, too, both times coming to pay his respects with tears flooding his hazel eyes.

Such a good man, a true humanitarian.

His grandson merely shrugged under Ora's gray-eyed glare. "You're well-loved here in town. Your friends will be happy to help you get around."

"I wouldn't dream of burdening my friends."

Undaunted, he handed her a schedule of the local bus service for seniors,

Ora handed it right back. "I don't go to those strip malls on Colonial Highway. Chains drive our mom-and-pop stores out of business. I shop locally."

"Well then, you're all set. The Commons is within walking distance for you. You can get your daily exercise while you're at it. Two birds, one stone." Young Dr. Duncan smiled at her.

Ora didn't smile back, resenting the implication that elderly people only venture out for doctor appointments and shopping errands. Her business—professional and personal—takes her to plenty of interesting locales beyond the town proper.

Tonight, she's following a dark stretch of Route 9G toward Hadley College, located a few miles north of Mundy's Landing. She finds herself gripping the steering wheel as yet another pair of headlights swing around an oncoming curve and bear down on her.

Why on earth are all the other cars giving off such a blinding glare tonight?

If she hadn't canceled her six-month checkup with Dr. Duncan, ignoring reschedule reminder calls from his nurse for months now, he'd blame her age and failing eyesight.

Hogwash. Headlamps are simply brighter on the luxury cars driven by all these fancy Hudson Valley newcomers, privileged sorts who don't bother to turn off their high beams for opposite-bound traffic.

If only they wouldn't drive so fast. Ora is in as much hurry as anyone this evening, yet cars are zooming up to tailgate in the rearview mirror before flying recklessly past on the two-lane road.

The latest gives her several nerve-jangling honks before crossing a solid line to get around her, resulting in a horn blast and harrowing swerve from an oncoming pickup truck.

Oh dear.

Ora turns on her hazards, eases her sedan onto the shoulder, and shifts into park. Her rib cage is cramped with anxiety, and she struggles to take a deep, calming breath.

Papa had a terrible accident on this rural two-lane highway many years ago, when another car slid into his path during a blinding snowstorm. Both Papa's legs were broken, and the other driver was killed.

That, Ora reminds herself, has nothing to do with this. The weather is perfect, and she's been driving this road without incident for sixty-five years now, though it's been a while since she's navigated it after dark.

"I know it like the back of my hand," she often said— until recently, when she realized she barely knows the back of her hand.

How odd to look down and see age-speckled skin draped over bony fingers, an old lady hand attached to what increasingly feels like an old lady body.

At least her mind is sharp as ever.

Weighing the wisdom of continuing on her way, she glances at the purse perched beside her like an expectant passenger. Turquoise pleather with a crocodile pattern, it clashes with her red top, denim slacks, and white Keds. But none of her other handbags would hold the bulky protective case.

She reaches over and takes it out.

In the dim light from a sliver of waning moon, the skull seems to give off a preternatural glow.

Ora typically doesn't go carting around human remains. The skull, inherited from Great-Aunt Etta, is usually stashed with other private relics that never go on exhibit at the historical society, like the gimmal ring that had once belonged to James and Elizabeth Mundy, and the locket that—

"Oh my!" she blurts as a truck speeds past, so ground-shudderingly close that Ora checks to make sure it didn't tear off her side mirror.

Watching its taillights disappear, she grasps the danger of lingering here, parked on the shoulder.

Make up your mind. Are you going to proceed, or turn back?

Home is tempting. This isn't a dire rescue mission. The teenage Jane Doe whose skull was bashed nearly four centuries ago will be just as dead in the morning, and a daylight drive to Hadley won't be nearly as harrowing.

But what if Savannah Ivers isn't available—or willing— to reschedule their appointment?

"We need her," she tells Jane Doe. "She's the only one who can help us."

Hadley College is just another mile or two up the road.

Jaw set, Ora drives on.

Having worked the overnight shift and spent most of this beautiful day in bed, Sully woke up starved, as usual— and found her fridge empty, as usual. Problem solved: al fresco dining on the Dapplebrook Inn's broad slate porch above the fragrant rose and honeysuckle border. Decadent lobster mac and cheese, an ice cold craft brew, a soothing Rachmaninoff piano concerto floating over speakers as a tangerine sun kissed the treetops and disappeared. It's just too bad the dusky candlelight forced her to set aside the paperback she was reading.

"Bring a book wherever you go," her grandfather, Big Red Sullivan, used to say, "and you'll never be alone."

A seasoned solo diner, she takes her grandfather's advice. And she never chooses a seat facing others, pre-ferring to avoid awkward eye contact, unwelcome conversation, or the occasional pickup attempt.

When she got here, the dining terrace was crowded. Now, sneaking a peek over her shoulder, she notes just one couple, sharing dessert in the corner behind her.

Maybe she should have skipped the dessert and tea she ordered. She's in the mood for both, but not alone, in the dark.

She takes out her cell phone, sees a new text message notification on the home screen, and raises an eyebrow.

Detective Stockton Barnes? Really? Out of the blue, after all this time?

It's been almost a year since he grudgingly helped pack her belongings into a newly purchased SUV that was more spacious than the studio apartment she'd just vacated.

"Who needs space? The more you have, the more you fill it with extra stuff you don't need." He gestured at the box he'd just dumped on the backseat.

"You mean like all my dishes and glasses you just shattered when you ignored my Fragile label?"

"*Every* box is marked Fragile."

"Because everything *is* fragile."

Including Sully herself, who might as well have scrawled the word in Sharpie across her own forehead.

For someone who said, "I'll miss you, Gingersnap," Barnes sure as hell hasn't been much of a correspondent.

Once in a while, they text. They had lunch at Christmastime, when she visited her large extended family and old friends in Manhattan, and she invited him to come see her some weekend.

"I will," he said, but he didn't.

She hasn't heard a word from him since the Thursday before Memorial Day weekend, when she snapped a photo of a steak on the grill and sent it with a text that read, Big enough for 2. Want some?

His response was instantaneous: Not even big enough for 1, & too well done for me.

I'll get more. Bloody rare. Come on up.

Now?

Holiday weekend & I'm off.

A row of flickering ellipses appeared in the text window, indicating that he was typing a reply.

After a moment, they vanished.

A long pause, and they reappeared. He was typing again.

Then he stopped.

At last, the ellipses came back and this time, stayed there, pulsating for a long time. What could he possibly be writing?

Anxiously awaiting what appeared to be a lengthy missive, Sully forgot all about her steak on the grill until the first-floor tenant poked his head out the door and asked if something was burning.

Her well-done sirloin had gone up in flames.

By the time she'd put out the fire and disposed of the charred remains, the ellipses had vanished again—that time, for good. She sent a row of question marks. Barnes never replied.

Now, almost a month later, he's materialized with a maddeningly casual: Hey, Gingersnap, what's up?

She starts typing. Hey, yourself. No. She deletes *yourself* and replaces it with *stranger.*

"Here you go, Sully." She looks up to see her favorite waiter here at the Dapplebrook Inn, a sandy-haired, bespectacled college kid named Trevor.

His white shirtsleeve rides up his wrist as he pours the tea into a china cup. Her never-off-duty, detail-oriented Inner Detective notes with interest the blue-black edge of a tattoo poking from beneath the cuff. She's glimpsed it before, intrigued by the hint of bad-boy edge behind the clean-cut, wholesome college student she's gotten to know since becoming a regular at the Dapplebrook last fall.

He's not the skull and crossbones type, so she imagines

that the ink depicts something innocuous or sweet—a heart and arrow, his mom's initials, a meaningful date. Maybe she'll ask him about it sometime. Or maybe it's more interesting to just keep wondering what it is and why he got it.

Tea . . . for two . . . two . . . for tea . . .

The Dapplebrook Inn brews it from whole leaves, just like her grandmother Colly always did.

But this is tea for one. Last month it was steak for one, big enough for two. It's always table for one, though pre-set for two. Trevor whisked away the extra napkin and silverware, but the vacant chair opposite hers reverberates solitude.

Most days, it's a much needed balm after hectic New York. But on beautiful summer nights like tonight, she wouldn't mind companionship. Not just male companionship, though a date once in a while would be nice. But her closest friend here, Rowan Mundy, is busy with work and family, and Sully has yet to find a circle of meet-for-margaritas pals like she'd had back in New York. Here, women in her own age group tend to be married, most with children. Men, too.

Fellow cop and coworker Nick Colonomos is a notable exception, but he falls into the same category as Barnes: off-limits.

Not to mention blatantly uninterested.

"Be right back with your cherry pie, Sully."

"Thanks." She thrusts her phone away, facedown on the table. "Maybe I'll have another beer, too. That goes with pie, right?"

"Goes with everything."

"Thanks. I promise I'll drink it fast."

"No worries. Much as I'd like to see you chug, I'm on till eleven, and we had a late check-in. The boss said she's coming down to eat, so I'm here anyway." About to walk away, Trevor gestures at the phone. "Something happen to make you need something stronger than Irish tea?"

"How'd you guess?"

"I hope it's not bad news."

"It's not. It's . . . I don't even know *what* it is."

"Sorry about that." Trevor heads back inside, scooping up a couple of check folders on abandoned tables.

Sully leans back in her chair, grabs her phone again, and shakes her head. Leave it to Barnes to intrude on her nice relaxing evening.

Hey, Gingersnap . . .

Hey, stranger . . .

Stupid response. It doesn't sound like her. She deletes and instead writes, Where the hell—

That sounds more like her, yet . . . too extreme?

Not in the old days, but now . . .

Delete.

She tries again: It's about time—

Delete.

It's not as if she's been waiting around for him to reach out again. She's barely thought about him.

Barely?

All right, she's missed him, but not consistently. She's been busy working her new job, settling into her new home, living her new life.

The couple in the corner departs, holding hands.

Sully stares at the blinking cursor, wondering what to say and why it feels like such a big deal. It's only Barnes.

But things are weird now. He made things weird when he didn't reply to her invitation back in May.

Or maybe she accomplished that—the weirdness—when she moved away.

Trevor returns, showing a tall, attractive woman to a nearby table, removing the second place setting. She's wearing white denim capris, a black cardigan, and black leather flats. Sully—similarly attired, though her capris are khaki, her sweater navy, flats brown—somehow feels underdressed.

The newcomer chooses the chair facing away from Sully. Clearly, this isn't her first solo dining experience.

Sully admires the brunette waves rippling down her back. She herself has always been plagued with wiry titian ringlets that frizz in the slightest humidity unless you tackle them with a brush and blow dryer and plenty of product. Who has time for all that? Most days—today included—she sports a ponytail.

Eavesdropping as the woman orders her meal, Inner Detective Sully notes that her accent sounds West Coast, and her health-conscious order screams California. No lobster mac and cheese for her; she's having chardonnay cut with club soda and a grilled chicken avocado salad, no cheese, dressing on the side.

If she went out for margaritas, Sully decides, she probably wouldn't want tortilla chips and guacamole. And she'd probably order hers frozen instead of straight up, no salt, hold the tequila.

Sully sips her tea, missing her old friends, tequila, New York . . .

Barnes?

Him too.

Departing for the kitchen with his order pad, Trevor aims an index finger at Sully. "I didn't forget your pie and beer."

"No rush."

"Pie and beer?" The woman turns to flash a smile at Sully. "There's a dessert combo I've never tried."

"Goes together like tea and crumpets, coffee and donuts . . ."

"Cookies and milk?"

"Yes. But I'll take a beer over milk any day."

The woman laughs. "That goes without saying. So are you staying here, too?"

"Me? No, I live around the corner. I'm Sullivan Leary."

"Emerson Mundy. Nice to meet you."

"Mundy? You're . . . ?"

"One of *those* Mundys?" She nods. "My dad's great-uncle built this place."

"So this is your hometown."

"Not exactly. I've never been here before. I'm from California."

Bingo. Sully fist-bumps Inner Detective Sully.

"How about you? Is this *your* hometown?"

"No, I'm from New York City."

"How did you find your way here?"

This is the part where Sully either admits she's law enforcement, or keeps that tidbit to herself for the time being. It's not that she's hiding anything, but when she meets new people, she prefers to be perceived based on *who*, and not *what*, she is.

"I was in the area on business about a year and a half ago," she says, "and I decided it would be a nice place to live. I moved last August."

"Do you miss New York?"

She hesitates. "Sometimes. Ever been there?"

"Today, as a matter of fact—I was at a teachers' conference in D.C. this week, so I flew into JFK from Dulles this afternoon and drove up here in a rental car."

"I bet your flight was delayed for thunderstorms and air traffic, and when it finally took off it was turbulent, after you landed you had to wait forever for a gate, there was a huge line at the rental car location, and when you got on the road you crawled along for hours in rush hour traffic."

Wide-eyed, Emerson digests that. "Either those are a lot of lucky guesses, or you're some kind of psychic detective."

Half right, Sully thinks.

"Nah. I just know how things are in New York."

"I guess life is better here, huh?"

"Yes. More affordable, too." Sully explains that she swapped her tiny studio with its sky-high rent and view of another sky-high brick wall for a much cheaper, much larger floor-through with a *real* view. Tucked behind the tall mansard roof of a Victorian home here in The Heights, her new place overlooks a charming cobblestone stretch of State Street.

"It sounds perfect. Wish I could do that."

"It was a long time coming. Are you here to visit family?"

"Hoping to find them. I never knew much about our roots and I've been doing some genealogical research that led me here."

"One of my closest friends is a Mundy, but it's her married name—her husband, Jake, is descended from the first settlers."

"So am I."

"Then I guess you're related. I can introduce you to Rowan tomorrow morning, if you'd like. I'm meeting her for coffee. It's her last day of school."

"School? How old is she?"

Sully laughs. "Rowan's a teacher."

"So am I." Emerson raises her eyebrows as if that's an astonishing coincidence.

It's not like you're both astronauts, Sully wants to say, but she swallows the sarcasm.

Sure you can take the girl out of New York *and* take the New York out of the girl. It just takes time, practice . . .

And distance from Barnes. He always brought out her inner wiseass, which doesn't go over so well here.

Embracing her kinder, gentler small-town self, Sully says, "I guess you and Rowan have more in common than just a last name. Come by Valley Roasters tomorrow at eleven. It's on the Commons—37 Market Street."

"You don't think she'd mind?"

"Not at all. She's—" Sully breaks off as her phone vibrates with a call. Seeing the number, she stands and hastily tucks three twenties beneath her teacup. "Sorry, I have to take this. Tell Trevor that'll cover my check. You can have the pie and beer. See you tomorrow?"

"Don't you want to check with your friend first?"

Sully waves away the suggestion, already striding toward the steps with her ringing phone. "She'll love it. Good night."

Ira is forty minutes late for her appointment when she finally spots the white-painted sign that reads Hadley College: Founded in 1825.

Leaving the highway, she drives between enormous stone pillars and follows a winding lane framed by ancient trees. She's no longer white-knuckled now that hers are the only headlights, illuminating lush foliage and a pair of deer grazing in a stand of trees.

During the school year, the campus is alive with traffic and young people. They stroll with backpacks, jog past, roll along on skateboards and bikes, or cruise around with windows down, music blasting. They wear shorts in inclement weather, foolish creatures, and no one seems to own galoshes anymore, much less an umbrella. On nice days, the men are shirtless and the scantily dressed women might as well be, all of them sprawled across the broad quad like a living room, staring at their screens, sleeping, reading, cuddling . . .

Imagine what Papa and Great-Aunt Etta would say about what goes on nowadays.

Ah, well. Tonight, with the vast majority of the three thousand students home for the summer, the campus is virtually deserted.

"We're nearly there, Jane. I do hope this young woman will be able to help us."

The question is, can Savannah Ivers be entrusted with a secret?

Perhaps. For a price.

According to the *Tribune* article, Savannah attended Hadley on a full, need-based scholarship, and will begin graduate studies in September.

Reading between the lines, Ora translated: *Savannah needs money.*

Ora isn't a wealthy woman, but she lives modestly and has more than enough to get by for another twenty years, God willing. She can afford to splurge on something as important as this, and it's time.

Until last summer, Jane was overshadowed by the Sleeping Beauties. The trio of 1916 murder victims were the focus of Mundypalooza; the reason people came from around the world to attempt cracking the case.

Now the Beauties are identified, their remains exhumed, tested, matched with descendants. All have been reburied; one transferred—with considerable controversy—to the family plot in Holy Angels cemetery. Case closed.

"Your turn now, Jane. I'll do for you what I did for the Beauties. I'll find out who you were, and what happened to you."

Steering around a bend, she sees massive Pritchard Hall perched atop a rise up ahead. A little over a century ago, the entire college was housed beneath its squared turrets, gothic gargoyles, and flying buttresses. Now only admissions and administration offices are located there.

For Ora, the spotlit granite castle is a beacon home.

If history is the family business, as the Abramses have always enjoyed telling people, then this campus is where it all began. Her father, Dr. Theodore Abrams, was a member of the one hundredth graduating class and later joined the faculty as a history professor. Hadley was Ora's alma mater, too, and was even Great-Aunt Etta's.

Past Pritchard, the buildings along the academic quad are either ivy-covered redbrick or unadorned rectangular concrete, representing opposing eras in twentieth-century architecture. Constructed in the 1980s, Muller Hall is a tall cube with sparse, narrow columns of windows on its white stucco face. Ora isn't fond of its contemporary style, but it, too, holds cherished memories.

Tonight, it might also hold the key to a centuries-old mystery.

This time, there will be no Mundypalooza. Plenty of James and Eliza's descendants, like former Mayor John Ransom, are locally prominent. The family would be reluctant, and understandably so, to drag skeletons out of the closet.

Or the purse, Ora thinks, wearing a thin smile as she pulls into the parking lot.

Emerson reaches over to the adjoining table and picks up the thin paperback Sullivan Leary left behind in her haste to take her phone call.

Perfect—this is a good reason to join her and her friend Rowan for coffee tomorrow morning.

Yes, she'd been invited. Yes, she'd been assured that Rowan won't mind. But she's never had a large social circle or been entirely comfortable meeting new people—a remnant of her lonely childhood.

Growing up, she saw her few friends at their own homes, where even if there wasn't an intact nuclear family, at least things felt . . . normal. Everyone else had a mother, and most had siblings, too. The fathers, regardless of whether they lived under the same roof, worked regular jobs. Flowers grew in window boxes, cars were parked in the driveways, visitors came and went . . .

In those houses, unlike her own, she saw the hustle and bustle of ordinary lives unmarred by the heartache—or stigma—of parental abandonment.

You grow up, you move on—

Yes, Dad, you move on . . . you taught me well.

Sometimes even now, memories stab like stray shards underfoot long after shattered glass has been swept away. If you let them burrow in, they'll fester, so you brush them off and keep going.

Tomorrow, she'll go to Valley Roasters to deliver Sullivan's book. If she feels like a third wheel, she'll make an excuse to leave.

If not . . .

Who knows? Maybe she'll make a couple of new friends. Maybe she, like Sullivan Leary, will decide to move here.

Smiling faintly, she starts to tuck the book into her purse, and does a double-take on the title.

Mundy's Landing: Then and Now.

Local history at her fingertips, a sign that she's meant to be here, and that . . .

Wait a minute.

Looking closely at the sepia-toned family portrait on the cover, she's almost positive she recognizes the parents' faces.

Flipping open the book to find a caption, she sees that it is, indeed Aaron and Sarah Mundy, along with their two daughters and three sons. According to the caption, the illustrious Horace J. was their second born, aged nine when the photograph was taken in 1880. He was a wisp of a boy, hovering close at his mother's side, wide-eyed behind wire-rimmed spectacles.

Only a year older, and far sturdier by contrast, ten-year-old Oswald seems to gaze back at Emerson. His mouth is solemnly set like the others', but the glint in his eye transforms his expression into a smirk. His right hand rests on his father's shoulder; his left is clenched at his side in a fist. It's missing altogether in the few photos Emerson found among her father's things—lost somewhere in his youth, and replaced with an iron hand.

Oswald's handsome face, too, was later transformed. He grew into a gaunt man whose grizzled beard couldn't entirely hide some kind of injury that had left a portion of his left jaw and cheek badly scarred.

But the smirk never left him. Emerson had glimpsed it in later photos, and he'd certainly handed it down to his grandson. She'd seen that same vaguely self-satisfied look on her father's face over the years.

She takes out her phone to snap a picture of the old photo, wanting to compare it later to the ones she left behind in California.

She'd powered down the phone at the airport in Washington. Turning it on now, she sees that she's missed several calls from Roy, and a string of text messages.

Where RU?

Keep trying to call . . .

Did you land?

Where RU?

Worried . . .

RU OK?

She quickly texts back Sorry, all is well, knowing the phone is going to ring a few seconds after she hits Send.

She's right.

She considers letting it go into voice mail. But Roy just wants reassurance that she's alive and well, and who can blame him?

She picks up the phone. "Hi, Roy."

"Emerson! Where have you been?"

The door opens, and the waiter steps out onto the porch, carrying a tray with pie, beer, and her own order.

"My flight was really late. I forgot to turn on my phone after I landed," she tells Roy. "Listen, everything is fine, but I'm in a restaurant, so I can't talk. I'll call you back in a little bit."

"What—" she hears him saying as she hangs up.

She turns to the waiter, looking puzzled beside the table Sullivan vacated. "She had to leave in a hurry, but she left you the money."

If she mentions that she also left the book, he might tell her to leave it here, and then she'll talk herself out of going tomorrow.

"Then you just got yourself a free dessert. And a beer."

"Oh, that's okay. I've already got my wine, and if I eat all that sugar, I'll be up all night."

As if she isn't up all night, every night, as it is.

"Are you sure?"

"Positive." She looks back down at her phone, buzzing with a text.

"By the way," he says, setting down her salad, "it's not like you're disturbing other diners. You didn't have to cut your phone call short."

"No, trust me, I did." She takes a long sip of chardonnay.

"Possessive ex-boyfriend?"

"Possessive current fiancé." She sets down the glass, picks up the phone, and glances at the text. "But it'll be okay."

"Are you saying that to me, or to yourself?"

Surprised, she looks up to see the waiter looking thoughtful.

"To you. I'm saying it to you."

"Well, that's good. Can I get you anything else?"

"Just the check, thanks. I'm going to gobble this and go."

"Take your time. Sure you don't want the pie and beer?"

"All yours."

He glances back toward the door, then says, conspiratorially, "Want me to sit here with you while I have it?"

"What? Oh . . . um . . ."

"Never mind. You have a fiancé. Now he's texting you?"

"How'd you guess?"

"He *is* possessive. I'll go get your check."

Watching him walk away with his tray, she reminds herself that he's only a kid, a good fifteen years younger—and, yes, she does have a fiancé.

A fiancé who's asking, Where RU?

She quickly types back, Restaurant. Will call you later.

She shuts off her phone, picks up her fork, and opens the book again.

"Barnes? What's up?" Sully asks, pressing the phone to her ear as she strides down the street, away from the Dapplebrook Inn.

"Can you talk for a second?"

"Yes."

"Are you alone?"

The street isn't entirely deserted. People are sitting on

porch swings with candles flickering. Several teenagers are shooting baskets at a garage hoop. A trio of women are chatting on a driveway. The only person in earshot is an elderly man in pajama bottoms and slippers, standing patiently as his leashed dog noses around a fire hydrant.

"Yeah, I'm alone," she tells Barnes, walking on toward the corner. "Why?"

"I need a favor."

"Okay." She waits.

He's silent.

"Hey, are you okay?" she asks.

"I'm . . ." A pause. "Can I stay with you for a few days?"

"Sure. When?"

Another pause.

She rounds the corner onto State Street.

Her address is two doors down. Like its neighbors, the house is a clapboard Queen Anne Victorian and sits close to the street on a small lot. While most of the other homes have elaborate paint jobs in charming vintage colors, Sully's place is white with black shutters and trim. The lot is heavily landscaped with blooming perennials. Dense shrub borders threaten to choke a white picket fence along the street and wrestle with the wisteria vines that crawl over an arched arbor gate.

"Hello? Barnes, are you there?"

"Yeah, I'm here."

"I said you can stay. When do you want to come?"

"I'm here," he says again.

"No, I heard that." Must be a bad connection. "I asked when—"

"I said I'm *here*."

"You're *where*?"

"Right here."

She hears his voice both in her ear and nearby.

The wisteria rustles, and a human shadow emerges.

Barnes.

But not the clean-shaven, impeccably groomed, well-dressed man she knows.

He smells of stale cigarettes, though he quit smoking three years ago, and of sweat. Not of musky, almost-pleasant masculine heat, but of the fetid BO that wafts from many a perp.

Even in the streetlight's dim glow she can see that his face is gaunt, eyes bloodshot and underscored by purple slashes, jaw and lip gray-stubbled. He's wearing dark jeans and sneakers with an untucked navy blue T-shirt that hangs on his frame. He must have lost a good twenty pounds.

"You look like hell."

His failure to respond with a sarcastic zinger is even more worrisome than his appearance.

He disconnects the call, shoves his phone into his back pocket, and meets her gaze.

"What happened to you?"

"I need a place to stay for a few days."

"Get your stuff and come on inside. Where'd you park?"

"I don't have any, and I didn't."

"What?"

"No stuff. No car. Just me."

"How'd you get here?"

"Train. And bus. There will be time for questions later, so can we . . . ?" He motions at the house.

"Why didn't you drive? And, wait—*you* took a bus?"

"I took three."

"Three buses? And a train? Why? There's an express bus that—"

"I know, Leary."

Not *Gingersnap*.

And no dig about Mundy's Landing being in the middle of nowhere.

"Why'd you take the long way here?"

He looks her squarely in the eye and gives the answer she already suspected. "To make sure I wasn't being followed."

"Because . . . ?"

"I'm in trouble. I didn't know where else to go, and I don't trust anyone but you."

She smiles faintly. "Someday, I'm going to remind you that you said that. I might even give you a hard time. But not tonight. Come on in."

October 24, 1955

My Dear Aurora,

I have instructed Mr. Duvane to deliver this letter to you upon my demise. He is also in possession of my last will and testament. I'm certain it is no surprise that I've bequeathed all of my worldly belongings to you, as my beloved grandniece and sole heir. In the pages that follow, I have provided itemized background information for some of my most cherished artifacts, which I entrust knowing you shall keep, preserve, and protect from exploitation.

It is my last wish that when my time comes, you will take my place as curator of the historical society, and live out the rest of your days in this village I have loved more dearly than I could ever have loved a spouse.

Thank you for the joy you have brought to my life. Carry on in my good work, and know that I shall always be with you, as will your dear papa, and that we will meet again in the great beyond.

Fondly,

Etta Abrams

Chapter 4

Ora drives across the broad parking lot behind Muller Hall, complimenting herself on her navigational skills though the pavement is largely wide open.

She has her choice of parking spots. She selects one beside the door, marked by blue pavement stripes, and hangs her disability parking tag from the visor. It expires in a month, and Dr. Duncan won't approve a replacement.

Silly man. She may be getting up there in years, but her mind, memory, and senses are as sharp as ever.

Aging is inevitable. Dementia is not. Aunt Etta remained astute until the end.

But Papa . . .

Ora turns off the car and snatches the keys from the ignition. It's time to meet Savannah Ivers. *Past* time.

She retrieves her antique rosewood walking stick from the seat and leans heavily on it as she steps out of the car. Dizziness swoops in like a bat, and her right hand tightens around the carved bone handle.

She's spent the latter part of her adult life fearing that her father's fate would one day become her own, and now—

No. No, it's simply the excitement. She's been so looking forward to meeting this young scholar, and to helping her poor Jane Doe.

She stands very still, eyes closed, willing the spell to pass. When it does, she makes her way around to the passenger's side to remove the large purse containing the skull. She slings it over her left forearm as if it merely contains lipstick, mascara, and knitting needles. She hasn't used any of those things in years, as her eyesight is . . .

Oh, it's not failing. No, her senses are sharp indeed. But who has time to fuss with cosmetics and hobbies when there are so many other important things to do?

"Come on, Jane. It's time."

Heading toward the door as spryly as her old legs and walking stick will let her, she notes that Miss Ivers failed to prop it open as asked. Did she ignore Ora's request? Or did she tire of waiting and leave for the night? Wouldn't that be just like this younger generation—not a shred of patience.

I don't like her at all, Ora decides abruptly. *I do wish I didn't need her help.*

Standing beside the closed door, she wonders whether she might indeed find the answer another way.

No, she needs an expert. One located in convenient proximity to Mundy's Landing, but without an emotional connection or preconceived notions.

Suitable candidates are hardly swarming the museum like high season tourists.

Resigned, Ora reaches out to knock on the door, but it opens before she makes contact.

"Are you Ora Abrams?" asks a young woman who can't possibly be Miss Ivers.

"Yes."

"I'm Savannah. Come on in."

She isn't wearing glasses or a lab coat, as she was in the *Tribune* photo. Her short skirt and tank top reveal long, shapely limbs. Her hair, pulled back tightly in her photo, now ripples past her bare shoulders in a mass of waves and ringlets. Unlike Ora, she seems to have time to fuss with mascara and lipstick. Eyeliner or shadow, too. She's wearing hoop earrings and a stack of bracelets, and a silver pendant dangles above daring cleavage.

She starts off down the corridor, bangles jangling, then turns back. "Sorry, am I walking too fast for you?"

"Of course not." Indignant, Ora thrusts the cane forward and takes a few brisk steps to prove that she's not feeble of body any more than of mind. "But I thought you worked in the lab."

"I do." Seeing Ora's pointed look at her attire, she adds hastily, "I don't usually dress like this. But I have a date, and you were late, so I had to get ready while I was waiting. In fact, I thought maybe you'd come and gone while I was in the restroom. The door is locked."

"Yes. I'd asked you to leave it open for me."

"I was afraid to. I'm not used to being here alone this late at night. Earlier, I could have sworn I heard footsteps in the hall, but when I looked, no one was there. Either this place is haunted, or someone is sneaking around. You probably think I'm losing my mind."

Ora doesn't deny it, pleased to note that if anyone is losing her mind around here, it isn't Ora herself.

She follows Savannah down the hall, past reproduction portraits of famous scientists and the closed door to the department chair's office. The name plaque has changed twice since Professor Malouf retired.

However, the forensics laboratory is very much the same. The perimeter is lined with cabinets, counters, and computers; sinks, screens, and scopes. In the center of the room, a row of tall steel tables await specimens. The wall art consists of anatomical diagrams. In one corner, a life-sized skeleton is propped in a chair wearing a tasseled mortarboard, gold braided honors cords draped around its bony shoulders.

Ghoulish grad student humor. Years ago, Ora arrived to find that every skull displayed behind the glass door of an antique cabinet had a blue-banded "It's a boy" cigar prodding from its gaping jaw. Professor Malouf explained that a colleague had just given birth.

Savannah pulls out a stool. "Have a seat. Or should I get you a regular chair?"

Of course she should, but she shouldn't ask. She should just do it. Young people today have no manners.

"No, thank you," Ora says stiffly. "I'll stand."

Savannah checks her watch, lifting her wrist so close to her face that Ora wants to ask about her glasses. Probably took them off for vanity's sake. Foolish, foolish girl—and quite clearly indicating that she's in a hurry.

Ora sets her bag on the table, switches her walking stick to her left hand, and opens the bag. She reaches past the skull for her checkbook. "As I said, I'd like to hire you for a special project."

"What is it, exactly?"

"I can't tell you until you're hired."

"How can I accept the job without knowing what it is?"

"May I please have a pen?"

"Excuse me?"

"A pen. I'd like to borrow one, please?"

As Savannah produces a Bic from a nearby desk, Ora glances at the stool, wondering if she should dare to climb onto it. Her legs are feeling a little wobbly, but the stool appears just as wobbly. The last thing she needs is to topple onto the floor and break an old bone.

Stoic, Ora thanks Savannah for the pen, writes a check, tears it out, and offers it to her.

"What's that?"

"The first installment on your pay."

As Ora enters the amount in the ledger, she watches from the corner of her eye as Savannah takes the check

and holds it a few inches from her nose. Pleased to hear a
startled gasp, she briskly folds the checkbook and returns
it to her purse. "That's half the fee. Yours unconditionally
if you agree to take the assignment. You'll receive the rest
when you've completed the assignment."

"What is it, exactly?"

"Are you accepting it?"

Silly question. No one in her position would turn down
that amount of money or the promise of more.

Yet she feigns hesitation. "I don't know. I'm really busy
right now with my research, so . . ."

Ora just looks at her.

"Um . . . my pen? Can I . . . ?"

"Of course." Ora hands it over.

Savannah returns it to the desk with more care than is
necessary. She's stalling, trying to figure what to do.

"I shouldn't have said 'unconditionally,'" Ora tells her,
and she whirls around. "There is a catch."

"What is it?" Savannah asks flatly, as if she knew it
was too good to be true.

"I would appreciate your discretion regarding the assignment."

Savannah looks around the empty lab and points at the
mortarboard-wearing skeleton in the corner. "Who am I
going to tell? Him?"

Her quip met with silence, she frowns. "Is this illegal?
Because I won't do anything illegal."

"Nor would I," Ora says haughtily. "What do you take
me for? I've been the director of the Mundy's Landing
Historical Society for seventy-five years now."

"Seventy-five years? Wow—how old *are* you?"

"A lady never asks. Nor does she tell," Ora responds,
masking her momentary confusion as she realizes the
numbers don't add up. Maybe it hasn't been seventy-five
years. But that isn't the point. "I can assure you that this

is a legitimate assignment, Miss Ivers. It's simply confidential. There are people on the faculty here who would be intrigued by it."

"Why didn't you hire them?"

"If I wanted to, I would have, long ago."

"Why now? And why me?"

It's time.

And you're an outsider.

"Because you're a brilliant young scholar with a bright future. Now then, do we have an agreement?"

"Sure." Savannah folds the check and puts it into her purse.

"*Sure?*"

"I'm sorry. Yes. We do." She extends her hand as if to shake on the deal. Ora's hands are otherwise occupied, lifting the skull in its protective case from the bag and gently setting it on the table.

Savannah gapes. "What is that?"

"If you don't know, my dear, then you should probably reconsider your future, and I shall certainly reconsider my offer."

"No, I mean, I know *what* it is . . . I just wonder why you have it."

Ora never knew how the skull had come into her greataunt's possession back in the late 1940s. She has her suspicions. Aunt Etta certainly wasn't above helping herself to precious artifacts in the name of historic preservation.

She once marched out of the Elsworth Ransom Library with a rare nineteenth-century classic first edition tucked under her arm. Ora was about ten at the time, and had borrowed her usual stack of Nancy Drew mysteries.

"Serves them right!" Aunt Etta had ranted as they walked several blocks toward Papa's brick house in The Heights. "This book should have been properly preserved, away from light and air and human hands. It's worth thousands of dollars, and they had it shelved in the main stacks where anyone could make off with it."

Somebody had. Aunt Etta hadn't bothered to check out the book with the librarian. But of course, she didn't consider it a theft and didn't intend to sell it. Infuriated that the library never even reported it missing, she later told Ora, "It just goes to show that the book is better off in my hands than in theirs."

She tucked it away in a protective case. She bequeathed it to Ora when she passed away in 1956, along with the rest of her worldly possessions—including the skull.

"It's part of my private collection—about three hundred and fifty years old," Ora tells Savannah now, lest the skittish girl misinterpret it as fresh kill and flee into the night. "It was found by a team of Hadley students in 1947 during an archaeological dig out at Schaapskill Nature Preserve."

"I've heard about that. It's the site of the first settlement. The cannibals—that couple who were hung in front of their kids. The Mundys, right?"

Ora purses her lips. Even the more intellectual young people retain the most gruesome details.

"So the college donated this skull to the museum?" Savannah asks.

"I suppose they must have. It was before my time."

"*Really?*"

"Why, yes. I was a girl when it was found, just like Jane herself." Miffed, Ora wonders just how old Savannah Ivers thinks she is—then realizes she cannot, in this moment, remember her own age.

"Jane?"

"Jane Doe." She indicates the skull.

"Oh, right."

"Additional human remains were found at the site during the same excavation. They're in the archives here on campus," she tells Savannah. "Years ago, a professor friend attempted to find out if the other bones included more of Jane. His work was inconclusive, but forensics have made great strides since then. I'd like you to reexamine them, along with the skull."

"I'm not authorized to go digging around in the archives and testing old bones. If you'd like to speak to a faculty member who can—"

"No. I would not." Ora isn't interested in playing by the rules, lest the Mundys—or the media—get wind of what she's doing. "I just thought you might have access, but if you don't . . ."

"I don't. Not officially."

Ora doesn't press the point. When Savannah is drawn into the mystery, she'll delve further of her own accord.

At last, the girl puts on a pair of glasses, along with blue gloves, trains an LED light on the skull.

"I can see that she was a teenager, probably fourteen to sixteen years old at TOD."

Time of death. Yes. The Hadley team determined that years ago.

Testing Savannah's skill set, Ora asks how she knows.

"Tooth emergence and cranial fusion. The hind molars haven't emerged from the mandible, and there are ridge bumps along the coronal and sagittal sutures," she adds, looking up, her eyes alive with interest.

Satisfied, Ora reaches into her purse again, takes out an envelope, and hands it to Savannah. "This is a complete list of the first group of settlers who landed here in 1665. I've crossed out most of the names by process of elimination, leaving only four young women. One of them was Jane."

"You want me to figure out which one."

"And whether her death was deliberate, or an accident."

"Got it. But will the answer to whether someone was murdered change anything now, centuries later?"

Ora considers the question.

The truth may change nothing.

The truth may change everything.

"There's really no way of knowing until we have the answer, is there?" she asks Savannah, who shrugs.

"I guess that makes sense." She looks again at her watch. "I'm sorry, but I'm meeting someone for drinks at the Windmill, so I'd better get going."

"The Windmill in Mundy's Landing?"

"Is there another Windmill?"

"I'm sure there are many in the Hudson Valley," Ora snaps. "Had I known you were coming to town, we could have met there."

"Sorry, but I didn't even know I had a date. I just met him this afternoon, and he texted me after you called."

A last-minute date with a virtual stranger who can't even be bothered to pick up the telephone? Incapable of masking disapproval, Ora shakes her head, and then Savannah's hand, taking her leave. She's had her fill of this conversation, and of standing on achy old legs.

She hobbles out into the night. The sky is black and clear with pinprick stars and a sharp-edged moon, yet she senses a familiar fog creeping in as she begins the long, harrowing drive back to Mundy's Landing.

The words with which she attempts to reassure herself make matters worse: *It's only in your mind.*

This so-called hometown of Emerson's is more off the beaten path than Roy thought. He never saw a gas station after he exited the highway, and rolled into this one on fumes. Standing at the pump filling his pickup, he checks his phone to see if Emerson answered his last message yet. He sent it while he was behind the wheel, keeping an eye out for cops along the highway as he typed. The last thing he needs today is another ticket.

Still no reply.

Frustrated, he shoves the phone back into the pocket of the ill-fitting cargo shorts he bought before leaving the Bronx. He stopped at a rest area on the road to change into them, along with newly purchased underwear and T-shirt. It's cheap polyester, the first one he saw on the clearance rack. Red, the only color in his size, and he wasn't about to browse around or pay more than five bucks.

The clothing he'd been wearing is sealed in the plastic shopping bag, tossed into the back of the pickup along with his duffel bag. His arms are coated in the pink lotion he'd bought, hoping it might soothe the itch. It hasn't.

She'd said she was in a restaurant. Is it here in Mundy's Landing?

This stretch of highway isn't exactly brimming with fine dining establishments. He surveys the array of fast food signs surrounding the Mobil station, trying to imagine his fiancée eating a burger, a donut . . .

A Slurpee. He watches a group of teenage girls emerge from the 7-Eleven next door and wander across the parking lot carrying large cups. They aimlessly volley a small rock across the pavement, passing it from flip-flop to flip-flop.

The gas pump kicks off. Roy replaces the nozzle, screws the cap back on the tank, and waits for the receipt to print.

The girls pass, snatches of their gossipy conversation reaching his ears.

". . . I don't know why she'd ever . . ."

". . . No way! He's such a . . ."

". . . and remember when they . . ."

". . . she made me swear not to tell you guys but . . ."

Small towns. Ugh. He's never liked them.

He lived in one during college. Less than two hours' drive from New York City, New Paltz felt like a foreign land to a kid who'd lived in every borough. Public transportation was almost non-existent. The only two restaurants that delivered were Chinese and pizza, and both were lousy. Most people spent an inordinate amount of time indoors, and the ones who didn't were outdoorsy types who enjoyed scaling cliffs or jumping off them.

Worse, small-town people spent an awful lot of time judging others and worrying about being judged themselves.

Roy lasted a couple of semesters, fell in love with a graduating senior, and followed her out to San Francisco. The romance didn't last, no matter how hard Roy tried to make things work. But he stayed on the West Coast. He eventually went back to school, got a degree in education, found a job.

Roy doesn't particularly like math, or high school kids. But he loves having summers off, and he's been looking forward to spending this one with Emerson.

Spending all of them with Emerson.

Only Emerson is slipping from his grasp.

He's been keeping an eye out for her since he left the highway, but he has no idea where she might be.

You never should have let her go in the first place.

But that's what you're supposed to do when someone you love wants to leave. His college girlfriend had a cheesy poster of a butterfly on her wall, with the saying, "If you love something, let it go. If it comes back to you, it's yours. If it doesn't, it never was."

Roy let go.

Emerson got away.

But she is mine. We're getting married. And I'm going to find her.

Emerson sets down her fork. She didn't eat much of her salad, too intent on trying to make out the photos in the book Sullivan left behind. Even with the votive candle close to the page, it was hard to see much detail. Now she picks up her phone again and turns it on, hoping to use the glowing screen to illuminate the open page before her.

There are more texts from Roy.

Jaw clenched, she decides she might as well get this over with, and calls instead of texting back.

He answers immediately. "Where are you?"

"In Mundy's Landing. I told you that."

"No, you didn't. You hung up on me."

"I didn't just hang up. I said I was in a restaurant."

"Which restaurant?"

"What difference does it make? I don't understand why you're acting like this."

"I'm worried about you."

"Because I'm traveling? I can't even go to a teachers' conference without—"

"How was the conference?" he cuts in.

"What?"

"The conference. How was it?"

"It was fine. Roy, this isn't normal. You're freaking me out, the way you're . . ." She trails off, seeing the waiter stepping back outside with her check.

"*You're* freaking *me* out," Roy is saying.

"Listen, I need to go."

"Just talk to me for a second, Emerson."

"I can't right now. Please. You need to let me go."

"But—"

"I'm exhausted. We'll talk in the morning." She hangs up, turns off the phone again, and meets the waiter's concerned gaze.

"Everything okay?"

She shrugs.

"Fiancé again?"

"How'd you guess?"

"Do you think he'll show up here?"

"No! He's in California."

"Are you sure about that?"

"What do you mean?"

"Nothing," he says. "Sorry. It just sounded like . . . I mean, I wasn't eavesdropping."

"No, I know. It's fine. He's just possessive, like I said." She pulls out a credit card and throws it into the check folder.

"Be right back," he says, and disappears inside with it.

He's in California . . .

Are you sure about that?

Roy's been known to show up at her doorstep on nights when she'd planned to be alone, longed to be alone, had *begged* him to leave her alone. When she asks why he's there, he gives her the same answer every time: "Because I'm concerned about you."

"Well, I'm fine, Roy. You don't need to worry."

Somehow, he always manages to talk his way inside. Once he's there, he asks too many questions, and she'll catch him staring at her wearing a strange expression.

"What?"

"Nothing."

"Why are you looking at me like that?"

"Because I love you."

It isn't just love, nor just concern.

It's something else, something that set off a warning within. Not urgent, but more like the faint, intermittent ping of a dying smoke alarm battery. You should do something about it, but it can wait until later, so you procrastinate and hope you won't regret it.

Roy would never hurt her.

Of course he wouldn't. He's her fiancé.

Still . . .

With a trembling hand, Emerson reaches toward the silverware alongside her plate. Grabbing the knife she'd used to cut the chicken in her salad, she wipes it quickly on her napkin and shoves it into her purse.

Roy sits in his truck, still parked at the gas pump. He'd been about to leave when Emerson finally called him back.

Seeing her number pop up, he thought everything was going to be okay, but . . .

But it isn't.

She hung up on him, and now her phone is ringing straight into voice mail again.

His head is spinning. He can barely think straight, and he's fading fast.

Coffee. He needs coffee, and something in his stomach . . .

Looking around, rubbing his forearms, he spots a Dunkin' Donuts. The parking lot is empty, but it's open twenty-four hours.

And there's a Holiday Inn right across the street—not the Ritz, but a step up from last night. He'll head over there with his food, grab a room, eat, freshen up, and then get back down to business with Emerson.

At the drive-through, he finds a handwritten Out of Order sign taped to the menu board.

He curses, slapping the steering wheel, hard. Nothing has gone right today. Nothing.

He pulls into a spot by the door and goes inside. The place is as deserted as the parking lot. A moon-faced young woman is standing behind the register. Her hair

is the color of scrambled eggs, and her name tag reads
Twyla.

He orders a couple of donuts and a cup of coffee.

"No problem," she says in the chipper server cadence
he's noted in his cross-country travels. Low, drawn-out
no, high-pitched emphasis on *prob*. "Cream and sugar?"

"Please."

"You got it." Low, drawn-out *you*, high-pitched emphasis on *got*. "Anything else?"

"No, thanks."

She rings it up, smiling hard, and Roy hands over a
five, wondering why the hell she's so chipper.

"And *heeeeere* you *go*, sir." She hands over his change,
probably expecting him to throw it into the plastic cup
marked Tips beside the register.

Roy doesn't believe in tipping at fast food places. Everyone wants a handout these days. He pockets the money,
yet Twyla remains cheerful, telling him she just put on a
fresh pot of coffee if he can wait a few minutes.

"We always get a huge rush after the late movie lets out
over at the Regal."

He wants to ask her how many people constitute a
"huge rush" around here—five? A dozen?

She bustles around, snapping open a small pastry bag
and setting it aside on the counter, apparently waiting
until the last possible moment to pluck his donuts from
the case, thus ensuring optimal freshness. She takes a hot
cup from a stack and places it near the bag, with a plastic
lid alongside. Busy, busy.

Chatty, chatty. "So what brings you here?" she asks,
because small-town servers always know who belongs
and who doesn't.

"I'm visiting a friend."

"Really? Who?"

Roy tilts his head at her. "Do you know everyone in town?"

"Lived here all my life."

"So that's a yes?"

"It's a *try me*."

"She's a Mundy. Know any Mundys?"

She grins. "Know them all. I'm one of them."

"You're a Mundy?"

"My great-great-grandmother was. Or maybe it was my great-great-great—anyway, I'm a Block but I know everyone around here. Who are you trying to find?"

Before he can elaborate, the door opens and they both turn expectantly. Has the huge rush begun?

A lone redhead walks in, phone and keys in hand. She's thin, wearing cropped khaki pants and a navy blue sweater, and her hair is pulled back in a ponytail.

"Sully!" Little Mary Sunshine is thrilled to see her. "We were just talking about you!"

"Crap."

"No, it was all good. We were thinking about going to New York City."

Raising an eyebrow, Sully glances from Twyla to Roy and back again.

"Not me," he says quickly, grasping her assumption, and Twyla bursts out laughing.

"No! Not him. He's a customer and we just met. I mean me and Dina. She was on tonight till eleven—you just missed her. We were looking at the new schedule and neither of us has to work on the Fourth of July, so we want to go see the fireworks in New York."

New York, where no one expects you to stand around making idle chitchat at midnight when you're exhausted and just want to dunk your damned donuts into some coffee and go on your way.

"That's a long way to go for fireworks," the redhead, Sully, points out.

"Yeah, but the ones around here aren't big fancy ones like they have in New York City. I bet you probably had a favorite place where you always watched them when you lived there."

"I did. My couch."

"You could see the fireworks from your couch?" Twyla is impressed.

"I could see the TV from my couch. If I ever watched the fireworks, and I'm pretty sure I haven't in years, that's the only way I did it."

"That doesn't sound like much fun."

"Sorry to be a party pooper, but the thing about New York is . . . the people who live there hate crowds."

Roy likes crowds. You can get lost in a crowd.

"Well anyway . . . you want a blueberry muffin and a mango Coolatta?" Twyla asks Sully.

She shakes her head, because why would anyone want that?

"Not tonight. I'll have a large black coffee and a ham egg and cheese on a bagel."

"You never drink coffee!"

"Never say never."

Looking unnerved, Twyla tells Sully what she told Roy—that she just put on a fresh pot in anticipation of the rush. "It's almost done, if you can wait for it."

"How long?"

"Like, two minutes. Trust me, the old one is stale and gross."

Sully trusts her and leans against the counter to wait.

Roy checks his cell phone for the time. If the coffee isn't ready in two minutes, he's out of here. He's starting to think he might need something stronger than caffeine.

"So why did you change your order?" Twyla asks Sully as she takes a bagel from the case. "Is it for someone else, or . . ."

"No, for me. Same old thing gets boring."

Twyla seems convinced, but Roy is not.

Sully is clenching her keys in her hand, her thumb beating a staccato rhythm against the ring.

Twyla motions at Roy and announces, apropos of nothing, "He's here to visit a Mundy."

"That's nice." Sully flashes him an uninterested smile—New Yorker to New Yorker—for which Roy is grateful.

"Where are you from?" Twyla asks him.

"California."

"Who did you say you were visiting again?"

He didn't.

"Her name is Emerson, but she's—"

"Emerson?" Sully snaps to attention.

"You know her?"

"I just met her, over at the Dapplebrook."

"Was she alone?"

Sully is still smiling, but something changes. It's as if a transparent shield has descended over her green eyes. "Why do you ask?"

"Just wondering. I worry about her."

"You're a friend?"

He nods, resenting the tone.

"Does she know you're here?"

"No, I'm . . . it's . . . a surprise."

"There you are—nice and hot." Twyla holds out Roy's coffee and pastry bag.

"Thanks." He grabs it, already on his way out the door.

"It was nice meeting you. Be sure to come back and—"

Her final words are lost on the closing door as he

makes a hasty exit, feeling Sully's gaze following him all the way to his truck.

"He was nice," Twyla comments. "Cute, too, right?"

"Not my type," Sully murmurs, keeping an eye on the departing stranger.

"You don't think the beard was sexy?"

Masculine movie-star-on-vacation stubble and even ironic hipster beards can be sexy. This guy's bushy beard and mustache were anything but, and he looked, at first glance, as if he'd been in a fight.

The angry red gashes along his arms pinged her Inner Detective radar. He was asking too many questions about Emerson Mundy.

Earlier, Sully had noticed an engagement ring on her finger. Can it possibly be from this guy? She seems out of his league. And the look in his eyes when he asked if she was alone—is he a jealous lover? Jealous ex-lover?

She and Twyla watch the pickup truck with California plates pull out of the restaurant parking lot and into the one diagonally across the road.

"I wonder if he's staying at the Holiday Inn?"

"He is."

"How do you know?"

Sully gestured at the other two businesses facing that lot. "Because he isn't buying tropical fish or doing Zumba at this hour."

"You're so smart. No wonder you're a detective!"

Oh, Twyla, Sully thinks, and smiles.

"So I guess he's going to wait until tomorrow to see his friend. She sure will be surprised."

Not if I have anything to do with it.

STATE OF NEW YORK
COUNTY OF DUTCHESS
In the matter of the estate of Oswald A. Mundy
Notice to Heirs

Donald X. Mundy
14130 Oxnard Street
Van Nuys, California

April 17, 1962

Dear Mr. Mundy:

   With regret, I provide formal Notice that your father,
Oswald A. Mundy, the decedent, died on March 11,
1962. As his only living offspring, you are sole heir to
Mr. Mundy's estate.

   Duvane and Associates has been appointed adminis-
trator of the estate. All documents, pleading, and information relating to the estate are on file in the Dutchess
County Courthouse under case number 0007697366.

   The assets of the Estate of Oswald A. Mundy will be
disbursed 60 days following the date of this Notice.

   Sincerely,

   Harold Duvane, Esq.
   Duvane and Associates
   129 Fulton Avenue
   Mundy's Landing 73, New York

Chapter 5

Tucked into the Jekyll Suite's cloud of a bed, Emerson listens to the ticking mantel clock and the night sounds that drift through the window.

Every time wind stirs the tall maple beyond the screen, she hears ghostly whispers—foliage grazing the mesh, she reminds herself. More pleasant are the steady cricket chorus, a barking dog, a passing car, the far-off clatter and whistle of a train.

She might hear the same noises back in her Bay Area apartment, she supposes. But when she thinks of being there, she remembers only the lonely ache that kept her awake so many nights, even when Roy was snoring beside her.

They dated for six months before he asked her to marry him, and she can no longer remember why she said yes.

Was it because his proposal caught her off guard? Because they were in a public restaurant, with beaming patrons waiting expectantly? Because it was Valentine's Day? Because it's what you do when a man is down on his knee? Because she loves him?

She thought maybe she did. He seemed like a good man, and he came along at precisely the right time. Her father's death allowed her to finally devote herself to a real relationship—one she wouldn't have to put on hold every time she had to make the trip to LA.

They had so much in common. Roy told her that he, too, had been raised an only child by a single parent. Like Emerson, he longed for roots, wanted to settle down, buy a home, start a family . . .

He seemed too good to be true.

Because he was.

How—*why*—had she overlooked his moodiness, and the occasional flares of temper? Had grief and loneliness distorted her judgment? Had she mistaken neediness and possessiveness for caring and nurturing?

Or is exhaustion confusing her now?

Glancing out the window before she climbed into bed, she could have sworn she spotted Roy's pickup truck driving slowly past the Dapplebrook.

It had to be her imagination—power of suggestion introduced by the tattooed young waiter. "Stay safe," he said as she headed upstairs to her suite.

Of course she's safe, behind locked doors and resting her head on a silky, eight-hundred-thread-count charcoal gray pillowcase.

Beneath the pillow, though, is the steak knife she swiped from the table downstairs.

Closing her eyes, she breathes deeply, reliving her arrival, moment by soothing moment.

The signpost: WELCOME TO MUNDY'S LANDING.

The village Commons, the climb into The Heights, the warm light glowing in the Dapplebrook's lace-curtained windows . . .

Home. Home at last . . .

Savannah Ivers parks in the municipal lot up at the top of Market Street and walks two short blocks to the Windmill. It's tucked into a row of stores and restaurants facing the Commons, all shuttered at this hour. Even Marrana's Trattoria, which seats people until ten on weeknights, has flipped its Closed sign and moved the sidewalk tables inside for the night.

But the Windmill's plate-glass windows are lit. An old Van Morrison tune spills onto the sidewalk, where a band of pretty girls loiter, simultaneously talking to one another, texting on their phones, and smoking. Manicured index fingers tap cigarette ashes into a terra-cotta sidewalk planter filled with vinca vine and geraniums. Strikingly similar short skirts, cropped camisole tops, and heeled sandals reveal a probable group wardrobe consultation, along with a lot of tanned, taut skin.

Avoiding eye contact with the Girls' Night Outers, Savannah senses their semi-disinterested regard as they note that she didn't get the super-cute-mini-and-cami memo, and her own nails are inadequate, short and free of polish. Why is it that females—her age, especially, but even elderly women like Ora Abrams—always seem to be sizing her up? It isn't just that they scrutinize her appearance, but she often senses a telepathic background check resulting in an instantaneous status report: *Outsider.*

The place looks jammed. Battling the usual insecurities, she pauses to look over the menu on a framed doorway placard.

No buffalo wings and cheese fries here, just locally sourced organic small-plate appetizers and "mixology"—aka drink—specials. The cocktails have creative names, like the signature "Dutch Kill," and are accompanied by intricate descriptions of herbal infusions and exotic-sounding liqueurs.

Unlike a regular college bar where the numeric costs listed on the food menu end in ninety-nine cents and there's nothing over ten bucks, the prices on this one are written in script and start at fifteen dollars.

No wonder she's only been here once in the four years she's attended Hadley. Last fall, her human behavioral genetics professor invited her here for drinks. Though he made it sound as if a group of students would be joining them, it was just the two of them.

His name was Tomas, but that night he invited her to call him Tommy.

The boyish nickname might have felt natural on a different kind of man, but he was thin and intense, with an enormous Adam's apple and John Lennon glasses. She tried "Tom," but he corrected her, so she didn't use his name at all.

He told her the Windmill used to be a dive bar where the students hung out. When the current owners bought it years ago, they got rid of everything but the name. The old pool table, dartboard, and neon Windmill sign—too gaudy for the modern incarnation—now reside in an off-campus fraternity house.

"Going in, or coming out?" a voice asks as Savannah hovers in the doorway, and she turns to see a bearded guy in a red shirt behind her.

"Oh, sorry. Going in."

He makes an after-you gesture, and she notices that his forearm is covered in angry-looking scratches.

She steps into the pub. Dark wood, exposed brick, flickering votives.

Last time, she spotted Tomas waiting for her at a table for two and wondered, with an almost idle curiosity, if he was going to make a move on her.

He did, later in the evening. He smelled of the garlicky smoked fish tapas he'd just devoured, and, oddly, of formaldehyde.

She rejected the advance. Not because of the formaldehyde. She probably smells of it, too, sometimes—occupational hazard.

But Tomas wasn't Jackson. She didn't want anyone else.

Not then, anyway.

Not until graduation day scattered her handful of Hadley friends like pollen on a warm May breeze, sending them to their hometowns or jobs in distant cities. After more than a month alone here on campus, she concluded that some new acquaintances—maybe even a new relationship—might not be such a horrible thing.

No one will ever replace the love of her life. But maybe it's time to let down her guard a little, think about dating again.

Hoping she hasn't been stood up, she searches the café tables along the wall where, according to Tomas, there used to be ugly, sticky vinyl booths.

"Sticky?" she echoed.

"Sticky," Tomas repeated.

Made queasy by the suggestive gleam in his eye, she said, "You mean from puke?"

That put a momentary damper on the romance.

She shouldn't have gone to meet him that night.

She shouldn't be here tonight.

She scans the other side of the room, where a long, backlit bar is lined by tall cushioned chairs instead of plain wooden stools. Every seat is occupied, with a standing crowd mortared between and behind them.

Her phone buzzes, and she glances down to see a new text. No message, just a photo, of . . .

Me?

Snapped a moment ago, it shows Savannah stepping through the door, with a blur of red-shirted guy behind her.

Noting the angle, she looks toward the bar and spots a hand waving at her. Aha! There he is.

She shoulders her way over, relieved to note that her

date, Braden, hasn't morphed into an unappealing jerk since they met.

She takes in his Mr. Nice Guy good looks: crinkly smile, burnt-sugar eyes, and the dusting of cinnamon freckles across the bridge of a slightly elfin nose. His hair, a burnished copper earlier in the sunshine, is more the deep shade of a vintage penny. It's long enough to wave around his ears, but just misses brushing the collar of his kiwi green polo. He's only a few inches taller than she is—maybe five-ten, five-eleven at most. He's fairly fit, in an average way—no ripped, muscular physique, but no hint of beer gut, either.

He tries to stand, but is boxed in by people crowding around waiting for drinks, so he leans over to give her a quick, cramped hug. "Sorry for the creepy text."

"I didn't think it was creepy."

"Sure you did."

"Maybe a little," she admits, and he laughs.

"You didn't hear me calling your name, and I was afraid to leave these seats to come and grab you. I had to stalk the bar for twenty minutes to get them."

She perches on the stool he saved for her, so close to his own that the padded seats are touching. The proximity makes her a little uncomfortable, but she resists the urge to tug her chair away. It's good for to let the walls come down a little bit, let someone in.

Braden summons a busy female bartender and manages to get Savannah a glass of wine, and a bourbon for himself.

"Cheers," he says, clinking against her glass.

"What are we drinking to?"

"My brother's crappy car, what else?"

She laughs.

This afternoon, engrossed in her work, she was startled by a knock on the lab window and looked up to see a lanky, freckle-faced redheaded kid outside. Incoming student orientation was under way across campus, and she correctly pegged him for a soon-to-be freshman.

"Lost?" she called through the screen.

"No, my car's dead. I left the stupid lights on again."

"They're not automatic?"

"Nah, it's an old car. Do you have jumper cables?"

She did not. Nor did the only other person in the building, a custodian whose laid-back name—Davey—belied a surly demeanor.

"Do you want me to call Triple A or something?" Savannah offered, after a scowling Davey had dumped a trash bag into the Dumpster and gone back into the building, leaving them in the parking lot staring at the crippled car.

"No, my mom will find out. This is the third time I killed the battery."

"Those stupid headlights, huh?"

"Yeah. I've only had the car since, like, Memorial Day but I'm sure I'll get used to it."

Three dead batteries in a month? Savannah didn't blame him for not wanting to tell his mother.

He decided to call his brother.

Savannah was privy to his end of the conversation with Braden, which went something like, "Hey, what are you doing? . . . Good, then can you come over and jump my car? . . . Yeah, I know . . . No, I can't, she'll kill me . . . Come on, please? It's not like you have anything better to do."

After some cajoling, he hung up and beamed a satisfied smile at Savannah. "He's coming."

She invited him inside to wait, and found a vacant office where he sat texting on his phone while she went back to work. An hour later, hearing a car and voices outside the window, she looked out and saw that a tan Jeep had pulled up beside the Honda. The driver got out with jumper cables—Braden.

He watched, with impressive patience, as Mick tried to figure out how to open the hood of his car. Then the patience evaporated and Savannah heard him snap, "Okay, get out of the way. I'll do it."

Hood open, he attempted to teach Mick how to connect the cables. They argued. Typical siblings—not that she has any.

She gave them time to get the car started, then combed her hair, put on some lip gloss, and went out to the parking lot.

Her efforts weren't wasted.

Now here she is, clinking her glass against Braden's.

"To your brother's crappy car," she says, and allows the cold, pricey French wine to ooze easygoing goodness all the way to her toes.

After leaving Dunkin' Donuts, Sully drives down the road to Wal-Mart. She'll run in, find some clothes for Barnes, and be on her way home while his coffee is still scalding hot. He probably won't even be out of the tub by the time she gets back. He warned her he was going to soak for a while.

"Good," she said. "Soak as long as you like. Just don't put those smelly clothes back on."

"What am I supposed to wear?"

"I'll buy you something."

"Where?"

"Didn't I tell you? There's an all-night Armani boutique on the Commons. Who says we don't have it all here in Mundy's Landing."

He didn't even crack a smile.

She sighed. "Where do you *think* I'm going at this hour, Barnes? I'll be gone fifteen minutes, tops. If you get out before then, borrow my robe. It's hanging on the back of the door."

"This tiny pink thing?"

It's purple, and one size fits all, and by the time she finishes shopping, she might just get to see him wearing it, or wearing nothing at all. Or maybe he's still in the tub, slowly wrinkling into a prune by now.

Picking out clothing for Barnes isn't the zoom-in-zoom-out task she'd envisioned. What does one buy a man who's so meticulous about his clothing, and needs big and tall sizes? She settles on a pair of powder blue shorts—shiny athletic fabric and elastic waist. Definitely not his style, but at least they'll fit. Searching a rack of athletic T-shirts, she briefly considers buying him a Red Sox one as a joke.

Very briefly. Under the best of circumstances, Barnes wouldn't find that funny. These are not the best of circumstances.

With some digging, she finds a navy T-shirt that bears the right team insignia: a white crisscrossed Yankees NY.

She finds it oddly intimate to buy him underwear, and belabors the boxers or briefs question far longer than she should. Then she heads to the personal care section to pick up a toothbrush, razor, deodorant . . .

What about bedding?

She has a pullout couch, but no sheets. She buys some, and pillows, and an extra long blanket so that his feet won't get cold. She wants him to be comfortable while he's staying with her . . .

Why *is* he staying with her?

Heading home, she drives up Prospect Street. At the historical society, she sees lights on in Ora Abrams's private quarters on the third floor.

They've been friends ever since Sully took the elderly woman to lunch last summer after the awards ceremony.

"Nice. She gives you twenty-five grand, you buy her a tuna sandwich," Barnes commented when she mentioned it.

"She loves tuna. And it was twelve thousand and five hundred bucks," Sully reminded him. Her half went to pay off her credit cards. He blew a good portion of his on an autumn cruise along the Danube with a woman he'd just met.

"That's some first date," Sully commented when he mentioned it.

"Jealous, Gingersnap?"

"I hate boats."

"This wasn't—"

"Yachts, ships . . . all boats. Anyway, I thought you were going to Cuba."

"In the spring. This is hurricane season."

While Barnes was living the good life in Europe, landlubber Sully was on the job in Mundy's Landing, no longer dodging bullets. Her first day, she and another armed officer responded to an emergency call from Ora Abrams, who said there was a jewel thief on the premises. They found her fretting over an empty velvet jewelry case she said had contained a valuable antique pearl and diamond necklace.

"I took it out of my safe and left the room for five minutes," she said, "and when I returned, it was gone!"

As it turned out, the necklace was fastened around her neck, hidden by the high ruffles of the flannel nightgown she was wearing . . . on a humid ninety-eight-degree day.

"Now how did that get there?" she wondered.

"Do you think she did it on purpose, to get attention?" Sully later asked Lieutenant Colonomos.

"I think she's lost her mind."

"There really was an intruder before, though, during Mundypalooza. Not just an intruder—a killer. The poor thing."

"If she calls again—and something tells me she will—you can have the privilege of handling it."

Ora did call—and Sully did go.

On her most recent visit, Ora claimed that a thief had attempted to break down her bedroom door with a battering ram.

The culprit was her cat, whom Ora had mistakenly locked out of the bedroom. She was stunned to see the fat orange feline in Sully's arms, sans battering ram. "But she was just right here in bed with me. She sleeps in the same spot every night, and I . . ."

Ora trailed off, seeing that the "cat" she'd been cuddling on the bed was actually a large fur muff. Her bewilderment gave way to scolding.

"Unhand my muff, Detective!" she bellowed, and Sully instantly missed Barnes, who'd have appreciated—and forever quoted—that admonishment.

Sully stepped back, arms raised like a perp who'd been caught reaching for a weapon.

"That's a priceless heirloom, a gift from Betsy Ross to Enoch Mundy. It belongs downstairs in a glass case," Ora added with an accusatory glare.

"Do you want me to bring it—"

"No, no, no! One doesn't go grabbing and transporting a delicate muff around the house as if it were a . . . a . . ."

Cat? Sully wanted to say, but refrained.

Ora donned white gloves to deliver the delicate object back downstairs to its display case, which was ajar, keys protruding from the lock.

"The thief must have snatched my purse to get my keys!" she deduced, and was gratified when Sully added that to the "report." Then she shifted gears and asked Sully if she'd like to see some of the other colonial artifacts on exhibit.

"Sure," Sully agreed, aware the poor thing didn't want

to be left alone just yet. Happens a lot on the job—you run into forgotten and forgetful senior citizens who only need your time and attention. She never had it to give until she got to Mundy's Landing.

Somehow, the befuddled little lady had transformed into an entertaining and brilliant hostess. Ora showed her, among other things, a cast-iron cauldron that first settlers James and Elizabeth Mundy had used to cook a stew made from the flesh of their dead fellow settlers to stave off starvation.

"They would butcher the corpses, throw in the bones, and boil it all up for dinner," she said matter-of-factly. "You're a police officer, so I know this kind of thing doesn't bother you."

When Sully pretended to agree, Ora told her she had something really interesting to show her and led the way back upstairs.

Wary, Sully watched her dig through a trove of presumably gruesome relics. Ora seemed harmlessly eccentric, but you never know.

She produced a disembodied human skull, and passed it to Sully like a bowl of chips. It was concealed in a protective case, but still.

"Where did you get this, Ora?"

"From Great-Aunt Etta. She was the curator here until she passed away back in '56. That's when I took over."

"But where did she get the skull?"

Ora looked around as if to ensure there were no eavesdroppers. Then she leaned in and confided that the remains had turned up decades ago, during an archaeological dig on the site of the original Mundy's Landing settlement.

"Was your aunt involved in the dig, then?"

"I'm not sure. I was very young at the time." After a pause, she added, "She was cannibalized, you know."

"Your *aunt*?"

"No!" Ora laughed delightedly. "Of course not. I was referring to Jane."

"Jane?"

"Jane Doe. It's what I call her." Ora pointed at a series of nicks along the cranium. "That's where they tried to get at her brain. It's one of the most nutritious parts of the human body, you know."

Sully did not know. "Guess you learn something new every day."

"And now I'm hoping you can tell me something I don't know."

Uh-oh.

"Can you tell if Jane was murdered, or died in an accident?"

"At a glance? No."

"What if you were to spend more time looking into it? Forensics have come such a long way, and you have so much crime scene experience. If this were one of your investigations . . ."

"Then the victim wouldn't have died . . . how long ago was it?"

"About three hundred and fifty years."

"See, that's the thing, Ms. Abrams. You don't need a police detective. You need a historian, or a forensic anthropologist. This isn't a crime."

"Two people were executed for it, protesting their innocence all the way to the gallows."

"So you want to know if James and Eliza Mundy were murderers after all? I'm sure you can find a professional who might be able to tell you more."

"Oh, I don't want to open that can of worms."

Cringing at her phrasing, Sully dutifully reiterated her promise not to reveal what she'd seen. But she's been reading up on local history ever since.

Reminded that she left her book behind at the Dapplebrook Inn, she sees that the porch is dark now, the restaurant closed for the night. There are no lights on in the guestroom windows above.

She thinks of Emerson Mundy.

First thing tomorrow morning, Sully decides, she'll come back to the inn to retrieve her book, and tell Emerson about the guy at Dunkin' Donuts.

In her dream, Emerson steps into the Dapplebrook Inn.

Lamplight has given way to flickering candlelight. Nancy Vandergraaf's voice is replaced by a masculine one. "You must be Emerson Mundy . . ."

It belongs to Horace J. Mundy himself. He's wearing a black coat with tails and a top hat, and Emerson is in a sweeping ball gown. He keeps a protective arm around her shoulders as he shows her around and introduces her to his wife and cherubic sons, who embrace her lovingly.

"You've been upgraded," Horace tells her.

"To the Jekyll Suite?"

"To live here with us."

"For how long?"

"Forever!" his little boy Robert tells her, and throws his arms around her waist. "Forever and ever and ever . . ."

Horace beams at her. "You're one of us. This is your home now."

"Home? I'm home?"

He nods, but then a shadow crosses his face, and she sees that he's looking at something—someone—behind her.

She turns to see a man, gaunt and bedraggled, lips a ghastly purple, ragged clothing soaked and dripping. He has no arm, and no prosthesis—just a stump of ragged, bloody flesh and bone poking from his torn shirtsleeve.

"Go away, Oswald," Horace commands. "You're not welcome here."

"You let me die," Oswald tells Robert, who has changed in a flash to a dapper young man. "You didn't save me. My name is Mundy, like yours. I'm your flesh and blood."

Horace intervenes. "You're nothing! Get out."

Oswald clenches Emerson's bare arm in a bony death grip. "If she stays, I stay."

"You'll go!" Horace bellows. "Both of you! Out!"

Emerson screams as Oswald pulls her roughly toward the massive front door. When he shoves her across the threshold, she falls, sprawling across the broad slate porch, skinning her knees.

"Get up!" a new voice instructs. "Stand and face your punishment."

She fumbles for the railing to pull herself to her feet, but the porch has disappeared. She's on a wooden platform of some sort, in the shade of a tremendous oak with low-hanging branches. A stage, she realizes. There's an audience below, their anticipation palpable as the shimmering heat.

Do they expect her to sing, or dance?

The sun glares like a spotlight, and the crowd glares, murmuring, waiting . . .

For what?

Someone is behind her—not Oswald, she knows instinctively. Oswald is gone. Horace, his wife and children, their home, the welcoming warmth . . .

All evaporated into a strange, still summer day, the air so thick with hushed expectancy that she expects to hear a rumble of thunder.

Rough hands yank her to her feet and nudge her closer to the edge of the stage. Her wrists are tied behind her, so tightly she can feel the fiber scraping into her flesh so that blood trickles down her hands. Another length of rope twines once, twice, three times around the hem of her long skirt, and a sturdy knot binds her ankles within the folds.

Rope . . .

More rope.

This time it drops from an overhead branch to dangle before her, knotted, looped . . .

A noose.

Panic zaps her like lightning.

This isn't a stage.

It's a gallows.

Those people aren't waiting for her to perform.

They're here to watch her die.

"No! Please! I'm innocent."

Her eyes are blindfolded. She feels the noose yanked over her head, and a hand shoves her forward.

The platform creaks, sways, gives way.

She's falling, falling . . .

Somehow, Oswald's voice is close in her ear. Or is it her father's? Roy's?

"You shouldn't have come here," he croons as she plunges to her death. "Now you'll pay."

The crowd at the Windmill has eased up a bit, as have Savannah's first-date jitters. With breathing room, there's no need for their chairs to be so close together now, but Savannah and Braden don't move them apart. Their elbows and knees brush as the conversation flows from music to politics to books.

As they talk, she can't help but notice the woman seated beside her, an attractive blonde, late thirties or early forties. She's alone, awkwardly so, and appears to want company. She seems to know quite a few people in the bar, greeting them by name in an eager way. Her name, Savannah discerns, is Kim. She has at least one child, and it sounds like she's recently divorced. Most of the men, including the few her age, are friendly, but obviously more interested in other, far younger, women.

That will be me in fifteen or twenty years if I don't let anyone into my life, Savannah thinks. *I'll either be alone in a bar drowning my sorrows in wine, or I'll be in a lab somewhere with a skeleton for company.*

She orders her second glass of rosé from a male bartender. He's handsome, though his face has seen too much sun and not enough shaving cream. His light brown hair is long, pulled back in a ponytail, with straggly wisps falling over his eyes. He's about Savannah's age and there's something vaguely familiar about him.

Maybe he's a student at Hadley, like the guy sitting next to Braden on the other side. Savannah has seen him around campus. Braden introduces him as Trevor. He's a waiter at the nearby Dapplebrook Inn, and just got off work for the night.

"Next time this guy takes you out," he tells her, keeping one eye on the baseball game being shown on the television above the bar, "make him take you someplace nicer. Cozy table for two at the Dapplebrook—I'll hook you up."

"They don't need you to hook them up," the bartender says, overhearing. "They've got me." He slides a wineglass to Savannah, filled with pink liquid. "I upgraded you from the house rosé this time. That stuff is vinegar compared to this, and I'm sure Braden doesn't mind paying for it."

"Meet Sean, the French wine expert," Braden says dryly. "He lived in Paris for a semester and came back a full-blown sommelier."

"Really? Me too!"

"You're a sommelier?" Sean asks, and she laughs.

"No, I was in Paris for a semester. When were you there?"

"Fall of 2015."

"I was there at the same time. No wonder—"

"Hey, Sean, I'm still waiting for my beer over here," Trevor cuts in.

She'd been about to say no wonder Sean looks so familiar. Did they cross paths in Paris? She'd probably remember that, or he would.

"Geez, haven't you ever heard of ladies first, dude? The beer is coming."

"With an upgrade? Or is that just for ladies, too?"

As Sean and Trevor tease each other, Savannah wonders if Sean just seems familiar because he looks a little like Braden—if Braden had a dark side.

It's not just that Sean isn't clean-cut. He has an edge, almost savagely gnawing on a plastic stirrer as he pours a round of shots for a group celebrating a bachelorette party. The bride, chunky and wearing a headband with a white pouf of veil, keeps falling off her high heels, bumping into Trevor. Several of the other girls flirt with him, and one asks him to take a group photo. Then she interrupts Braden and Savannah to ask him if he'll take a photo of Trevor with the group.

He shakes his head, but they cajole him.

"Here," the bride slurs, "you can even wear my veil." She plunks the headband on his head. He scowls, and Braden takes the photo, then hands the phone back to the bachelorette brigade, who embark on a ladies' room excursion.

"You know," Braden says, turning back to Savannah, "when you were late tonight, I thought you were standing me up. I'm really glad you didn't."

"Sorry about that. I had a meeting that ran long."

"A meeting? At night?"

"Yes, some crazy old lady from the historical society wants to pay me a boatload of money to do something for her."

"You mean Ora Abrams?"

"You know her?"

"All my life."

"So you're . . . wait, are you from Mundy's Landing?"

"Where else would I be from, with a last name like Mundy?"

"Your last name is *Mundy*?"

"Didn't my brother tell you that when you met him?"

"He didn't tell me anything, except that you were coming to get him. Oh, and that your mom would be upset if she knew he had a dead battery again."

"That's so Mick." Braden shakes his head. "I've got my own stuff to worry about, and all I've done since I got back home is bail out that kid."

"Back home from where?"

"New Hampshire."

"Why were you in New Hampshire?"

"College. I just graduated in May with a degree in history. I had a job lined up with a museum in Boston. But they lost their funding at the end of April and the position was eliminated so . . . back to square one, and back home."

"That stinks."

"Yeah."

"Don't feel too sorry for my cousin," Sean the bartender pipes up. "He's got an Ivy League degree, so I'm sure he'll find something."

Ivy League plus New Hampshire equals . . .

"Dartmouth? And you two are cousins? So you grew up together?"

"Dartmouth, and we're cousins, but we didn't grow up together," Braden tells her.

"But *we* did," Trevor pipes up.

"You're a cousin, too?"

"No, Trevor and I graduated high school together," Braden says.

"But who knows? Maybe we're related somewhere back in the family tree. A lot of people around here are connected, right, Bray?"

He shrugs. "Small towns. All I know for sure is that Sean and I are cousins."

"Roommates, too, right now," Sean says with a mirthless laugh. "Aunt Ro is letting me stay for the summer. She used to be a black sheep, like me. But she turned out all right, so maybe there's hope for me."

Savannah finds herself feeling sorry for him, even relating to him on some level, beyond the Paris connection. If Braden's charmed home life—despite the job snafu—has made her acutely aware of all that's missing in her own, his cousin must feel the same way.

With a lull in the drink demands, Sean pops open a beer for himself, gulps it, and looks at them.

Rather, at her.

"So what's your name?"

"Savannah."

"Never been there."

"Neither have I."

"Yeah? Then why is it your name?"

"Savannah is my father's hometown. I guess my mother thought that if she named me after it, he might like me." She lifts her glass to her lips, and adds before she sips, "Didn't work."

"Know the feeling."

"Not fun, is it?"

"Hell, no. But here's to hanging in there." He lifts his bottle, and she clinks her glass against it.

She isn't flirting with Sean. She just wants to make him feel better about his own situation, and she needs to let Braden know that they come from different worlds, in case it matters to him.

He's focused on his cousin, eyes narrowed. "Come on, Sean, your dad isn't such a bad guy."

"You're the only one who thinks that."

"Everyone makes mistakes. He loves you. Give him a chance."

"That works both ways."

"He's given you plenty of chances."

"And every time I talk to him, he lists all the ways I'm letting him down."

"He's just disappointed that you didn't stick it out at Notre Dame."

"Yeah, well . . . that makes one of us." Sean shrugs. "College isn't for me."

"It was for you before—"

"Don't go there. Okay? Just don't. Please."

"Sorry. I just hate to see you—"

"*Stop.*" Sean drains his beer, plunks down the bottle, and busies himself wiping down the bar, chewing, chewing, chewing a plastic stirrer.

The woman seated beside Savannah rises, throws down a twenty and heads for the door, calling, "Later, guys," as if she'd been hanging out with them—or anyone at all.

"See you, Kim." Sean swoops in for the cash and her empty glass like a seagull on a French fry.

"Do you know who that was?" Braden asks Savannah.

"Is she an actress or something?" A number of celebrities live here in the Hudson Valley, but she never recognizes any of them.

"No, that's Kim Winston. Her daughter Catherine was involved in that mess last summer."

"The copycat killer thing?"

"Yeah."

"Wow. It must be hard to get your life together after something like that."

"I feel sorry for her. They were a nice family. Now her marriage is over and she's a single mom, trying to get back on track. People talk, you know? They say she drinks too much, and she gets around, and she's looking for a new husband—"

Sean leans in. "All true. Can you blame her? Take it from me—you don't go through what she did and then get on with life as usual."

Braden toys with his glass, tight-lipped, as a man takes Kim's vacated seat.

"Hey, Dutch Kill Phil," Sean greets him. "Want another one?"

"Why not. My name's Roy, by the way."

"Roy doesn't rhyme with what you're drinking, so . . ." Sean shrugs. "You know. I like to give my customers nicknames."

Even if the customers don't appreciate them.

Savannah glances at the man, the one who followed her in to the bar, wearing the red shirt. He's looking at Sean like a mosquito he can't decide whether to wave away, or squash flat.

"Hey, Roy, don't worry, we have a nickname for him, too," Braden says. "It's Buzz Kill Bill."

Trevor snickers. Sean does not.

"Lousy nickname for a bartender." Roy looks down at his cell phone as if it just alerted him with a call or text.

Savannah can see that it didn't. He's just looking at a map that was already open on the screen. Again, she notices the red scars on his arms. His nails are bitten all the way down, with raw-looking scars where the fingertips probably bled.

Sean mixes the Dutch Kill cocktail using three different liqueurs, a lemon, a hand of fresh ginger, and a grater.

After disappearing into the kitchen to grab another ingredient, he finishes the drink, and hands it over.

The bachelorettes have returned at last to order another round of shots, continue their futile flirtation with Trevor, and take more group photos and selfies.

Savannah looks at Braden, sipping his beer, staring into space. He's probably wishing they hadn't come here. Or maybe he's wishing he hadn't asked her out in the first place.

When he finally glances her way, she offers a faint smile. "So. Alone at last."

"Around here? Don't count on it."

"I heard that," Trevor says.

"You hear everything. Everyone hears everything. That's the problem with this place."

"Or the beauty of it," Trevor says. "It's all in how you look at things. Come on, Mundy. You used to be a glass-half-full kind of guy."

Braden picks up his drink and gives Trevor a pointed stare as he drains it, then sets down the empty glass.

"Well played, my friend," Trevor says. "Well played."

Braden turns to Savannah. "I'd say we should get out of here and go somewhere else, except . . . there is nowhere else."

"That's okay, this is fine."

"Not really. This place is killing me."

"The Windmill?"

"This town. Being back here, living at home . . . I wasn't supposed to be here this long. I should be in Boston right now with a great job, friends, a place of my own . . ."

"Sorry. That stinks."

"Yeah." He rests his chin on his knuckles and looks at her. "So."

"So."

"So Ora Abrams has a boatload of money, huh?"

"And a three-hundred-and-fifty-year-old skull."

"I've heard."

Good. She wasn't supposed to mention the skull to anyone, but a wine-fueled need to reconnect with Braden undermined her discretion.

"You heard she gave me the skull?"

"Wait, she *gave* it to you?"

Oops. "You said you heard."

"I meant, everyone in town knows Ora has a skull that was dug up out at the first colony, but she never talks about it. I can't believe she just handed it over to you."

"Not to keep. She wants me to take a look at it."

"Why?"

"You know I'm studying forensic anthropology at Hadley, right?"

"Right, but what is it that you're supposed to be looking for?"

Savannah stall-sips her wine. She shouldn't have said anything in the first place, but now that she has, she might as well tell him the rest. There isn't much, and anyway, what's the big deal? The others don't seem to be eavesdropping at the moment, caught up in discussing a controversial play in the televised baseball game.

"Ora wants to know who Jane Doe was," Savannah explains in a low voice, "and whether she was murdered by . . ."

Only then does it occur to her that he's a Mundy.

Maybe it is a big deal. To him. To some.

"Murdered by my ancestors, the cannibals?" he asks.

"Does that bother you?"

"Nah. It's not like I knew them, right? I have enough real problems to worry about. Who doesn't? No one in their right mind gives a crap about a murder that happened in 1666."

"Ora Abrams does."

"Yeah, well . . . like I said . . . no one in their right mind." Seeing her expression, he says, "Hey, you're the one who called her crazy."

"I know . . . but maybe *eccentric* is a better word."

He thrums his fingertips on the bar. "All I know is that she hired me to do some yard work around the grounds last week, and she kept calling me Asa."

"What's a *sa*?"

He laughs. "You're adorable, you know that?"

Maybe she should find the comment insulting, coming from a guy with an Ivy League degree. But he stops thrumming and gives her hand an affectionate squeeze, explaining, "I meant the name. Asa."

"*Asa?* I never heard it before. Why would Ora call you that?"

"I guess she thought I was my dad—Asa is his real first name, but everyone in the world calls him Jake."

"Except Ora?"

"She usually calls him Jake, too. I must have corrected her ten or twelve times. And she had this strange look in her eyes. I told my mom someone should check in on her. She doesn't have any family and my mom kind of looks out for her."

"Did she check in?" she asks, noting that he hasn't let go of her hand. She doesn't want him to, enjoying the sturdy warmth of his grasp.

"Not yet. She's a teacher and the end of the school year is busy, and my aunt's been . . . uh, sick. That's pretty much why Sean is staying with us for a while, so, you know . . . my mom kind of has her hands full right now trying to help everyone. Enough about this stuff. It's depressing. What were we talking about?"

Ora's skull. Not exactly more cheerful.

Savannah changes the subject, asking him about Dartmouth, and his job hunt, and where he wants to live.

His answer to that last question is flippant. "Anywhere but here."

"Why?"

"Because people my age don't stick around."

"I'm here."

"Not for good, though."

"Who knows? I don't really have a long-term plan."

"How about a short-term one?"

"What do you mean?"

He leans in, his breath whispering against her ear. "You want to go somewhere else?"

"I thought there was nowhere else?"

"Well, I can't ask you to come to my place, unless you like parents, dogs, kids . . ."

"Sounds great."

She means it sincerely, but Braden rolls his eyes, interpreting sarcasm. "Do *you* have a place?"

"I do."

"Can we go there?"

She hesitates, considering it. This might be the beginning of something great, or it might be a huge mistake. Only one way to find out.

"Sure," she says. "Why not."

Mundy's Landing sleeps beneath a black dome hung with glittering stars and moon. Summer air, heavy with honeysuckle and roses, stirs with an occasional ripple of wind off the river and, at precisely 3:27, the long whistle and rattling rush of a passing freight train.

The hangman, wearing a dark hood with eyeholes, waits in the shadow of a ten-foot-tall rose of Sharon hedge along the Dapplebrook Inn's western wall. Rooted a good three feet from the foundation, the leafy bank creates a dim corridor stretching from the mansion's back mud porch to the massive maple tree in the front corner.

At this late hour, standing in this spot, the hangman is concealed from the street, the yard, and the driveway. Even if someone were to peer out through a first-floor window from a darkened room, the sills are about seven feet off the ground. They'd have to lean in to see straight down into the leafy crevice. Not likely, unless they're searching for a lurking intruder.

Mundy's Landing has seen its share in recent years, but no one is anticipating more violence. Guests staying at the inn tonight aren't trying to solve a hundred-year-old murder case. They're ordinary vacationers, or perhaps business travelers.

Outsiders . . . all but one.

Lamplight glows in the Jekyll Suite's corner window, infiltrating the dense maple limbs directly overhead. It burns valiantly as a settler's campfire fending off bitter cold, a pitch black forest, a feral wolf pack.

It burns like flames stoked to boil a nourishing human stew.

The hangman swallows hard, stomach churning, holding a length of rope coiled as tightly as the garden hose that hangs from a pretty wrought-iron bracket by the porch.

Starvation can do appalling things to a person—not just physically, but mentally.

If ordinary people in ordinary circumstances become short-fused when they're deprived of just one meal, imagine what it was like for the settlers of Mundy's Landing.

One end of the rope is already slung over a sturdy branch high overhead, the other end looped into a noose like the one that sent James and Elizabeth Mundy to their doom.

They'd long since cheated the Grim Reaper, narrowly escaping London's plague to make a death-defying ocean voyage to a strange, hostile land. Surely they believed they'd survived the worst, only to endure six months fending off feral forest predators and hostile Native Americans. Then came the barrage of fierce winter storms and agonizing starvation.

How far did they go to save themselves, and their children?

How far would anyone go?

The truth gnaws, ferocious, cruel as human teeth on human flesh.

Day after day that winter, storms howled through the Hudson Valley and snow piled up as if bent on burying the settlers alive. Day after endless day, young Jeremiah dug his way out the door to swing an axe into wood that fed the fire, and James Mundy butchered their neighbors' corpses, and Elizabeth stirred the grisly porridge.

How could they?

How could *she*?

Did hunger consume her ability to reason, her sense of morality and human decency? Was she left with only a desperate need to feed herself and her family, some primal urge fed by maternal instinct, self-preservation . . .

Murderous rage?

Oh, Elizabeth. I know what you did.

Three and a half centuries ago, she made a terrible choice and met her fate at the end of the noose, and now—

The hangman hears a sound.

Footsteps, out on the street. Purposeful footsteps, drawing closer, closer, closer . . .

Rustling boughs. A whisper.

"Hey, are you there?"

"Yes," the hangman says softly, gloved hands tightening on the coil of rope. "I'm here."

Mr. Horace J. Mundy
68 Prospect Street
Mundy's Landing, New York

November 29, 1928

Dear Mr. Mundy:

Several weeks ago, I recognized your name and photograph in the New York Times alongside our newly elected governor, Franklin Delano Roosevelt. You do not know me, but on this Thanksgiving Day, I ask you to accept my gratitude for the greatest blessing in my life.

Sixteen years have passed since my sister, brothers and I left England with our parents, traveling in steerage on board the Titanic. Though I was only seven years old, I clearly remember that before the ship left Southampton, my brother Bobby's boarding documents were briefly confused with those of a first-class passenger who shared his name.

That young man, as you may have guessed, was your son Robert Mundy. He later came to our quarters deep in the bowels of the ship to meet my brother. He said he wanted to shake his namesake's hand. He did just that, as we all looked on in awe. I can see him now, in jovial spirits, a handsome young man with most unusual eyes—one blue, the other gray.

Later, when the ship struck the iceberg, the crew awakened the first-class passengers and told them to go out on the deck in their life vests. When your son Robert Mundy got there, he realized that no one had bothered to alert the steerage. He came down, banging on doors all the way. We shall never know how many lives he saved.

My parents were not among them. Although your

son personally escorted us onto the deck, there weren't enough seats in the lifeboats. Robert insisted that we children and our mother take his place. But as he was helping my mother on board, an angry mob of first-class passengers intervened.

I was allowed to stay, with my infant sister Mary, and my brothers Paddy and Bobby. Our mother was lost at sea along with my father, your son, and hundreds of other souls.

We survived, though the years have not always been kind. Little Mary did not live long in the orphanage. Paddy was lost in the Spanish influenza epidemic, Bobby in the Great War. Yet I take comfort in knowing that he, too, was a hero, like your son Robert.

Please accept my belated gratitude and condolences. May God bless you and your family all the days of your lives.

Sincerely,

Margaret Mundy Kramer

Chapter 6

"**G**ood morning!"

Hearing a cheery greeting as she descends the wide stairway just past 7 a.m., Emerson spots Nancy Vandergraaf at the desk, looking fashionable in a cotton candy pink Lilly Pulitzer shift emblazoned with splashy kelly green paisleys.

"How did you sleep?"

"Great," Emerson lies.

She dreams often, but usually forgets them upon waking. Last night's nightmare startled her from sleep, and stayed with her through the remainder of the night. Even now, she can feel the rope tightening against her neck . . .

No. Not your *neck. And it was a terrible nightmare, but it's over.*

Get moving.

Moving on . . .

Nancy gestures at her jogging shorts and sneakers. "Going out for a run?"

"Yes."

"Careful. Wherever you go, it's all downhill from here."

For a moment, confused, she wonders if she's dreaming again. She looks down, expecting to see skirt folds, bound ankles and rough-hewn planks, and is reassured by her Nikes and polished hardwoods.

"What do you mean?" she asks Nancy.

"They don't call this The Heights for nothing. You're starting from the highest spot in town. The return trip could be more of a workout than you bargained for."

"I spent yesterday cooped up in a conference room, a plane, a car . . . I definitely could use a workout."

"Well, if you want some nice flat terrain with a lovely view, there's a trail along the river out near Schaapskill Nature Preserve. It used to be an old rail track, but they paved it over for runners and bikers. It's less than a mile away, straight west. Do you need directions?"

"I'm sure I'll find it."

"Breakfast goes until eleven, so come back hungry!"

By eleven, she'll be on her way to Valley Roasters to meet her first Mundy.

She steps out into a beautiful morning. Prospect Street is quiet, its sidewalks and parallel rows of stately homes bathed in foliage-filtered sunlight. Cars are parked in most driveways and blue-bagged newspapers wait on porch steps. Butterflies flutter-browse picket fence cottage gardens, and a sprinkler's *ch-ch-ch* joins chirping songbirds.

Through an open window, a good-natured male voice calls for someone to wake up and get moving. A father trying to rouse a sleeping teenager, Emerson guesses as she jogs past.

Get moving . . .

Moving on . . .

She follows the steep brick-paved street past the grand old historical society mansion, down into the business district.

Here, too, the cozy town stirs to life. Delivery trucks

idle in front of several nineteenth-century storefronts, doors open as drivers unload supplies. A man in a suit is using the sidewalk ATM beside the bank's front door. A young woman writes tonight's specials on an A-frame chalkboard in front of Marrana's Trattoria, chatting with the stock boys arranging produce in outdoor bins at The Market on Market.

Along the Commons, trailing pastel petunias spill like tie-die popcorn from terra-cotta buckets, and hot pink impatiens fill window boxes and bracketed hanging pots. Over at the police station, a ruler-straight row of scarlet geraniums stands sentry.

The broad green is damp with dew. Clumps of white webbing dot the grass where spiders have overnighted.

Spiders . . .

She thinks of the crawl space in her father's house, where she found the box containing the letter from Priscilla to Jeremiah. She left it safely zipped beneath the lining of her suitcase just in case someone—Nancy?—slips into the Jekyll Suite and goes through her things.

We shall never tell . . .

As is often the case, the thought of that ancient family secret leads her to a far more recent one. She thinks of her mother, buried so deeply by her memory—and by her father—that Emerson can barely remember what she looked like.

Other than fleeting snippets, she has just one solid recollection.

She remembers contentedly lying on the floor, chin propped in her hands, watching a beautiful blond woman put on makeup. They were in an alcove off the master bedroom that her mother called her dressing room. Seated at a movie star vanity with light bulbs all around the mirror, Didi gushed to Emerson about big-time Hollywood actors.

She sounded like an infatuated teenager, calling them by their first names as if she knew them personally.

Maybe she did, Emerson decided when she grew old enough to speculate. Maybe she left her husband and child to be with another man. But Emerson didn't dare ask her father for the whole truth. Not in childhood, and not as an adult.

All she wants, all she's ever wanted, is the kind of ordinary life people take for granted. A real home, a real family, a sense of community . . .

It's here. This is where I belong. I never want to leave this place.

On weekday mornings, Savannah wakes to the marimba tone of her cell phone alarm, perpetually set for seven-thirty.

Today, she wakes to the sound of someone rummaging around, and to the smell of coffee—strange, as her coffee machine's timer setting broke last year.

Opening her eyes, she sees Braden Mundy standing at the fridge. His hair is damp and he's naked from the waist up, wrapped in a blue bath towel. It's the one she's already used twice this week, and hung over the bathroom door to use again today. The rest are heaped in the bag of dirty laundry that's been piling up for two weeks now.

Every morning, she looks at it and tells herself she'll get it done tonight. Every night, there are far more interesting things to do.

Especially last night.

Braden Mundy isn't the first guy who's spent the night with her since she arrived at Hadley, but he's the first one she doesn't want to kick out first thing the morning after. And this is the first time she doesn't feel guilty when she thinks about Jackson, the love of her life.

He was killed four years ago this week, the summer before her freshman year.

He was handsome, with a wiry build and dark eyes and long lashes. So smart—not book smart, because he never had the chance to study much, but he knew a lot. Quick-witted. Everything about him was quick—the way he'd burst into a smile, or blow up in anger. The way he spoke, and moved, and drove . . .

Yeah. He drove like he did everything else.

Fast car driven by a devil-may-care eighteen-year-old on a hot summer night . . .

When it happened, she was at Hadley orientation, being introduced to a new lifestyle that was never meant to involve Jackson. Core curriculum, residence halls, financial aid, study abroad . . .

She received the devastating news while she was having breakfast with a rising senior who'd just returned from a semester in Paris. In the moment before her phone rang, Savannah was imagining herself eating *chocolat* beneath the Eiffel Tower in springtime.

Only later did she realize that that she hadn't even been picturing Jackson in France with her.

Had she already known, on some level, that he would die young?

Or had she already taken the first subconscious step away from him, toward the inevitable long-distance, different-worlds breakup?

Sometimes, she finds it oddly comforting to imagine that she'd have lost him sooner or later even if he hadn't died—that this is how her life was meant to be, and tragedy hadn't altered her path.

Other times, she misses him terribly, and is certain she'll never fall in love again.

Maybe that's not the case.

She attempts to finger comb her tangled hair. It smells like last night—the bar, his aftershave.

Braden turns and grins. "Hey."

"Hey." She smiles back. "How long have you been up?"

"I didn't sleep much. But you were out like a light right after—"

"Right," she says, embarrassed. "Wine always knocks me out."

"Sure, sure. Blame it on the wine. Listen, I was going to make some breakfast, but you're all out of . . ."

"Everything? Yeah, I know. Help yourself to whatever you can find."

She's still getting used to living on her own after four years in the dormitories. This studio apartment is a summer sublet in a dated stucco complex two miles from campus. In August, she'll have to find another place to live. By then she should be able to afford something much nicer, thanks to Ora Abrams.

Braden has gone back to rummaging through her refrigerator. "All I see is yogurt—and a little container of something goopy and red."

"Leftover sweet and sour sauce from Chinese takeout."

"That's good. I was afraid it might be blood."

"Did you eat it?"

"No. *Is* it blood?"

"Why would it be blood?"

"You know . . . for work."

"I'm not a vampire. I'm a forensic anthropologist." She sits up, holding the quilt against her shoulders, feeling exposed nonetheless. "My work doesn't involve storing blood in my home fridge. It usually doesn't involve blood at all."

"Sorry. I don't know much about it. Want to go out for breakfast? There's a great diner over in Kingston, and then afterward, we can—"

"Wait, Kingston? I mean, that sounds good, but I can't—I have to get to the lab."

"Right. I guess I'm the only one who doesn't have anything going on."

She wants to tell him to stop feeling sorry for himself. It can't be easy to graduate from an Ivy League college with high expectations and find yourself living at home, jobless. But this is just a blip in what seems like an otherwise charmed life.

"Are you going to look at Ora Abrams's skull this morning?" he asks.

"Yes." It's her first priority today, and not just because the woman is paying her more money than she's ever earned, research grant included. She's curious about Jane and wants to find out what happened to her, and who she was.

"When are you leaving?"

"As soon as I can get ready." She looks around for the clothes she'd worn last night, hoping they're in arm's reach. They aren't. Everything is strewn across the floor, evidence of their date's passionate conclusion.

"Can I come?" Braden asks.

Technically, no. Visitors aren't allowed.

But she already bent the rules last night for Ora.

And maybe it's a good idea to show him what her work entails. Either it'll scare him away, or it'll dispel his assumptions.

Besides, Muller is quiet at this time of year. The second summer session ended earlier in the week, and classes won't begin again until August. Now the focus is on admissions tours and orientation sessions, and those events don't bring prospective students anywhere near the inconveniently located basement anthropology lab. The main floor facilities are designated for other sciences, pre-med in the prime position.

Chances are, no one will be around this morning when she swipes in the back door with her card key. Nor is it likely that anyone will stop by the lab to catch her entertaining a visitor on the job, or doing a job that isn't exactly her job.

"You can come for a while," she decides. "Toss me that sweatshirt hanging over the doorknob, will you?"

"This?" He grabs it. "Why?"

"So that I don't have to parade around naked."

He grins. "A naked parade sounds good to me."

"Toss the sweatshirt."

He does, but only after pretending to a couple of times, then dangling it just out of reach. If he were someone else, she might find the playfulness immature and maddening instead of irresistibly charming.

Fifteen minutes later, she's showered and ready for work, her damp hair pulled back in a bun. Reservations came raining down in the stream of hot water that washed away his scent, and she decided Braden had better not tag along after all.

For one thing, she has a lot to do.

For another, she wants to see him again. If they part ways now, nothing will get in the way of that. The more time they spend together, the stronger the chances that something might go wrong. Either she'll say something stupid, or he'll be turned off by her job, or he'll turn out not to be the great guy he seems to be. He'll move on to someone more suitable, someone with an Ivy League degree and no baggage and a career that doesn't involve human remains.

Stepping out of the bathroom dressed in her lab coat, glasses perched on her nose, she finds him lounging on her couch wearing last night's rumpled clothes.

He looks up from his phone. "You look hot."

"You're kidding, right?"

"Are you sure we have to leave right this second?" he asks, and his gaze travels from Savannah to her unmade bed, then back at her.

She laughs. "Yes. I can't—"

He's up off the couch to curtail her protest with a kiss, and she somehow allows him to propel her back to the bed.

It feels right, but it's wrong, she thinks as it all comes tumbling away—her lab coat, the pins in her hair, her resolve to go their separate ways.

Reaching the stone markers on either side of the dirt road leading into Schaapskill Nature Preserve, Emerson slows to a trot, careful not to turn her foot on the rutted dirt lane.

At a fork, a sign indicates that the paved riverfront trail is off to the right. She heads in the opposite direction, toward the original settlement site.

Her sneakers crunch along the mulched path. It's cooler here, shaded by dense woods. Bumblebees and butterflies nose an undergrowth of wildflowers.

The breeze rippling the overhead boughs is somehow dank and floral, simultaneously dead and alive. She can't see the river yet, but she can smell its muck and water and she can *feel* it: dark currents churning around her, within her.

Rounding a bend, she spots a clearing ahead. Beyond a cluster of Canadian geese feeding in the field, an enormous oak tree shades the stone monument marking the spot where the first settlers lived—and died.

Some more violently than others, she acknowledges, feeling her pulse pick up even as she slows her pace, approaching the spot as if she might stumble across something terrible, like . . .

A gallows?

Cannibal stew?

As a California public school teacher, she's well-acquainted with the ill-fated Donner Party's experiences while snowbound during the winter of 1846–47. Her students are fascinated by the survivalist cannibalism details, and many focus on the topic for their Wagons West unit reports.

Through them, Emerson has become privy to gruesome details—everything from how to butcher a human corpse to which organs provide the most efficient nutrition. One student, a young woman who was later hospitalized with an eating disorder, wrote vividly about the physiological stages of starvation. The account, complete with case studies, haunts Emerson to this day—especially here, and now, on the very spot where her ancestors endured epic suffering.

James and Elizabeth were executed on a warm July day, probably very much like this one. The date is only a few weeks off.

Did they climb a platform beneath this very tree? Did they feel the sun's warmth beating down as they stood listening to the charges against them? Were their last gasps infused with this tincture of wild honeysuckle and marine life, rotting bark and leaves? Was their last glimpse of this world tall grass and wildlife, oak branches and a wide blue sky?

There were people here that day, though. The hangman. Their three children—those brave Mundy orphans. And their fellow English settlers, the ones who couldn't know what it was like here that winter. The ones who had condemned poor James and Elizabeth.

Emerson stares at the well-fed flock, cloaked in drab browns and blacks, feathers ruffling, beady black eyes regarding her with suspicion.

"They were my family," she calls out. "My flesh and blood! My . . ."

Flesh and blood.

Flesh.

Blood.

Flesh . . .

They ripped human flesh from bone of their brethren and roasted it over the fires of Hades!

"They were starving! Their children were dying!" she protests to the phantom voice. "They did what they had to do!"

Admit thy guilt!

Trembling, she hugs herself, whispering, "They were starved, desperate . . ."

She knows too well the hollow ache, not for food, perhaps, but for other things that are just as crucial—kinship, a shared home, someone to love, someone who loves you so deeply that they would die for you, kill for you.

Guilty! Guilty!

"Noooooooooooo!" The howl surges within her and spills over. Its force catapults her across the field toward the accusers, waving her arms, screaming a shrill, word-less scream. With a great squawking and flapping of wings, the creatures scatter to the heavens.

Then Emerson is Emerson again. Panting hard, she watches peppery specks, mere geese again, disappear into the wide blue sky above oak branches that reach toward her like sturdy, outstretched arms.

What is it about Barnes, Sully wonders as she awakens on a boulder of a couch, that whenever he's around, she finds herself breaking her own rules?

Rule #1: Don't be quick to forgive someone who hasn't given you the time of day.

Broken.

Rule #2: Never give up your bed for an overnight guest.

Broken.

Like my back.

At least Rule #3—Never kiss a fellow cop—remains intact.

Though the idea did cross her mind for a split second when she got back last night and found Barnes sound asleep in her bed.

She let him stay there. He looked so peaceful, and so . . . Naked.

Realizing he probably had nothing on beneath the covers, she felt a forbidden longing stir, and made a tip-toed beeline for the couch.

With a grunt, Sully attempts to twist her stiffened spine into any kind of position that will allow her to stand. Nope.

She stretches and flexes her toes, wondering what time it is. At least ten, judging by the sunlight falling through the window across the room. Not good. She's supposed to meet Rowan Mundy at eleven. And she wanted to go over to the Dapplebrook first thing, to get her book and talk to Emerson Mundy.

Right now, rolling and straining, she can't even get off the couch.

"Need a hand?" A large black one closes over her own.

"Wait! Don't pull," she tells Barnes, wincing as a spasm seizes her lower back.

"I won't pull."

"*I'll* pull."

"Fine. You pull." He pauses. "You're not pulling."

"When I can move," she says through clenched teeth, "I'll pull."

They wait in silence.

"Now?"

She curls her pinky finger. "Owwwwww!"

"That bad?"

"Worse."

"Okay, don't pull. Push against my hand to brace your-self. Ready? Go ahead. Push!"

"I . . . can't . . ." she bites out. "Get me . . . an ice pack. And . . . drugs."

"What?"

"Medicine cabinet . . . top . . . shelf."

Fifteen minutes later, she's in a chair with a bag of frozen peas between her hip and the cushion, waiting for the outdated painkiller to take full effect.

The doctor had prescribed the medication last year for her bullet wound. She soon discovered that nothing that came in an orange bottle could ease the agony of being shot and watching a kid die.

It can, however, ease her sciatica.

Barnes sits on the offending couch, drinking the re-heated coffee she'd brought him last night and left on his bedside table.

It can't be any worse than the nasty cup of tea he just brewed for her. She's not complaining, but only because it still hurts to talk.

She watches him brood, noting that he hasn't used the razor she bought for him at Wal-Mart. At least he show-ered and used the toothbrush, because he smells a lot better than he did when he got here.

She still has no idea what the hell happened to him. Time to find out.

She opens with an icebreaker. "Hey, good thing we never had a baby together, Barnes."

He doesn't ask why.

Seriously? An opener like that, and he's silent? Not just silent, but he almost seems angered by the quip. Either this is worse than she thought, or he spaced out and didn't hear her. She persists.

"I mean, you'd make a lousy labor coach." Using ex-aggerated inflections, Sully paraphrases their earlier conversation, making his voice guttural, her own high-pitched and anguished. "'*Push*' . . . '*I caaaaaan't!*' . . . '*Okay, here, have some drugs.*'"

She's baiting him, trying to rouse a comeback that will prove Barnes—*her* Barnes—lurks somewhere within this glum shell of a man.

Nothing.

Alrighty then.

"Why aren't you saying anything?"

"What am I supposed to say?"

"You know . . . insult me, mock me, tell me to go to hell . . . the usual."

"I thought you said it hurt you to talk."

"It's getting better by the second."

"Yay," he says flatly.

"I see you found the clothes I left you."

"Yes. Thanks."

"Gotta love one-stop shopping. I guessed on the sizes." The navy blue T-shirt hangs in folds on his not-as-broad-as-usual shoulders. "And boxers instead of briefs—also a guess. Was I right?"

He shrugs.

"You mean you're a tighty-whitey guy?"

Bait.

Wait.

Nothin'.

Sully shifts her tactics and her position in the chair—still *ouch* but improving. "Are you going to tell me why you're here? Because as much as I want to think you just missed me, this doesn't feel like a last-minute vacation, and I feel like you'd rather be in Cuba."

He almost seems to wince at that comment. "I don't want to talk about it right now."

She shrugs. This time, it doesn't hurt quite as much. The prescription medication really is dulling the pain.

Maybe her common sense, too, because she's not going to press Barnes for more information.

"Fine, it can wait. I have to be someplace anyway."

"Work?"

"No, I'm meeting someone."

"A date?"

She shrugs. It's not the kind he's thinking, but let him assume there's a man in her life, because . . .

Because, dammit, having him here is . . .

It's inconvenient, that's what it is. And worrisome, concerning his safety.

It's nothing more. She doesn't regret leaving Barnes and New York; not at all.

She heaves herself to a standing position and cautiously arches her back. "I'll bring back some lunch for you. But if you get hungry in the meantime . . ."

He makes a face, looking down at the bag of peas she thrusts toward him. "Freshly thawed and squashed by Sully butt? No, thanks."

"Not butt. Hipbone." She starts out of the room, then turns back. "One last thing . . ."

"No means no. You get on out of here with your butt peas, girl."

It's so good to have him back—a tiny hint of him, anyway—that she holds up the bag as if it was, indeed, her one last thing. "Sure I can't tempt you?"

"You mean threaten me?"

Smiling as she walks away, she swallows the original question she was going to ask.

She knows the answer already.

Yeah, he's in danger. And despite three buses and a train . . .

That probably makes two of us.

10th July 1665

Dearest Sister Felicity:

Two months have passed since we bade each other farewell in London. I shall not recount the arduous, perilous weeks at sea, lest you decide against fulfillment of your promise to make the journey to this bountiful new land so that we may be reunited.

I expect that Mother has passed on by now. I do hope that her suffering was not great, and that you did not take ill while caring for her in her final days whilst this scourge ravaged the population. I must thank you for allowing me to take her gimmal ring. I wear it on my own finger now, and one day, I shall give it to Jeremiah for his bride.

Daughter Charity remains frightfully frail. Though Priscilla is several years younger, she is a more stalwart child and her health is good. Jeremiah is becoming a fine, strapping young man. However, he has taken an improper fancy to the Dowlings' young servant girl. He does not speak of it, but it gives me great cause for concern. I cannot ensure space between them in cramped shipboard quarters, but surely when we reach our destination, he will come to his senses.

I shall post this letter in the morning when our ship docks. Did you know that this great harbor, known as New Amsterdam until September, has been renamed New York? I viewed its smoky rooftops in the distance from the deck this evening as the sun slipped into the sea. Tomorrow, we shall disembark to set foot on New World soil, and to prepare for the final leg. Our journey shall continue north from the mouth of the river to fertile ground our country has reclaimed from the Dutch and the savages who inhabit its forest. There, we intend to build a home where we shall welcome you one day. I will send word of our location when we are settled.

Until we meet again,

Your sister,

Elizabeth Mundy

Chapter 7

Showered, wearing makeup, dressed in cuffed white denim shorts and a sleeveless periwinkle blouse, Emerson lingers in her suite at ten minutes to eleven, listening to the old mantel clock.

She doesn't want to arrive at the café right on the dot. That would make her seem too eager. She sits at the desk in the windowed alcove overlooking the street, hands clasped on the polished top, legs crossed beneath it.

Mundy's Landing: Then and Now lies before her. She gave it a thorough read, though the text was limited to captions beneath old photos. Not all are of Mundys—most aren't. She studied the ones that are, struck by the resemblance between herself and her ancestors—maybe because you see what you want to see.

Tick . . . Tick . . .

Ten more minutes.

Nancy hadn't mentioned the desk last night when she'd shown Emerson the table, clock, and bench, but she'd said there were other original pieces in the room. Could this be one of them?

It certainly looks authentic, but the silky mahogany surface is unmarred by evidence of longtime use. Her own classroom desk at school was only ten or fifteen years old, yet unmistakably timeworn with ink stains and nicks.

Antique furniture is sturdier, though. And Horace probably used a blotter. Wanting to believe he'd sat in this very spot, she stares out into the network of sturdy limbs that seem to strain toward the house like strong arms and splayed fingers.

Back in Horace's day, the leafy screen might not have obscured neighboring rooftops along Prospect Street's steep slope to the heart of town. Maybe he could see all the way out to the fringe of towering evergreens on the river bluff.

She imagines him working on his financial paperwork, pausing every so often to gaze out at Schaapskill, pondering their ancestors' plight during that tragic winter.

Tick . . . Tick . . .

She opens a drawer, seeking some evidence, like . . .

What? Fingerprints? The phrase "Horace was here" scribbled inside? Yellowed, faded paperwork caught way in the back?

She finds only a glossy white folder imprinted DAPPLE-BROOK INN above a simple line drawing of the building's façade. Maybe there's stationery inside—letter paper and envelopes bearing the address, even a picture postcard or two.

No.

Just as well. Who but her father would appreciate the significance of correspondence from here?

The folder contains a couple of take-out menus, a page of coupons for local businesses, and a photocopied hand-drawn grid of area streets, a relic of the days before smart phones and Google Maps. There's a glossy trifold brochure outlining the inn's history, but even the modern photos appear dated, and it contains far more information about the architecture than the family that built it.

Shoving everything back into the folder, she checks the clock.

Six minutes to eleven.

Tick . . . Tick . . .

She returns the folder to the drawer, closes it, and stands, restless. Too bad she couldn't spend the morning exploring the first floor of the inn as she'd planned.

Nancy Vandergraaf is a nice woman, and last night Emerson did welcome her insight into the family history. But she isn't in the mood to chat right now, and Nancy seems like the kind of person who craves conversation.

Earlier, when Emerson reached for the front doorknob upon returning from her run, it turned from the inside. There was Nancy, smiling and holding out an icy bottle of water.

"Welcome back!"

Had she been watching for Emerson to come back up the street? Roy sometimes does that when she shows up at his door, waiting like an anxious puppy.

"How was your run?"

"Tougher coming home, like you said."

"I told you! Those hills are killer."

Emerson agreed with her, though that's not why the return trip was more difficult. She'd walked most of the way back up to the inn, pondering what had happened out by the river.

"There's a continental breakfast in the dining room. We usually serve it on the porch, but there are hornets or yellow jackets buzzing around, so I'm going to spray the whole area. It should be fine by lunchtime."

Emerson thanked her and grabbed an apple and a piece of toast to eat in her room. Under a hot shower, she thought about the strange experience at Schaapskill.

For a few crazy moments—*crazy!*—she felt as though she might somehow have gone back in time. It was almost as if she'd actually become . . . whatever, *whoever* Elizabeth Mundy is to her.

Her great-grandmother, at least nine *greats* over.

Time travel is impossible. But out there, in the middle of that clearing, she was Elizabeth, trapped like a hunter's prey, facing certain death.

She could feel her racing heart pumping desperation with every beat, could see the crowd, could hear the voices condemning her to death.

Now, she paces across the room, scowling.

Come on. The crowd was a flock of geese, and the voices were only in your head.

Yes, of course she knows that now. On some level, she must have known it then, too.

As she told Nancy Vandergraaf, she doesn't believe in ghosts.

Then again . . .

She doesn't *not* believe in ghosts, either.

Maybe the place is haunted. The field, the inn, the whole damned town.

Mouth dry, she grabs her water bottle and takes a long, tepid sip. About to set it back on the table, she realizes that she should have used a coaster when she put it down the first time. The condensation left a faint ring on the wood.

Terrific. It's one of the room's original antiques, like the bench and the . . .

She can hear Horace's disapproval reverberating through the room.

Tsk, tsk . . .

But of course, it's only the mantel clock.

Horace's clock, ticking . . .

Tick . . . tick . . .

Tsk . . . tsk . . .

Horace wouldn't want her here. That was his voice in

the nightmare, telling her she shouldn't have come, condemning her.

She tucks her room key, phone, and some cash into her pocket and grabs Sullivan Leary's book, hoping Nancy Vandergraaf won't be lying in wait at the foot of the stairs.

Luck is with her. The front hall is deserted. She can hear dishes rattling in the kitchen at the back of the house, and voices of the waitstaff as they prepare to open the restaurant for lunch.

As she descends the front steps, she decides to detour around the block and kill a little more time. Turning right instead of left, she hears someone call, "Hey, are you trying to sneak by me without saying hi?"

Emerson turns to see Trevor, the nice waiter from last night, setting tables on the porch.

"Sorry! I didn't even see you there."

"Sure, that's what they all say."

"Who?"

"You know. The beautiful women who pass me by."

She can't help but smile at that. She's not beautiful by any stretch of the imagination, especially to a kid his age. She's almost old enough to be his mother.

Almost? Come on. You're closing in on forty, and he doesn't look a day over twenty-one.

Still, it's been a while since anyone flirted with her, unless you count Roy.

A chill creeps over her at the thought of him.

"We've got some great specials today," Trevor informs her, "so I hope you're not going out to lunch."

"No, just coffee."

"Enjoy!" He waves, or maybe flashes a peace sign, and she strolls off into the breezy sunshine, making a right onto Prospect Street.

"Hey!" Trevor again.

She turns back.

"You're going the wrong way."

"How do you know that?"

"Because you said you were going for coffee. Everything's that way." He points in the opposite direction, toward the business district.

"*Everything?*"

"It's Mundy's Landing. There's not much, but what there is, is down there, around Fulton and Market."

"Not if you like taking the long way around." Smiling more to herself than at him, she turns away. She can feel Trevor's eyes following her until she turns the corner onto State Street.

Small towns.

Holy cow.

If she moved here, would she ever get used to everyone noticing and weighing in on her every move?

It's better than no one ever noticing you at all. Strangers' friendliness may occasionally cross the line into nosiness, but at least they care. It's been a long while since Emerson has felt as though anyone cares, other than . . .

Dammit.

She pushes Roy from her mind, trying to focus on the lovely old homes that line State Street. Making a left at the corner, she notes the large Second Empire Victorian about halfway down the block.

Forty-six Bridge Street is another of the three notorious Murder Houses where the Sleeping Beauty Killer struck during the summer of 1916. The current residents, the Bingham family, figured prominently in last summer's news coverage.

Emerson spies a woman in the side yard. Tall and slender, with short dark hair, Annabelle Bingham is easily recognizable. Her picture was all over the news a year ago, along with photos of her husband, her son, their house . . .

Back then, she looked fragile and haggard. Today, she appears fully healed, serenely cutting tall white flowers from a blooming border. But as Emerson walks past, Annabelle flicks a wary gaze at her.

Not surprising.

Once you've been stalked by a murderous sociopath, you're probably suspicious of every stranger who crosses your path.

Not just strangers.

Sometimes, people you know, or even love, are capable of heinous acts. Emerson picks up her pace, leaving the Murder House behind.

Bridge Street ends at Fulton Avenue, the eastern perimeter of the town square. Market Street runs parallel, across the green that was so quiet earlier this morning. The bucolic paths have become pedestrian thoroughfares. Every bench is occupied. In a grassy corner, the spiderwebs are gone, and a teenage magician in a cape performs for a group of children wearing lime green Mundy's Landing Day Camp shirts. At the fountain, chubby-fisted toddlers throw pennies at their mothers' urging, then attempt to climb into the rippling water after them.

"No, Carlton!"

"Vincenza, get out of there!"

"Stop splashing, Montgomery!"

Emerson walks on past, as amused by the mother-child splash match as she is by the lofty names that burden Mundy's Landing's pint-sized citizens.

"Your mother wanted to name you Emily," her father once told her, after Didi was gone. "But I insisted on Emerson."

"Why?"

"It's better."

The answer was insufficient, but she lived with it, like everything else.

Valley Roasters, at 37 Market Street, occupies the first floor of a plate-glass storefront on the square, and has—like most other East Coast cafés Emerson has visited—a West Coast café vibe.

Ella Fitzgerald croons in the background. Couches and easy chairs mingle with round café tables beneath high tin ceilings and low-hanging pendants that cast ambient light. Behind bakery case glass, doily-topped trays display an impressive assortment of muffins, scones, and pastries. The air is singed with burnt toast. Anywhere else, the char might assault one's nostrils; here it wafts in a pleasant potpourri of freshly ground beans and hot brew.

She looks for Sullivan Leary in the large crowd that—unlike Emerson herself—so obviously belongs here.

The baristas are without exception in their late teens or early twenties, wearing perfunctory smiles as they take orders, relaying them behind the scenes in rapid-fire staccato shorthand. Businesspeople in dress slacks check their phones while waiting for their to-go. At the tables, earnest types type Great American Novels on laptops. Yoga moms converse on couches, sipping frothy dairy-free, gluten-free, sugar-free, fat-free hot beverages that at steep prices are anything *but* free.

There's a palpable camaraderie among them—even the silent, solo patrons. They populate this café, this town, like the Hollywood extras she used to see shooting on-location shoots back in LA. Central casting at its finest, and she's wandered onto the wrong set.

She should go. She doesn't belong here.

Bitter disappointment clogs her throat.

It's no big deal—really, it isn't.

But she can't help it. She so wanted . . .

Everything. A friend, a family, a home . . .

Sure. Coming right up, along with your latte and scone. Did you want that to go?

Oh, I'm staying.

No. She's not.

Turning toward the door, she sees a familiar face.

"Hi, Emerson." Sullivan Leary grins at her. "Glad you made it. Sorry I'm late."

Savannah places the skull on the tall laboratory table.

Braden, perched on a stool beside her, leans in to look. "So that's Jane Doe?"

"That's Jane Doe. Only we can just call her Jane, like Ora does."

"Nice to meet you, Jane."

"I'm sure she'd shake your hand, if she had one."

He raises an eyebrow, and she offers an unapologetic shrug.

"Gallows humor. Comes with the territory."

She turns her attention back to the table. But she's conscious of Braden's eyes on her, and of all the reasons why he shouldn't be here right now. In fact, she can't think of any reasons why he should, other than that he spent the night in her bed. A good portion of the morning, too, so far, giving her a much later start than she intended.

As she trains a bright LED light to get a better look at the remains, she hears his phone vibrate with a text.

"My mother. *Again*."

"Everything okay?"

"She's wondering where I am, even though I texted her last night that I was staying with a friend, and I texted her this morning that I was still with the friend."

"Did she ask which friend?"

"Yep." He grins. "You're John, my rich college buddy who has a summer place in Rhinebeck."

"In that case"—she reaches for the sliding calipers with a blue-gloved hand—"we should head over to my estate after this and see if the household staff can whip up some lunch while we take a dip in the pool."

"Great idea. Or we can slum it and go out for pizza at Marrana's. Mick works there. He can thank you for helping him yesterday by putting extra-extra cheese and pepperoni on our pie."

"And extra-extra-extra mushrooms?"

"Hungry?"

"Famished. We forgot about breakfast."

"Yeah, but it was worth it."

Smiling, she begins measuring the skull, jotting the results on a yellow pad as Braden finishes his text.

"There. That should hold off my mom for a while." He shoves his phone back into the pocket of the same jeans he was wearing last night. "Sometimes she forgets that I'm twenty-two."

"Because you're living at home."

"True. If I were hundreds of miles away, she wouldn't forget that."

No—but she might forget you.

Then again, his mother seems nothing like Savannah's mother. Most aren't.

"If I don't find a job and get a place of my own," he says, "she's going to drive me crazy. They all are."

"All?"

"My parents, my brother and sister, my cousin, the whole damned family. Even the dog. He keeps hiding my underwear. Only mine. Hey, don't laugh. I'm serious. I'm wearing my brother's boxers."

"Day-old boxers at this point."

"Also worth it."

Smiling, Savannah bends over the table again, imagining parents who ask too many questions, siblings who need endless favors, and even an underwear-stealing dog so stupid, as Braden told her, that they'd long ago changed his name from Rufus to Doofus.

She never had a life like that. She always thought she'd create it for herself one day. She and Jackson used to talk about getting married, settling down in a big old house in a small town, having a bunch of kids . . .

"What are you looking for, exactly?" Braden's question startles her.

Oh. Wait. He's referring to the skull, not her hopes and dreams for her future.

"I'm trying to determine what happened to Jane."

"You mean the cause of death?"

"Blunt force trauma to the skull, see?" She indicates the gaping hole in the cranium. "Now I need to figure out whether it was accidental."

"How can you tell?"

"Lots of ways." She leans in, examining the wound. "I look at the location, wound pattern, internal staining . . ."

"How'd a nice girl like you get involved in gory stuff like this?"

Uh-oh. Here we go. Here comes the part when he decides you're a weirdo.

"My mom," she tells him.

"She's a forensic anthropologist?"

"No, she never went to college. She works in a hospital lab, and every night when she gets home, she watches TV."

No need to elaborate that basic cable was one of the few luxuries in their lives, or that her mother has always paid far more attention to the television than to her daughter.

"*CSI* was her favorite show. So, you know . . . I thought it was fascinating."

That's true, but she also thought that she and her mother might have more in common if she, too, worked in a lab. Or that her mother might notice her more if she were like the characters she admired so much on TV. Smart, in control, always finding the answers—always answers to be had.

Not so in real life. It took her a while to figure that out.

"Do you miss her?"

"My mother?" She focuses again on the skull, and the calipers that have been poised over the same spot for too long. "Sometimes."

In truth, Savannah doesn't miss her at all, and is pretty sure it's mutual. On rare occasions when holidays close the dorms and she's forced home, her mother seems to resent the disruption. Ironic, considering that her daily routine still consists only of work, an overindulgence in food and television, and not enough sleep. Savannah interferes with none of it, and is always relieved to get back to Hadley.

"What about the rest of your family?" Braden asks. "Your dad? Brothers and sisters?"

Her dad lived fifteen minutes and a world away when she was growing up. He worked menial jobs to make court-ordered child support payments for Savannah and the other kids he'd had with other women, half siblings she'd never even met—her choice, and theirs, and her father's.

But sisters . . . ?

She thinks of Jackson's twin, Cher.

When Jackson was killed, she was an unmarried, unemployed high school dropout, carrying the nephew her brother couldn't wait to meet. She planned to name him Kanye, after the rap star.

"This kid is going to be a great musician, too," Jackson had told Savannah. "I can tell."

"He's not even born yet."

"But he's got great rhythm when he kicks. You watch. Little Kanye will live up to his name and be a superstar."

Savannah didn't point out that Little Kanye's mother hadn't lived up to her own iconic name. Bearing no resemblance to the star for whom she'd been named, Cher was blond, though not naturally, and fat even when she wasn't eight months' pregnant.

One day a few weeks after Jackson's death, Cher lumbered down the block to find Savannah sitting outside, absently watching greasy-haired, dirty-elbowed neighborhood kids blowing up bottle rockets in the street.

"I heard you're not going to college after all," she said, heaving her huge self down on the concrete steps. "How come?"

"Because it doesn't matter anymore."

Who cared if she let go of that dream, and the scholarships that went with it? Not Savannah, not then. And certainly not her mother, ever.

A bottle rocket exploded too close for comfort, and Cher's arms flew to protect her belly.

"What the hell is wrong with you?" she shrieked at the kids in the street, then turned back to Savannah as if nothing had happened. "Why doesn't it matter?"

"Because he's gone. Nothing matters."

"That's a shitty reason to stay. There ain't nothing for you here now. Get out like you're s'posed to. I wish you could take me with you. Both of us," she added, and gave her swollen stomach a loving pat.

The baby, who was named after his late uncle instead of after Cher's favorite musician, was born the day before Savannah left for Hadley.

She got to hold him in a hospital room that smelled of body odor and vegetable soup.

"I'm going to visit you every chance I get," she crooned, stroking his square, red little face with a gentle fingertip, "and tell you all about your uncle."

She broke the promise.

"No big deal," Cher wrote back a year or so later, when Savannah sent a guilty text message on the anniversary of his death. She added that "Jacky" was almost big enough to wear the Hadley T-shirt Savannah had sent her first week on campus.

By now, he'll have long grown out of it. By now, they're probably calling him Jack. By now, he would have been, should have been, calling her Auntie Savannah.

Braden clears his throat. "So, uh . . . I take it you're not big on talking about your family. Forget it. What are you seeing?"

She's seeing a little boy and a man she'll never know, and a future she wasn't meant to have.

But Braden is talking about Jane—another life cut short by violent death.

"I'm not finding anything indicating that she fell."

"Like what?"

"A V-shaped pattern in the wound from hitting a hard corner," she says, writing down measurements and adjusting the light. "Or a weblike network indicating a wide, flat point of impact."

"The ground?"

"The ground, the floor . . ." She turns over the skull, adjusts the light again, and peers at the underside. "And if she'd fallen, the internal staining from the bleeding and pressure would be much bigger and more spread out than it is here."

"So it wasn't an accident?"

She shakes her head, pointing to multiple trauma points.

"Someone hit her hard, at least three times, with something long and thin."

"Holy crap. Like with . . . what? A broom handle or something?"

"Heavier. If I had to guess, probably an iron tool—

maybe a fireplace poker, something like that. The hit point is narrow, see?"

He comes over and leans in, standing so close behind her that his breath stirs the wisps of hair that have escaped the hairpins she hastily repositioned before they left her apartment.

Is that what Jane experienced a moment before the first blow struck the back of her head? Was she aware that someone had come up behind her? Someone she knew, or at least, thought she knew?

There were no strangers lurking in the settlement at the time she died. Only twenty-five, maybe thirty settlers had traveled together from England to find themselves cut off from the rest of the world. The quintessential locked room mystery, except . . .

Savannah briskly moves away from Braden, stepping around to the opposite side of the table as if she needs a different angle to examine the skull.

All these years, historians speculated that James and Elizabeth Mundy were, like the Salem witches, victims of Puritan vengeance in an era when crime and sin were intertwined, defined by the eyes of the beholder, and punishable by death.

What if they were guilty as charged?

If so, then what if, as Tomas, her genetics professor, once lectured, there really is a "murder gene"?

The theory is that certain genetic variants are linked to violent mental illness. Tomas cited plenty of case studies to support it.

"Do you think she suffered?"

Savannah looks up sharply, wondering, perhaps illogically, if Braden *wants* the girl to have suffered. His expression is suitably somber.

"No, she didn't. Not for very long, anyway."

"How can you tell?"

"Bleeding to death from a head wound would leave significant staining. You can't survive losing more than about fifty percent of your blood, but it takes a long time to drain. As you bleed out, your blood pressure drops and the bleeding slows as the heart rate slows."

"Like opening a faucet in an old house. In our house, anyway. When you run the water for a while, the water pressure drops."

"It's actually more like a garden hose. As the tank drains, the flow slows and the water pools. Cutting a major artery is like unkinking the hose—it speeds up the death and limits the internal cranial staining."

"So . . . you're saying someone cut her artery after she was knocked out with the poker?"

"Yes. See this?" She points to the mandible, noting that there are only a few teeth.

"The jawbone?"

"The nick on the jawbone." She rests a gloved fingertip beside the barely visible groove. "It's hard to find unless you know what to look for."

"What is it?"

"A mark from the blade that sliced her throat."

He looks up, startled by the brutality of it.

"She was murdered in cold blood?"

"I think so."

He clears his throat. "By my ancestors. The cannibals."

"We have no way of knowing who did it."

"Yeah, well, they were the last men standing, you know? Who else could it have been?"

She reaches for the envelope sitting on a nearby desk and unfolds the sheet of paper inside. It looks as though it was typed on an old-fashioned typewriter, with some of the letters slightly smudged or raised above the others.

She hands it to Braden.

"What's this?"

"A list of the English settlers who were living there that winter."

"You mean dying there."

"That, too. The murderer could have been anyone on this list."

"Why are most of the names crossed out?"

"Process of elimination to identify Jane. The four that remain are females in the right age range—roughly fourteen to sixteen years old at time of death."

Tabitha Ransom, born 1650, died February 12, 1666
Ann Dunn, born 1649, died January 29, 1666
Anne Blake, born 1652, died February 21, 1666
Verity Hall, born 1650, died February 3, 1666

He studies the list. "Where did the dates come from?"

"I guess someone was keeping track."

"So one of the crossed-out names belongs to the killer?"

"I think so."

"And if you use process of elimination . . . I mean, a lot of these people were dead by January, and of the ones that remain—it's not going to be a toddler, so . . ."

"Right. You can rule out at least half these names based on age alone."

He looks at the list for a long time, then hands it back. "You're going to tell Ora about this?"

"That Jane was murdered? I have to."

"Terrific."

"Hey, I thought you didn't care. You said you had other problems to worry about."

"I do. But when you look at her . . ." He shakes his head, gesturing at the skull. "She was a real person, you know?"

"They're all real people, Braden." She gestures around the lab, at the skeletal remains and jars of specimens.

"How the hell do you do this every day?"

"I don't necessarily do *this* every day."

"But how can you stand it? I mean, maybe you've never been through anything that would make you realize—"

"Like what? Realize what?"

"You know. I've been through some stuff . . . well, my family's been through some stuff—and I guess that when you lose people in a violent way, it's hard to—"

"*Everyone's* been through *stuff*, Braden."

How can she tell him that loss has made her even more dedicated to doing what she does? She can't, unless she bares her soul about Jackson.

Ah, the dead boyfriend. Now there's a cheerful topic guaranteed to make him want to stick around.

She weighs her words. "The way I look at it, someone has to piece things together for the victims and their families."

"Piece things together?"

"What?"

"You know . . ." He gestures at the skull, making an attempt to smile. "Forget it. My stab at gallows humor. I was referring to the fact that the rest of her is out there somewhere, but . . . I guess *stab* is a poor choice of words, too."

For a long moment, they stand there staring down at Jane.

Savannah detaches herself from the human beings whose remains enter this lab, but some cases are easier than others. You'd think that this one wouldn't feel personal—an unidentified young woman who's been dead for centuries.

Braden pulls his car keys from his pocket. "I should go. You have work to do." He doesn't meet her gaze.

She shouldn't be surprised, should she? She was expecting this. It's probably for the best. He doesn't belong here, in the lab, in her life. He doesn't *get* her.

Still, she makes a feeble protest.

"We were going to go get pizza."

Extra cheese, and pepperoni, and mushrooms . . .

"Yeah," he says. "I kind of lost my appetite. Another time, okay?"

"Sure."

He looks at her, puts his hands on her shoulders, and leans over to kiss her forehead. "I'll text you later."

"Sure," she says again, and watches him go, wondering whether she'll hear from him, wondering whether she wants to.

Valley Roasters is crowded, as always. Too crowded for Sully to bring up the guy last night as she and Emerson wait for their orders at the counter, shoulder to shoulder with the rest of the world.

She spots a familiar red head and points out Rowan Mundy, sipping an iced tea and checking her phone at a table for two in the corner.

"You didn't tell her I was coming?" Emerson asks.

"I didn't have a chance, but it's fine."

"I should probably go. I just wanted to give you back your book and say a quick hello."

"You can't leave before you meet your cousin."

A smile lights Emerson's eyes. In the dim light last evening, Sully didn't notice that one is a piercing, January blue, the other a November slush-gray. Seeing her again today, she noticed it right away.

Heterochromia is the kind of rare physical condition that makes Sully's job a little easier. Witnesses who cross paths with a missing person or a suspect later tend to remember someone whose irises are two different colors.

"*Sally?*" The pretty brunette behind the counter peers at the Sharpie scribbling on a paper cup. "*Sally?*"

Seeing a tea bag tag and string poking from beneath the plastic lid, Sully reaches for it, grinning. "That's me."

"Oh hey, Sully." She hands over the cup and gestures at the boy taking orders behind the register. "Sorry. Theo's new. I guess he doesn't know you."

"I'm not that new. I know her," Theo protests. "That's a U. It says Sully."

"Sure it does." The girl picks up another waiting cup, squints at it, and calls. "Um, *Edifice?*"

"I'm going to guess that's her." Laughing, Sully points to Emerson. "We just call her Eddie."

They head over to the crowded seating area, where Rowan smiles and waves. Fresh from her elementary school classroom, she's wearing a summery floral print dress. Sully, who shares her coloring, wonders how she managed to find splashy shades of pink that somehow don't clash with her hair and freckles.

"I'm free!" Rowan calls, and several people nearby turn to look at her.

"Don't mind her, she just got out of jail," a middle-aged man at the next table announces with a grin.

Rowan returns it good-naturedly. "You know it, Joe."

"I assume you're here to arrest her again, Sully."

"Not this time," she tells Joe. "Rowan somehow always manages to cover her trail."

"The trick is to stay one step ahead of her."

"I'll try to remember that. Emerson, this is Rowan Mundy, and these nice people"—she gestures at the man and his female companion—"are Joe and Sonia Goodall."

"Hey, I'm a nice person, too," Rowan protests.

Joe Goodall teases her again, then asks Emerson where she's from.

"California."

"Oh! Then you must be a Mundy," Sonia Goodall comments.

"I am. How did you know?"

"She knows everything."

Sonia swats her husband's arm. "Don't listen to Joe. He makes me sound like a busybody."

"If the shoe fits, hon . . ."

A second swat is less playful. "Cut it out, *hon.* Anyway, Emerson, someone mentioned you at my last garden club meeting."

"Was it Nancy Vandergraaf?" Rowan asks. "Because she's the one who told me that one of Jake's relatives was coming to town from San Francisco."

"I don't think so. Nancy hasn't been to a meeting in a while. Anyway, word travels fast around here. You'll see."

Emerson smiles faintly. "I'm seeing."

The Goodalls go back to their coffee, and Rowan asks Emerson how, exactly, she's related to Jake.

"I have no idea. I've been doing some genealogy research, and it led me here. I just know that I'm descended from the first settlers."

"So is Jake. We'll have to figure it out. Have a seat."

Looking around for a chair to borrow, Sully spots three teenagers at a table for four. She chats briefly with them, and exchanges greetings with a couple of other acquaintances.

The muscle spasm in her back is gone, thanks to the pain medication. Unfortunately, it left her brain feeling slightly numb and cloudy. Or maybe that's for the best, considering that Barnes is dragging her into his problems.

"Wow, you know everyone in town," Emerson comments as she rejoins the table. "Did you say you've only been here a year?"

"Not even, but I pretty much knew everyone in town my first day."

"That's great."

"Sometimes it is," Rowan says, "and sometimes it isn't. Mundy's Landing can feel a little suffocating if you're not used to it."

"*You* must be, though," Emerson says, "if you've lived here all your life?"

"Not all of it. Jake and I were down in the New York suburbs for a while."

"Why would you ever even leave?"

"The suburbs?"

"No, here. I mean, it's so . . . you know. It just seems like a great place to live."

"It is, unless you're young and looking for excitement. Just ask my oldest son. Anyway, Jake and I moved back after we had all our kids."

"How many do you have?"

Rowan laughs at Emerson's wide-eyed question. "Three. But when they're all home, it feels like a lot more. My nephew is staying with us this summer, and all the kids' friends are around. Plus, we have the dog, and a stray cat just had kittens under our porch that my daughter thinks are now ours, so . . ."

"And here you just said you were free." Sully peels the lid off her cup to fish out the tea bag.

"I know, what was I thinking?" Rowan shakes her head. "The kittens *are* free, by the way. Want one?"

"Um, for the tenth time, no thanks."

"Sorry. Forgot I already asked." Rowan turns to Emerson. "Kitten? They're super cute."

"I'm sure they are, but I'm allergic."

"So is my husband. Guess it runs in the family. Not that my kids care if Dad is clogged and congested and crippled with sneezes for the next . . . how long do kittens live?"

"Twenty years, if you take care of them," calls an older

woman seated in a nearby chair. "You need to set up household barriers, and tell Jake to see an ENT and look into allergy shots so the kids can keep their kitties."

Rowan thanks her for the suggestion, then turns back to them, rolling her eyes. "Shots and barriers? That'll be the day."

"So how old are they?" Emerson asks.

"About ten days."

"I meant your kids."

When Emerson smiles, Sully thinks, she's truly lovely. But she doesn't smile often enough. She seems troubled.

Does that have anything to do with the man Sully encountered last night?

I have to tell her. If some guy showed up in town to surprise me, I'd want to know.

Some guy like Barnes?

"Braden is twenty-two," Rowan is telling Emerson. "He just graduated from Dartmouth. Kind of going through a rough time—he thought he was moving to Boston with a great job, but that fell through so he's back home for now. My daughter, Katie, just finished her sophomore year at Cornell. She has an internship this summer and I've barely seen her. And then there's Mick. He just got out of high school by the skin of his teeth."

"With a little help from me." That comes from Joe Goodall at the next table.

"Hey, are you eavesdropping again?"

"Not on purpose, Ro. Close quarters. So don't go saying anything nasty about me."

"I never badmouth anyone. Unless they deserve it," she amends, seeing his dubious look. "Some people . . ."

"Watch it, there, Ms. Mundy. The walls have ears."

"Don't I know it." Turning back to Emerson, Rowan tells her Joe is the local high school principal. "He's always been in Mick's corner, even when that wasn't

exactly a great place to be. And he made sure he graduated."

"And now he's going to college." Sully pats Rowan's
hand. "You did good, Mom."

"Team effort. Jake and I pulled a few strings to get him
into Hadley, just like my parents did for me. I just hope he
makes the most of this opportunity. He doesn't always."

"He's been through a lot. You all have." Sully thinks
of the cold December day when she and Barnes arrived at
Rowan's house out at Riverview Road to find a 10–31—a
crime in progress, and a bloody one at that.

She asks Rowan how her sister Noreen's most recent
surgery went.

"Really well this time. She's getting around just fine
now. In fact, the other night, the nurse called to ask if
I'd seen her, because they couldn't find her. It turned out
she'd decided to go out for a walk."

"Is she supposed to do that?"

"Nope." Rowan smiles, but Sully sees through it, and
asks how Noreen's son Sean is doing.

This time, the reply is an uncharacteristically curt
"He's fine."

On that fateful December day, her nephew was an
honors student at Notre Dame, returning from his fall semester in Paris. He was the perfect kid with a perfect life
that had shattered in his absence.

It would have been disturbing enough for anyone to
discover that his parents' seemingly solid marriage had
dissolved. But on top of the news that the Chapmans were
separating, their son came home to a family tragedy. His
mother, Rowan's sister Noreen, had barely survived the
brutal attack at his aunt's house.

Once a beautiful and brilliant attorney who capably
mothered four overachieving children in a luxurious Long
Island home, Noreen Chapman now resides in a Hudson

Valley rehabilitation hospital. She's making a slow physical recovery, but her mental condition is deteriorating. She'll never be the same.

Nor will Sean.

In the aftermath of the attack, his three younger sisters' lives resumed a level of normalcy at home with their surgeon father. Sean took off his spring semester to be with his mother. Last fall, he returned to Notre Dame and failed every class. Given a second chance, he spent the spring loafing around South Bend.

Though Rowan didn't share much detail about his time there, it was plain to Sully that he'd gotten into some kind of trouble. No longer welcome in his father's house, the long-haired, grungy young man staying with the Mundys is clearly troubled. Sean bears little resemblance to the clean-cut, well-scrubbed scholar Sully had met at his mother's bedside eighteen months earlier.

Green eyes shadowed, Rowan changes the subject. "How about you, Emerson? Do you have kids, a husband . . . ?"

"No kids. No husband . . . yet." Emerson holds up her left hand, where the engagement ring sparkles. "We haven't set a wedding date."

"Congratulations," Rowan says, smiling.

"Is your fiancé here with you?" Sully asks.

"*Here?*"

"Yes, here in town."

"No. Why?"

"Because I met someone last night who said he'd come here from California to see you."

"*What?*" Emerson's high-pitched question draws stares. "Where?"

Sully tells her about the encounter and describes him. Clearly, Emerson doesn't welcome the news that he'd asked if she was traveling alone.

"That's Roy. Did you say that I was?"

"I didn't say anything."

At least, not about that.

Why did she have to mention they'd met at the Dapplebrook Inn? Ordinarily, she'd be more prudent about sharing information with a stranger. But she was tired last night, preoccupied with Barnes's sudden arrival. Her guard was down—unlike Emerson's. Spotting a telltale wariness in those unusual blue and gray eyes of hers, Sully asks, "Are you having problems with him?"

"I'm not sure." Emerson exhales, gazing at her cup that may or may not say *Edifice*.

Sully thinks of her favorite aunt, Ida, who was fun-loving and bubbly before she married her second husband, a man Sully will never consider her uncle. He doesn't beat Ida, but he controls her so completely that no one in the family has seen her alone in years.

She often looks just like Emerson does now—worried, and cagey.

"Are you afraid of Roy?"

"No."

"That's not very convincing."

"Maybe I am a little afraid. But really, I just wish I knew what he was doing here."

"He told us he wanted to surprise you, and I—"

"Wait, *us*?"

Sully nods. "Twyla and me. She works at Dunkin' Donuts."

Rowan, who'd been checking her phone, looks up. "You mean Twyla Block?"

"Katie's friend? Yes."

"How do you know her?"

"I met her at your house on New Year's Eve."

"Every kid in town was at that party, but she and Katie aren't really friends."

"I thought she said she was related, too."

"She probably did, and we probably are, somewhere back in the Mundy family tree. She and Katie played together when they were really little, but Twyla was one of those girls who . . ." She shakes her head. "I had her in my classroom, and I've seen other kids like her—the ones who latch on to their friends and smother them. Know what I mean?"

Sully nods. Growing up, she'd transferred into an all-girls parochial school at eleven. Surrounded by inseparable pairs, thieves-thick threesomes, and clubby quartets established in kindergarten, Sully was miserably alone. The uniform added insult to injury: a tartan skirt with a scarlet Saint Brendan's sweater and necktie that clashed with her hair.

One day, her nun-assigned reading partner asked her to share a lunch table. The invitation morphed into regular after school playdates—which no one ever called playdates back then—and sleepovers every weekend.

Sully no longer remembers the other girl's name—probably Mary-something. Saint Brendan's was an army of Mary Beths and Mary Anns and Mary Claires. No one else's hair was red, or curly, or cut above their shoulders.

Yet one day, Sully's only friend showed up with her blond hair dyed pinker than Frenchy's in *Grease*, puffy with corkscrew curls.

"I did it myself," Mary-something whispered over their shared *Oxford Junior Reader*, and Sully heard the other girls snickering. "My mother wouldn't let me cut it, but I slept on her sponge rollers. Isn't it righteous? Now we look like twins."

God, no. They didn't. And *righteous* was Sully's own personal catchphrase back then, one that the Saint Brendan's girls didn't quite grasp and weren't yet using—until that moment.

"She's such a copycat," she heard someone say later from behind a bathroom stall. She eavesdropped in horror on a discussion of Mary-something's long history of smothering, imitating, and eventually alienating every friend she'd ever had.

That day, she feigned a stomachache, went to the nurse, and got sent home before lunch. She didn't answer the phone when it rang incessantly after school, glad her father was at work and her mother out buying Jell-O and soda crackers for her sick daughter. She took the phone off the hook and smothered its rapid bleating with a pillow until it stopped. By that time, her stomach really did hurt.

Lost in the memory of the awkward end to her childhood friendship, she half listens as Rowan describes a similar situation between her daughter Katie and Twyla Block.

Emerson has fallen silent, toying with a straw wrapper.

Sully thinks about Barnes. If he hadn't shown up here last night, she never would have been in Dunkin' Donuts blabbing about the Dapplebrook Inn.

She clears her throat. "Emerson, I have to tell you something."

"What is it?"

"I mentioned that you were at the Dapplebrook. I'm sorry."

"To Roy? He asked you where I was staying?"

"Not exactly." She thinks back over the conversation. "Twyla was doing most of the talking."

Rowan says, "That's not surprising. She can be a chatterbox."

"I guess I didn't say you were *staying* there," Sully tells Emerson. "Just that I'd met you there."

"But how did he even know you knew me?"

Barnes. It's all his fault.

The illogical answer thunks around in Sully's head like a sneaker in a dryer.

"I'm sorry, I wasn't really thinking when I said it. But if he's dangerous, you need to let me know. I'm a police officer."

"And a damned good one," Rowan says. "She saved my life, and my son's and my sister's."

Watching Emerson Mundy digest that information, Sully can guess what she's thinking.

I just hope she didn't endanger mine.

15th August 1675

Dearest Brother Jeremiah,

   Scarcely two days have passed since you left me our little settlement. I know not when a southbound messenger might make his way here, but I shall have this letter prepared to post so that my apology may reach you in haste.

   I do regret, dear Jeremiah, the harsh words we shared on the eve of your departure. I was distraught that you have chosen to desert me here, even if just until the spring, and set off with strangers for a distant city. We have protected each other all our lives. Without you, I am vulnerable.

   Yet I am content to stay within the confines of this population. I have no desire to explore the lands beyond. I was not tempted, as you were, by the Dutch traders who entertained us with vibrant accounts of the pleasures to be experienced in New York.

   I know that you long for a proper education and a selection of eligible young women to court, and that you have felt isolated here in the northern wild. I do not share your yearning, for this is the only home I have ever known. Though I was a mere child of seven when we left London with Mother and Father and sister Charity, I remember not the city we left behind, nor the journey across the sea.

   I do recall the day we sailed into the New York harbor, and our brief wanderings before we continued the journey upriver. I recall muddy streets teeming with strangers and livestock, rife with stench and vermin. I knew then that I never wished to return, and I expected that you would share my sentiments.

I perceived a betrayal when you, my brother, accepted our visitors' invitation to accompany them on their journey downriver. I selfishly feared for my own well-being, and turned deaf ear upon your parting assurances that all will be well, and that you will return in the late spring. I felt, in that moment, that you alone should understand the perils I might face without you in the months ahead. I feared that I might go mad when the snows begin to fall, bringing cruel reminders of the winter so long ago, with no one to comfort me in the night. No one who knows the terrible secret we alone share.

However, now that I have grown accustomed to the idea, I have come to accept my plight. I am safely settled in the Goody Dowling's home, and they are all pleased to have me here. Dorcas, in particular, has said she has always longed for a sister. I suspect that she longs for a husband as well, and she is wistful when she speaks of your decision to venture beyond our humble population in your search for a wife.

Worry not about my safety, Jeremiah. As you stated, our settlement is much larger and stronger than it was in its infancy. We are fortified to outlast the stormy months ahead, just as we have every winter since that dreadful first.

I shall miss you. No other being in this world can comprehend the horrors we endured, nor the drastic measures our parents took so that we all might survive. Dear sister Charity could not bear it. But you and I are hardier souls. Until your return, we must each bear the terrible truth alone. I promise that I shall not, in your absence, unburden our secret upon another person, and I pray that you will not, either.

I wish you well as you devote the months ahead to

furthering your education and finding a suitable wife who will wear the gimmal ring Mother intended for your bride.

Do you remember that Mother wore it daily to remind her of her mother and sister and England? When word came that both grandmother and Aunt Felicity had died of the plague, she sobbed for the first time that I could ever recall. I feel that I share a bit of that mournful desolation now, dear Jeremiah, for with you gone, I feel quite alone in the world.

I shall look forward to welcoming you home in the springtime.

With affection,
Your sister,

Priscilla Mundy

"It was great meeting you, Rowan." Emerson reaches out to shake her hand, but Rowan embraces her.

"You too. I'll check with Jake and be in touch later about dinner."

"That would be nice, but no pressure."

"I think tonight would be good. We have plans tomorrow night, and weekends are always crazy in our house. You come, too, Sully."

"What?" She looks up from typing a text on her phone.

"Dinner tonight. Our house. I'll make the Sully Salad."

"There's a salad named after you?" Emerson asks.

"It's this Asian salad she loves. I make it whenever she comes over, but last time someone in my house had eaten the ingredients."

"You really think ramen and peanut butter are going to last with three college kids around?" Sully's smile seems a little forced, and she quickly looks down again at her phone. Someone had texted her when they were back at the table, and after checking it, she announced she had to get going.

"Four college kids, with my nephew," Rowan corrects her. "And I'm stopping at Price Chopper on the way home, so this time, I'll lock up the ramen and peanut butter."

"Thanks, but I think I have to take a rain check."

"Working tonight?"

"No, just tied up."

"Hot date?"

"Who," Sully asks, "would I be dating?"

"I thought maybe Nick Colonomos finally—"

"Oh please. If it hasn't happened by now, it's not going to happen."

Rowan turns back to Emerson and explains, "Nick is pretty much the only eligible bachelor in town, and Sully is—"

"Sully is *not* the only eligible bachelorette," says Sully. "He's not interested."

"You never know. He's the one who recruited you for the job."

"Yes, for the *job*. Not to marry him and bear his children—which, for the record, if he were asking, I wouldn't be interested in doing, no matter how beautiful those babies would be. And it's not just because he's a cop."

"Sully has a lot of rules, and one is that she doesn't date cops," Rowan tells Emerson. "But that would change if Nick hit on her."

"Hello—I'm right here." Sully waves. "I can hear you."

"You *hear*, but you never *listen*."

"No, *you* never listen, Rowan. I'm perfectly happy on my own. I don't need a man in my life."

"Whatever you say."

Emerson marvels that they've barely known each other a year. The way they banter, you'd think they were lifelong friends. Envying Sully's easygoing relationships with the locals, she wonders if she, too, would be welcomed into the fold if she were to move here.

"Jake can tell you more about the family tonight," Rowan tells her, "although he's not the expert. You really need to go see Ora Abrams at the historical society."

"Do you think she's there now?"

"She's always there. In fact, I've been meaning to check in on her for days. If you go, tell her I'll come by soon."

Rowan heads for the door, and Sully puts her phone back into her pocket. "I'll introduce you to Ora on the way back up Prospect, Emerson, if you want to wait for me. I just need to grab a couple of sandwiches to go."

"A couple?"

"I'm starved. My cupboards and fridge are bare, and I don't even have college kids to blame."

Now that it's lunchtime, the café is even busier. Emerson leans against the brick wall to wait, watching Sully slip into the line at the counter and chat with two businessmen in front of her, and then with an older woman behind her.

Emerson takes in the crowd: women in sandals and skirts or pumps and hose, men in dress shirts and khakis, and a few in suits and ties. Even the few who are alone seem to be engaged in conversation. Scrubs-clad medical workers gossip among themselves, as do overdressed teenage girls who seem conspicuously aware of the teenage boys checking them out. A jumpsuited mechanic stirs coffee with an oil-stained hand, conversing with construction site guys wearing hard hats and orange vests. At a nearby table, a priest is lunching and laughing with an elderly couple.

If Emerson lived here, she wouldn't be alone.

But you wanted to be alone, remember?

Roy wasn't the only one who reached out after her father died. Colleagues invited her to lunch, to dinner, to the movies. They meant well, particularly the ones who'd also lost a parent and said they knew how she felt.

They didn't, and not just because most still had one parent living, or a wide circle of family and friends. Many were married, and nearly all had at least one sibling to share the burden of grief, and the memories.

When they met, Roy already had a plane ticket to New York for Thanksgiving with his mother. He invited her to come, but she wasn't ready for that. He offered to stay, but she talked him out of it.

"You shouldn't be alone," he said.

Thinking he might be right, she accepted a fellow teacher's invitation to Thanksgiving dinner. It was Norman Rockwellian: flowers, candles, and wedding china in a wallpapered dining room, cousins squeezed in on folding chairs, a rousing Trivial Pursuit game after pumpkin pie.

Emerson compared it to Thanksgivings past: a wobbly kitchen table, Stove Top stuffing, and a couple of broiled supermarket drumsticks. Those holidays for two never felt right, yet neither did the picture-perfect version with someone else's family.

"Sorry about that!" Sully is back, with a white paper bag and a hot cup. "I didn't think it was going to take so long, or I'd have told you to go ahead."

"It's fine. I'm not in a rush."

As they head out, Sully nearly crashes into a lanky man in glasses about to step into the café. "Trib! I almost spilled coffee all over you."

"You mean you're finally coming over to the dark side?"

"I was *born* on the dark side."

"No, I meant the coffee. I thought you were a tea drinker."

"Good catch. If you ever get tired of the newspaper business, you'd make a good detective." Sully turns to Emerson. "This is Trib Bingham, the editor of the *Mundy's Landing Tribune*."

She knows who he is. He lives at 46 Bridge Street with Annabelle and their son, Oliver, and probably more than his own share of nightmares.

"Trib, this is Emerson Mundy. She's here visiting from California."

As they shake hands and make small talk, Emerson wonders about the coffee. And two sandwiches, for such a small person?

Out on the street in the sunshine, Sully falls into a pre-occupied silence. Maybe she, too, has secrets.

They cross the brick-paved street and cut through the Commons. No sign of webs on the broad lawn now. The spiders are there, though, lurking among blades of grass like enemy soldiers in a jungle.

Beneath a tree, a young couple unloads the contents of a wicker hamper onto a colorful patchwork quilt.

"How charming—a picnic," Emerson comments.

"Fifty bucks' worth of charming. The Market on Market sells packaged picnics to go. You order online and pick it up at lunchtime."

"That seems reasonable. I bet the blanket and basket are worth at least that much."

"The fifty is for the food, and you leave another fifty as a deposit for the setup. When you return everything, you get it back." She smiles at Emerson's expression. "Sorry to burst your bubble. Charming doesn't come cheap. But at least things are more peaceful around here now. Last summer during Mundypalooza, this place was a zoo and the traffic around the square was gridlocked. See that corner? We had an officer there every day directing traffic."

Emerson follows her gesture to the intersection of Prospect and Fulton, where a single car is braking for a flashing red light. No police officer now. She glances over her shoulder, scanning the street behind them.

Sully catches her. "You okay?"

"Just achy." She reaches back to rub the spot between her shoulder blades. "Yesterday was tough—lugging heavy bags through airports, the long drive in all that traffic, and I didn't sleep very well, so . . ."

Sully isn't buying that for a second. "You're looking for him, aren't you?"

"Roy?" She hesitates. Is now the time to admit that it isn't just Roy?

"I know this is none of my business, but I don't like this," Sully says. "The man is your fiancé, and you look terrified."

"It's just, I'm not used to always having someone around, and sometimes, I need space, and Roy doesn't always like to give it to me. That makes me want to pull away, and then he . . . holds on even tighter."

"Is he violent?"

"No, it's not like that. He's just . . . possessive. Or maybe it's obsessive."

"Maybe both. I know he's your fiancé, but following someone across the country is extreme. A romantic gesture would be one thing, but something tells me you're not seeing it that way. How long have you been engaged?"

"Since Valentine's Day. We met last September."

"So you haven't known him long."

"Well, it was the beginning of September," she clarifies, as if a few weeks make a significant difference.

"How does your family feel about him?"

"They—*he* never knew Roy. My father, I mean. I met him right after my dad, uh, passed away."

"I'm so sorry. That's tough."

"Yeah." She wipes her eyes with the back of her hand. "I know I'm acting like a big baby. Pushing forty, and I still feel like Daddy's little girl."

"Losing a parent is tough no matter how old you are. How about the rest of your family? Your mom? Siblings?"

"No siblings. No Mom. I mean, I had one, but she walked out on us right before my fourth birthday and never looked back. Not a visit, a phone call, a birthday card . . .

"I'm sorry. Where is she now?"

Emerson pauses, wondering how to answer that, and decides on a shrug—for now.

"Ever tried to find her?"

"My father would never have wanted me to do that."

"Your father isn't here anymore, sweetie," Sully points out.

"Yeah. I, um . . ." She clears her throat. "I used to think she might try to find me, but then, the older I got, the more I realized, you know . . . that she never bothered, because she'd have found me right where she left me."

"So you still live in the same house?"

"My father did, until . . . he died there, in the house, last summer."

Died, as if he just closed his eyes one day and went to sleep.

That isn't how it happened. A fist clenches her heart.

"Have you sold it?"

She's trying to sell the house, trying to keep strolling down the street as if nothing's wrong, trying to keep breathing around the familiar strangling sensation in her chest. Trying, trying, trying to move on.

"I . . . the house . . . I listed it last winter."

It's going to be a hard sell, even in this hot market—and not just because it needs a heap of TLC. Clearly, the Realtor knew what happened there last July, and potential buyers might have heard as well.

She looks over her shoulder again as they cross to the opposite sidewalk and turn down Prospect Street.

Sully looks, too. "It's okay. He isn't there."

"It . . . it isn't just him."

"What? What do you mean?"

Emerson closes her eyes and takes a deep breath.

"Sometimes, I see someone who looks like *her*. I mean, who looks like I think she might look now. Like, last summer, when my father was first sick in the hospital, I'd see this nurse and I'd think . . ." She shakes her head. "This sounds insane."

"You'd think it was your mother?"

"Yes. Like she was there, not just watching him—us—but watching over us. I got this vibe . . . but then if she saw that I'd spotted her, she'd always sort of duck away."

Sully nods. "It happens."

"What happens?"

"I was with the NYPD Missing Persons Squad before I came here. It's not uncommon for families to think they've caught a glimpse of a missing loved one from a distance—or to actually see them."

"You mean . . ."

"I mean, sometimes, people who leave willingly do come back from time to time, for whatever reason—not to reconnect, but just to check in, sight unseen."

"So you're saying it really might have been her."

"Maybe. Is that the only place it ever happened? In the hospital?"

"No, there were other times—a few times before that, over the years—and then a lot more often after, when I got back to Oakland. But I was grieving, and it was a tough time, so I figured . . . anyway, Roy said the same thing."

"He said what?"

"When I told him I thought I'd seen my mother hanging around, he told me I was crazy. He said it was the grief, and I was seeing what I wanted to see. But lately, something changed with him, and . . . I started to feel like he was getting paranoid."

"How so?"

"I'd catch him checking the rearview mirror when we were driving, or, you know, looking over his shoulder . . ."

"Like you've been doing here, today."

"Yes. I thought maybe he'd seen her, too." She looks up, into Sully's eyes. "Do you think she's been around all this time, keeping an eye on things? Especially now that . . . my dad is gone?"

"I don't know. Do you want me to see what I can find out about her? I have access to certain resources that might help figure out where she is. Closure might be healthy, after all you've been through. What's her name?"

"I'm not sure. I called her Didi."

"So that's a nickname you had for her? Or it's a shortened version of her given name?"

"I have no idea. Maybe it's her initials. D. D."

"Your father never told you?"

"He didn't like to talk about her."

"That's not surprising, but he must have had some documentation somewhere."

"Not in the house. He got rid of everything years ago. I went through the whole house after he died"—this time, she manages not to stumble over the innocuous word—"and there wasn't a trace of my mother."

"What was your father's name?"

"Jerry Mundy."

"With a G or a J?"

"J. It was Jerome."

"I'll see what I can come up with using his name and hers and the address, if you can text it to me. And you said she left before your fourth birthday? When was that?"

"I was born on New Year's Day in 1980. When my father told me she was gone, I was sitting on the floor by the Christmas tree playing with my new Cabbage Patch doll. Remember those?"

"Yes. Never had one, but my cousins wanted them and they were impossible to get—Christmas of '83, right? My dad was a cop, and he was on the job at a toy store riot when a shipment came in."

"All I knew when I got mine was that Santa left a cute little doll on Christmas morning, and my mom left right after that. Kind of felt like he swapped them out."

"Well, someone must have loved you very much to get ahold of that doll for you that year," Sully tells her. "I'm going to see what I can find out."

"I could never afford to pay—"

"You wouldn't be *paying* me. It's a favor for a friend."

"But—you barely know me, and . . ." She shakes her head. "That kind of generosity—I'm just shocked that you'd do that for me."

"It's not a big deal, truly. Sometimes I really miss this part of the job."

"I guess people don't go missing very often around here."

A shadow crosses Sully's face, and Emerson wishes she could take back the comment.

Last summer. The copycat. The Sleeping Beauties.

And before that, Brianna Armbruster.

"Sorry. I forgot."

"I wish everyone around here could forget, too. Sometimes I think this town is scarred forever."

"Scars heal."

"Not all of them." Sully touches her forehead, looking pensive again. Then she asks, "Let's get back to Roy. How much do you know about his past?"

"I know the basics—where he came from, where he went to school, that kind of thing."

"In other words, you know what he told you."

"Yes."

"I think it would be a good idea if I did some check-

ing into his background, too. Just to make sure he doesn't
have a history of . . . trouble."

Sully's cell phone rings, and she juggles the coffee and
sandwiches into one hand as she pulls the phone from her
pocket with an apology to Emerson.

She follows that with a brusque "Sorry, I'll be there in
two minutes," to the caller.

Hanging up, she looks at Emerson. "I know I said I'd
introduce you to Ora Abrams, but I've got a friend waiting for me, so . . ."

"So you didn't switch over to coffee after all?"

"No, and I'm not eating both these sandwiches. But
keep that to yourself, okay? Around here, people talk—
and I'd rather they didn't talk about me."

Emerson nods. That's her private business.

And my mother and Roy are mine.

Now Sully is going to dig into the past and turn up God
knows what.

*But you can handle anything life throws at you, just
like your ancestors did. Jeremiah, James, Elizabeth . . .*

Sure. Just look how things turned out for them.

In the ladies' room down the hall from the lab, Savannah splashes cold water on her face and presses a wad of
scratchy brown paper towels against her eyes.

Unfortunately, it fails to erase the evidence that she's
been crying.

Staring at her puffy-eyed self in the mirror above the
sink, she's grateful the building is quiet today. There's no
one around to ask her what's wrong, or offer unsolicited
advice or judgment upon hearing she's upset over someone she hasn't known even twenty-four hours.

Maybe it isn't even about her disappointment in him,
but in herself. She ignored her better judgment, took a
stupid risk, and almost believed, when he stuck around

this morning, that he was interested in more than a physical connection.

If only she'd followed the lab rules instead of bringing him to work this morning.

If only she'd followed her own rules instead of bringing him back from the bar to her apartment.

If only Ora Abrams hadn't shown up with her skull until after Savannah had made a real connection with Braden, the complicated kind that takes more effort to dissolve than walking out the door.

If only, if only . . .

Oh well. Braden Mundy isn't in the market for a ghoul friend.

It's one thing to mention that you're studying forensic anthropology, and another to let him see you in action. Next time, she'll keep dead people out of the relationship until a man has gotten to know her for who—as opposed to what—she is. And she sure as hell won't sleep with him on the first date.

She's lucky she emerged relatively unscathed. The vast majority of one-night stands end as this one did. Yet with her chosen field comes innate awareness that some end in violence courtesy of sexual predators, or worse, disguised as Mr. Nice Guys.

Back in the lab, greeted by Jane Doe's murdered skull, she tells herself that she should never have let a stranger into her past, her lab, her head, her bed . . .

Brows furrowed, she opens her laptop and scans her files for her human behavioral genetics course materials.

It takes her a few minutes to find what she's looking for—there, under the heading "Murder Gene."

According to her notes, a genetic mutation can impact neurotransmitters such as serotonin, causing an imbalance that can, in some people, lead to an inability to control violent behavior.

There's documented evidence, too, that psychopathic impulses might be inherited due to irregularities in areas of the cerebral cortex that generate empathy.

She reads through a series of case studies about cold-blooded killers who were, according to the research Tomas cited, predisposed at birth to become violent criminals.

Unsettled, she sets aside her laptop and looks again at the skull on the table.

Yes, maybe she should be glad—at least until she discovers more about what happened to Jane—that Braden Mundy has left the building.

2nd February 1676

Dearest Jeremiah,

Much has happened in the six months since we bade farewell.

I pray this letter finds you safely passing the winter at the home of the Widow Ames's brother in New York. Perhaps by the time you have received these pages, the warm spring breezes will have brought a thaw, and you shall be preparing to make the return voyage with a fine wife in tow.

If you have not found a bride in New York, I daresay Dorcas Dowling will be pleased. She still fancies you and mentions you often. She is becoming quite tiresome. Yet I am tolerant, and remain so very grateful to Master Dowling for allowing me to board with their family in your absence.

Goody Dowling has been so very kind, as always. I shall never forget that she alone took pity upon our tormented sister Charity after Mother and Father were lost, when it seemed as though all others here would have preferred that we, too, mount the gallows.

Though harsh snows and brutal cold have been pervasive this winter, I have scarcely noticed, warmed by the tender companionship of Mr. Ransom's eldest son, Benjamin. He took it upon himself to escort me to Sunday services in your absence, and our friendship has blossomed. He has asked for my hand in marriage. I ask, in turn, for your blessing.

With affection,
Your sister,

Priscilla Mundy

Still enveloped in the fog that chased her home last night, Ora slept away the entire morning. It's a good thing there's no Mundypalooza this summer. Last year at this time, she'd have had to rise before the sun to greet the long line of visitors already stretching from the front door and down the sidewalk.

Today, her cat leaped upon the bed at 5:45 as usual, purring and tapping Ora's face with a fat orange paw. *Time for breakfast.* The message was clear; Ora's head was not.

"In a few minutes," she crooned, and drifted back into a dream where Papa was waiting.

He was so handsome, wearing his favorite camel hair sport coat, his hair neatly combed, healthy and smiling and young . . .

Well, Papa was always young on the outside. It was his brain that aged, much faster than his body. Early onset Alzheimer's disease, they call it these days. Back then, they called it other things.

Senile . . .

Bonkers . . .

Losing your marbles . . .

But dream Papa's brilliant mind was intact, and he

held her on his sturdy lap and told her wonderful stories about the olden days, and her mother.

"You can't possibly remember her," Papa and Great-Aunt Etta used to say. "You were too little when she died."

For a long time, Ora was certain she could remember. But when she got older, she realized that sometimes, stories of the past can be so vivid that you feel as though you were really there.

Just like dreams.

Her cat, Briar Rose, woke her several more times this morning, no longer purring, green eyes fixed on Ora's in an accusatory glare. It isn't like Ora to ignore her, but she just couldn't seem to make her old bones obey her brain's—and, more surprisingly, her cat's—commands to get moving.

She wanted to see Papa again, and he was there.

Briar Rose disappeared, and Ora woke on her own to find that it was growing late. Eight o'clock . . .

Then nine . . . ten . . .

Still the dream beckoned her. Only when she heard the steeple bells at Holy Angels clanging the noon hour did she regain consciousness. A few minutes later, the grandfather clock two stories below chimed twelve times.

For years, she tweaked the pendulum in an effort to regulate the hour, but finally gave up. A clock that's always a little behind the current time seems fitting for this house, and her life.

At last, Ora has managed to rouse herself, yet she can't seem to function properly. It's as if someone came in the night to swaddle her brain, and body, too, in a thick blanket.

Maybe she has a bit of a hangover. In the winter months, she occasionally enjoys a nip of brandy to warm her before bed. Perhaps she got the season mixed up last evening. It happens from time to time. Though she doesn't recall a nightcap . . .

But then, she doesn't remember driving home, either.

Nor does she remember opening the secret drawer beneath her bookshelf to remove several of Aunt Etta's precious artifacts, but there they are, scattered about the room.

Heading into the bathroom, she tells herself that she'll put it all away just as soon as she's washed and dressed.

Emerging a short time later, still trying not to fret about the holes in her memory, she descends the first flight from her private quarters. As always, she stops for a rest on the maroon velvet bench in the wide second-floor hall. Today, especially weary, she lingers a little longer than usual, thinking about Papa.

Not the virile, vibrant man she'd seen in her dreams. Rather, the man as he'd been when she last saw him alive. A man whose thick head of hair rose above his forehead like a cockatoo's crest; a man who strolled downtown one snowy morning wearing the camel hair sport coat with only boxer shorts and a pair of antique spats over bare feet.

That version of her father argued with friends who weren't really there, and seemed not to see or hear those who were. He conjured senseless missions that entailed endlessly wandering the house, and if he could escape, the neighborhood as well. He occasionally forgot Ora's name, and eventually his own.

You've never forgotten your *name*, Ora assures herself. *And you don't imagine things. Just because no one else has seen the intruders around the mansion . . .*

Well, of course they're really there.

Last summer's traumatic violation remains so vivid that she probably shouldn't worry so much about losing her memory, and her mind. Then again, she sometimes wonders if her close call with the copycat killer caused her problems in the first place.

Years ago, the first Dr. Duncan theorized that Papa's car accident triggered his illness.

"Most times, dementia comes on so gradually that even the patient isn't aware anything is amiss," he told Ora one day in his office, behind closed doors as Papa conversed with Rip Van Winkle in the empty examination room next door. "But occasionally, we see a precipitating factor."

Tormented by the other driver's violent death, Papa had been wheelchair bound with both legs in casts for the duration of that winter and most of the spring. He'd intended to use the convalescence for reading, researching, and writing, but instead sat staring out the window at the bleak landscape, brooding as his true self slipped away and an erratic stranger crept into his broken body.

Unsettled, Ora positions her cane and heaves herself off the velvet bench to continue her journey to the kitchen.

There, she opens a small can of Fancy Feast Chicken Hearts & Liver and spoons it onto a bone china saucer sprigged with purple pansies. "Rosie? I know you're hungry! Rosie?"

Briar Rose usually comes running, regardless of her mood, when she hears the top pop from a can of food. Today, she's holding a grudge.

"I don't blame you, my dear," Ora warbles. "My behavior was inexcusable."

She leaves the saucer on the counter, not wanting to put it on the floor until the kitty presents herself. Otherwise, the food will draw mice or ants, both of which have recently made their presence known in the kitchen.

In summers past, the constant parade of Mundypalooza visitors inspired Ora to be meticulous about keeping the place clean, and she always had plenty of volunteers to help. Now that she's alone so much of the time, so weary and forgetful, it's all she can do to sponge spills and crumbs from the counter.

She isn't hungry, but she supposes she must eat, so she opens the refrigerator to find the tuna salad left over from yesterday's lunch. Pushing things around as she looks for the familiar yellow Tupperware container, she counts . . . three, four, *five* half-full containers of orange juice!

How strange.

Even stranger, she recalls buying milk for her coffee the other day, but she doesn't see it. The lemons she keeps for her tea are also missing, although she does see a lime in the crisper.

Upon closer examination, she realizes that it is, indeed, a lemon gone green with mold.

Nose wrinkled in distaste, she's about to take it out and throw it away when she spies the tuna. Leaving the lemon for later, she closes the fridge, sets the container on the counter, and opens the breadbox. How curious. No bread, but there's a carton of milk lying on its side.

"If I didn't know better," she tells the still invisible Briar Rose, "I'd think you were playing tricks on me."

Does she know better?

Of course. A cat can't do such a thing.

Perhaps one of the volunteers . . .

But there are no volunteers this summer. Mundy-palooza is history.

"*Everything* is history," Papa loved to say. "Even the future, if you wait long enough."

Papa.

With an uneasy twinge, Ora picks up the carton. It's warm, and the expiration date is a few weeks old.

Someone is playing tricks on her. It isn't Briar Rose. And it isn't a ghost. Ora doesn't believe in such things, even living here.

She carries the milk over to the trash can in the corner and wedges it in, pushing down on the lid to keep it there. One of these days, she'll need to take the garbage outside to the Dumpster. She hasn't done that in quite some time. Every so often, she thinks it should be starting to stink, but so far, she hasn't smelled a thing.

Returning to the task at hand, she decides that one doesn't need bread in order to make a tuna sandwich. One can use crackers.

But when she takes the box of saltines from the cupboard, a confetti of shredded cardboard, cracker dust, and mouse droppings rains onto the countertop. Oh dear. They've gnawed the bottom corner from the box.

It's a shame Briar Rose hasn't been much of a mouser since Ora invited her into the house a few years back.

Before that, she belonged to Augusta Purcell, who lived out her life in the Murder House over at 46 Bridge Street. The proverbial crazy old cat lady, Augusta collected pets and strays, frustrating the neighbors as well as the local rescue shelter, which doesn't advocate letting cats roam to dine from garbage cans and the rodent population.

Ora, too, found the band of felines a nuisance, with one exception.

Briar Rose, she's convinced, is directly descended from Marmalade, the orange kitten Augusta had owned as a child in 1916. Present in the house when the Sleeping Beauty's corpse was discovered, Marmalade is mentioned in historic news accounts about the case.

Ora always provided her with celebrity treatment, showering her with doorstop kibble. In return, Rosie would bestow an occasional rodent carcass on the back porch mat.

When Ora heard that Augusta had passed on, she added Briar Rose to her private collection, so to speak, in much the same way Aunt Etta always helped herself to important artifacts.

Like her late great-aunt, she doesn't feel guilty about it. Rosie is much better off here than she was on Augusta's watch. It's just a pity that regular meals served on fine china have destroyed her appetite for rodents.

"Rosie, you aren't earning your keep! I might as well put mousetraps on my shopping list."

A bleat of sound reverberates through the house, but it isn't the indignant meow Ora anticipated.

It takes her a moment to recognize the doorbell.

She always unlocks the front entrance first thing in the morning so that museum visitors can walk right in. Discombobulated when she finally made it downstairs today, she forgot all about it.

"I'm coming! Don't go away!" Grabbing her walking stick, she hurries to the foyer eager to greet her visitor—or preferably, visitors. It's been much too quiet around here.

How lovely it would be to see a tour van parked at the curb, or perhaps a yellow bus filled with children, although . . .

Is school out for summer?

She seems to have lost track of the seasons again, but no matter. It will be splendid to have the museum filled with people, just like old times.

Reaching to turn the burnished bronze lock, she's startled to see Great-Aunt Etta's hand attached to her own arm. Arthritic, blue-veined, and liver-spotted, it's familiar: the very hand Ora clasped through the long days and nights back in 1956, before her aunt drew her last breath.

Oh my. Has she become delusional?

Of course not. Her arm hasn't gone and sprouted Aunt Etta's hand. She herself is in her eighties now, so that must be her own appendage, withered with age.

That deduction brings only momentary comfort.

Who, she wonders, will hold this hand when it's Ora's turn to depart this world?

Such morbid thoughts for someone who has plenty of living left to do!

She stretches on a smile and throws open the door, prepared to greet a traveling family, a group of boisterous children . . .

Alas, a lone woman stands on the doorstep. She's brunette, tall and slender, casually dressed and wearing sunglasses.

"Yes? May I help you?"

"Yes, I . . ." The woman looks from Ora to the museum hours posted on the door to her wristwatch. "Sorry, I thought you would be . . . are you . . . is this . . ."

"This is the Mundy's Landing Historical Society, and I'm Miss Aurora Abrams." Yes. She is the curator, and this is her home, and it's her duty to share its treasures with the public.

"Are you open?"

"We are indeed. Do come in."

Do come in . . .

She may not have sprouted Great-Aunt Etta's body parts, but she sounds just like her.

Perhaps she always has. When you're raised by an elderly spinster—particularly one who embraced a bygone era as she did—you aren't always hip to the latest slang. Or whatever it is that kids are saying these days, or said then. She wouldn't have known.

They teased Ora, back in her school days. They laughed at the way she talked, the way she wore her hair, even the way she dressed. All the girls wore dresses and skirts back then, but Ora's were somehow wrong—too frilly, too short when they should have been long, too long when they should have been short. She didn't have dungarees and gym shoes for play. She couldn't wear lipstick. She couldn't listen to music, other than Papa's ragtime piano records. Great-Aunt Etta had countless rules, and Ora followed them all. No wonder she spent so much time lost in books about the past. She was living in it.

And you loved it, she reminds herself, ushering her visitor into the hall. *You still do.*

Funny. She spent so many years longing to go back in time, yearning to relive days she'd never lived. Great-Aunt Etta and Papa shared memories so vivid she felt as though they were hers, as well.

"Why did I have to be born in modern times?" she once asked Papa, who laughed heartily.

"I used to ask Aunt Etta the same question."

"But you weren't!"

"I thought I was. One day, you'll have a child who thinks you were born in the good old days."

And so she was. Only there is no child. No family. No one left but Ora, all alone in a big empty house that doesn't belong to her.

Most days, she feels as at home in the old Conroy-Fitch mansion as she does in her own body. But when she finds herself missing her childhood and family or fearing what her future might hold, familiarity takes flight. Just as she occasionally seems to be inhabiting someone else's body, she sometimes feels as though she's been buried alive in a stranger's mausoleum.

A lovely mausoleum of carved woodwork and marble, guarded by a massive grandfather clock. She stares at it across the foyer's mosaic tiled floor, watching the pendulum sway in time with her heartbeat, ticking away the moments until . . .

"This is beautiful."

Hearing a voice behind her, she whirls around to see a woman standing there.

Again, she reminds herself that there are no such things as ghosts. Then who is the woman?

Maybe she isn't really here. Maybe Ora swiveled too quickly, and it made her dizzy, and . . . and . . .

But why would she have swiveled in the first place,
unless she'd heard a voice?

For a terrible moment, she considers Papa and Rip Van
Winkle.

Then she notes that the person standing before her certainly seems real. An imaginary person wouldn't waste
time quietly looking around the room the way this woman
is. Papa's delusions behaved in a much more interesting,
and often disruptive, manner, rousing him into animated
conversation.

This isn't like that. This almost seems like . . .

Her thoughts whirl until—*Yes! Yes, of course!*—the
truth is ejected.

She's a visitor. She rang the bell. You invited her in.

"I love the way that window is painting a rainbow on
the stairway." The woman gestures at the staircase, an
ornate half spiral that rises to a wide second-floor balcony
facing an exquisite crystal chandelier.

"A rainbow," Ora echoes, following her gaze to the
hexagonal stained glass pane that casts a fluid, vibrant
spectrum across the well-worn oak landing.

"Do you live here, Ms. Abrams?"

The question seems to come from miles away. Disori-
ented, still dizzy, Ora repositions her walking stick for
better support.

It doesn't seem to help. Perhaps the room really is listing. Old houses settle. This one might be settling right
now, all at once.

The visitor seems oblivious, though, asking, "Ms.
Abrams? Do you live here?"

She clears her throat. "I . . . I . . ."

"Oh my goodness, are you all right?" The woman
clasps Ora's upper arms in both her hands. "You look like
you're going to pass out."

Ora wants to tell her not to be ridiculous. She's never been the sort of woman who faints.

"We come from much sturdier stock," Great-Aunt Etta would say. "We can take care of ourselves, and each other, and everyone else."

"Ms. Abrams?"

No. *Miss.*

When Ora opens her mouth to correct her, the right word comes out of it, but it's unexpectedly framed by two others.

"I . . . miss . . . him."

The woman stares at her. "Who? Who do you miss?"

Papa.

Overcome with longing, Ora cannot speak. Tears trickle down her cheeks.

It's been so long since she's seen him—the way he used to be, erudite, clever, logical . . .

The way he was in her dream this morning.

Oh, I want to go back to sleep.

I want to sleep and sleep, and never wake up. I want to . . .

The harsh word jangles into her brain like a cartoon alarm clock.

She does *not* want to *die*. Goodness, no. She has far too many things left to do, another mystery to solve . . .

For years, she's been leading museum tours through the colonial exhibit, telling visitors about the starving first settlers, the survival cannibalism, the execution. She shows them the cast-iron pot where James and Elizabeth Mundy were presumed to have cooked their stews of human flesh, points out the faded trial transcripts under glass, and discusses various relics archaeologists unearthed on the settlement site: buttons and jewelry, tools, coins, pottery.

Inevitably, when Ora asks for questions at the end of a

tour, someone asks whether the Mundys really did commit the crimes for which they were convicted.

"Did they kill the other settlers so that they could eat them?" People—especially children, who are fascinated with blood and gore—want to know. "Or did they just eat the ones who had already died?"

Ora always responds with a well-rehearsed shrug and line: "The truth has been lost in the mists of time."

The dramatic statement seems to satisfy her visitors.

As for Ora herself . . .

"I need to call her right away!" she blurts.

"Call whom?" her visitor asks, looking startled.

"Savannah Ivers."

"Is she a friend of yours?"

"She has my skull."

"Your . . . skull?"

"Yes, and she may have been trying to reach me while I was asleep."

The visitor digests this, then suggests, "Why don't you lie down for a minute? Is there a couch in the next room where you can—"

"No!"

"No couch?"

"There is, but I don't want to lie down." Ora moves toward the kitchen, trailed by the woman. "I want to eat. I was just making myself some breakfast."

"Breakfast? Have you not eaten yet today?"

"No. I was so tired from the drive last night that I slept most of the day away."

They've reached the swinging door marked Private. Ora pushes it open a crack, hoping she left it fit for company, and is startled to see it in disarray.

"Oh dear," she says, stepping around a stained, sodden wad of paper towels on the floor. "The place has been ransacked again."

Cabinet doors are open. Dirty dishes overflow from the sink onto the counter. The garbage she thought she'd left tidily in the can seems to have fallen out onto the linoleum, along with a couple of potatoes that must have rolled off the counter.

She bends to retrieve them. They're spongy, nubby with sprouted eyes, skin tinted green in some spots, growing blackish white mold in others.

No reason to waste perfectly good food, Aunt Etta would say. *Just peel it all away, and the potatoes will be good as new.*

Setting them on the counter, Ora spies the pretty white china plate sprigged with purple flowers. Ah, her lunch. It doesn't look very appetizing, but she's famished.

Remembering her manners, she asks her guest, "Would you like some tuna salad? There's enough for both of us if you don't have a big appetite."

"No, thank you." Her tone is polite, but her eyes are on Ora like searchlights, one gray, the other blue. How very unusual. She reminds Ora of someone.

"Um . . . did you say that's tuna salad?"

Ora nods, browsing the past, sorting through the faces she used to know. They far outnumber the ones she knows now, even if you don't count the historical figures who mingle with very real acquaintances in her mind's eye.

"Are you sure about that?"

"Yes, I do love tuna fish. I was going to make a sandwich, but someone has stolen the bread, and . . . I'm sorry, I've forgotten your name, dear."

"I don't think I told you. It's Emerson."

"Lovely to meet you." She extends a hand. "I am Miss Ora Abrams."

"Yes, I . . . I know."

Ora smiles, pleased. Back in her Mundypalooza days, she was often interviewed by the press, and recognized by strangers. How nice to know that her stellar reputation is intact even now that the hullabaloo has died away.

"Did you say someone stole your bread, Miss Abrams?"

"I'm afraid so. Ever since the break-in last summer . . ." She shudders, remembering the frightful night she awakened to glass shattering. "Well, that was very different. But I remain on the lookout for criminal activity. And now, look. Look at my kitchen."

"Have you called the police?"

"Oh yes. I call all the time."

"And what do they do?"

"Investigate," she says, spotting something crawling underfoot.

She lifts her black oxford to stomp on it with a satisfying crunch, and explains, "Those sugar ants are everywhere at this time of year, and they're enormous, and so fast. Most mornings I'm up before the sun, and you should see them try to get away when I turn on the kitchen light."

Her visitor makes a strange sound. "Are *you* feeling faint, Miss—or is it Mrs. Emerson?"

"Emerson is my first name. My last name is Mundy."

Mundy!

The word jolts Ora like a defibrillator zap. No wonder she seemed so familiar. Ora has never met her, but she's seen those eyes many times before, in a manner of speaking.

She sets aside the plate of tuna salad, her appetite vanishing like fleet-footed insects into a shadowy crevice. "I should have known you were a Mundy the moment I saw you. You look just like Artie."

"Like who?"

"Artie—his full name was Arthur H. Mundy, of course, same as his father. Heterochromia runs very prominently through every generation of your family, going all the way back to your ancestor Elizabeth Mundy. She's the one who was executed here back in—"

"Sixteen sixty-six. I didn't realize that her eyes . . ."

"One blue. One gray."

"How do you know that?"

"It's well documented. If you read the trial transcripts—they're on exhibit upstairs—you'll see that it was used as evidence against her. Back in Puritan times, any physical aberration was considered a sign of mental imbalance or even worse, wickedness."

Now she sounds more like Papa than Aunt Etta. Papa, delivering a brilliant lecture back in the days before the accident.

Warming to her subject, she goes on, "In 1665, the very year Elizabeth and her family sailed away from England, an English doctor named Thomas Jameson published a beauty manual called 'Artificial Embellishments,' and made specific reference to 'a crooked body.' You can imagine that Elizabeth's unconventional appearance didn't help matters when she was accused of murder."

"That's terrifying—an innocent person condemned to death for what she looked like."

Ora shrugs. "Well, in Elizabeth's case, it wasn't just for that. But death sentences were doled out for plenty of questionable reasons during that era. The Salem witch trials took place not long after your ancestors were executed."

"Twenty-seven years after."

"Yes, it was . . . 1693." She nods, pleased with her guest and with herself now that the world—along with Ora's own memory and math skills—seems sharp once more. "Very impressive. Not everyone knows that fact off the top of her head."

"I'm a history teacher."

"A history teacher *and* a Mundy?"

"Yes, and I was hoping you could tell me about my family."

"Do sit down. I'll make us a cup of tea. What is that you'd like to know?"

"Everything."

Ora beams. "You've come to the right place."

Seated across her small kitchen table from Barnes, Sully watches him finish the last bite of the ham and cheese sandwich.

She'd been surprised when he texted her at Valley Roasters to ask when she'd be home.

Everything OK? she wrote back, and he responded that he was just hungry.

For all he knew, he was interrupting her on a date.

A part of her wanted to believe that was the point. Romantic sabotage is far more appealing a prospect than the always self-sufficient Barnes holed up in her apartment like a famished, hunted fugitive.

Fresh from her conversation with Emerson, Sully was already wary when she came through the door. She found Barnes, back against the wall, hand on his gun, poised for a sneak attack.

"Only me," she said breezily. "Who were you expecting?"

"Only you."

Yeah, sure. She let it go then.

Now she watches Barnes sip the coffee and make a face.

"Not good?" she asks in surprise. Last summer, he said the brew at Valley Roasters was acceptable—the highest compliment he'd offer anything in Mundy's Landing.

"Not hot. But it's okay." He leans back and chews the plastic stirrer, legs crossed under the table, bare foot tapping the air.

"When did you start smoking again?"

"Who says I'm smoking again?"

"Either you're being a decent houseguest and not lighting up in here because you know I hate it, or you're out of cigarettes."

"What are you, some kind of detective?"

"Not a very good one, because I don't have a clue what the hell's going on with you."

No comment.

Through the open screen, she can hear the squeals of children playing in a backyard pool.

"Marco Polo," she says. "They never get sick of it."

"What?"

"The game."

"Game?"

"You're a million miles away. Last summer, we heard kids playing Marco Polo all day, every day, in the pool. Remember?"

He shrugs.

Sully leans forward, rests her chin on her clasped hands, and levels a look at him. "What's going on? You have to tell me. Seriously."

A pause, and then, "I did something stupid."

She sighs. "Oh, Barnes. Do you know how many great comebacks I have for that? It kills me to waste this opportunity. *Kills* me. But if we're playing this straight . . . are we playing this straight?"

He nods.

"Bummer. What stupid thing did you do? And I swear if this involves a woman . . ."

Another pause. "It doesn't."

"Good."

Still, he hesitates, drinking more coffee, avoiding eye contact. Not his style.

Outside the window, a loud splash and delighted laughter.

"Marco!"

A children's chorus of "Polo."

More splashing, more laughter.

Oh, to be a kid again. But she'd settle for a few years ago, before Mundy's Landing and Manik Bhandari and burnout, when she was still fulfilled by New York and being on the job with Barnes, and Barnes was his old self.

"You've got to tell me," she says. "Just tear off the damned bandage. It's the only way."

He takes a deep breath and looks at her like a bungee jumper double-checking the harness before leaping from a precipice.

"It happened a long time ago. Before we met."

"So it was . . . when did we meet? Ninety-eight?"

"Ninety-nine. But this happened back in '87. I was right out of the academy, working a case with Stef."

Now retired, Frank DeStefano was Barnes's first partner, a barrel-chested old-timer. "Before or after he saved your life?"

"After. There wasn't a whole lot of *before*."

"Right, you met him, and he saved you . . . what was it? Your first five minutes on the job?"

"Third day. October 4, 1987, 4:36 a.m."

"That's precise."

"It's not something you forget."

"Not something you ever let *me* forget when we started working together. You loved to remind me that your old partner took a bullet for you."

"He didn't take the bullet. He dove on top of me a split second before the perp fired."

"Because you were green enough to open your mouth and not keep your head down in the first place."

"Rookie mistake. They happen."

"They can get you killed. You were lucky."

"It wasn't luck. It was Stef."

Sully shrugs. She hadn't known the man well, but he had a little too much bravado for her taste. Maybe she was just jealous of his relationship with Barnes—like a second wife resenting the first, even though everyone had moved on.

"So a few weeks after he saved my life, we were working the Wayland case."

"Should I remember it?"

"It was in the tabloids. Perry Wayland—ring a bell?"

She shakes her head. "I was a mere tyke back then, Barnes."

"Wayland was a Wall Street guy. Came from old money, had an Ivy League degree, the whole package. He disappeared not long after Black Monday. Do you remember that, or were you too busy stacking LEGO blocks?"

"I'm a girl, remember? I played with dolls."

"You played with LEGO. And little Matchbox squad cars," says Barnes, who knows all her secrets, just as she thought she knew his.

"So the stock market nosedives," she prompts, "and this Wayland guy disappears . . ."

"And his Mercedes turns up parked on the GWB."

George Washington Bridge.

Sully knows what that implies. "Jumper?"

"His wife swore he wasn't suicidal. You really don't remember this? She was in the press all the time. Aristocratic-looking, attractive blonde from Boston. Her maiden name was Billington, descended from one of the *Mayflower* Pilgrims."

"I don't remember any of this."

"Okay, so the wife—her name was Kirstie—said he'd never kill himself. Swore he wouldn't put her and the kids through that hell."

"Yeah, well . . ."

They all say that, the bewildered families trying to make sense of a loved one's disappearance.

My husband would never . . .

My daughter would never . . .

My sister would never . . .

All too often, they would.

"Kirstie was convinced it was foul play. Said he'd been acting strange, preoccupied, making phone calls at all hours, that kind of thing."

"Not suicidal, so . . . an affair?"

"She said no way."

Of course she did. They often do.

My husband would never . . .

"The family offered a huge reward, we set up a telephone hotline. We got the usual cranks and a few mistaken sightings—you know how it is."

"I do. Little old lady calls and says she saw the guy hanging around on her porch and it turns out to be the mailman?"

"Or a stray dog."

"Flower planter, shadow, sheer imagination . . ."

She nods. Been there, done that.

"But then an anonymous female caller leaves a tip that the guy's staying at a dive beach motel in Rhode Island. Wayland's from New England and went to college up there—undergrad at Brown, Harvard MBA. So Stef and I drive up there to check it out . . ."

"And it's him?"

"I didn't see him. Stef did. I was in the motel office talking to the night clerk, showing her pictures—of course she said she's never seen the guy. Meanwhile, Stef's out in the parking lot taking a leak when he spots a guy getting out of a beat-up car . . ."

"Wayland."

"Lost some weight, has a beard, wearing a crappy stained T-shirt, but yeah. It's him."

Same old story. "Let me guess. He's with another woman."

"No."

She raises an eyebrow. "Another man?"

"Stef said he was alone."

"You didn't see him?"

"No."

"And you don't believe Stef?"

"Of course I believe Stef. Why wouldn't I?"

"Just the way you said it, like there was something more going on. Never mind. So he faked his disappearance, left the wife and kids, and I'm assuming he had a bundle of cash to make it happen. Why?"

"Why do people take off?"

"For love, but you said he was alone. Or for hate," she adds, wondering if Kirstie Wayland's husband saw her as a nagging shrew. Maybe she *was* a nagging shrew.

Been there, done that, Sully thinks, remembering her own ex-husband's accusations. During their final miserable months together, he wasn't so far off the mark.

"What else?"

"They're trying to protect themselves or save their own life. They're running from someone or something. They're living a lie, and they're willing to exchange it for another lie." She thinks of Emerson Mundy's mother, wondering which it was for her, as she asks aloud which it was for Wayland.

"Pretty much all of the above," Barnes tells her, "and then some."

In the neighbor's yard, splashing, and someone hollers, "You're it!"

"Okay, ready? Marco!"

Sully envisions the child, waist deep in water, eyes closed, arms outstretched, flailing toward the elusive voices and splashes, trying to grab hold of someone just out of reach.

She looks at Barnes.

Why do people take off?

"So what was the stupid thing you did?" she asks, though she can probably guess that more accurately than she did his underwear style. It's written all over his face.

"I kept my mouth shut."

"Dammit." She shakes her head. "Wayland paid you off?"

"Wayland paid Stef. Stef gave me a cut. He told me it happened all the time, no big deal."

"*No big deal?*"

"Stef said it, not me."

"And *you* said, 'My money comes the old-fashioned way. I earn it,'" she points out, remembering that night at the pub last summer, when she told him about the reward.

"It was a long time ago. Obviously I know better now, but I—"

"You knew better then! Come on, Barnes. Right from wrong. That's straightforward stuff! Didn't you think of that poor woman—and her children? How could you let them believe their father was dead?"

"Wayland's a scumbag. Stef said they were better off not knowing the truth, and—"

"Was that up to Stef to decide?"

"No. But—"

"Or you?"

"It was—"

"I can't believe you're—"

"Would you let me defend myself for two seconds? Please?"

She clamps her mouth shut, certain nothing he says will make a difference. But she lets him talk.

"You know I lost my dad when I was twelve. He used to hand me a few bucks for the ice cream truck—'Get us both a Drumstick,' he'd say, 'but don't tell your mom because she has me on a diet.'"

Sully's heard about his father before. He was a good

man, young and afflicted with heart disease. A walking time bomb, and it exploded—a massive heart attack killed him before his fortieth birthday.

"I blamed myself when he died. My mother was always so worried about his health, because she knew what could happen. But I thought she was a nag, and my dad would brush it off. He'd take me to the park to shoot hoops, or to a ball game—huffing and puffing to the upper decks, eating hot dogs. I thought it was fun. It was killing him."

"Those were his choices. He wanted that time with you." She wonders what this has to do with anything. They've been over this before, countless times. Squad car therapy.

Barnes's marriage crumbled in part because his ex wanted a family, and he didn't. The job was too demanding for him to devote the time to parenting that his father had, and it's dangerous. He couldn't stand the thought of his own child growing up fatherless.

His ex-wife considered his reasons "a big heap of BS." Sometimes, Sully does, too. Wee hour colic, spit-up, and Gymboree wouldn't just conflict with the job—they'd conflict with Barnes's off-hours lifestyle, wardrobe, white sofa, exotic travel, and all.

"What does all this have to do with taking a payoff from Wayland?"

"Do you know what it's like to lose the guy who's supposed to have your back?"

Yeah, Barnes. I do.

She considers pointing out that after years of partnership, friendship, kinship, he abandoned her. He might say it was the other way around. But she's the one who tried to maintain contact after she left New York.

We aren't talking about us, though. We're talking about his father, and I'm still not sure why.

Anyway, Barnes doesn't wait for an answer. "After my

dad died, my mom fell apart. That kind of grief can ruin your life. It ruined hers."

"Not yours."

"It could have. I had a lot of anger, and my dad wasn't around to keep an eye on me, and my mother kind of gave up. I was headed to a bad place before Wash set me straight. You know that."

She nods, familiar with that story, too—how an older neighbor, a retired cop named Washington, had caught Barnes trying to break into his car parked on the street. Instead of scolding him or reporting him, Wash took him under his wing. He guided a troubled kid onto the right path, becoming a father figure.

"Wash was the first guy who saved my life. Stef was the second. I owed him."

"That doesn't excuse what happened."

"No, but maybe it explains it. You've been there. You know how it is. Inner city cop. Us and them."

She shakes her head. No. She may know that, but she doesn't know this. Doesn't know *him*.

"You did this stupid, *stupid* thing, what? Twenty-five years ago?"

"Almost thirty." He graces her with a brief smile, a flash of the old Barnes. "You never were a math whiz."

"It's the painkillers."

"That was hours ago."

"They're strong. So it's been almost thirty years, and you're just now getting around to feeling guilty?"

Poof! The old Barnes vanishes.

"I've felt guilty for thirty years. But I had my reasons."

"Yeah, you said. You owed Stef."

"Not just that."

"Then what?"

He shakes his head.

"I deserve more than this, especially from you."

"I know you do."

"But you're not going to give it to me?"

"It's not that simple. I need you to be patient until I—"

"If you wanted patience, you should have shown up on a saint's doorstep."

"You're no saint, and neither am I. We all do things we wish we hadn't done. Sometimes we don't have reasons, sometimes we do."

"Tell me yours."

He sighs. "I didn't know until recently that Wayland isn't just some guy who took off on his wife."

"No? Who is he?"

Barnes tilts his head, as if considering whether to confide in her. "It's complicated."

She waits for more, and doesn't get it.

"Has he resurfaced? Is that why you're here?"

Ignoring the first question, he says, "I'm here because I need time to sort this out and figure out what the hell I'm going to do about it."

"You came barging into my life to sort things out? You couldn't do that at home?"

"No," he says simply, "I could not."

So he's hiding. Possibly in danger. Why else would he go to such lengths to make sure he wasn't followed here?

"I know you deserve the rest of the story, and you'll get it, I promise, just as soon as I figure out what I need to do. Right now, the less you know, the better off you'll be."

"Like Kirstie Wayland was better off?"

"Does it help you to know that it didn't take her very long to lose interest in finding her husband? She moved on and was shacking up with an even richer guy a few months after I saw Perry in Rhode Island. She had him declared dead. Collected the insurance money, too."

"Did it help *you* to know that?"

"You know what? It did. Yeah. And I—"

He breaks off at the sound of a scream.

When Ora Abrams offered her a cup of tea, Emerson refused as politely, quickly, and firmly as possible. She has no intention of ingesting even boiled water amid filthy dishes and rotting garbage that stinks to high heaven.

No wonder the place is infested with roaches, mice, and heaven knows what else.

She'd assumed Ora had made up the story about the kitchen having been ransacked because she was embarrassed. Now it's apparent that the poor dear is senile.

Such a cliché, a little old lady eating cat food. A tragic cliché. Why isn't someone helping her? Rowan, or Sully— surely someone must realize what's going on here.

But then, how would anyone suspect?

The rest of the first floor is exquisite, the front rooms furnished with fine antiques and glass display cabinets. The air might be a little musty and dusty, and there's more cat fur on the horsehair sofa than can possibly remain on the cat. Still, everything appears to be in order.

You'd never know the truth unless you ventured beyond the public museum space, or captured Miss Abrams in a less-than-lucid moment.

"Now, where do you fit into the family, dear?" Perched on a chair, gray eyes alight with wonder, spry Ora looks like a children's librarian about to embark on story hour. There's no evidence of dementia, as if it, too, has been safely tucked away behind a closed door marked Private.

"My father was descended from Aaron and Sarah Mundy."

"Oh my goodness! Your father is Horace? No, that can't be right. You're much too young, and Horace has only sons."

Should she remind Ora that Horace and his sons are long dead?

No. "My father is Jerome."

"You mean *Jeremiah*."

"*Jerome*."

"But he was named after Jeremiah himself."

"How do you know that?"

"It's only logical, as your grandfather's middle name was Jeremiah."

"I'm pretty sure my grandfather's middle name was Xavier."

"'Pretty sure?'" Ora shakes her head. "My dear, Xavier wasn't—"

"No, I'm positive. My grandfather was Donald X. Mundy."

X marks the spot.

Ora shakes her head in denial, her wispy white bun wobbling like a tipsy crown. "That's incorrect."

"My grandfather's father was Horace's brother, Oswald." Emerson feels like a frustrated mother trying to convince a stubborn two-year-old to open up and swallow.

"That's impossible."

"Why—" Something grazes her legs beneath the table, and her question gives way to a shriek.

Ora stoops to investigate. "Rosie! There you are, my sweet girl. Where have you been?"

Emerson half expects to see her petting an enormous rat, but it's a fat orange cat.

"Don't worry, she's very friendly."

Unsure whether Ora is referring to the cat or to her, Emerson watches the old woman gently petting the tabby.

"Are you afraid of cats, Miss—or is it *Mrs.*—Mundy?"

"It's actually Ms." Seeing Ora's mouth tighten, she adds, "And I love cats. I'm just allergic."

"Yes, well, that runs in your family."

"So I've heard."

"Oh?"

"Yes, Rowan Mundy mentioned it."

"Rowan is a darling girl." Ora is on her feet again, heading toward the cupboards. "Her husband Asa is descended from Jeremiah."

"Asa?" Looks like the confusion is back. "I thought her husband's name was Jake."

"That's what they call him. His name is Asa Jacob Mundy IV, descended from Aaron Mundy's brother Ezra, born in 1842."

"You know this off the top of your head?"

"Oh yes. I know everything."

Emerson bites back a smile. "That's why I'm here. I'd love to hear about my family."

"It would take weeks to tell you *everything*. Shall we start at the beginning?"

"Why don't we start with my great-grandfather and his brother? Did you know them?"

"Oh yes, but not well. You see, I was born in '35, and by then, the boys were getting up there in years. Horace's youngest son, Arthur, used to come visit from Philadelphia with his family in the summertime, and his boy, Artie, was my age. We were playmates. Poor Artie was just as terrified of his grandfather as I was. I remember Horace as an elderly man with white hair, sitting in his rocking chair on the porch of the Dapplebrook Inn. That used to be his home, you know. It's where we used to play."

"What about Oswald?"

"Oh, he was a terrifying creature."

"Terrifying?"

"Ranting through the streets with his iron arm detached, waving it around like a billy club . . ."

Emerson is as disturbed by that image as she is to see

Ora take a can of cat food from one cabinet and a small china plate from another.

"Papa told me to stay away from him, and even Aunt Etta avoided him," she goes on. "Of course, she'd known him and Horace all her life. She always said it was a terrible pity, the way the tables had turned."

"How so?"

"Oswald was the firstborn, and he was Aaron and Sarah's favorite as a child." Ora opens the can and takes a spoon from a drawer.

"What about Horace?"

"The boys were only fourteen months apart, but so very opposite. Oswald was dark and athletic and dashing. Horace was fair and scrawny and terribly nearsighted, with thick glasses. He didn't have much personality back then—quiet and studious, a shadow of his big brother. But oh, how he idolized Oswald. Everyone did."

"How did Oswald feel about Horace?"

"Oh, he was very protective of his little brother, and an excellent role model in the early years—he was an avid horseman, and a champion oarsman. He excelled at academics, and he was the most popular boy in school. He graduated first in his class and was accepted to Dartmouth."

"It must be a family tradition. Braden Mundy just graduated from there."

"Who?"

"Rowan's son."

Ora smiles absently, poised with the plate and spoon. "That's nice. And was he on the crew team, as well?"

If she digs in to eat that, I'll have to stop her.

Aloud, she says, "I have no idea."

"Oswald was going to be on the team, but then he had his accident, and everything changed."

"He was hit by a train, right? What happened, exactly?"

"It was late at night, and he was walking alone. He must have tripped and fallen." She stoops over to put the plate on the floor, and Briar Rose begins devouring it.

Crisis averted. Phew.

"Oswald was lucky he survived, but he lost his left arm. So tragic. And of course, that was when everything changed with Horace."

Emerson watches her put the dirty spoon back into the drawer, and the empty can back into the refrigerator.

"Um, Miss Abrams . . ."

"Yes, dear?"

If she interrupts the tale, she may never get to hear the rest—at least, not from the old woman who knew her great-grandfather and uncle personally.

"You said Oswald had an iron arm?"

She shudders. "Yes. The doctors fitted him with it, a hideous thing, virtually useless. Rowing was out of the question. And his face was scarred after the accident. One cheek and his jaw were like the pulp of a blood orange."

"It must have been painful for him."

"Well, back in those days, they prescribed laudanum to manage the pain."

"That's opium."

"Yes, and highly addictive. It impaired Oswald's cognitive skills. The following year, he did enroll at Dartmouth alongside Horace, but he didn't last very long."

"He failed out of college? What did he do then?"

"What else was there to do but come home to Mundy's Landing?"

Emerson can picture the former hero, maimed, addicted, and depressed, a disheveled has-been.

"But he did eventually fall in love and get married and have a son," she remembers—her own grandfather.

"Love? I don't know about that. He had a dalliance with a teenage hired girl, and that resulted in a pregnancy and a shotgun marriage. An utter disgrace to poor Aaron and Sarah."

"I'm sure it was," she murmurs. "What about his son, Donald?"

"Born just four months after the wedding. He was the same age as Horace's youngest, Arthur."

"I wonder if it made Oswald happy, for a little while, anyway. Being a father, having someone to love," she adds, seeing Ora's quizzical expression.

"Oh no. Not at all. There was no love. That baby made him miserable, and his wife, as well. She ran off with another man, never to be seen again."

Thinking of Didi, she marvels that history had repeated generations later with her own mother's abandonment.

No wonder her father had been so unhappy. So damaged, and angry.

So am I.

"How do you know all of this?"

"Aunt Etta told me."

"How did she know?"

"She knew everything." Ora shrugs.

"And the baby? Donald?"

"What about him?"

"Did she know him? Or did you? Did you know what became of him after his mother left?"

"Horace's poor wife had to nurse him alongside her own infant, Arthur, so that the poor thing wouldn't starve to death. She'd have taken him in and raised him, and Oswald probably would have handed him over in a heartbeat, but Aunt Etta said Horace wouldn't allow it. He sent them away when the boy was weaned."

"Away . . . where?"

"They were nearby at first. And then I don't know whatever happened to them."

"Did you ever meet Donald?"

"Not that I recall."

Ora, who prides herself on knowing everything, gives an offhanded shrug to indicate the insignificance of the child who grew up to become Emerson's grandfather.

No wonder Donald didn't like to speak about his past. No wonder he was estranged from Oswald, a bitter embarrassment by the time he died in his nineties.

"I feel sorry for him," she tells Ora.

"For the father, or the child?"

"Both. They were victims of a terrible tragedy."

"Plenty of people survive traumatic injuries and go on to live productive lives. Oswald's unfortunate accident didn't have to result in his becoming such a . . ."

"A train wreck?"

The irony in her comment doesn't escape Ora, who flashes an appreciative smile.

"Precisely. Oswald made bad choices that led to colossal failures, including his marriage."

"His marriage led to the birth of his son."

"A miserable marriage, and a miserable child, Aunt Etta said. It cried all the time."

"Of course it did! Because its mother was gone, and its father was broken! And it was not an *it*. You're talking about a human being."

"I'm aware of that, my dear."

She's talking about Donald Mundy.

Not about you.

Yet Emerson can't help herself. She goes on, "A child can sense when her parents wish she'd never been born."

Ora catches the slip. "*She?*"

"*He*. Thank goodness that little boy was born, or I wouldn't be here."

"That isn't true, my dear. Oswald's failings had very

little impact on Horace's family life. His marriage was stable, and his children were—"

"*Oswald* was my great-grandfather. Not Horace."

"No, he wasn't."

"Yes, he was."

They're toddlers playing tug of war with a plastic sandbox shovel, and Emerson can't let go.

"My grandfather, Donald Mundy, was Oswald's son."

"That can't be."

"It *is*. It *was*. I don't know why you keep insisting—"

"Because of your eyes, Miss Mundy. It's very simple. "

"What do you mean?"

"Oswald's eyes were dark. Horace had one blue eye, and one gray. Heterochromia is passed from parent to child, and it appears in every generation. Aaron had it. So did two of Horace's boys, and my little playmate, Artie. Oswald's son couldn't have had heterochromia, so he couldn't have been your grandfather."

"But my father said . . ."

Her father.

Her father, who had piercing blue eyes.

If Ora really does know everything, then not only can Oswald not be Emerson's great-grandfather, but—

Her mind's meandering along that treacherous path is curtailed by a scream.

This scream, Sully knows, is not swimming pool child play.

It's an adult voice, a woman in trouble, and it came from somewhere on Prospect Street or beyond.

She jumps up, grabs her badge and gun, and heads for the door.

Barnes starts to follow.

"No!" She whirls to stop him. "Stay."

"You stay, too." He steps around her, blocking her path.

"What the hell, Barnes! This has nothing to do with you."

"How do you know? I haven't even told you—"

"Get out of my way!

"Don't go blasting out of here until you know what's going on."

"I need to go do my job!" She gives his chest a push, a feather duster attempting to budge a concrete wall.

"Dammit." He steps aside, but again tries to follow her.

"I'm not the one who's hiding. You are. If you set foot outside, people are going to know you're here. Do you really want that?"

Another scream, shrill and terrified.

Leaving him behind, Sully races down the steps and out onto the sidewalk.

Barreling around the corner onto Prospect, she spots a knot of people gathered in the front yard of the Dapplebrook Inn.

The manager, Nancy Vandergraaf, is at the center of the group. She's obviously the one who was screaming. The others are trying to calm her, and Nancy keeps gesturing at the behemoth maple tree several yards away.

"Sully!" Trevor, her waiter pal, spots her. "Hurry!"

She sprints toward them.

Trevor keeps one arm wrapped around Nancy's thin shoulders and points toward the tree with the other. His shirtsleeve has ridden up, and this time, she can see his tattoo. So much for his mother's initials. At a glance, she thinks it's a swastika, but a shocked double take reveals an ugly black spider.

"What's going on? Nancy, are you all right?"

She wails unintelligibly.

Trevor translates: "There's a dead person hanging from the tree."

Horace J. Mundy
68 Prospect Street
Mundy's Landing, New York

August 8, 1894

Dear Horace,

This morning, Mrs. Anderson told me I had a letter. I was certain it would be from you, and that it would contain the funds I requested.

Bully for me. I was half right.

In response to your written request that I never again darken the doorstep of your fine new summer home, I shall remind you of two incidents.

Do you recall the time three horrid older boys cornered you in the schoolyard? They were bigger and stronger than you, as most were. Yet they were also bigger than me. I heard you shouting for me and I took them on. Three against one. Those bullies went home wailing, with black eyes and fat lips all around. You told me that day that if ever I needed a favor—anything at all, even a tremendous one—I should call upon you.

Now I have, only to be denied. I remind you that I requested a loan, not a handout. Heaven knows you have more than enough money to spare. If you can provide the means to get me by for a few months, I shall turn things around, look for work, perhaps heal from these terrible injuries at last.

If you cannot . . .

Ah, yes. There was one other memory I wanted to share. Forgive my lapse. My brain hasn't functioned properly since the accident. I fear nothing has.

Yet for all that I forget, one memory stubbornly persists.

After the accident back in '88, you were at my bedside, and Mother, too, in despair over my condition.

She believed I was comatose. You both did. The doctors confirmed it was the case. Yet I heard every word.

I heard Mother asking you how it could have happened. I heard you tell her that we were fishing down by the river, and quarreled about some silly thing, and you left to walk home alone.

You neglected to mention that we'd been sipping Father's bourbon—imagine Mother's fury if she knew that he kept a hidden flask, or that we had helped ourselves to it, intending to learn to drink spirits like a man. You see, Horace? I remember far more of that night than you do. Or perhaps, just far more than you want me to.

You told Mother I must have stumbled while I was crossing the railroad trestle, and fallen onto the tracks.

After she left the room, I felt your hand squeeze mine— the only hand I had left. I heard you sobbing pitifully. I heard you apologize for what you had done, praying that God would forgive you. That I would forgive you.

I did not know then what you meant.

Now, all these years later, I do.

As a boy, you used to look at me with great admiration and respect. Somewhere along the way, it turned to envy. On that last night by the river, I saw pure hatred— unleashed by drink, but hatred nonetheless. When I last looked into those mismatched eyes of yours, I see pity and disdain, and guilt.

You came up behind me as I was walking home, didn't you? You pushed me in front of the train.

You wanted me to die.

It would have been better for both of us if I had.

But you have achieved your goal. You've replaced me as the favorite son, golden boy of Mundy's Landing. And so you shall remain, as long as you can see fit to help a fellow to whom you do, after all, still owe a tremendous favor.

I await your response.

Your brother,

Oswald Mundy
c/o Mrs. Anderson
162 Academy Street
Poughkeepsie, New York

Chapter 10

"Ora? Ora!"

A voice, not Aunt Etta's, but a female voice, steals through the darkness. She feels a cool, moist cloth dabbing at her forehead.

Someone is gently tending to her.

Mother?

She must be dreaming, or . . .

Perhaps her time has come. If so, then it isn't nearly as traumatic as she'd expected. One minute, she was sitting in at the table, the next . . .

She opens her eyes, hoping that Papa is here, too. Heaven looks very much like her kitchen, and her mother looks very much like . . .

"Thank goodness!" the woman says, her eyes—one blue, and one gray—wide with concern.

"What . . . ?"

"You fainted."

Fainted?

Ah, then this really is her kitchen, and the woman is Emerson Mundy.

Ora feels oddly disappointed to find herself alive and well.

Or perhaps not entirely well. She doesn't seem to

have the strength to sit up, and her eyes insist on closing again.

"Ora? Ora, can you hear me? I'm going to call . . ."

Untethered, she allows herself to drift into the darkness again.

Sirens are wailing before Sully can call for backup.

"I called them when I heard Nancy," Trevor tells her.

Sully touches his arm, grateful that the ugly black ink spider has crawled back up his sleeve for now. "Tell me what happened."

"Nancy went outside to water the flower beds, and—"

"I do it every morning!" Nancy's interjection is a shrill protest, as if someone had expressed doubt. "Every single morning! I water those flowers, and today . . ." She shakes her head.

Sully has never seen Nancy Vandergraaf disheveled, and this moment is no exception. Though trembling and shell-shocked, the woman doesn't have a hair out of place. Her mascara isn't even running.

Trevor resumes his account. "When I heard Nancy scream, I was thinking, you know, about the yellow jackets. There's a hive in the window well back in there by the hose." He indicates the rose of Sharon hedge alongside the house. "She got stung the other day, and I thought she'd been stung again, till I looked out the window and saw . . ."

He points to the maple tree growing at the corner of the veranda. A human hand, swollen and blue, pokes from behind the thick trunk, motionless, suspended a few feet off the ground.

"There's a note on the tree," Trevor says as a squad car pulls up at the curb.

"A suicide note?" Sully asks.

"Not really. Some kind of game. Here, I'll show you."

"No, Trevor, we need to wait right here for backup."

Sully finds herself scrutinizing him, all of them—
Nancy, and the neighbors who have gathered around.

A shivery old woman hugs herself as if she's frightened or freezing, the latter unlikely given her hunter
green velour tracksuit that's too warm for June. Wide-
eyed adolescent boys whisper to each other, skateboards
under their scrawny arms. A ponytailed mom balances a
baby on her hip and a cell phone in her hand, texting as
her child whimpers.

More neighbors are heading in this direction, others
are out on their porches, passing cars are stopped in the
street, their drivers gaping at the commotion.

Sully recognizes only Dr. Yamazaki, the plastic surgeon who lives in the Murder House across the street.
She usually sees him coming and going from the hospital
or office wearing scrubs or sport coats. He must be off
today, dressed down in a turquoise St. Barts T-shirt. He's
carrying a pooper-scooper and a knotted plastic bag, and
is accompanied by his Akita, Rita, straining on a leash.

Lieutenant Nick Colonomos steps out of the police car
and strides toward them, accompanied by Officer Meagan
Johansen, who steps in to hold the new flood of gawkers
back from the property.

"What's going on, Detective Leary?"

"DB over there," she tells Nick.

Dead body. His dark eyes widen.

"Did you confirm?"

"No, I just got here myself, but I was about to—"

"Let's go take a look. Officer Johansen, you stay here
with the witnesses. Take statements."

Sully doesn't miss the spark of envy in Meagan's eyes.
An attractive brunette with a bikini body that's prominently featured in her social media photos, she often
gazes at Nick Colonomos . . . well, probably the way Sully

herself looks at him. He doesn't seem any more interested in Meagan than he is in Sully.

Her cell phone vibrates with a text as she and Nick walk across the grass. She pulls it out of her pocket and sees that it's from Barnes, and consists only of several question marks.

Not breaking her stride, she writes back, All OK.

It isn't, but she is, and that's presumably all he wants to know.

"Did they say whether it was a local or a guest?" Colonomos asks Sully in a low voice as they approach the tree.

"No."

Spotting the corpse, though, she stops short in shocked recognition.

"Suicide. And it's a partial," Colonomos mutters.

Partial—the word registers, and she grasps it somewhere in the back of her mind, in the part that's not reeling with disbelief.

Partial hanging, as opposed to a complete hanging, in which the body dangles from the noose. In a partial, the body is asphyxiated by a ligature, but maintains contact with the ground.

She's seen both on the job. Neither is pretty.

The victim is kneeling at the base of the tree, head bent at an unnatural angle. A length of rope is embedded around the neck and rides up the bark, disappearing into the branches overhead.

Colonomos needlessly checks for a pulse and shakes his head. "Must be someone staying here at the inn."

Spotting the aforementioned note on the tree trunk, Sully steps closer.

A sheet of paper is stuck to the tree with a thumbtack. It's small, about four by six, and lined, with ragged edges that indicate it was torn from a spiral notebook.

She gapes at the crude lines, circles, and slashes drawn in a bold purple marker. A game, Trevor had said.

"Suicide note?" Nick asks.

"No. And I don't think it's a suicide, either."

"Why? What does it say?"

"It says we've got our hands full, Lieutenant."

He's beside her, looking over her shoulder at the paper. "What the hell is that?"

"That," Sully tells him, as a sick shiver runs through her, "is hangman."

The telltale nick of a blade on Jane Doe's jawline isn't the only disturbing evidence Savannah has discovered today.

Though the girl couldn't have been older than sixteen, she's missing most of her teeth.

In the days before toothbrushes, colonists who practiced oral hygiene—and not all of them did—would have used soft twigs to scrape away the plaque on their teeth and gums. Jane's remaining teeth show no signs of decay that would cause a young person's teeth to fall out, and Savannah can see faint scraping marks that indicate she took care of them.

Calcium loss was the probable culprit.

Given access to more of Jane's remains, she'd likely find additional signs of calcium theft—osteoporosis in the vertebrae and pelvis. With just the skull, she's left to theorize, but the evidence is strong that Jane's story is even more tragic than being butchered to provide human flesh for starving neighbors.

Strange—you can't mourn a person you never met, let alone one who lived centuries ago. But when she imagines a young girl in the throes of starvation, being brutally murdered, her remains cooked and eaten—not just hers, but . . .

During that era, significant tooth loss in such a young

woman is a strong indicator of pregnancy. Nutrition was severely limited under the best of circumstances, particularly in a developing colony in the dead of winter. A fetus would have robbed its mother's body of calcium anywhere it could be found.

Wondering whether she'd already delivered a child upon her death, Savannah again refers to the list of settlers. Three babies had been born that summer and fall, but all were named and listed in tandem with their mothers, who were in their twenties and thirties. Sadly, the babies perished along with everyone else that winter—in one case, birth and death coming on the same day.

Jane must have been pregnant when she died.

Did she even realize?

Did others?

Could the pregnancy have had anything to do with her murder?

Chilled by the thought, Savannah remembers that day last summer on the street. Bottle rockets, and Cher's maternal instinct for the child in her womb.

"I'm so sorry," she whispers to Jane Doe. "For you, and for your unborn child."

A cockroach skitters from under the refrigerator and darts past the spot where Emerson kneels beside Ora, disappearing into a crack into the grimy shadows beneath the stove.

"Ora? Can you hear me?"

The old woman remains still, eyes closed, but she's breathing.

Her head is propped on a pillow Emerson had snatched from a velvet sofa in the next room. She strokes the wrinkled face with the dish towel she'd grabbed from a hook and dampened at the sink. It smells like a wet sock left for a week in a dark closet, but it was the nearest thing at hand, and she thought it might revive Miss Abrams.

It did, for a few moments, but then she faded away again, and Emerson dialed 911.

She listens to the sirens, unable to tell whether they're heading here, or still part of the wailing entourage responding to the crisis unfolding down the block.

The fat orange cat sits nearby, grooming its ears with a saliva-dampened paw, pausing to solemnly regard its stricken mistress, and then—with suspicion—Emerson.

"It's okay," she tells the cat. "I'm trying to help her."

The cat stares at her, and then, satisfied, goes back to grooming.

"Hang in there, Ora. Help is on the way."

How long has it been since her collapse?

Five minutes? Ten?

It happened moments after they heard those urgent screams outside.

Before that, Ora had informed Emerson that she couldn't have descended from Oswald Mundy.

Heterochromia is passed from parent to child, and it appears in every generation.

Is it true?

Now isn't the time to consider the implications, but Ora is stable, and help is on the way, and . . .

She has to know. Now.

She tosses aside the smelly towel and reaches into her pocket for her phone. Opening a browser window, she types in *heterochromia* and hits Enter.

She doesn't bother to scan the results, just clicks on the first link and searches for something that will prove that Ora Abrams's senility has tainted her knowledge of genetics, if not history.

She doesn't find it.

Ora was right.

Blue-eyed Jerry Mundy could not have been her biological father.

Sully spent a good chunk of her childhood at her grandparents' apartment.

If her grandfather wasn't home, she and her grandmother sipped tea together and watched police dramas on television. When her grandfather was around, the TV stayed dark and silent. He didn't consider those shows entertainment.

A large-boned, flame-haired beat cop, he was known to everyone, including Sully, as Big Red. When Colly was busy in the kitchen, he taught Sully to play gin rummy and seven-card draw.

"Not for money," he'd assure his wife if she came buzzing around with criticism. "Just for bottle caps."

"Lord knows you've got enough of those," Colly would huff, and Big Red would just sip from his ever-present bottle of beer and wink at his granddaughter.

Per their secret agreement, every beer cap was worth a quarter. The more beer Big Red drank, the more Sully won. One profitable night, her grandmother heard her jangling away from the table and asked her to turn her pockets inside out.

"Red!" Colly bellowed as quarters rolled across the worn linoleum, to the delight of her three cats. "It's a sin to gamble with an eight-year-old!"

That put an end to the card games, but not to Sully's fun with her grandfather.

The most interesting thing about Big Red—well, there were many interesting things, but Sully was particularly fascinated by his passion for language and literature. She'd never seen her own father, also a burly cop, pick up a book. Nor, for that matter, her mother, or Colly.

Big Red's appetite for books was so voracious that he'd read almanacs and romance novels and even some of Sully's children's books—any genre, as long as it wasn't a detective novel. For him, crime fiction—like TV cop dramas—did not provide adequate escape from daily life.

Big Red and Sully spent a lot of time sitting on the old chintz sofa in companionable silence, reading. Once in a while, they worked a crossword puzzle together, and they often played word games. Scrabble, Boggle . . .

Hangman.

That was the most fun, because all they needed was a pen and a pad of paper. There were no game pieces for the cats to dive-bomb and scatter. Hangman was portable. On nice days, they could play outside on the stoop, or even on the subway if Big Red had an errand to run.

When Sully stayed overnight, she and Big Red had hangman tournaments into the wee hours. They never tired of trying to stump each other with unusual or long words for the other to guess. Once, Big Red turned the paper sideways and drew the gallows in the center, and across the top created a wide row of dashes, each representing a letter in his secret word.

"Hey!" Sully counted the dashes and accused him of cheating. "There aren't any thirty-letter words in the dictionary!"

"There's one."

Pseudopseudohypoparathyroidism.

Her little stick man was hanging from the gallows long before she figured it out, even though Big Red added eyes, nose, mouth, and a little hat to the stick man to allow her extra guesses.

Now, she stares at a chilling version of the childhood game, affixed to a tree from which a real person hangs.

Along the top is a partially solved word diagram:

_ _ N _

Beneath it is a crude depiction of a stick figure hanging from a gallows.

Sully stares at it, half listening to Nick Colonomos's

cell phone conversation with Ron Calhoun, who'd left this morning for a golf trip to Lake George.

Every suicide, no matter how obvious, is investigated as if it were a homicide. Thus, the chief must be informed, and the crime investigation team summoned. Sully doesn't see them nearly as often here as she did the C.S.I. team in New York.

After hanging a couple of large tarps to conceal the body from anyone out in the yard or inside the house, they began taking the measurements and photos that go along with an unattended death, careful not to disturb the evidence. Also on the scene are paramedics who'd arrived far too late to help the victim, whom they estimate to have been dead for ten to twelve hours. No longer needed here, they've lingered to talk baseball, barbecue sauce, and weekend weather with the forensics guys.

All in a day's work. No one seems concerned about the piece of paper tacked to the tree.

Sully can't seem to ignore the irrational, perhaps egotistical part of her brain that suspects the note was planted by a killer, perhaps for her own benefit.

Who has she told about Big Red and the hangman tournaments?

Barnes, of course. Barnes knows every detail of her life, far more than her ex-husband, who even if she'd told him probably wouldn't remember her grandfather's nickname, let alone their special games.

She mentioned hangman at the Mundy home on New Year's Eve, too. Rowan and Jake's kids had a party, and she invited Sully and a few of the parents over to help supervise. Nancy Vandergraaf was there, as was her son Christian, whom Mick Mundy and their other friends call Van for short.

The adults played Scrabble in an out-of-the-way corner. Though Sully drank her share of champagne that evening, she remembers talking about having played Scrabble with Big Red, and hangman, too.

Was there a crazed killer at the party who might have overheard?

That's far-fetched. Sully can't imagine that the high school and college kids were capable of anything more criminal than smuggling beer into the house—which they did. At that point, Jake Mundy confiscated car keys, Rowan headed upstairs to find bedding for a horde of un-expected overnighters, and Sully was left listening to a tipsy Nancy Vandergraaf badmouthing her ex-husband.

Trevor was there, too—friends with Rowan's oldest son, Braden.

Now he and Nancy are both here.

She tilts her head back, following the length of rope that climbs from the corpse's neck into the leafy maple boughs. The other end is anchored to the garden hose spigot protruding from the house.

"He's not coming back."

She looks up, startled to see Nick standing beside her, phone in hand.

"I'm sorry, what was that?"

"I just hung up with Ron. Told him it looks like a sui-cide."

She nods, though not in complete agreement, looking again at the note.

Did some twisted predator seize the game's signifi-cance in her life? Is he trying to make a mockery of her precious childhood memories, by . . . by . . .

By lynching a person to whom you have virtually no connection? Come on. That makes zero sense.

This has nothing to do with you.

But if it did, it wouldn't be the first time she'd played a role in a murderous ritual.

Eighteen months ago in Mundy's Landing, a killer

became fixated on her because she, like his victims, had red hair.

"Detective?"

She looks up at Nick.

"You're not convinced," he says.

"It's just that note. I look at it, and I think—"

"I know. I'm thinking the same thing."

"You are?"

"There were notes under the Sleeping Beauties' pillows."

She widens her eyes. She'd been focused on her own connections, but he's right. The 1916 killer, and last summer's copycat, had left the same cryptic handwritten message at every Murder House. *Sleep safe till tomorrow*—a line from a William Carlos Williams poem.

"I mentioned it to Ron," Nick goes on, "but he pointed out that a weird note at a death scene doesn't mean homicide. This could just be a unique version of a suicide note. They aren't always coherent, you know? You don't kill yourself if you're of sound mind."

She nods. She, too, has seen her share of missives left by people who have taken their own lives. Some are rambling accusations, some containing only pertinent information for survivors, and some consisting of only a few words—usually *I'm sorry*.

"We need to look at the facts."

"Yes, but as a detective, you rely as much on instinct as on evidence."

"In this case, is your instinct—and mine, I'll be honest—a knee-jerk reaction? See a note, assume murder. That doesn't add up."

"I know."

"Do you know how rare a homicidal hanging is? Especially when you're talking about a full-sized adult." He gestures at the victim, engorged face frozen in horror, pupils dilated, black tongue protruding.

Sully looks, too, and suppresses a shudder. She's seen worse, but in most cases, she'd never known the victim alive.

"It would be hard to hang someone this size," she agrees, "but not impossible if you incapacitate the person first. And this is a partial hanging. You wouldn't have to pull all that weight off the ground. All you'd have to do is get the ligature into place and tighten it until they asphyxiate."

"That's true. The victim could have done it that way, too, though. Kneel and fall forward. I've seen it."

"So have I."

A pink rose of Sharon bloom lies in the dirt between the hedgerow and the foundation. The woody stem is jagged at the base, as if torn away. Several other twiggy blossoms dangle from the boughs above, broken but not severed.

The ground around the spigot is thick with bark mulch. At a glance, it doesn't appear to have been disturbed. But several gardening rakes and shovels are propped against the house a short distance away.

"Someone could have smoothed over the mulch to cover evidence of a struggle," she tells Nick.

He looks at the ground, the snapped stem, the shrubs, and back at her.

"And the victim could have bumped into those branches walking through here." He indicates the forensics team. "They'll be able to tell us more. But let's go back to the note. I've never played hangman, so tell me about it. You said before it's a four-letter word . . ."

"Yes, and the third letter is N, see?" She points at it, not touching it though her hand is encased in the obligatory rubber glove. "The other three letters haven't been guessed yet."

"I can think of a few four-letter words," Nick mutters, "and none of them have an N in them."

"Maybe the next of kin know what it means."

"Right. You're going to handle the notification, then?"

"Yes, I'll take care of it now." Sully removes her gloves and shoves them into her pocket, taking a long last look at the dead man in the red shirt.

Just hours after she saw him in Dunkin' Donuts, Roy Nowak came to the Dapplebrook Inn and took his own life, or was murdered.

What the hell happened in between?

Savannah finds Ora's number listed in her outgoing calls and hits redial, then listens to it ring . . . and ring . . .

Just as last night, it's answered with an electronic click and the now-familiar measured enunciation of a recorded outgoing message.

"Hello, you have reached the personal answering machine of Miss Ora Abrams at the Mundy's Landing Historical Society. Do leave a message at the tone, and I shall return your call just as soon as I am able. Thank you. Good day."

Savannah can't help but smile at the detailed instructions, wondering if this is, indeed, an actual answering machine and not voice mail. The lengthy beep certainly sounds like it.

"Hello, Ms. Abrams, this is Savannah Ivers over at Hadley. I'm down in the lab with the cranial remains of your Jane Doe. I haven't been able to identify her yet, but I have some . . . um, fairly shocking information to share with you. I'll come by the historical society this evening to discuss it in person if you—"

Interrupted by another loud beep, she frowns.

Definitely an old-fashioned machine, the kind with limited storage. Her mother has one and it's always cutting people off mid-sentence. She screens every call—Savannah suspects her own included. Whenever her mother doesn't pick up, she pictures her sitting a few feet away from the phone, engrossed in a television program and ignoring the caller's voice being broadcast through the room.

Now she can't leave Ora her number and tell her to call back and confirm this evening's visit. Oh well. She'll just try again later.

After hanging up, she puts her gloves back on and places the skull into a cupboard for safekeeping. About to leave the list of settlers, too, she thinks better of it and tucks it into her bag. She takes out her keys, locks the cupboard, and locks the door to the lab behind her.

Time to head home for lunch. Her stomach rumbles with hunger, still protesting the unfulfilled promise of Marrana's pizza. She hasn't had anything but coffee and wine in a good twenty-four hours.

What was it like for poor Jane that bleak, barren winter? Had she, like the others, resorted to survivalist cannibalism in an effort to save herself and her unborn child?

The settlers really were, as Braden pointed out, dropping like flies as the winter wore on. From mid-January into early February, people were dying daily.

Dying . . . and being butchered and eaten.

Lost in thought about Jane's fate, she walks down the empty ground-level hallway past darkened offices, storage rooms, and labs. Pushing through the door to the parking lot, she blinks into the midday sun, looking for her car.

Unable to find it in the glare, she feels around in her bag for her prescription sunglasses and swaps them with her regular glasses.

Somehow, she still doesn't see her car among the few that are parked here.

For a wild moment, she imagines that it's been stolen. Then she remembers—it's back in the parking lot behind her apartment. She'd been so absorbed by Jane's plight that she'd forgotten Braden had driven her over here this morning, and she'd assumed they'd leave together.

Now what? During the school year, buses make a regular loop from campus to surrounding shopping centers and student housing complexes. They don't run in summer, and as she told Mick Mundy, there are no cabs.

Terrific.

Does Braden even realize she's stranded here?

Will he be in touch when he does?

He'll probably just assume she has a way to get home on her own.

She might as well go grab some lunch before she begins the long, lonely walk home in the heat.

Hearing sirens yowling through the streets of Mundy's Landing on this warm, sunlit afternoon, the hangman experiences a twinge of regret.

Shame it had to be this way. Such a waste of time, and energy, and, oh yes, a life . . . if you're the kind of person who believes that every human life has value.

Unconvinced of that, the hangman is nonetheless uneasy recalling the mighty struggle that unfolded in the shadows beneath the historic maple.

Not everyone goes to his or her death in a resigned and dignified manner, as James and Eliza Mundy did. Then again, they weren't caught off guard. They knew it was coming. No one had to wrestle with them in an effort to inject a drug meant to make it all easier, on them and on their executioner.

Last night, the needle found its mark, dispensing medication to render the victim unconscious.

The hangman wasted no time fixing the noose and tightening it. Within a few minutes, the deed was done.

Now, it seems, the deed has been discovered.

Hearing the commotion, the residents of The Heights must suspect that this matter is far more serious than another fender bender at the corner of Fulton and Prospect, a false alarm at the savings and loan, underage kids drinking in the gazebo . . .

Surely they're flashing back to last summer's tragic events, and those of the winter before. Surely they've witnessed enough drama over the past eighteen months to sense that another catastrophic event is unfolding.

How much more heartache, they must wonder, can the village endure?

They must believe that Mundy's Landing has seen far more than its share of violence, as last summer's *Tribune* editorial claimed.

How easily, and conveniently, they've forgotten that their little village wasn't founded in peace and harmony. That its founding fathers literally consumed each other, sipped human blood, ripped flesh from bone. And then, when the long nightmare was over—should have been over—three children were forced to witness their parents' public murder.

Does it matter, in the end, whether justice was served?

Vengeance begets vengeance just as violence begets violence.

This, then, is their legacy.

Theirs, and mine.

Oswald Mundy
Boarder
162 Academy Street
Poughkeepsie, New York

August 9, 1894

Dear Oswald,

> *Enclosed please find the sum of one thousand dollars.*
> *It is not a loan, but a gift.*
> *I wish you all the best, and I stand firm in my request*
> *that you not return to my home, or to Mundy's Landing.*

Sincerely,

Horace J. Mundy
68 Prospect Street
Mundy's Landing, New York

Chapter 11

Emerging from the hedgerow horror to the Dapplebrook's now cordoned-off front yard, Sully sees that the crowd on the street has grown. There's another squad car now, and an ambulance, both parked with red dome lights twirling in silence.

Roy's pickup truck is conspicuously missing. She looked for it parked on the driveway with the guests' cars and it wasn't there. Nor is it on the street. A quick phone call to the Holiday Inn on Colonial Highway revealed that it isn't in the parking lot there, either.

So where's the truck, and how did he get here?

A scenario pops into her head—Roy parks blocks away, creeps over in the dead of night to see if he can find Emerson, and . . .

Either he didn't find her, or he did, and saw something that upset him enough to take his own life.

Or . . .

Or Emerson Mundy lied.

She's the last person Sully wants to suspect. But emotions aside, it makes sense. The vast majority of homicide victims are killed by someone they knew. Roy Nowak was, presumably, a stranger in town—to everyone but her fiancé.

He'd driven thousands of miles to find her even though

she'd asked him to stay away. He had scratches all over his arms. Where did they come from?

And why hadn't Emerson wanted him here?

Because something had happened between them—something physical—before she left? She'd said he isn't violent, yet there was no mistaking the fear in her eyes.

Back up. Look at it from a different angle. Roy as victim, Emerson as suspect.

All right. Say she's lying. Is it possible that she's traveling with another man?

She ate alone last night, and didn't mention a companion this morning, when Sully told her about Roy. There was no mistaking the haunted vulnerability in her eyes, the way she looked over her shoulder as they walked back from the café . . .

Not just for Roy.

What if he wasn't the only one watching Emerson? What if he'd crossed paths here with someone who had a vested interest in keeping her safe?

I have to talk to her, right away.

Officer Johansen has sequestered the witnesses on the porch of the inn, well away from curious onlookers now lining the sidewalk. Sully checks to see if Emerson is among them. There's no sign of her, but she was going to stop at the historical society to visit with Ora.

Sully ducks under the police tape, heading in that direction.

"Hey, Sully!" a neighbor calls from the sidewalk.

"What's going on?" someone shouts. "Is it another Sleeping Beauty?"

She ignores the questions, spotting another ambulance parked a few doors down.

"Hey, guys, we've got a DOA and we're waiting for the ME," she calls to the paramedics positioning a stretcher. "You don't have to—"

Then she sees that the stretcher isn't intended for the victim at the inn. It's already occupied by someone whose identity is made obvious by the tuft of white hair against the sheet.

Ora Abrams.

For an illogical instant, Sully imagines that the old woman, too, was found in a noose, the handiwork of an evil hangman who'd worked his way along the block in the dead of night.

What if it was—

Speak—*think*—of the devil.

Emerson Mundy emerges from the mansion, accompanied by a third medic. Visibly shaken by whatever is going on with Ora, she does a startled double take at the scene in front of the inn—crime team, squad cars, a crowd . . .

She looks around wildly before she spots Sully. There it is again—the same vulnerability, fear, wariness. She's looking for Roy, or for . . .

"What's going on?" she calls as Sully hurries toward her.

"I was about to ask you the same thing. What happened to Ora?"

"I was visiting with her, and when she heard someone screaming, she fainted."

"Is she all right?"

"She hit her head." A medic slams the ambulance doors closed after the stretcher. "Still out cold. What the hell is going on over there? I heard—"

"Investigating an incident on the property," Sully cuts him off. "It's under control."

"Can you lock up here, Sully?"

"I looked around for her keys," Emerson tells her, "But I couldn't find them."

"Know anyone who might have a set?" the medic asks.

"Rowan Mundy. I'll call her. Just go. Take good care of Miss Abrams."

She and Emerson stand in silence, watching the ambulance depart with a fresh wail of sirens.

Then Emerson turns to Sully. "What happened at the inn? What kind of incident? Those screams . . . it sounded like Nancy. Was it?"

"Why don't we go inside?" Sully leads her past a few unkempt perennials poking from an untilled bed with all the cheer of leftover funeral flowers.

The interior is dim. Last winter, Sully placed timer devices on several first- and second-floor lamps—a simple and effective burglar buster, she told Ora. But the lights won't come on until this evening, so she flips an overhead switch.

"Did something happen to Nancy?" Emerson asks as Sully closes the door behind them.

"Not Nancy."

"Then who?"

Sully hesitates.

Every house in The Heights seems to have a ticking grandfather clock presiding over the entry. She's always found them elegant. This one strikes her as ominous, the atmosphere so suffocating that she fights the urge to throw open the tall windows. Frightened of prowlers, Ora refuses to sacrifice her perceived safety for fresh air, even on the warmest summer days.

"You might want to sit down, Emerson."

"*I'm* not eighty years old. I'm not going to faint, I promise. Whatever it is . . ."

Sully gestures at a bench.

Glancing at it, then back at her, Emerson is stoic. "How bad can it be? I barely know anyone here, and I've already lost my dad, unless . . ."

Wide-eyed, as if something awful has just occurred to her, she sinks onto the bench. "Is it about my mother? Did you already find her? Is she—"

"It's not your mother. It's Roy."

"*Roy?*"

"When was the last time you saw him?"

"When I left California. Why?"

"You said he was calling and texting. When did you last hear from him?"

"Last night. He texted, but I didn't—"

"Can I see, please?"

Shaken, Emerson pulls her phone from her pocket and hands it over to Sully, who scans the one-sided list of messages.

RU in NY yet?

Where RU?

Hope UR OK?

The final one arrived just after eleven o'clock last night.

"Did he come looking for me? Did he hurt Nancy?"

"No, Nancy is okay. But she found him. I'm so sorry to tell you this, but Roy died."

"*What?*"

Breaking tragic news is the worst part of her job. No matter how many times you do it, you can't completely detach. At least, she can't.

She does compartmentalize, of course. You have to. You can't survive this job if you absorb the agony of every life that shatters before your eyes. But she isn't a robot. She empathizes with the people for whom her presence, and her words, will forever after mark a grim turning point, even when the loss isn't a complete shock.

When a loved one has gone missing, people are often anticipating bad news, and some almost seem to welcome acknowledgment of what they've long suspected.

Even so, there's no easy way to accept confirmation of a death, any more than there's an easy way to deliver it.

In a case like Emerson's, when the deceased has been estranged, or the relationship complicated for whatever reason, you might expect the person to react with less raw emotion, or even with an underlying measure of relief. But in Sully's experience, most broken relationships are accompanied by a subconscious need for resolution. Just . . .

Not this kind of resolution.

Emerson buries her head in her hands, quietly crying.

Sully wants to put a comforting arm around her shoulder, but if Roy didn't commit suicide, then Emerson isn't just the bereaved. She's a suspect.

Sully steps into the small powder room under the stairs to look for tissues. There are none, and an empty cardboard tube sits on the toilet paper roller.

Her phone stirs her pocket with another text.

Barnes again.

Where RU?

Ah, irony. It's identical to one of the texts Roy sent Emerson. Sully, too, opts to ignore it—for now, anyway. She puts away her phone and moves on toward the kitchen in search of a napkin or paper towel.

It's been a while since she ventured past the door marked Private. When Ora calls her to the house, it's usually because she believes someone is trying to steal the personal belongings kept in her third-floor quarters. Sully leaves her in her room and goes through the motions of a thorough search below, but there's no need to comb the house from top to bottom. Ora takes her at her word, and has peace of mind to sleep through another night.

Today, the moment she sets foot into the kitchen, the smell hits her, along with a wave of guilt. How long, she wonders as she stops short and looks around in dismay, has Ora been living this way?

Pressing her nose and mouth against her shoulder the way she does when she's protecting herself from the stench of a rotting corpse, she spies a roll of paper towels on the counter. She hurries across the room to unspool a length and returns with it to the front hall, where she hands it over to Emerson without comment.

"How?" she asks, looking up, her eyes flooded with questions and tears.

"It looks like he took his own life."

The news brings a fresh wave of tears, and she presses the paper towels to her face, sobbing something that sounds like "Not him, too."

Sully gives her a moment to compose herself, thoughts spinning wildly.

"Did you lose someone else to suicide?"

"My father."

"Oh no. I'm so sorry."

"He'd been sick, and he just couldn't take it anymore, so he . . . he hung himself."

The last two words drop like bricks.

Hung himself?

Again, Sully's phone vibrates with a text.

Again, she ignores it, not bothering to see whether it's from Barnes again. Even if it isn't, it's not more important than this.

Emerson clears her throat, hard. "I never put the news out there in public, but word gets out."

"I'm sorry. I had no idea," Sully murmurs, trying to figure out where this fits into the scenario she'd begun to work through her mind. It doesn't.

"I don't like to talk about it. It's not easy to find out that the man you thought you knew . . . Well, I guess I didn't know him so well after all."

Is she talking about her father, or Roy?

Maybe both.

Despite everything, despite ignoring the texts, Sully finds herself thinking of Barnes. He has nothing to do with this. Yet he might as well have appeared in front of her, conjured by the phrase "the man you thought you knew."

"Sorry. I just can't get my head around this." Emerson, who has radiated emotional and physical strength from the moment Sully met her, seems small and fragile, tears flowing.

"I understand. Deep breaths."

She watches Emerson inhale, exhale.

Inhale, exhale.

"We need to notify his family. They're in New York?"

"I guess. Yes."

"Do you have any contact information for them?"

"No."

"His mother's name, maybe?"

"It's not the same as his. She's been married a few times. I don't know. I'm sorry."

"It's okay, we'll find her. Just breathe."

Inhale.

Exhale.

"How did he do it? Was there a note?"

Sully hesitates. "Yes."

"What did it say?"

If this turns out to be a homicide, then that piece of paper is evidence.

"Sully?"

"I'm sorry, it just . . . I can't discuss this yet."

"The note? Was it . . ." Emerson's hands clasp over her mouth, and she asks through her trembling fingers, "Was it hangman?"

Stunned, Sully backtracks through the last few moments of their conversation. Had she inadvertently said what she was trying not to reveal?

Of course she hadn't. She'd been careful.

As possibilities fast forward through her brain, her phone rings. It might be Colonomos, or something related to the investigation.

Nope. Barnes.

She apologizes to Emerson and answers the call with a curt "What?"

"Where are you?"

"On the job."

"Are you okay?"

"I'm talking to you, aren't I? I mean, I *was* talking to you. Later, Barnes!" She disconnects the call and apologizes again.

"Who's Barnes?"

She ignores the question. "You asked if the note was about hangman. Why would it be?"

"Sorry. It wouldn't be. I just had this crazy thought."

"I don't understand."

"You would think . . ." She pauses, makes a little choking sound. "I mean, he was leaving me alone in the world, and all he left me was a little piece of paper with a hangman on it."

Sully is too astonished to speak.

"There are things a parent should know to say, you know? Even just *good-bye* or *I love you* would have been meaningful. Especially after my mother left me. Yes, she left *us*—but he was her husband. Marriages fall apart. But I was her own flesh and blood. She chose to abandon me without warning, without a good-bye, and he hated her for it—and then he went and did the same exact thing."

"Your father. You're talking about your father."

"Yes."

"He left a note, with the game? Hangman?"

"Yes."

"Did you ever play it together? Did it have some special significance?"

"Not at all. It means nothing to me." Emerson inhales deeply and clamps her mouth shut, cheeks filled with air. Tilting her head back to stare at the delicate crystal chandelier high overhead, she holds her breath, maintains her composure.

"Was there a word?" Sully struggles to keep her voice level, respectful. "In the diagram, I mean?"

Emerson lowers her head to look at a Sully, allowing the air to escape her mouth on a burst of sorrow, frustration, anger . . .

Typical emotions for someone whose loved one has taken his own life.

Her father, and now Roy.

"A word? Not really. I mean, there were spaces for four letters, but only one was filled in."

"What was it?"

"An E. Why?"

"Was there anything else?"

"A little gallows with a stick figure hanging there, like it was saying, 'You lose this game.' And you know what? It's true. I lost. Not just the game, but everything. Everyone."

As she speaks, Sully's brain whirls like a lottery spinner, irrational thoughts bouncing through, refusing to settle.

Four letters.

A hanging victim.

A stick figure on the gallows.

Wait a minute. She's overthinking this. The logical answer drops into place like a numbered ping-pong ball.

You win.

"You told Roy about it." Of course she must have.

"Told him about what?"

"About your father's note."

"No, I didn't. Like I said, I met Roy afterward. He didn't know him. I didn't tell anyone."

"You mean your friends?"

"I mean *anyone*. It was a slap in the face."

"What did the police say about it?"

"About . . . ?"

"About the hangman note!"

"They didn't know, either. After I found him, before I called them, I . . . you know. I put it away."

"So no one else knew about it."

"Right."

Wrong.

Roy knew. He had to have known, because . . .

If he didn't know, then how could he have left the same peculiar note?

Unless Emerson did this herself.

Is she playing me?

"Did you keep the note your father left?"

"Yes."

"Could Roy have seen it?"

"Roy? Why?"

"Where is it? Do you have it here with you?"

"Yes, it's—Wait a minute." The light dawns. "Why are you asking me so many questions about this?"

"I can't—"

"Did Roy—did he leave a hangman note, too?"

Sully can only stare at her, pity and an acrid splash of dread pooling with bile in her gut.

Her hunger semi-sated by a parched chicken cutlet on a mayo-sodden roll, foggy brain revived by two cups of black coffee, Savannah exits the dining hall to find the quad equally deserted. A freshman orientation meeting is under way in Pritchard Hall, but it isn't scheduled to let out until mid-afternoon.

Now that she's had some time to reconsider, her earlier fears about Braden Mundy and the murder gene seem almost ludicrous.

Most guys—most people—would be spooked by human remains, let alone by remains that bear clear evidence of murder, and speculation that his own distant ancestors might have been responsible . . .

Well, it hardly made for a romantic morning after. She can't blame him for taking off, but he said he'd call. Maybe he will, and if he doesn't . . .

Live and learn.

She follows the brick path toward the library on the opposite corner, housed in a stately brick box of a building with white-paned windows.

Out of habit, she silences her phone as she steps through the tall double doors. There's no security guard today at the threshold, where backpacks are searched on the way in and out. A lone student sits at the tall desk beyond, so engrossed in the book she's reading that she doesn't even glance up.

The adjacent information desk is unmanned, but Savannah has a general idea what she's looking for and where to find it.

She makes her way across the vast seating area at the center of the main floor. Usually crowded with students rustling papers and exchanging stilted whispers, it's hushed and empty today. The low lamps scattered along the wooden tables are unlit, as are the ones beside comfortable couches and chairs, and uncomfortable vintage study carrels.

The space is open to a vaulted ceiling mural three stories above, where sunlight filters through tall windows. White spindled second- and third-floor balconies line the overhead perimeter, with a network of built-in book stacks branching away into the deep shadows beneath.

Savannah heads for the stairwell at the back wall, vaguely remembering having seen a local history collection located in a dim corner somewhere above.

After a bit of wandering, she finds it on the third floor behind a wall of glass. The lights are off, and the research librarian's desk is empty. Trying the door, she finds it unlocked, and enters.

The room is no-frills compared to the grandeur below, and smells musty. Maybe the research librarian is merely out to lunch, but Savannah doubts it. Lit by just a dim shaft of light falling through a window facing the taller building next door, the room has an air of neglect.

She considers turning on the overhead fixture, but decides against it. No need to alert passersby to her presence. For all she knows this spot is off-limits at this time of year.

Free-standing shelves lack the ornate moldings of those below, though at a glance, their contents appear to be far more valuable. She surveys rows of archival periodical boxes, microfiche cases, and fragile old volumes. Most appear not to have been disturbed for decades, perhaps even centuries. The sections are labeled on thin red plastic strips with raised white lettering, organized according to locale and time period.

Zeroing in on the large area devoted to Mundy's Landing, she sees that a significant part of the collection relates to the 1916 Sleeping Beauty murders. Another time, she'd pause to peruse it, but she might be kicked out of here at any moment.

Instead, she finds the section marked Colonization: 1665–1700, and gets down to business.

Emerson keeps her head down as Sully escorts her over from the historical society, past the gawkers and gossipers gathered on the sidewalk. The lovely grounds of the Dapplebrook Inn are beribboned in yellow tape like a macabre gift.

Her father's death last summer had unfolded far more subtly. If the neighbors even noticed the ambulance and police car in the driveway, they didn't bother to check in to see if Dad was all right. No one came to the door afterward with food and sympathy.

Things are different in Mundy's Landing. People care.

Or is it that here, people hear sirens and suspect the worst?

"How are you doing? Hanging in there?" Sully touches her arm as they approach the front steps, and she nods, unable to muster a suitable response.

She'd told Sully before that scars heal, but she could see that Sully didn't believe it.

Neither do I. Not now.

So much has happened in such a short time that she has yet to grasp the full impact of what happened back there in Ora's kitchen. Shocking revelations buzz around her brain like trapped hornets preparing to swarm and sting.

She follows Sully across the slate veranda. Nancy is there, and so is the waiter from last night. They're sitting at a table with a few others, a uniformed police officer standing over them. Emerson avoids meeting anyone's gaze, wondering whether they know her connection to the dead man hanging in the tree.

Sully opens the door and peers warily into the house, almost as if she's expecting to find an intruder. Then, for the second time today, she escorts Emerson into an elegant entry hall where an antique clock ticks away the minutes in somber cadence.

"Where's your room?"

"Second floor."

"Okay, let's go."

Emerson leads her up the stairs, past the family photos of heroes and perhaps a scoundrel or two. She longs to pause and stare at Horace and Oswald. But black and white photos won't verify Ora's claim that Oswald's eyes had been dark, and it was Horace who had one blue eye, and one gray.

Emerson had always assumed her heterochromia came through her absent mother's side of the family. She had no way of knowing that it was a Mundy trait stretching back centuries—one Jerry Mundy did not share.

So he couldn't have been her biological father. Her stomach roils with the betrayal from the man who'd raised her. Yet he wouldn't be the first Mundy to keep a dark secret.

We shall never tell . . .

Was he even a Mundy?

Her heart is pounding. Had the man she knew as Jerry Mundy stolen her real father's identity, his life . . . his daughter?

"Emerson?" Sully's voice intrudes on her thoughts.

They've reached the top of the stairs.

"Sorry. This way." She turns toward the Jekyll Suite at the far end of the hall, feeling as though she's wading through quicksand in the dark. As she passes the grand portrait of Horace, she longs to pause and examine his eyes.

Ora Abrams is a senile octogenarian. She could have imagined the heterochromia in Horace, along with other things. After all, she was talking as if he were alive, and she mistook Emerson for his daughter . . .

Horace didn't even have a daughter. He had three sons. Ora said two had heterochromia.

Riddled with questions and an abominable array of possible answers, she fumbles in her pocket for the key to her suite.

"Hanging in there?" Sully asks.

Hanging in there . . .

The phrase dangles in Emerson's muddled brain, and she swallows a surge of inappropriate, hysterical laughter.

"Emerson?"

She manages a simple, and probably unconvincing, "Yes."

Nothing makes sense. She longs to lock herself away to sort through the facts.

Later. After the commotion has died down and she can make her brain function properly once more.

She unlocks the door and opens it.

"Wait." Sully touches her arm. "I'll go first."

She takes a pair of gloves from her pocket and pulls them on, then keeps her right hand poised at her waist as she enters the room.

Emerson recognizes the position. She's prepared to pull out a weapon if need be.

Does it mean she isn't convinced Roy killed himself?

Does she suspect he was murdered? That his killer might be hiding here? Maybe Emerson should tell her about last night—that she'd been spooked, trying to fall asleep. That she'd felt as though she wasn't entirely alone in the suite, as though someone might be lurking.

She watches from the doorway as Sully gives the rooms a quick check. Then she lingers at the window, looking out thoughtfully into the maple branches.

"Did he hang himself from that tree?"

The question startles Sully, and she turns as if she'd forgotten Emerson was there.

"Never mind. He did. I can tell by the look on your face. Oh God."

"I'm sorry." Sully reaches to pull down the shade to shield her from the ghastly sight of Roy's corpse hanging from the tree.

"You don't have to do that. Before I came down to

meet you and Rowan, I was sitting right there at the desk looking out. I didn't see a thing. Just leaves."

Sully pulls down the shade anyway, with a bold snap that hangs in the air.

Unnerved, Emerson looks around the room, making sure everything is just as she'd left it a few hours earlier. It's so easy to imagine someone—Nancy Vandergraaf—here, rifling through her belongings, searching . . .

But even if Nancy—or someone less unlikely—wanted to steal jewelry or electronics, she wouldn't look inside the lining of the empty suitcase on the floor of the closet. Sure, she might feel her way along the fabric to see if anything bulky is tucked away. But she'd find nothing, and move on.

Her fingers wouldn't detect the hangman note, or the ancient letter, one of many Priscilla Mundy Ransom sent to her brother, Jeremiah Mundy. This is the most incriminating.

Sully watches her open the suitcase and unzip the cloth lining. Slipping her hand into the seam, she leaves the old letter in place, but removes the hangman note and hands it over.

Sully turns on a lamp and holds it to the light, intently focused.

"You said Roy didn't know about this note, but where did you keep it for all this time?"

"In a drawer by my bed in my apartment back in Oakland."

"Could Roy have snooped through your things and found it?"

"Not unless he somehow got in when I was gone. We don't live together."

"He didn't have a key?"

"No. He wanted one after we got engaged, but . . ." She shakes her head. "I hadn't gotten around to it yet. We mostly hung out at his place. Unless . . . I mean, he could have borrowed my key and copied it."

Sully's eyes narrow. "Is that something you thought he might do?"

"Maybe. I don't know. I mean, he's not a criminal. He's a teacher. I can't imagine that he'd have . . ." She trails off, seeing the look on Sully's face. "*You* think he would?"

"I didn't know him. But the way you described him— obsessive, jealous . . . and he wasn't violent, you said? He never laid a hand on you, and you never laid a hand on him? Even in self-defense?"

"No! Why—wait a minute." Emerson lowers herself into a chair and places a hand beneath her left collarbone, feeling her heart racing along with her thoughts. "Even if Roy had come across that note in my apartment, he couldn't have known what it was. Who'd look at a piece of paper with a hangman game on it and think it was a suicide note?"

"Where was it when you found it?"

"I told you. It was with my father."

"I know this is tough for you, but . . . where? Was it . . ."

"You mean, was it clenched in his cold, dead hand?" The words are harsher than she'd intended.

"I'm sorry, I—"

"No, *I'm* sorry. It's just that I'm still so angry at him, and . . ."

And the anger has more to do with what she learned today than with what happened last year.

But you have to be in this moment, not in that one. You have to tell Sully what she needs to know. Help her understand what happened to Roy.

She takes a deep breath. "I found my father in his bedroom. The note was on the floor nearby. It was . . ." She closes her eyes, remembering the room, the house, her childhood.

"Take your time. It's okay."

"It was under a paperweight I gave him one Father's Day. I made it myself, when I was a little girl. It was just a rock that I covered in red paint, but I thought it was shaped like a heart. My heart. That's what it was supposed to be."

Her heart.

Hard, deformed, with jagged edges.

"I'm sorry."

She opens her eyes and sees Sully, sympathetic yet doggedly on task, holding up the note so that it faces her.

"Look carefully. You're sure your father is the one who wrote this?"

"Who else would it have been?"

Sully doesn't answer the question, just waits for an answer to her own.

Stomach churning, Emerson fears she might vomit as she studies the lined sheet of notebook paper.

Scrawled in bold purple Sharpie, it's a simple word diagram above a hanging stick figure.

$$\_ \_ \_ E$$

"It's not like it's handwriting," she finally says with a shrug. "I mean, anyone could have written it, I guess. But it was there, with my father. That's all I know for sure."

"Is there any word you can think of that has some significance and ends in an E and has four letters?"

"No."

"Anything at all, a name, maybe?"

She reaches back to rub the aching spot between her shoulders. "There's nothing."

"What if the third letter was an N? Something, something, N-E. Does that make any sense?"

"Off the top of my head? No. I mean . . . wait, why are you asking about an N?"

Sully gives her a long, hard look, as if she's trying to figure out whether she can trust her.

Then she says, "An almost identical note was found on the tree where Roy hung himself. Hangman, but the third letter was an N."

Emerson sits quietly, allowing the news to sink in, before voicing the obvious. "My father couldn't have written the note Roy left."

"No."

"Do you think Roy wrote the one I found with my father?"

"Do *you*?"

"Why would he . . . I just don't get what you're thinking."

"Are you sure?"

No. She knows exactly what Sully is thinking. She doesn't want to say it, but Sully isn't going to be the one. Unaware that Emerson has already been dealt a harsh truth today, she's trying to protect her from just that.

This, she can handle.

"If the same person wrote Roy's note and my father's note," she says slowly, "then one of the suicides might not have been a suicide."

"One," Sully agrees grimly, "or both."

11th April 1676

Dear Jeremiah,

I received your letter, and your refusal to permit my marriage, with bitter disappointment. I beg you to reconsider your decision.

Have you lost recollection of your pain when Mother and Father would not condone your affection for Anne Blake? Do you not recall the bitter consequences?

I cannot fathom what my life would be without Benjamin. He is my reason for living. At last, I know what it is to deeply love another human being, to be willing to give my own life for his.

Brother, I recall your uttering the same words when Father bade you to do what was necessary. I remember that you threw yourself at his knees, begging mercy for the woman you loved, asking that you be sacrificed so that she instead might live, that we all might feed upon your own flesh instead of hers. I was far too young to fathom then what you felt for her.

Now, I understand your desperate, selfless act. I ask in return that you grant me your compassion, along with your permission, and your blessing, for my marriage to Benjamin.

Your sister,

Priscilla Mundy

Chapter 12

Stepping back outside, Sully finds only Nick on the porch, seated at a table, writing on a clipboard. Beyond the yellow tape, most of the neighbors have shuffled home to resume their lives, leaving just a few bystanders to linger on the street. Judging by their casual posture and a burst of animated laughter that reaches the porch, they might as well be planning a fall block party.

Nick looks up at her. "Detective Leary. Did you . . ."

"Yes. I told her."

"We'll need her to make a positive ID."

"She's willing. I told her I'll call later tonight when the ME is ready for her."

Obviously it can't be done here and now, given the state of the corpse. The medical examiner will take it away, clean it up, make it presentable, and place it on a refrigerated slab. It's all designed to make the morbid process as easy as possible on people forced to identify their loved ones.

"Did you interview her?"

"Yes. She said she hasn't seen him since she left California and she didn't think he was suicidal."

"Where is she?"

"Upstairs pulling herself together. The news hit her

hard. She and Roy had their problems, but he was her fiancé."

"Did she react when you asked her about the scratches on his arms?"

"I didn't ask her specifically. She said there was no physical violence, and I believe her."

"Really?"

Sully nods, and extends her gloved hand. "Look at this, Nick."

"What is it?" Nick takes gloves from his own pocket and pulls them on. "Another so-called suicide note. Her father's."

She hands it over, watching Nick's eyes widen with recognition as he takes in the similarities—same sized sheet of spiral-bound notebook paper, same hangman diagram drawn in the same shade of purple ink.

"Where did you get this?"

She explains quickly. Nick is on his way down the porch steps before she finishes, beckoning her to follow.

The crime scene investigators, both of whom happen to be named Bob, have moved over to the area where the rope attaches to the hose spigot. They're still shooting photos, along with the breeze, but their inane conversation grinds to an immediate halt when they see Nick and Sully.

"What's up, Lieutenant? Detective?" asks the taller, heftier, round-faced Bob.

"Found anything that would indicate a homicide?"

"Only the scratches on his forearms."

"But they might be self-inflicted," says the other Bob, much younger and smaller with a wiry build. "Some kind of dermatitis. The guy's fingernails are bitten down to the quick. He might have driven himself crazy trying to scratch an itch."

"Crazy enough to commit suicide?" Sully shakes her head.

"Imagine that you have a bad case of poison ivy, and no fingers."

"He has fingers."

"I'm trying to make a point."

"So am I." Sully points at the broken rose of Sharon branches on the ground and dangling from the shrub, all now marked by numbered yellow evidence placards. "Could there have been a struggle?"

"Could have been, but based on TOD, we know he did this in the dead of night, Detective."

Time of death. She knows what they're getting at. "It would have been dark out here."

"Yes, and he could have done the damage to the area just by fumbling around here alone."

"Especially since he was drunk as a skunk."

Sully raises an eyebrow at Small Bob's comment. "How do you know that?"

"Found a receipt in his pocket. Looks like the stiff had a couple of stiff drinks at the Windmill."

Large Bob cracks a smile at the quip.

Sully does not.

The Windmill—not surprising. It isn't the only bar in town, but it's the oldest, the most upscale, and by far the most popular with tourists and locals alike. The others include a waterfront dive that draws the tugboat crowd, a few no-frills social clubs, and the lobby bar over at the Holiday Inn. Maybe he worked his way over from there.

"What time did he leave the bar?" she asks Small Bob.

"Stayed until just about closing time. The receipt is stamped at 1:47 a.m."

"Can I see?"

He rummages around a small bin with gloved hands,

going through the contents of Roy's pockets: a crumpled napkin, a set of car keys, some cash, all encased in clear plastic pouches, as is the crumpled slip of paper he shows Sully.

Peering at it, she can see that Roy bought three expensive drinks and left what amounts to a dollar a drink as a tip—three bucks on a bill that was almost fifty.

"I'm guessing the bartender will remember him, if no one else does," she says.

"Especially if he was upset about the fiancé," Nick tells her. "He wouldn't be the first idiot to pour his heart out to anyone who will listen, drink himself into a stupor, and make a suicide attempt."

"A lot of them live to tell about it," Small Bob says. "But you gotta wonder about the ones who don't. Were they just trying to get some attention and win back someone who's lost interest?"

"Girl I knew growing up did that. She told her friends her ex-boyfriend would dump his new girlfriend and come see her in the hospital . . ." Large Bob shakes his head. "She jumped off the Tappan Zee."

Small Bob responds with a wince and a whistling sound. "Did he come to her wake instead?"

"Along with everyone else in town. Including the new girlfriend."

Sully barely listens.

A significant amount of alcohol is not just capable of rendering someone suicidal.

It could also have made him vulnerable to a predator on the prowl.

Sitting cross-legged on the floor in the local history room, Savannah isn't sure what she's looking for. She only knows, as she leafs through one book after another, that she has yet to find it.

Some are scholarly volumes with a general focus on Dutch and English settlements of the Hudson Valley. Many are fairly recent, but a few are at least a hundred years old, with old-fashioned text and a damp must wafting from the yellowed pages.

All devote chapters or at least a few pages to Mundy's Landing, but she finds no new information about the settlers themselves. Most provide a general—and in the older books, perhaps melodramatic and embellished—account of their tragic fates.

Frustrated, she moves past the traditionally published volumes to a low shelf containing mostly homegrown materials.

Here, she finds something far more interesting.

The thick pamphlet written by local historian Etta Abrams, Ora's great-aunt, contains far more relevant detail. Curator of the historical society back in 1915, Miss Abrams published the pamphlet to mark the two hundred and fifty years since the first settlers came ashore at Mundy's Landing. The booklet is little more than a bound manuscript hand-typed on the typewriter used to create Ora's list of settlers. Digging it out of her purse to compare, Emerson confirms that the same letters are smudged or raised.

Ora had said the skull belonged to her aunt, and she'd probably inherited the list from her as well.

The pamphlet features biographical information about each of the early settlers, including the four young women who could possibly have been Jane Doe.

Sixteen when she died, Tabitha Ransom had married John Ransom the previous spring in England. The young couple made the transatlantic journey with John's older brother, William. The Ransom brothers' parents and two additional sons were scheduled to follow, arriving in the fall. They were on board the ship stranded by ice many miles south of the settlement, and arrived in May to find their family members dead . . . and devoured.

Ann Dunn, also married, was the wife of Richard Dunn and mother of five-month-old Henry Dunn. She lost them on the same day, and outlived them by what must have been a ghastly month.

Anne Blake, little more than a child at fourteen, was one of three servants traveling with the Barker family—parents George and Mary, children also named George and Mary. All four died around Christmas, Anne not until the last week of February.

Verity Hall and her younger sisters Patience and Honor had lost their mother before leaving England, and were orphaned when their father, Josiah, became the first casualty in the New World. Long before famine struck, he was fishing at the river's edge in October 1665, lost his footing, and drowned.

Savannah uses her cell phone to photograph the entries about Tabitha, Ann, Anne, and Verity, none of whom survived the winter, and at least one of whom was brutally killed.

Maybe it will be easier to identify Jane Doe if she narrows the lineup of suspects.

She grabs a pencil and Ora's list of settlers, placing checkmarks beside every child twelve and younger. Then she checks off everyone noted as having died before January 29, when Ann Dunn, the first of the four possible Janes, passed away.

That leaves her with ten adult suspects that includes a remaining trio of Jane candidates, and James, Elizabeth, and Jeremiah Mundy. In addition, there are two other men, John and William Ransom, and two additional women. One was a middle-aged spinster named Jane Carroll, the other, Verity's fifteen-year-old sister, Honor.

Verity herself died on February 3.

John Ransom died February 5, one week before his wife Tabitha. On dates between their deaths, several young children perished, as did Honor Hall. Jane Carroll followed, on Valentine's Day.

That left only William Ransom, Anne Blake, and the five Mundys.

For one week, the seven survived.

Anne Blake's death, the final among the colonists, was recorded on February 21.

For the first time, Savannah notices that there is no death date listed for William Ransom. Yet he wasn't among the five survivors, and . . .

Hmm. Despite pertinent information on the individual settlers, Etta's pamphlet includes no specific death dates. Only Ora's list has that information. So where did she—or her Aunt Etta—find it?

There must have been another resource.

Combing the shelves row by row, Savannah finds books about survivalist cannibalism, Hudson Valley traders, European immigration, Native American tribes . . .

All interesting, but not relevant to her search. More promising are a couple of published journals from later settlers, and several folders containing old letters and research papers about the Mundy family legacy and their descendants, none published earlier than the 1920s.

Achy from sitting on the floor, she carries them over to a desk. Wondering what time it is, she fishes her phone out of her bag to check the clock, and sees that she missed a call while it was silenced. No, a couple of calls, and a text, too. All from Braden, eager to reconnect.

Forgot you don't have a car. Sorry. Will pick you up. What time?

She starts to text back, then decides to step outside and call him instead. If they have an actual conversation, maybe he'll ask if she's free this evening.

She looks at the stack of folders. Should she leave them out on the table while she's gone, or put them back, for now, where she found them?

A third option enters her mind, and she glances at the glass walls to see if anyone is visible beyond. She was the only one on the third floor when she got here, and it still appears deserted.

After a moment's consideration, she opens her backpack and tucks the folders inside one of her binders. No one was inspecting bags, and even if the guard is here now, he'll take a quick peek and wave her past.

She isn't stealing the materials, Savannah promises the library, and herself, as she zips the backpack. She's borrowing them to aid in solving a historical mystery.

Outside in the sunshine, she sits on a bench and dials. Maybe they can have that Marrana's pizza after all. Maybe this is one reckless fling that will end in happily-ever-after.

"Hey, this is Braden."

Voice mail.

Optimism snuffed as quickly as it ignited, Savannah hangs up.

Sully stares at the corpse, still in the same position. The hands have been bagged for evidence. The rope remains intact, and will until the investigation is complete and the body removed.

"Do you have his cell phone?" she asks the Bobs.

They don't.

"Did you check his pockets?"

"Where else would we look?" Large Bob asks, and Small Bob snickers a crude suggestion.

Sully looks at Nick. "He had his phone when I saw him at Dunkin' Donuts."

"Maybe he left it in his truck when he went into the bar?"

"Who does that?"

"Maybe the battery was dead. Maybe it's charging back at the Holiday Inn."

"Maybe someone took it to conceal evidence."

"Maybe. But it looks like a straightforward suicide."

"Hangings almost always are," Small Bob says.

The *almost* echoes in Sully's head as she heads back toward the house, thinking about Emerson.

She's worked a number of cases where a female domestic abuse victim became a murder suspect based on motive, opportunity, or circumstantial evidence.

What if her own Aunt Ida's husband were to die under suspicious circumstances? Though Sully is ninety-nine percent sure that her kind, gentle aunt is incapable of even reciprocal violence, she'd wonder whether the years of abuse had taken their toll. People can snap under duress and become violent in self-defense.

But you don't stage a homicide as suicide in the heat of the moment.

Either Roy Nowak took his own life in a way that was meant to mimic Jerry Mundy's death, right down to details Emerson said he couldn't have known, or . . .

Or she killed him in a fit of rage, or self-defense . . .

Or someone else did. Perhaps someone who wanted to protect Emerson from a man she perceived as dangerous.

Savannah had considered returning to the library after she failed to reach Braden, but she didn't want to risk having to smuggle the historic papers back in—and then out again if he decides to return her call before she's finished with her research.

Instead, she's back in the lab with Jane Doe, combing

the files for relevant information, and setting aside several documents she'd like to re-examine.

Among them are the ship's manifest listing the original settlers who traveled up the Hudson River in the late spring of 1665, and a collection of letters the colonists had written to loved ones back in England over the course of that devastating winter. The messages, initially laced with hope and reassurance, grew desperate as the winter wore on. Later dates bore agonizing details of starvation and heartbreaking accounts of loved ones dying one by one.

Months later, rescuers arriving far too late discovered the poignant missives along with a scattering of worldly belongings and a litter of carnage.

Wading through archaic prose, searching for mention of the Mundys or any detail relating to her four Jane Doe candidates, Savannah has momentarily forgotten about Braden when her phone rings.

"Hey," he says when she answers, "I saw that you called. What's up?"

"I was returning *your* call. And you texted, too. A few times."

"What?"

"I mean . . . you did, right?" She couldn't have imagined it, could she?

"Sorry, I can't hear you very well. I'm on the road."

Realizing he must already be heading over to pick her up, she says, "I was just calling you back, but you didn't answer."

"I was in the middle of a phone interview."

"That's good. How'd it go?"

"It went great. I'm pretty psyched. So anyway, I was going to give you a ride home—I forgot that you don't have your car . . ."

"*But . . . ?*" she prompts, sensing a big fat one hanging in the air.

"But now I can't."

"You can't give me a ride home?"

"No, sorry—I'm on my way to Hartford right now."

"Hartford . . . ?"

"Connecticut."

She listens in silence to his explanation that he'd sent his résumé to a large insurance company there over a week ago, in answer to an advertisement for an opening in research. This afternoon, their human resources rep called him for an impromptu phone interview, liked what she heard, and invited him to meet with the person doing the hiring.

"Today? Isn't that short notice? Especially for a job that's so far away."

"It's not even a two-hour drive," Braden says, "and she was going to schedule it for Tuesday morning because this guy is going away tomorrow for a long weekend. But I figured I'd better jump on it, so I offered to come right away. You never know what's going to happen between now and then."

"I'm sure the job will still be there on Tuesday."

And I'll still be here *if you don't come get me like you said you would, you jerk.*

"Don't count on it. This is the first opportunity I've had in weeks."

"But . . . an insurance company? Your degree is in history. I thought you wanted to work at a museum."

"Museums don't want me," he says curtly. "Listen, I'm sorry you're stuck there. Can you get a ride from someone?"

"No."

"Oh well . . . can you walk? I mean, it's not that far."

He's right, and it isn't as if she didn't consider walking. But she's not going to make this easy on him.

"It's a few miles. And there aren't even sidewalks the whole way."

"Can you take a cab? I'll pay for it."

"There are no cabs. If there were cabs, your brother could have taken one yesterday."

And we never would have met. And that would have been better for everyone.

"My brother didn't need a cab. He needed a jump."

"I don't need a jump, Braden. I need a ride."

"Sorry. Listen, I'm going to find one for you. Sit tight."

"But—"

He's already hung up.

Alone in the Jekyll Suite once again, Emerson opens the window shade Sully had lowered.

Morbid curiosity getting the better of her, she leans forward over the desk, pressing her forehead against the glass, trying to glimpse Roy somewhere below. Maybe if she sees him, she'll be able to grasp the fact that it really happened—that he *did* follow her here to Mundy's Landing, that he *is* dead.

But all she can see are the leafy maple boughs that scratch the screens like whispered truths she doesn't want to hear.

She sinks onto the edge of the bed, head buried in her hands.

"I'll call you when it's time," Sully promised before she left. "It won't be until later this evening. I'll come get you and drive you over. I know it won't be easy."

No, it won't.

Death is disturbing no matter when or how it happens, but this isn't like the first time, with her father—or rather, the man she believed was her father.

Hearing her phone chime with an incoming text, she lifts her head to see that it's from an unfamiliar number.

25 Riverview Road—see you at 7:30!

Rowan Mundy.

If Emerson tells her what happened, will she cancel the dinner plans?

When Emerson returned to Oakland after her father died, she wanted to be left alone. This time, it's different. This time, she wants to be with people, with *family*.

Of course, when her so-called father died, she didn't even know she *had* family. Nor did she have reason to suspect that he *wasn't* family.

She needs to uncover the truth. Maybe Rowan's husband, Jake, can help her.

Can't wait! she texts back.

Earlier, with Sully, she'd managed to dodge the bizarre scenario her imagination fired at her. Now it blazes in like a saloon cowboy.

Was she raised by an imposter—some sick predator posing as Jerry Mundy?

She looks so much like him . . . is it possible that they're not related?

Is that why he'd isolated her from the rest of the world? Why he'd gone to such great lengths to hide evidence of the past?

No wonder there were no old documents, no vintage photographs. No wonder they had no extended family in their lives.

He'd claimed to be an only child, that his father was estranged from his grandfather, that his parents had passed away before she was born. She'd never thought to question him, never thought to research any of it, never . . .

Wait a minute.

She's seen her grandparents' graves. Inez and Donald X Mundy.

Unless the cemetery, too, was staged to perpetuate an elaborate hoax?

No. *That's* far-fetched.

Okay, they really did pass away before she was born. Yay. The lone indisputable fact in this mess.

Had she buried a stranger beside them? Are those poor dead souls spending their eternal rest with someone who'd impersonated their son, and her father?

If so, then what happened to the real Jerry Mundy? And what about her mother? Where does she fit into the lies Emerson had been fed by the man who raised her as his own?

Her phone rings.

Sullivan Leary already?

No—Rowan Mundy. She's probably heard about Roy and is calling to postpone tonight.

"Hello?"

"Sorry to keep bothering you. It's Rowan. I just heard about Ora."

"Ora! Oh, I'm so sorry. I was going to tell you, but then . . ."

Then came the chaos of Roy, and her own drama.

"I just ran into the Yamazakis' housekeeper in the supermarket parking lot. They live across the street from the historical society. She said Ora fainted and was taken to the hospital in an ambulance, and that a young woman was with her. I'm so grateful you stopped over there. Otherwise, God knows how long she'd have lain there alone on the floor. I feel terrible that I haven't checked in on her lately. She doesn't have any family, and I've been worried about her."

On her end, in the background, Emerson can hear a dog barking, dishes rattling, voices. A normal home, the kind she never had.

"Wait a second, sorry, Emerson. *Guys!* Quiet down! I'm on the phone! And can someone please feed Doofus?"

Emerson would have been unsettled enough to discover that she'd been adopted as an infant. But at least that would make sense.

If you're adopted, your imagination can conjure noble birth parents who gave you up because they couldn't provide the life you deserve, instead of—

"Sorry about that." Rowan is back on the line. "I have to go referee before they kill each other. See you at seven-thirty, okay?"

There's nothing to do but hang up, hoping Jake Mundy will shed some light on her past, and help identify her birth father.

Because if Ora is right about the heterochromia, then I wasn't just raised as a Mundy. I am a Mundy.

1st July 1676

Dear Jeremiah,

Benjamin and I were married yesterday.

I regret that you did not grant your permission, but I do hope one day to receive your blessing.

I suspect that you endeavored to forbid my marriage because you feared that I would share with my spouse the truth we promised never to divulge.

I do believe the burden of that terrible secret was too much for Charity's frail little body, and that it, and not the plague, did kill her in the end. But I am far stronger than she was. I have kept the truth safely to myself in your absence.

If Benjamin ever discovered the role his brother William played on that terrible day, he would never forgive me. I cannot bear to lose him, nor to hurt him. Thus, our secret will remain safe. I hope you shall find your way back home soon.

Your sister,

Priscilla Mundy Ransom

Chapter 13

At last, the commotion on Prospect Street has ebbed. The neighbors have gone back into their houses, most of the emergency vehicles have driven away, and a lone officer remains at the curb in front of the Dapplebrook Inn. The medical examiner's van awaits the body, its driver smoking a cigarette and talking on a cell phone.

He waves at Sully as she leaves the property.

She waves back, wondering if he's talking about the case. Or is he convinced this situation is exactly what it appears to be: a suicide, and nothing more?

Her sneakers make a hollow, staccato thud on the concrete as she hurries back up Prospect Street, headed home to see what she can find out about Emerson's missing mother, and thinking about Barnes.

What if someone found him here?

Wayland? Stef?

Sully enters the house, walks quietly up the steps to her apartment, and slips the key into the lock with her left hand, her right closing over her weapon. She opens the door swiftly, poised for trouble, and finds none.

Unless you count Barnes, waiting for her.

"I thought something happened to you," he snaps.

"I told you I was on a case."

"I got a text from your phone saying you were on a case. Anyone could have sent it, and you didn't pick up when I called."

"Why would you think someone else texted from my phone?" She strides past him toward her bedroom.

He's right behind her. "It happens."

"I'm a cop, Barnes, not a thirteen-year-old. Who's going to get ahold of my phone and text you?"

"What happened out there? Why all the sirens?"

"Suicide that looks like a homicide, or vice versa. I'm thinking vice versa."

"Who? Where?"

"At the Dapplebrook."

"Does it have anything to do with—"

"No."

"You don't even know what I was going to say."

"It doesn't matter. It has nothing to do with you, or anything you'd know about." Seeing the hurt look in his eyes, she softens her tone. "You haven't been here in a year. It's not connected to what went on last summer."

"Okay. But—"

"What about me?"

"What about *you*?"

"What do *I* need to know, Barnes?"

He remains silent, looking at her.

"You showed up here, and you're obviously hiding, and you thought something happened to me just now— something that had something to do with you. Why? Am I in danger because you're here?"

"No one knows I'm here."

"How can you be sure?"

"Because if they know where I am, I'd already be dead. Or someone else would."

"Me?"

He shrugs.

"Beautiful," she mutters, shaking her head.

"No," he says, "not you, okay?"

"Who else is there?"

"In my life? Besides you?"

"That's not how I meant it. I meant—"

"Look, if they're still looking for me, they aren't going to find me here."

"Who's *they*? Wayland?"

"I told you, it's complicated. But now that I have some distance to think—and sleep, and eat—I'm feeling like I can handle it better."

She throws up her hands. "Fine. Handle it. Whatever. I don't have time right now for complicated. I have to look up something before I go interview some witnesses."

"Where?"

"The Windmill."

Her bedroom door is ajar. She can see the quilt untucked and tangled, one of her pillows on the floor.

"Sweet of you to make my bed," she says.

"I was going to change the sheets so you can sleep there tonight. Sorry about your back, and . . . everything. I should have thanked you before for letting me have your bed, for buying me clothes, for bringing me lunch. Look, I owe you a huge favor. When the dust settles—"

"Wait a minute, you know what? I need a huge favor right now."

"From me?"

"No, I was talking to him." She points to the empty spot beside Barnes.

"Must you always be so sarcastic?"

"I must." She crosses the room to her desk, grabs a pen and pad of paper from a drawer, and flips open her laptop. As it boots up, she jots some hurried notes on the pad, tears off the top sheet of paper, and hands it to him.

"Didi Mundy . . . Los Angeles . . . What is this?"

"I need you to find her. She went missing between Christmas and New Year's in 1983."

"Who is she?"

"A suspect." She bends over to type on the keyboard, accessing the database. While it loads, she jots more notes on another sheet of paper.

"What kind of suspect?"

"Murder."

His eyebrows shoot up, and she quickly explains her theory—that Emerson's absent mother might have re-surfaced and is responsible for staging the deaths of her father and Roy.

"But what's the motive?"

"I'm not sure, but the romantic relationship may have been abusive. For all I know, the father-daughter one was as well." She tears off the second sheet of paper. "Maybe the missing mother's been keeping an eye on her daughter all along, and she's trying to punish those who have wronged her, or just protect her from further harm."

She holds out the paper. Barnes just looks at it and then at her, wearing a strange expression.

Patience, especially at a time like this, doesn't come easily to Sully. If at all.

"This is a cakewalk for you, and it'll take your mind off your problems. Here." She thrusts the note at him. "A few more details and names—Emerson's father, Jerry, born in 1940, and the victim. Roy Nowak. School teacher from New York, lives in Oakland. See what you can find out. One more thing . . ." She quickly writes out the hangman diagram.

_ _ N E

"While you're at it, see if you can solve this puzzle, okay?"

"Oh sure, why not," he says, having snapped out of his

funk, at least momentarily. "Anything else? Errands? Foot massage?"

"That'll do it for now. I need to change and get out of here." Shoving the third piece of paper into his hand, she thanks him and hurries toward her room.

"Wait, Sully—"

Her phone rings, cutting him off.

Nick. She answers it, continuing on to her room. "Detective Leary."

"We found the truck."

"Where?"

"Parked in the municipal lot at the north end of Market. Forensics is going through it now."

"Was his cell phone in it?"

"No. There was a charger plugged in, but no phone attached."

"Either he lost it, or someone stole it, or he left it at the hotel."

"Well, it wasn't the Holiday Inn. I called. He wasn't a registered guest there last night, which explains why we didn't find a room key."

"That's odd. I saw him pull into the parking lot. I figured he was either staying there, or about to check in." She balances the phone between her shoulder and ear, about to unbutton her shirt. Remembering Barnes somewhere behind her, she stops.

"Maybe didn't have any rooms available?" Nick suggests.

"The sign said there were vacancies. Unless . . . what if he wasn't checking in? What if he was meeting someone there?"

"That's possible."

"One other thing, Detective. There was a big bottle of calamine lotion in the console of the truck. Looks like he did have some kind of itchy rash."

"Meaning the scratches were self-inflicted."

Meaning, most likely, that Emerson hadn't lied about a physical altercation between them.

Relieved, though it by no means clears her as a suspect, Sully says, "We need to get ahold of his call and text records."

"You know that takes a while, Detective."

Yeah, she knows. *Complicated* seems to be her theme today.

It's hard enough to get a warrant when you have an active homicide investigation. In this case, they'll need to provide paperwork and justify a court order.

"Maybe he just lost the phone and it'll turn up at the Windmill," Nick suggests.

"Yeah, and maybe Roy Nowak will rise from the dead and solve the hangman puzzle, too. Did you find his mother?"

"Still looking. We'll need Emerson Mundy to make the ID."

"She's aware."

"And you're keeping an eye on her?"

The question has nothing to do with concern for Emerson's emotional well-being. She tells him that she knows where Emerson is, and where to find her.

"See you later, Lieutenant."

She hangs up, strips off her shirt, tosses it into the wicker hamper, and reaches into the closet.

What if Roy really was meeting someone at the Holiday Inn? Or what if he was about to check in, and something happened that made him change his mind? Was he being followed? Did someone waylay him in the parking lot?

She doesn't recall seeing another car enter after his. But she wasn't paying close attention, unaware that she was witnessing the prelude to a suicide, or homicide.

Did Roy get a phone call, maybe, or a text? Did some-one lure him to the Windmill?

Maybe he decided to have a drink over there on his own, looking for female company, or for Emerson herself. If he were trying to find her, though, why wouldn't he have gone straight to the Dapplebrook?

That's sure as hell where he ended up, but—

"What was that all about?"

Barnes's voice stops her in her tracks. She'd forgotten he was even here. Standing with her back to the doorway wearing only a bra, she presses the uniform shirt against her, not turning around. "What?"

"The call."

"Just . . . more about the case. I've got to get going."

"You need to be careful."

Yeah, she thinks. *I do.*

She sighs, her back still to him, trying to sound cava-lier. "You want me to barricade myself in here with you? Or can I go out and do my job?"

"Do your job. Business as usual. Just . . ."

"Yeah, I'm always careful." She pulls on the shirt, but-tons it swiftly, and reaches back for the knob to close her bedroom door between them. "Listen, I'm changing in here, so unless you want an eyeful of Sully butt . . ."

"Hey. Look at me."

She turns, reluctantly. "What?"

"I mean it. Be careful."

She sees something in his eyes that was never before so stark.

Stockton Barnes is afraid—and he cares about her more than he should.

To Savannah's surprise, Sean knocks on the window of her lab a scant half hour after Braden called back to tell her he'd be picking her up at some point this afternoon.

"You're sending your cousin?" she'd asked in disbelief, having expected Braden to say he'd canceled his interview and was on his way.

"Yeah, he's just hanging around the house. He doesn't mind. I told him to knock when he gets there."

"Any idea what time that might be?"

"What's that?"

"What time should I—"

"Sorry, I'm having a hard time hearing you . . . the signal is spotty here . . ."

As he hung up, he added something that sounded like *Wish me luck*, though for all she knows, it could have been *I don't give a . . .*

"But if he didn't care," she told Jane Doe's skull, "he'd let me find my own way home, right?"

Jane Doe seemed to stare back, saying, *If he cared about you, he wouldn't have volunteered to go to Hartford today.*

Jane Doe, she decided, is childish and petty.

Now Sean is here, in broad daylight appearing even more careworn than he did last night in the bar. He's wearing the same black T-shirt. She wonders if he slept in it; wonders, too, how he went from Paris and Notre Dame University to bartending and living at his aunt's house.

"Ready?" he calls.

She glances back at the skull and the old papers spread out on the table, along with a notebook and magnifying glass. She'd been planning to return the research documents to the library before closing, but she hasn't worked her way through them all yet. She'll have to drag everything home with her overnight—and she can't jam fragile documents into her bag and dash out the door.

"I just have to put some stuff away," she calls back to Sean. "Do you want to wait in the car, or . . . ?"

"I'll come in," he says, as though she'd intended that as an option. "Is that door unlocked?"

"No. It's . . . uh . . ."

"Locked?" he asks with a smirk, or maybe a smile.

She nods and hurries out into the deserted hallway toward the back door.

How can she make him wait outside after driving all this way? He probably already knows Braden was here with her this morning.

He isn't Braden. There's something about him that makes her feel . . .

The opposite of safe.

Meaning what? In danger?

No.

Just . . . not entirely safe. Not with the murder gene research fresh in her mind. Is she really going to get into a car alone with him?

She should just thank him for offering a ride, and tell him she'll find another way home.

Opening the door, she says, "Listen, thanks for coming. I feel bad about this, and—"

"*You* feel bad? Why? You're the one who's abandoned."

Abandoned.

Instead of sending him on his way, she pauses to feel sorry for herself. Poor, abandoned Savannah. Story of her life.

"If anyone should feel bad," Sean goes on, "it's Braden."

"Does he?"

He shrugs—not the answer she was hoping for.

"Listen . . ." she begins again.

"Hey—Ambroise Paré!" Sean points at the wall behind her.

"What?" She turns to see that he's indicating one of the framed portraits that line the hallway.

"He was a sixteenth-century French surgeon."

"No, I know *that*." Paré was one of the forefathers of forensic pathology. "I'm just surprised you do."

"Well, I visited the Musée d'Histoire de la Médecine a few times when I was in Paris. Ever go?"

"Yes! A few times."

They discuss a couple of exhibits, and the next thing she knows, he's following her into the lab, and she's feeling okay about that—at least until he asks, "Is that the skull Ora Abrams gave you?"

"How do you know that?"

"I heard you telling Braden about it." He gives an unapologetic shrug. "You hear a lot, working at the bar."

"I'll bet."

He leans in to give the skull a closer look.

"Can you, um . . . I mean, you can't touch it unless you're wearing gloves."

"I'll pass. So the Mundys killed her and ate her?"

"No!" She hesitates. "I mean . . . someone did."

"Someone killed her or someone ate her?"

"Both. Not necessarily your family."

"That's good news," he says, and again she spots the traces of a grin, "considering that I'm not a Mundy."

"You're not? But . . . I thought you and Braden were cousins."

"On our moms' side. They're sisters."

So much for her psycho killer fears, at least where he's concerned.

He asks how she can tell Jane Doe was murdered, and she shows him the same evidence she showed Braden yesterday. He seems compelled, and asks a couple of well-phrased scientific questions.

"You didn't learn all this stuff from a few visits to a museum abroad. How do you know so much?"

"I took some bio courses, and anatomy, too. My father's a surgeon. I was pre-med."

"Then . . . why are you here?"

"Because my cousin asked me to pick you up, remember?"

"No, I mean, why are you staying with your aunt and uncle? What happened with your family?"

"You want the long version or the short?"

"I—"

"Short is, my parents split up."

"That's—I mean, that's rough—but for some reason I thought—"

"Oh yeah, and at the tail end of my semester in Paris, my mother was attacked by a lunatic who just about stabbed her to death."

Savannah's jaw drops.

"She survived," Sean goes on. "And my dad left her. He's a bastard."

"What about your mom? Is she . . . ?"

"Rehabilitation home. She's not the same. Maybe she will be eventually. My aunt hopes so."

"What about you?"

"I hope so, too."

That wasn't what she meant.

"What—"

"And that concludes the short version. Trust me, you don't want to hear the long, and if you do, I'm not in the mood to tell it." He looks again at Jane Doe, changing the subject. "Think you can find out who hurt her?"

"I'm trying. I'm waiting to hear back from Ora Abrams, because she might have access to some information that will help. But meanwhile I've got this stack of research to go through, and I have a list of people it could have been."

"Can I see?"

"Got a few minutes?"

"I've got all day."

She pulls up a stool and sits on the one beside it, reaching for the borrowed folder.

Papa!

At last, Ora has found him.

He's just as she remembers him, dashing and wise, waving to her from across a vast green distance.

The Commons?

Perhaps it's Schaapskill Nature Preserve, out by the settlers' monument.

"Papa!" she calls. "I'm coming! I've missed you so!"

"I've missed you, too, darling!"

She starts toward him, but the grass is thick, tangling around her feet so that she can barely move, and the lights . . .

The lights are blinding.

"Papa! I can't see you! Where are you?"

"I'm here, darling!"

But his voice is distant, and she can't catch her breath, can barely speak.

"Papa! Wait!"

"I'm waiting . . ."

"Aurora! Stop this instant!"

She knows the voice.

Great-Aunt Etta.

She squints into the glare, seeing only a shadow in the distance, blocking Papa.

"Aurora, you must go back!"

"I'm so tired . . ."

She longs to see them again—Aunt Etta, and Papa, and her mother—

"It isn't time! Not until you've told them!"

Told them . . .

Told them . . .
Told who?
Told them what?
Filled with despair, she struggles to make sense of it.
"We'll be here waiting for you when it's over," her aunt's voice floats across a great green distance. "Go back and tell them. You're the only one who knows."

TO BE DELIVERED UPON MY DEMISE

Mrs. Rowan Mundy
25 Riverview Road
Mundy's Landing, NY 12573

December 31, 2016

Dear Rowan:

As a most eventful year draws to a close, I am think-ing fondly of you and your family. It was so kind of you to invite me to ring in the new year at your lovely home. I regret that I was unable to accept your invitation, but I've had a cold and am afraid to catch a chill. At midnight, I shall reflect not just upon the momentous—indeed, notorious—events of the old year, but upon its many unexpected blessings. You have always been a good friend to me and to the museum. I have enjoyed your annual visits with your fourth-grade class, and your commitment to teaching local history to our young-est residents.

Your concern and support, especially after all that unfolded this summer, have meant far more than you will ever know. I appreciate your regular visits, and your ongoing assistance with museum matters and my own personal affairs. As I look ahead to the new year, I hope that I shall live to see it through, sound in both mind and body.

Whenever my time does come, this letter will make its way to your hands courtesy of my attorney. While the historical society, and its collections, are not mine to give, you will inherit my personal estate. I'm certain that the money will be put to good use with your growing family, and that you will care for my possessions, and guard the secrets you will find among them.

With warmest friendship,

Aurora Abrams

P.S. You mentioned that your oldest son is studying history. Perhaps when I am gone, he will want to take over as curator, and carry on in my footsteps and Aunt Etta's.

Chapter 14

Tucked into a corner of the small lobby, the Holiday Inn bar consists of little more than a couple of stools, counter, and beer tap.

Sully starts there, wondering whether Roy might have done the same last night. Maybe he really was meeting someone.

But the tired, middle-aged female bartender, like the tired, middle-aged female desk clerk she just interviewed, didn't see him. Both were on duty from 6 p.m. until 2 in the morning.

"It was deadsville in here last night," the bartender tells her. "Just me and the regulars."

Sully thanks her and heads back out to her car, pocketing the photo she'd printed off the Internet—a headshot of Roy from the Web site of the school where he teaches.

Hoping Twyla is on duty, she drives across the street to the Dunkin' Donuts. She's in luck—doubly so, because the place is empty.

"Sully! Hey, I'm glad you came back. Dina's having a cigarette break out back, but let me go grab her, because we wanted to talk to you about our trip to New York for—"

"Wait, Twyla, I just have a few quick questions for you. Official business, okay?" She flashes her badge.

Rimmed by thick liner and clumpy mascara, the girl's eyes widen, then narrow.

Sully knows guilt when she sees it. Wheels are turning beneath that bad blond dye job. Twyla went from wondering if she's about to be privy to some scandalous gossip to realizing she might have gotten caught doing . . . what?

Handing free donuts to her friends at the drive-through? Smoking weed at a concert? Meddling in murder?

Sully's gut tells her the last option is highly unlikely, but she's been fooled before.

"Twyla, do you remember the man who was in here last night?"

"There were a lot of men in here last night."

"He was here when I was. Had a beard. Red shirt. You thought he was hot."

"I don't know. I meet a lot of people." Now she's gone celebutante, inspecting her nails, fingers folded, palm up.

"Twyla? He's dead."

"What?" She looks up. "Car wreck?"

"No. Did you see him again after he left here?"

"No."

"And he didn't come back?"

"No."

"You didn't see him leave the parking lot across the street?"

"No." She takes a box of sugar packets from beneath the counter and begins restocking a container, her movements guarded. "But I was busy. We got a rush when the movie let out. Why are you asking me all of these questions?"

"Like I said, he died, and I'm investigating. This is one of the last places he was seen alive."

"Yeah, but you saw him, too!"

"I know. I'm just hoping you might have noticed something I didn't."

When it becomes clear that Twyla will shed no additional light on the case, Sully hands over her card. She tells the girl to call if she remembers anything, just as she told the women over at the Holiday Inn.

She doesn't expect to hear from any of them, though once in a while, someone surprises you.

She gets back into the car and drives down the highway into town. A ripe mango sun casts a late-day glow over the village. She parks in front of the Windmill, finding the door propped open onto the street, as always. Later in the evening, music will be blasting out onto the sidewalk. At this hour, she hears only clinking glassware and the chatty voices of the staff setting up for the evening rush.

Again, she wonders what brought Roy here, and what happened to his cell phone.

When you've got a dead body and no phone, chances are someone made it disappear because it contains evidence. Sure, it might have been Roy himself. He could have taken his own life, upset over what he perceived as Emerson slipping away. He could have found out the details of her father's suicide, and mimicked them to punish her.

But what about the note Jerry left behind? Even if Roy had stumbled across it, could he have understood the hangman puzzle with only one letter available? If he didn't know what Jerry Mundy was trying to say—if indeed Jerry had written the first note—why would Roy bother to duplicate it? And if he did know what it meant, wouldn't he have solved it in his own final message, instead of doling out one more letter?

That's the ominous part of the whole thing. Two different notes, each containing one letter of a four-letter word . . .

It implies that two more notes, two more letters are still to come.

But not if I solve the puzzle, and the case, first.

"**C**ontinue . . . straight . . . for . . . one . . . mile . . ."

Obeying the electronic GPS command, Emerson at last guides her rental car up the steep, winding stretch of Riverview Road toward the address Rowan provided earlier.

Though she's wearing sunglasses, she squints into the glare of late-day sun with every westward turn as she follows the winding road along the Hudson's bluffs.

She's running late. It's almost a quarter to eight. Emotionally and physically drained, she'd fallen asleep sitting on the couch in her suite, brooding about her discovery. When she woke up, it was after seven. She hurriedly changed into jeans, a crisp white blouse, and a blue linen blazer. After checking the brightly lit bathroom mirror, she took a few minutes to put on a little makeup, trying to hide the haggard circles a short nap couldn't erase.

Oh hell, after what she's been through, a weeklong nap wouldn't help.

There was no sign of Nancy downstairs. A placard on the porch stated that the restaurant will be closed for the evening—no explanation given.

Emerson detoured through the business district, planning to pick up a box of cookies, but the bakery was closed. Instead, she stopped at Price Chopper and got a chocolate layer cake. Not fancy, but better than showing up empty-handed.

Never properly educated in social manners as a child, she grew up unaware that hostess gifts are customary until she was the only one of her college suite mates who didn't bring something to a friend's parents hosting them all at their beach house for a weekend. That was just one of countless embarrassing lessons learned over the years, yet another acute reminder of her mother's abandonment and her father's social ineptitude.

"You . . . have . . . reached . . . your . . . destination."

It takes her a moment to spot the house. Set back from the road, the Queen Anne Victorian is as charming as the vintage homes back in The Heights, rising three stories with dormers, turrets, and a wraparound porch.

Of course. Yet another storybook home for the fortunate residents of this storybook village.

Turning into the driveway, she sees nearly half a dozen vehicles already there. She'd assumed she'd be the only guest, but a full-blown dinner party appears to be well under way.

How will she manage a private conversation with Jake about their shared ancestral connection?

Maybe she should just leave. No one would blame her for going back to the hotel alone after all she's been through today.

But if she doesn't stay, her questions won't be answered anytime soon—not with Ora incapacitated for who knows how long. And she'll have to find a place to eat yet another solitary dinner, waiting to be summoned to the morgue, followed by another nightmare-plagued sleep in the Jekyll Suite, windows scraped by the shadowy boughs that sheltered Roy's lifeless body.

No. No way.

She parks the rental car behind a tan Jeep already blocking a beat-up Honda, and heads for the front door carrying the cake.

A wide porch runs along the home's façade and angles beyond the turreted windows at either corner.

Climbing the steps, Emerson notices that the potted red impatiens could stand to be watered. White paint is peeling in spots on the wicker furniture, and several blue cushions are askew. The fanned pages of a book lying facedown on the table are swollen as if from rain or a dunk in a swimming pool. An apple core someone left nearby is teeming with ants.

Yet this is different from the pervasive neglect in her own childhood home, or what she witnessed earlier in Ora Abrams's kitchen. This house is lived-in, well-used, appreciated.

Ringing the bell, she's aware that the ache in her shoulder blades has crept over the rest of her. The day's events are finally taking a toll, and she still has a long night ahead. Any second now, Sullivan Leary is probably going to be in touch about the morgue.

Again, Emerson thinks of Roy, not just dead in the tree, but presumed murdered.

Who can Sully possibly suspect?

Come on, who do you think?

She'd asked so many probing questions. Yet she can't possibly believe Emerson is capable of such a heinous crime, can she? She knows Roy was dangerous, mentally unstable, likely to have made enemies who might have taken his life if he didn't do it himself.

What about the hangman notes? What about a pair of identical suicides?

What about my missing mother, lurking in the hospital, and God knows where else? If Sully—

The door opens, curtailing the thought, and she finds herself face to face with a smiling man.

"You must be Emerson. I'm your cousin Jake."

Walking into the Windmill, Sully recognizes the waitresses on duty. Both are clad in black jeans and T-shirts, and both have long, straight dark hair and red matte lipstick. They look like sisters, but she's enough of a regular here to know that they're not. The taller of the two, Ellie, is a local girl, a teacher's aide over at Mundy's Landing Elementary School by day. The other, Jenna, lives in Kingston and has tattoos, a pierced nose, and a boyfriend who plays in a band.

The faint smell of last night's wine and beer hangs in the air, and dust floats like golden glitter in late sunshine falling through the plate-glass window. Ellie is lighting votive candles on the tables as Jenna writes the specials on the chalkboard.

Ellie winces as the chalk squeaks. "Do you have to keep making that sound?"

"You mean this?" Jenna does it again, grinning.

"You're evil!"

They have yet to notice Sully, standing just inside the door.

She clears her throat. "Hello, ladies."

"Hi, Detective Leary. We're, uh, not open yet," Jenna tells her, lifting a bony, well-inked wrist to check her watch.

"Don't worry," Sully says. "I'm not here to eat."

"Bartender's not here yet."

"Not drinking, either," she says, though she wouldn't mind a stiff whiskey right now.

And she does need to talk to whoever was bartending last night. First things first, though. "Has anyone turned in a lost cell phone?"

"We find cell phones all the time," Ellie reports, and winces as the chalk squeaks again.

"Sorry! Accident, I swear!"

"Yeah, sure." Rolling her eyes at Jenna, Ellie tosses aside the lighter and walks toward the bar, beckoning Sully to follow.

She crosses the room, for the first time noticing the finish on the wide-planked hardwood floors, and the rich red leather on the tall-backed barstools. The bar itself is nice, too—a carved, vintage piece with inlaid Italian marquetry, backlit mirrors, and glass shelves lined with liquor bottles and decanters.

The place is always so jammed when Sully's here, she's never had a chance to get a good look at the backdrop.

What are the odds that anyone working last night got a good look at Roy?

Ellie takes an orange cardboard Nike shoebox from a shelf and plunks it onto the bar. "Here's the lost and found."

Sully watches her rifle through the contents, pausing to try on a silver bangle, proclaiming it "Adorbs. What do you think, Jenna?"

Her friend looks over. "I think that blond bitch who works at Tru Blu had that on last night. I'm sure she'll notice if you go around wearing it."

"I wasn't going to *steal* it. I was just admiring it." Ellie puts it back with a mindful glance at Sully, takes a cell phone from the box, and holds it out. "Here you go. Is it yours?"

Seeing that the device is nested in a pink and white striped case, her flash of optimism vanishes. "Not the one I'm looking for, but—"

"Hey, that's Amy Gusset's," Jenna says, and pulls her own phone from her pocket. "She was here last night for someone's bachelorette party, and I saw her taking a ton of pictures with it. I'll text her and tell her."

"How's she supposed to get a text if she doesn't have her phone?"

"Some people can get them on laptops."

The pink and white phone dings with a text. Ellie looks at Jenna with a smirk. "It's you. There's no passcode on it. Want me to reply?"

"Don't be a wiseass."

"All right, ladies, I have a few more questions for you." Sully shows them the photograph of Roy. "Ever seen him before?"

They haven't.

"And you were both working last night?"

They were.

"But it was crazy-busy," Jenna adds.

"It's always crazy-busy," Ellie agrees, and takes another look at the photo. "Oh hey, is he the dude who hung himself over at the Dapplebrook?"

"How did you know about that?"

"My friend Trevor's a waiter there. I saw him on my way over here a little while ago."

"Where?"

"Just sitting on a bench over there, doing nothing." She gestures at the plate-glass window.

"Out on the Common?"

"Yeah. He looked super upset. I asked him what was wrong, and he told me someone killed himself, which sucks. Trevor said he was supposed to work, but Nancy told him to go home because they can't open the restaurant now. He was bummed because he really needs the money, you know?"

"Wow, that does suck." Jenna shakes her head. "Poor dude."

Sully isn't sure whether she's referring to Trevor or the dead man, but she'd guess it's the former. She looks out the window, scanning the Common for Trevor, but there's no sign of him now.

"He was telling me that he's super broke," Ellie is saying, "and he can't afford to pay his tuition for the fall unless he makes a lot more money."

"Where did you see him last night?" Sully asks, remembering that he'd waited on her at the Dapplebrook, and on Emerson Mundy, too.

"He comes in here for a beer sometimes after work. He sits at the bar."

"Yeah, I saw him, too, when he got here," Jenna says, "but I didn't get a chance to talk to him."

Sully wonders whether Trevor's path intersected with Roy's. Maybe they got to talking. Maybe he'd asked

Trevor about Emerson, and Trevor mentioned that she was staying at the Dapplebrook.

She thinks about Trevor's spider tattoo, and she tries not to wonder whether it's an ominous indicator of a dark side, much darker than she'd suspected. It's just a tattoo. Intellectually, she knows it means nothing. Does her trusty gut beg to differ?

"Who else was working last night?" she asks, pen poised on paper.

"Laura Vronsky and Sean Chapman were bartending. Sean was on till close, but I think Laura left at midnight. She should be back here any second."

"How about Sean?"

"He doesn't come on till nine."

Sully needs to talk to Rowan's nephew before then, but she doesn't want to drag Rowan into this—particularly with Emerson due at her house for dinner.

"Can one of you give me a cell phone number for Sean?" she asks the women.

"I have it right here." Jenna checks her phone and reads it off to Sully, who dials it quickly.

He answers on the second ring.

"Sean, this is Detective Leary."

There's a pause, and then, "Sully?"

"Yes. Are you at your aunt and uncle's house?"

"No, I'm . . . with a friend. Why? Did something happen?" he adds, with the dread-laced inflection of someone who knows too well what it's like to get a life-changing phone call.

"Nothing like that. I'm down at the Windmill, and I was wondering if I could talk to you for a few minutes."

"Oh. Um, okay, sure. I'm on my way into town, so I'll stop by there if you want."

She thanks him, hangs up, and looks back at the waitresses.

"He's on his way. Did you recognize anyone else in here last night?"

"You're kidding, right?" Ellie asks. "I mean, I recognized pretty much everyone."

"Can you give me some names? Start with the people you saw sitting at the bar, and—" She remembers something. "Can I please see that cell phone you found?"

"You mean Amy's?" Ellie takes it back out of the shoebox and hands it over.

"Is Amy a friend of yours?"

"Not really. I mean, I know her."

"I'm friends with her, sort of," Jenna says. "She works at the mall in Kingston."

Sully half listens. This isn't necessarily about Amy, or a group of young women celebrating someone's bachelorette party.

Her thumb is poised over the photos app. No, she shouldn't search the phone without the owner's consent or legal permission, but she isn't tampering with it, and she isn't looking for evidence, nor expecting to find any. This is gray area. An investigation.

Mind made up, she opens the photo file. Jenna's right—there are a ton of pictures. Sully is aware of the two women watching her as she scans through them, looking for Roy's red shirt in the crowd. Most are of a group of partying girls, one of whom is wearing a headband with a little white bridal veil. She spots Trevor in one of the photos, scowling with the headband on his head. Rowan's nephew Sean is visible in the background in many.

She flips back through, enlarging each photo, and spots Rowan's son Braden sitting at the bar next to Trevor in the background of one picture. There's a woman sitting next to him, and . . .

There.

That's Roy.

He's sitting on a bar stool next to the woman. Who is she? Are they together?

Roy is looking down at a phone in his hand.

Sully enlarges the photo until it's a grainy blur, trying in vain to see what he's looking at.

She flips to the adjacent photos, but she still can't tell. In one of them, though, she sees that Braden Mundy is holding hands with the woman seated next to Roy. She's with him, then, and not with Roy.

"Are you, um . . . done with that?"

Sully looks up to see Jenna watching her with a pointed expression. Ellie, too.

Before she can reply, her own phone rings.

Barnes.

She puts Amy's back in the shoebox and hurries toward the door, wanting to answer it in private. "I'll be back," she tells the waitresses, and imagines them rolling their eyes at each other.

"I found her," Barnes's voice greets her as she steps outside and across the street to the Common.

"You found who?"

"Come on, think about it. Who did you ask me to find?"

Sully's brain catches up to the conversation. "Emerson Mundy's mother?"

"You're *good.* How'd you guess?"

"Cut the bullshit," she says, though a part of her welcomes it, evidence that Barnes is semi-back to normal. She plops herself down on a vacant bench and flips to a new page on her pad of paper, prepared to write down a name, an address. "What's her name? And where is she?"

Barnes gives her a one-word answer she should have expected, but doesn't see coming.

"Dead."

"I think I've got something," Sean says.

Savannah looks up from the hand-drawn map she's been examining. Enshrouded in a transparent acid-free sleeve, it shows the layout of the first settlement. Each rectangle represents a dwelling and is labeled with a family name. The diagram was found among John and Tabitha Ransom's belongings.

So was the similarly protected document Sean is showing her. "This is a letter William Ransom wrote to his father on February 12, 1666."

"He died a few days later," Savannah tells him—just one of the facts she's committed to memory over the past few hours of intensive research.

"Yeah, it sounds like he knew his time was about up. Read this."

He hands over the letter, along with the magnifying glass they've been passing back and forth in trying to glean information from the old papers. In some cases, the text is smudged or faded. In others, the unfamiliar syntax might as well be a foreign language one has studied, but not to fluency.

Savannah reads the letter, then looks up at him.

"What do you think?" he asks.

"I think it's pretty clear who Jane Doe was. I have to show this to Miss Abrams. I was planning to head over there tonight."

"I can drive you over there before I drop you off at home. I don't have to be at work until nine."

"It's out of the way for you, isn't it?"

"Yeah, but I'd like to hear what she has to say, and . . ." He shrugs. "This is the first time in a while that I've thought about anything other than my own problems. Makes my life seem not so bad, you know?"

She nods, feeling the same way, glad he's coming along with her.

12th February 1666

Dear Father,

    I am writing to tell you that our beloved John and his wife, Tabitha, have perished.

    One week has passed since my brother fell into a deep sleep from which he did not awaken. When the morn dawned, Tabitha was distraught upon discovering him, and grew frantic when she realized that our neighbors would soon feed upon her dead husband's flesh as they have the others.

    Together, we wrapped him in muslin and carried him out of doors and a little ways away from our dwelling. I had not the strength to bury him even if the earth was not frozen solid, as it has been for many weeks. I scraped a long trench in the snow and gently lay my brother within, knowing he would soon be covered by falling snow, and they would not find his corpse.

    The following day, the storm abated and the Goody Mundy came 'round to offer us the last of the porridge she had concocted from the heart and liver of Verity Hall, who had succumbed just days ago.

    We refused the grisly brew as always, and she warned us that we will not survive unless we resort to nourishing ourselves with the remains of our departed friends, as the Mundy family has.

    She is right. Yet I shall remain strong, like my brother and his wife and the others who have stood strong against this sinful temptation, only to die and have their flesh devoured by those who will survive this miserable life only to find eternal condemnation hereafter.

    Goody Mundy reminded us that the others are all gone now, saying only we three remain, along with Anne

Blake, the Dowlings' young servant girl. Then, belatedly, she noted that John was not present in our small room. When we told her he had passed away, a strange glint came into her blue and gray eyes, and I believe I glimpsed Satan himself as she inquired greedily after his remains.

When I boldly told her we had buried him so that he would never be found, she grew enraged and took her leave. Tabitha was quite fearful. I calmed her with this Bible verse from Jeremiah 19:9.

"And I will cause them to eat the flesh of their sons and the flesh of their daughters, and they shall eat every one the flesh of his friend in the siege . . ."

Goody Mundy has not returned, though her husband and son have been by to check on us. We have assured them, through the closed door, that we are quite alive, but have not let them in.

Tabitha endured just six days without her husband before she, too, closed her eyes forever on this dark afternoon. I could not rest her remains alongside my brother, as the white blanket had long since enfolded him, but I dug a small spot in the same vicinity. The harsh wind pummeled me as I lay down Tabitha's withered frame, and I shall confess that I contemplated settling myself there with her. My body so ached with bitter cold and hunger and grief that only the thought of you and Mother forced me back indoors. I cannot leave you to wonder ever after what became of your family, or to hope that perhaps we might return to you, as we have waited in vain for your ship's arrival for many months now.

I shall add this to my previous letters, in the hope that you will discover them one day. I can only pray that my own death will come as gently and swiftly for me as it

*did for Tabitha and John and the others. Now, Father,
my last deed has been accomplished. May we meet again
in heaven.*

Your son,

William Ransom

Chapter 15

With one unexpected word, Barnes has effectively blown Sully's burgeoning theory about Jerry and Roy and the hangman notes.

"Emerson's mother is *dead*?"

"Yes," Barnes says.

"For how long?" Sully holds the phone clamped by her shoulder against her ear, hands prepared with paper and pen to write the information she's certain he's about to deliver—that the woman was found dangling from a noose somewhere, a hangman note at the scene, and . . .

"Thirty years."

"*Thirty!*" She curses softly.

"She died around December 27, 1983."

"But . . ."

This changes everything.

It happened right after she walked out on Emerson and her father.

Or *did* she walk out?

Did she die, and Emerson's father couldn't bear to tell her the truth?

Sully's seen the reverse—one parent leaves, and the other fabricates a death for the children, thinking it's better to grow up thinking your father or mother would be there, given the choice.

That lie, as Sully has learned over her career, can come back to haunt a grown child.

What about this one? People make irrational choices under duress. If Jerry Mundy told his young daughter that her mother had abandoned her, he must have had his reasons.

Or maybe it was simply what he believed to be the truth.

"Barnes, let's back up. Tell me how you know all this."

"Records. Birth, death, newspaper . . . it's all there. It fits."

"What was her name?"

"Deirdre Davies Mundy."

Deirdre Davies.

Didi, a nickname for Deirdre.

Or D. D., her initials.

"That makes sense." She writes it down. "Keep talking."

"Born in Philadelphia in October 1964. Parents met at Princeton, mother a Main Line debutante, father from a New York banking family that—"

"Wait, this can't be right. Nineteen sixty-four means she was just a kid herself when Emerson was born in 1980."

"A woman calling herself Gerry Mundy gave birth to a daughter named Emily in Los Angeles on New Year's Day, 1980."

"Gerry? Emily? See, that's not right. Her father's name is Jerry, and her name is Emerson."

"Maybe she decided to change it to something more exotic. Happens all the time."

"I'm sure she would have told me if that was the case. She knew I was going to look for her mother."

Sully pencils a big X over the page of notes she'd just scribbled. "You've got the wrong person, but thanks for giving it a shot."

"Hear me out. There's more. The dates line up, and—"

"Not exactly."

"Close enough. Maybe the hospital got the baby's name wrong, maybe the mother changed it later. The dates fit, and the address on the birth record matches the one Emerson gave you."

"But I thought you said her mother's name was Deirdre?"

"It was. She wouldn't be the first teenager to show up at the E.R. in labor and give birth under an assumed name. She was alone."

"No husband?"

"No husband, no ID, no insurance. Walked in off the street. Things were different back then. They admitted her, they released her. In between, she had a baby and she paid her bill."

"With cash?"

"A check. It was good."

"What was the name on the account?"

"Jerry Mundy. No red flags. Gerry. Jerry."

She mulls it over. "This is crazy."

"Come on. Round peg in a round hole. Why are you trying to make it square?"

"Because it eliminates my prime suspect in a murder. Maybe two murders."

"You're sure you're looking at homicide?"

"Not a hundred percent, but . . . my gut is telling me yes."

"Okay, well then now you can stop wasting your time on a dead end and start looking elsewhere."

She looks back over the notes she'd just crossed out, making sure everything is still legible. "Any idea where?"

"Maybe. Let's back up again. Deirdre went missing

from Philadelphia in the summer of 1979, five months before Emily Mundy was born."

"Holy crap."

"Yeah. I found her in the missing persons database."

Hearing a text come in on her phone, Sully tells Barnes to hang on a minute. She lowers it to see a message from the medical examiner's office.

DOA ready for ID.

Terrific.

She responds with a thumbs-up emoticon and goes back to her phone call.

"So, Barnes, you're saying Deirdre Davies was a pregnant fifteen-year-old who ran away to California in the summer of '79, had a baby girl named Emily on New Year's, and the baby later became Emerson, and . . ." She does the math and wrinkles her nose. "Deirdre was the teenage bride to a guy who would have been . . . um, forty when Emerson was born? Ick."

"No, that's not what I'm saying. She didn't marry Jerry Mundy. She *was* a Mundy."

"Wait, *what*? I thought you said she was a Davies."

"That's her middle name, not her maiden name. Actually, it's her mother Lilith's maiden name. The Davies are a prominent Main Line family. Lilith Davies married Arthur Horace Mundy Jr. in 1957."

"Arthur *Horace* Mundy Jr.?" Sully writes furiously on her pad. "So he's connected to Mundy's Landing."

"Yes. Their wedding was written up in the *New York Times*, and it mentions that the groom's grandfather was the famed financier Horace J. Mundy. The bride and groom were both twenty-two, right out of Princeton. Oh, and the family was big on nicknames. The bride's was

Lili, the groom's was Artie. Deirdre was their youngest child. Maybe they called her D. D.—her initials."

"But this means Jerry Mundy . . ." Sully is too flabbergasted to continue.

Barnes says it for her. "Jerry wasn't Deirdre's husband. He was her cousin."

Jake Mundy looks to be in his late forties or early fifties. Handsome, with dark hair graying at the temples and a nice smile. He's wearing a dress shirt, top button unfastened and knot of his tie loosened.

Emerson searches for some physical similarity on his face, and finds none.

Yet despite the discrepancy in her lineage, one thing is certain: she, too, is a Mundy, descended from Jeremiah just as Jake is. Otherwise, she wouldn't have inherited the letter that reveals the truth about the early settlers . . .

Or, more importantly, the heterochromia.

If, say, she'd been adopted as an infant, odds would be astronomically stacked against her possessing the same rare genetic aberration that runs in this family.

Emerson shakes the hand he offers, hoping he can't feel hers tremble in his grasp, or the wobble in her voice as she apologizes for being late.

"No worries. We're pretty informal, and we never eat before eight, even when we're aiming at five. Come on in."

"I wasn't sure where to park—I didn't realize you were having more company, so I'm kind of blocking the driveway."

"That's not more company. Just me, Ro, and the kids. If anyone needs to get out, believe me, they'll let you know about it, loud and clear."

Relieved, Emerson shoves her car keys into the pocket of her jeans and steps inside.

The home might once have been as grand as the Dapplebrook Inn and the Conroy-Fitch mansion, but it's far more comfortable. The lower steps of the elegant staircase are stacked with things that obviously need to be carried up—a book, a stack of folded towels, a couple of plastic supermarket bags, a six-pack of toilet tissue. A dog's chew toy bone is half buried beneath the Oriental area rug, and its fringed border is bedraggled as if it, too, has been chewed. A sweatshirt hangs by its hood from the newel post. A basset hound noses a pair of oversized basketball sneakers that are lying just inside the front door.

That explains the faint smell of dog and locker room that mingles with a delicious savory aroma wafting in the air.

"Sorry about the mess. Careful, don't trip," Jake kicks them aside and yells, "Mick? Come down here and get your shoes out of the front hall before Doofus eats one again!"

No response.

"Kids." Jake shakes his head, untying his tie and draping it, too, over the newel post. "I'm sure he's plugged into headphones. If I really need to be heard, I have to go up there, or text, crazy as that seems. But sometimes, yelling makes me feel better, you know?"

"I do know. I'm a teacher," she says, pushing her sunglasses up on her head.

"Just like Rowan. No wonder she likes you so much. She—well, we're definitely related," he interrupts himself to say, peering at her face.

Her heart skips a beat. "How do you know?"

"You have the Mundy eyes—one blue, one gray, just like Jeremiah Mundy. My grandfather told me about that when I was little. The trait died out in our branch of the family, but not in yours."

So Ora was right about the heterochromia.

What about everything else?

"Come on into the kitchen. Rowan's busy cooking."

She is indeed. Pots bubble on the stove, the oven timer is beeping, and a steaming, foil-covered pan sits on the granite-topped island in the center of the large room. A pile of corn on the cob, some peeled, some not, waits on the counter beside a heap of husks and silks.

"Welcome!" Rowan turns away from the sink and dries her hands on her cut-off shorts. Her feet are bare, and she's changed into a sleeveless orange T-shirt that clashes with her coloring and reads—quite aptly, Emerson decides—Life Is Good.

Rowan resets the stove timer, gives Emerson a quick hug, and asks if she drinks white, red, or beer.

"Oh . . . um . . ."

"Or water," Rowan adds, "if you're a teetotaler. I bought a big thing of iced tea this afternoon, but the kids wiped it out already."

"Better that than the beer." Jake opens the fridge.

"Don't count on it. I bought a twelve-pack of Coronas and there are nine left."

"Let's just hope the culprit was legal age." Her husband pulls out a bottle of beer and offers it to Emerson. "Or would you rather have wine?"

"Whatever's easiest."

"I'll have wine." Rowan shoves strands of sweat-dampened red hair away from her flushed face. "It's too hot for red, so make it white. Anything but chardonnay."

Her husband pokes through the fridge. "Riesling?"

"Anything but Riesling and chardonnay."

He pulls out another bottle. "Pinot grigio."

"Anything but pinot grigio, Riesling, and—"

"You're kidding, right?"

"Of course." Rowan laughs, lifting a lid to stir something on the stove. "Emerson, is pinot grigio okay?"

"Sure." She's not much of a drinker, and she wants to

keep her wits about her, especially tonight. But she goes with the flow, as if she's used to dropping by people's homes for dinner, hanging out in kitchens like this, filled with clutter and food and banter and life. As if she's just one of the family . . .

I am. I'm a Mundy. My eyes prove it.

Jake opens a drawer. "Where's the good corkscrew?"

"Haven't seen it. Use the bad one."

"Is this the bad one?" He holds one up.

"That's the one that doesn't work."

"Why do we have it?"

"In case we lose the other ones. Did you feed the babies, by the way?"

"I'm allergic, remember?"

"You don't have to bury your nose in their fur, just— forget it. You open the wine. I'll feed them." She grabs a can of food from the cupboard, pops the top, dumps it into a bowl, and heads out the back door.

"They're not babies," Jake tells Emerson as he twists the metal spiral into the wine bottle. "A stray cat had kittens under the porch. Want one?"

"I'm allergic, too."

They smile at each other. Emerson watches his muscular forearms strain until the cork pops out, and she imagines what it would be like to be married to a man like him—easygoing, capable, handsome . . .

So different from Roy.

But Roy is gone. Nausea rolls into her gut.

Did he think about her in his last moments, clinging to his ideal of the marriage they could have had . . .

Remembering his questions, and his scrutiny, she reminds herself that it's over. No one will ever look at her that way again.

Rowan breezes back in. "Those kittens really are adorable. I wish—"

"Don't even think about it," Jake says.

Listening to them tease each other about kids and kittens, Emerson feels a nagging sense of foreboding, as if it's not really over. As if any second now, someone is going to pounce.

"Hey!" Jake is on his tiptoes in front of a high, glass-fronted cupboard filled with stemware. "We have Mallomars?"

"So that's where I stashed them! I knew I had one more box around here somewhere. I know it sounds bad, hiding food from my kids," Rowan tells Emerson.

"And your husband," Jake puts in.

"And my husband, but they're eating us out of house and home this summer."

"That's because we have twice as many as we were counting on with Sean here and Braden back after all."

"More the merrier." With a shrug, Rowan grabs her wineglass and holds it out in a toast. "On that note . . . welcome to the family, Emerson."

"You still there?"

"Yeah," Sully tells Barnes, "I'm still here."

Still here, clutching the phone to her ear, sitting on a bench on the Common, watching a young man toss a Frisbee to a puppy that should be on a leash, and a group of kids splashing in the nearby fountain posted with a No Wading sign. In the center of the fountain is a statue of Horace J. Mundy, Emerson's great-grandfather . . . on her *maternal* side?

"Talk to me," Barnes says.

"I'm just . . . I can't believe Emerson's parents were cousins."

"There's no father listed on the birth certificate. Maybe it wasn't Jerry. Could have been some kid in Philly. She was about four months' pregnant when she took off."

"Then who is Jerry, exactly? Sorry, I'm just trying to get my head around this."

"Jerry would be the great-grandson of Horace J's crazy brother Oswald Mundy," Barnes explains. "Deirdre was his cousin Artie's daughter. Artie was a few years older than Jerry, born in 1935."

"So you're saying that Jerry might not have been Emerson's father, or even her stepfather? He wasn't romantically involved with Deirdre?"

"That, I don't know. Maybe he was more like an uncle."

"That makes sense. He took in his cousin's runaway pregnant daughter . . ."

"And apparently never bothered to call Artie to say Deirdre was safe."

"Really?"

"Really. Her parents were looking for her throughout the early eighties, offering a huge reward. They said she wanted to be an actress and thought she might have run off to Hollywood. According to the case files and the newspapers, they almost seemed to expect her body to turn up in California."

"And that was . . ." She looks back over the scribblings. "December 27, 1983. How did she die?"

"Ready for this? Strangled. Her body was killed elsewhere and found on the shoulder of a canyon road, rope ligature around the neck."

Welcome to the family.

Rowan Mundy's toast warms Emerson like a morning sunbeam. So does the cautious sip of tart white wine.

Rowan sets her glass aside and goes back to dinner prep. "Get busy, Jake, or it'll be midnight before we get this food on the table."

"Wouldn't be the first time." He puts down the beer bottle and asks Emerson, "So, how are we related?"

"I'm . . . not sure." She isn't ready yet to tell him about the discrepancy in her lineage. Better to first see what he has to say. "I was hoping you could tell me."

"Ever seen a complete family tree?"

She shakes her head. "Have you?"

"My grandfather made one years ago. Nothing elaborate, just a penciled chart on a sheet of notebook paper. But I remember finding it when I was a kid, stuck in the old family Bible."

"I'd love to see it."

"Is it with your grandfather's old photo albums?" Rowan asks him.

"No, my mother has it in Texas. I texted Liza earlier when you said Emerson was coming over. She promised to scan it and send it—the family tree, not the Bible," he adds with that ready grin.

Rowan explains to Emerson that Liza is Jake's sister, who lives in Houston. Their mother moved down there, too, a few years ago, after Jake's father passed away. "She's kind of losing it, and we worry about her. That reminds me—I called the hospital to see what I could find out about Ora."

"How is she? Is she conscious?"

"All they'd say was that she's been admitted. They couldn't release any information over the phone. I'm going to go over there after dinner."

"Can she have visitors?"

"I have connections if she can't. My friend Zoe is a nurse there, and her shift starts at seven on weekdays. Do you want to come along?"

If she tells them about Roy, and the morgue, they'll have questions. Jake will be sidetracked from his mission to show her the family tree.

But if she doesn't mention it and they find out later—of

course they'll find out later—they might think she has something to hide.

Better to be honest, she decides, and opens her mouth.

Before she can say a word, the stove timer goes off, and Rowan shouts, "Doofus! No!"

Neither of those things has anything to do with the other, or with Emerson, who swallows back the news about Roy.

"He's got a clump of corn silk! Come on, boy. That's not good for you!"

"Who says it's not good for him?"

"The vet!"

"The vet said *cobs* aren't good for him. I'm sure the rest is fine."

"We don't know that, Jake! Help me get it out of his mouth!"

Amid the marital argument, repetitive beeping, jangling dog tags, and growls from Doofus, they wrestle him for the soggy clump of green and brown.

"Got it!" Rowan holds it up, triumphant.

Doofus barks and makes a jump for it.

"Sit!" The dog ignores Jake's command. Jake grabs his collar and escorts him into the next room.

Rowan turns off the stove timer, gathers the corn, and begins dropping the ears into the pot of boiling water.

"Sorry about all that, Emerson. I was hoping tonight was going to be perfect, but this is pretty much the way things go around here. When you meet my kids they'll be bickering, and I'm sure any second now the dog will barf up corn silk or someone's shoe—or there will be corn silk barf *in* someone's shoe."

"Why don't you let me give you a hand? Can I stir something, or make something, or . . ."

Rowan gratefully accepts the offer, and she pushes aside her guilt over not mentioning Roy.

Rowan hands her a whisk and small bowl and sets out bottles of oil, vinegar, and soy sauce. "If you can just throw together the dressing for the Asian salad, that would be great. I'll get more soy sauce. That's not enough."

"Um . . . is there a recipe?"

"Somewhere, but just wing it. I always do."

Emerson rarely cooks, and when she does, she follows step-by-step instructions.

She splashes some oil into the bowl, wonders if it's too much, decides it's too little, and adds some more. She looks over to see if Rowan is watching her in horror, but she's dragging a stool over to the cupboard.

"I'm probably going to regret this," she says as she climbs up, and begins to rummage around. "But I know I bought another bottle of soy sauce a few weeks ago."

"Why would you regret buying soy sauce?"

"I mean, I'll regret looking for the soy sauce. You know how sometimes, you need that one thing that's stashed way in the back, but you can't get to it without everything else tumbling out? Or does that only happen to me?"

"It happens to everyone. Believe me."

Footsteps creak down the stairs, and Jake reappears in the kitchen. He's changed into blue plaid shorts, a polo shirt, and flip-flops.

"Ro, the natives are getting restless. Well, two of them. One says he hasn't eaten in 'days,' and the other says she has a date so hurry up."

"What about the third native?"

"Asleep. Think he's the one who drank the three Coronas?"

"Could be. He was upset when he got home from that interview." She shrugs, climbing off the stool sans soy sauce. "And he stayed over at his friend's house. I'm sure they were up all night."

"He needs to start keeping regular hours and sleeping when the rest of the world does."

"He will, when he finds a job."

"This wasn't even something he wanted. He was a history major."

"He'll take what he can get. Entry level in anything. This is a hard time in his life. When I was his age, I was miserable."

"Hey! When you were his age, you met me."

That results in more teasing banter, and then Rowan explains to Emerson that their older son, Braden, had a job interview in Hartford this afternoon.

"He drove all the way there, and the guy talked to him for ten minutes and sent him packing. It doesn't mean he didn't get the job, but . . ."

"Yes it does," Jake says.

"It probably does. I can't find the soy sauce. But at least the whole world didn't come raining down on our heads. That cabinet is a mess, and I really need to—" She breaks off and sniffs the air. "Is something burning?"

"Is it dinner?" Jake asks.

With a curse, Rowan spins toward the oven and yanks open the door. "Crap, crap, crap! I turned off the timer and forgot about the tenderloin."

She grabs potholders, pulls out a roasting pan, and sets it on the counter. Poking at the meat, she declares it perfect—and herself "crazy."

Jake turns back to Emerson with a little smile and shake of his head, as if the two of them are in on a private joke. Anyone can see that he's crazy about his crazy wife, and who wouldn't be?

Rowan is wonderful. So is he. Longing to be a part of their lives, Emerson feels a lump rising in her throat. Why should she go back to California? There's nothing there for her now. Why shouldn't she just stay here in Mundy's Landing forever?

Welcome to the family . . .

Jake waves a piece of paper at her. "My sister sent the family tree."

"Am I on it?" She tries to make the question light, but it comes out sounding like someone's beaten it out of her.

"You're probably too young, but I bet your dad is."

"Can I see?"

Rowan steps in. "I can finish the dressing. Why don't you guys go look at that in my office?"

"Are you sure?"

"Positive. I've got everything in control here."

Emerson doubts that, but Jake is already on his way out of the room, and she follows, eager to see if the key to her past lies in his grandfather's notes.

"Don't forget your wine." Rowan hands it to her. "I'll holler when dinner is ready. You can close the door so no one interrupts you."

Reminded that Sully might very well interrupt, summoning her to the morgue to view Roy's body, Emerson impulsively does something she hopes she won't later regret.

It's only for a little while, she tells herself as she turns off her cell phone. *Just until I can find out the truth and figure out where I go from here.*

"Deirdre Mundy was strangled with a rope?" Sully is incredulous. "Don't tell me there was a hangman note."

"Not mentioned in the case files. It took a while for LAPD to ID her—no central missing persons database back then."

"No DNA testing, either. They were sure the victim was Deirdre?"

"She had one blue eye and one gray eye. That's how they eventually made the connection."

"Like Emerson." Sully jots it down.

"Like Emerson. The parents, Artie and Lili, flew out west, confirmed the victim in the morgue was their daughter, and brought her home. She's buried in the family plot in Philly, according to her obituary. Oh, and something else about that . . ."

"Yes?"

"The obit doesn't mention she even *had* a daughter."

"You said they were wealthy society people. They probably didn't want to publish something like that."

"Or they didn't know about it."

"What makes you say that?"

"There's no mention of a pregnancy in the missing persons case files. That's not the kind of detail you keep from the police if you're desperate to find your daughter. She found out she was pregnant and took off so that she wouldn't have to tell her parents. Happens all the time."

"Maybe she really did leave Emerson and her father. Maybe she was killed the night she took off, and Jerry never knew what happened to her."

"That's hard to believe. She was found a few miles from his house, decent neighborhood. It was big news."

"Maybe he missed it."

"Maybe. But he still never contacted Deirdre's parents to tell them they had a granddaughter."

"And he never told Emerson about her family in Philadelphia. She told me her father was all she had."

"Except he possibly wasn't her father."

"Except he told her he was," Sully returns, writing notes, shaking her head sadly.

She'd been thinking Emerson was lying, but it turns out everything Emerson herself believes about her past is a lie, right down to her own first name. Three homicides with a similar MO—strangulation by a noose—might indicate that the same person who killed her mother had resurfaced decades later to do the same to her father and fiancé.

It's an unlikely scenario, but one she has to consider.

"For all we know, Didi Mundy wasn't a runaway," she muses. "Maybe she was abducted."

"I don't know if I'd go that far. There were quite a few reports about a girl matching her description spotted in the bus terminal in Philly the night she disappeared, and a bus driver remembered that she took a Greyhound to the Port Authority in New York."

"Just like a gazillion other runaways. Okay, still . . . Jerry passed his dead cousin's daughter off as his own. There's a lot more to this story."

"You're thinking what I'm thinking," Barnes says.

"I sure as hell am."

Could Jerry Mundy have killed Didi?

"I don't suppose you found possible solutions for that hangman puzzle that would tie this all together?" she asks Barnes.

"You mean blank-blank-N-E words? Sorry. I'll keep looking."

She thanks Barnes, hangs up, and prepares to call Emerson. She won't tell her over the phone that her mother is dead and her father is, at the very least, not the man she thought he was. No, she'll pick her up, take her to the morgue, and wait to break the news until after she's identified Roy's body.

If her father and Roy—and her mother, too—were murdered, then her own life might be in danger.

Who, Sully wonders as she dials the number, would have a reason to kill the people closest to her? Her mother, her father, her fiancé . . .

Only when the phone rings right into voice mail does a terrible possibility enter her head.

She hangs up without leaving a message.

4th December 1676

Dear Jeremiah:

In the wee hours this morning, as a harsh wind blew from the west and the season's first snowfall blanketed our little village, I found myself weeping violently in our marital bed. My Benjamin begged me to tell him why.

As I lay there in the dark, I could not unsee the gaunt, sunken faces of our parents and sister. Do you recall that Charity's hair dropped out in clumps? That Father's skin grew sallow, and Mother's hands were rough and gnarled, no longer soft and gentle. Her fingers wasted into claws, even her thumb too thin to wear the gimmal ring she cherished.

Do you remember how she sobbed the day she realized it had slipped from her skeletal hand and been lost? How we searched and searched the room in vain?

'Twas on that day, Jeremiah, that I believe our Mother slipped into madness.

I am often able to put such dark thoughts from my mind. When you were here with me, I could purge my soul to your ears. Now you are gone, and I have borne the burden alone for too long.

I now take pen to paper confess that I did this morning betray part of our secret to Benjamin. While I did not dare reveal his brother's role in our trials, nor that William had chosen a cowardly, frozen death, I told him of our parents' terror as our grisly supply of human flesh ran low when the colony had dwindled to only seven of us.

I told him Anne Blake became, in our parents' eyes, our final hope—our last possible source of sustenance.

I did not say that I am sure Anne's life might have

been spared, had his own brother not become suspicious of Father's intent on the eve he visited to persuade him to nobly offer himself.

If only William had volunteered to lay down his pitiful life to save us all. He was dying anyway. As a bachelor, he would leave no one to grieve. Instead, he took flight into the blizzard like a cowardly rabbit fleeing the hunter.

Is it any wonder that Mother flew into a fury, knowing that William had surely perished alone in the wilderness? And for naught. His useless, frozen waste of flesh might have fed our family for a month, and your Anne might have been spared on that terrible night.

As I reflect, Jeremiah, I cannot blame our parents' actions. All those weeks, as our companions became stricken and died, we were provided with protein. When that supply had been exhausted, the only way we might live was for another to be sacrificed.

Yet I can imagine the anguish you felt when Father commanded you to accompany him to the Barkers' abode where Anne was staying. I pity you for the beating you received at your refusal.

I told Benjamin of the blood that stained your clothing where the whip shredded the fabric to wound your tender flesh. I recounted your despair when your willingness to sacrifice yourself instead fell upon deaf ears. How could any of us have devoured the flesh of one of our own? For that reason, it had to be Anne.

Even then, I could not bear the look in your eyes when Mother snatched up the blade and went along in your place.

Hearing your anguished sobs, I convinced myself, and our sister, that you, too, had gone mad.

Benjamin comforted me as I described how Mother

and Father returned with their murdered bounty. Anne was a kind, gentle soul. She did not deserve to die. Yet, my husband now assures me, neither did we.

I shall never forget the hideous moment when Mother made the dreadful discovery—that her own gimmal ring was on Anne's finger. That you had given a servant girl our mother's cherished heirloom, meant for your bride.

I did not understand Mother's anguish, whilst savagely butchering the girl's flesh for the cauldron, when she saw the fetus. I did not understand, then, that it was your child growing in Anne's womb. That the stew Mother made that day, the very nourishment that saved our lives, was of our own flesh after all.

I remember that you refused to partake, that they held you down and forced you to swallow. For your own good, they said. If you did not eat, you would not live.

I am thankful, Jeremiah, that you came to your senses and survived. 'Twas not long after that the snows abated, and Father was able to hunt and provide for us until the ship came.

This is where I concluded the tale I told my husband. He bore it with great sorrow, and without judgment.

No matter when or whether we meet again, or what happens to us in the years that lie before us, Jeremiah, I assure you that my Benjamin has given his word to carry our secret to the grave. We shall never tell.

Your sister,

Priscilla Mundy Ransom

Chapter 16

Rowan Mundy's home office is off the foyer, a surprisingly orderly oasis tucked behind French doors.

Jake closes the doors after them and turns on a couple of lamps. Though the sun is a long way from setting, its angle doesn't reach through the room's lace-curtained bay windows overlooking the shadowy front porch.

"Sit down," he tells Emerson, "and we'll see what we have here."

Feeling as though her legs are about to give out, she sinks onto the nearest seat, an aptly named fainting couch. She sets her cell phone on an adjacent table, wanting to set down the glass of wine as well, but she doesn't dare without a coaster. Instead she takes a sip, hoping it might settle her nerves.

Jake sits in the cushioned leather desk chair, finds a pair of reading glasses in a drawer, and puts them on. Then he rolls the chair across the carpet, parks next to her, and holds the sheet of paper so that she can see it.

"This is my grandfather, Asa Jacob Mundy II. His father was the first Asa Jacob, and I'm the fourth."

"You didn't name either of your sons after you?"

"Nah, they have enough problems," he says with a

smile. "My grandfather's grandfather was Ezra Mundy, born in 1842."

So old Ora Abrams was right about that, too.

"You said you're descended from his brother, Aaron, right?"

Emerson nods, following Jake's forefinger as he traces it along the faded penciled lines. "Aaron had five children. Your last name is Mundy, so you were descended from one of his sons. He had three, but only two lived past childhood, Horace and Oswald."

Leaning in, she sees that Oswald is listed as having had a wife named Ramona—the teenage hired girl? He had one son, Donald Mundy, born in 1900, the same year of the marriage. Donald married his wife, Inez, in 1924, and had one child, a son named Jerry, born in 1940.

There he is. At least he's real—though there's no record of her mother, or her own birth.

"You've probably heard of Horace," Jake is saying. "He was pretty famous, and pretty full of himself, my grandfather always said—sorry. No offense, in case he was your grandfather."

"I'm not sure if he was. You wouldn't happen to know . . . did he by any chance have two different colored eyes?"

"Yes, he did. My grandfather told me that. His own father, the first Asa Jacob, was born the same year as Horace, and they were first cousins. They played together as kids."

"What about Oswald, Horace's brother? Did he have the same eyes?"

"No. Only Horace. He was the charmed son, according to my grandfather, although he didn't start out that way as a kid."

"What about Horace's sons?"

"He had three. Robert, Joseph, and Arthur, and they—"

"No, which ones had it?"

"Had what?"

"Heterochromia. This." She points at her own eyes.

"Joseph did not. I met him once, when I was a little kid. He looked almost exactly like my grandfather. Same bright blue eyes. Those run in the family, too."

The man she knew as Jerry Mundy also had bright blue eyes.

It means nothing, she reminds herself.

"What about Robert?"

"He went down on the *Titanic* long before my time."

"And Arthur? Did you ever meet him?"

"No. My grandfather said he used to come to visit his father when Horace was still alive, but that was long before my time. I did meet his son Artie and his family, though. They came for a family reunion once, back in the late seventies. We have pictures of that day."

Emerson follows the lineage from Arthur Sr. to Arthur Jr., born in 1935.

He had two children.

His older daughter's name was Deirdre.

Deirdre . . .

She can hear a faraway voice calling the name in her head.

"Can I see the pictures?" she asks Jake, above the roar of blood pounding in her veins. "Please?"

"Sure. Let me see if I can find them."

She watches him stand and walk over to the built-in bookshelves beside the fireplace.

Deirdre . . .

Can it be?

"Here it is." Jake walks toward her carrying a large album bound in burgundy leather. "This was my grandfather's. The family reunion pictures are someplace in here."

"When was it? You said the 1970s?"

"Late seventies—wait, it must have been 1979," he says, setting the album on the desk and leafing through it. "That was the spring my high school baseball team went to the championships, and my parents made me miss a game to be there. The reunion was in April. It was a hundred degrees out and humid, and they made us pose for pictures in every combination you can imagine. Individual families, generations of cousins, old people who didn't even know their own names, let alone who they were sitting with . . ."

He chuckles, shaking his head.

Emerson stands behind him, looking over his shoulder at the blur of old photos encased on sturdy pages beneath clear plastic sheeting.

"I was pissed off the whole day," Jake recalls. "We saw my local cousins all the time, and I didn't see the point in meeting a bunch of strangers who came in from out of town and were probably never going to come back. By the way, no one ever did—except you."

"Me? But I wasn't . . . I wasn't there. I wasn't even born yet."

"No, but your family must have been invited. Everyone was. Oh, here we go. Look, there I am . . ."

She leans in to see a glowering young man in a large group shot. "Wow." Jake lifts the plastic to remove the picture and examine it more closely, adjusting his reading glasses on his nose and holding it up to the desk lamp. "This could be my son Braden. People always say he looks like me, but I usually don't see it."

Emerson hears him talking, but the words don't register. She's scanning the other photos on the page, searching, searching . . .

There.

Two faces jump out at her from a candid, so vividly familiar that the air is squashed from her body.

They're sitting in webbed lawn chairs under a tree—a young girl and a middle-aged man. He has long sideburns, but his blue eyes are unmistakable, and the girl . . .

The girl . . .

"Jake!" His name escapes her like a high-pitched cry for help. Maybe it is.

"What's wrong?"

"Who are they?"

He looks at her, startled, and then down at the photo she's pointing to.

"Oh! I thought you were—"

"Who are they?" she asks again, more urgently.

"I don't know. The names are probably on the back. Let's see." He sets aside the picture he was holding with maddening, painstaking care.

She clenches her fist around her stemmed wineglass and holds her breath as he removes the other photo.

"When something is over, Emerson, you move on."

"I'm not Emerson, Daddy. I'm Emily."

"Your mother wanted to name you Emily . . ."

But her mother was gone.

And after she was gone, Emily became Emerson.

She watches Jake turning over the picture and squint, trying to read the old handwriting. "Looks like it says cousins Jenny Mundy and Deirdre Mundy."

Frowning, he flips it back to the front. "That can't be right." Checking the back again, he chuckles. "Not Jenny. *Jerry.* It's cousins Jerry Mundy and Deirdre Mundy. Recognize them?"

Yes.

Her father.

Her mother.

She hears a thud, and feels something wet against her legs.

The wineglass—it fell from her hand, spilling on the carpet.

She stammers an apology.

"No big deal," Jake says. "It's white. It won't even stain. I'll go grab some paper towels."

He puts down the photo and hurries from the room, reaching back to close the French doors behind him.

He doesn't want me to hear him tell Rowan that something's wrong with me. Just like Roy. Just like . . .

Emerson hesitates only a moment.

Then she grabs the photo and goes straight to the French doors. As she pulls one open, she can hear voices in the kitchen. They sound concerned.

She opens the front door and slips away, out into the night.

So . . .

Tired . . .

So . . .

Late . . .

"Ora?"

A voice reaches her, so close, much closer than Papa's, and even Aunt Etta's.

But they were out there somewhere, calling to her.

Yes. Morning had broken with dazzling light, and she was out at Schaapskill, and grass was green, and they were there, they were . . .

They were telling her something.

I must . . .

I must . . .

When night swooped in, she lost them again. Now she's feeling her way back home in the darkness, all alone, alone . . .

"Ora? Can you hear me? It's Rowan."

Rowan . . .

Ah, Rowan, the youngest of Mickey and Kate Carmichael's brood, a pigtailed imp with a mischievous smile—missing her two front teeth, Ora recalls, and complaining that the tooth fairy had left her only a dollar.

"All my friends get two dollars, Miss Abrams."

"Two dollars? For a tooth? Oh my. Why, a few pennies could buy a sack of candy when I was a girl . . ."

When I was a girl . . .

Aunt Etta, showing her a secret drawer filled with treasures.

The skull . . .

"One day, Ora, you'll solve the mystery . . ."

The gimmal ring . . .

"I've written it all down for you here, see, Aurora? So that you'll know . . ."

You'll know . . .

You're the only one who knows . . .

About the ring, the skull, but there's something else, something else . . .

Go back. Tell them . . .

She doesn't want to go back. She's weary.

Rowan is here to listen.

If she tells Rowan, she can return to Papa and Aunt Etta and the beautiful, beautiful morning.

"I'm so sorry, Ora," Rowan is saying. "I had no idea you hadn't been feeling well, or taking care of things, until Emerson Mundy—"

Emerson Mundy.

Yes.

The rest of Rowan's words are lost in a loud, rattling sound from within—a gasp as Ora remembers.

She struggles to breathe, to find her voice, to tell them . . .

To warn them.

Clenching the steering wheel, Emerson navigates the curves along Riverview Road.

She'd been as stunned to glimpse that face in the old family album as she'd have been if her mother had walked into the room.

Didi . . .

Deirdre . . .

She was just a kid in the photo, but the face was unmistakable. She later—though not much later—sat at her Hollywood mirror and gushed to her little daughter about movie stars, sounding like a star-struck teenager . . .

Because she *was* a star-struck teenager.

Emerson's father really *was* her father; really was a Mundy. It just never occurred to her that her mother was, too.

So her parents were cousins, her father decades older . . .

He always did like little girls.

You know how sometimes, you need that one thing that's stashed way in the back, but you can't get to it without everything else tumbling out?

It doesn't only happen to Rowan, with her kitchen cabinets.

And Emerson's father wasn't the only one who wanted to forget her mother.

If she had ever allowed herself to search back in her mind for one missing item—her memory of her mother—other, darker things might come to light.

When Didi was gone, she cried at night. Her father came to comfort her, and he stayed, and . . .

Eventually, she stopped crying.

Stopped feeling.

Stopped remembering.

Until last summer.

Sully clutches her phone against the steering wheel as she turns into the driveway at 25 Riverview Road. Barnes should be calling back any second now with the information she asked him to find.

Yes, any second, he's going to confirm that the crazy idea that popped into her head back there on the Commons is just that. Crazy.

Sully parks on the road in front of the house, thinking of Rowan's nephew Sean, of Roy Nowak, of Emerson, her mother . . .

She slams the car door, possibilities screaming through her brain like the crows startled from the overhead branch. Fat and black, they lift with a flapping commotion and then settle again in the boughs of a nearby maple. Beyond its branches, a curtain flutters in an upstairs bedroom window, and she sees the shadow of someone looking out.

Come on, phone, ring.

She hears only the peaceful hum of a boat on the river far below, and a tree frog croaking in time with her footsteps along the walkway toward the front door.

The first time she entered the Mundy home, she discovered Rowan's sister Noreen, throat slit, scarcely alive. Rowan, too, barely escaped with her life.

The next time Sully walked through that front door, she found it hard to forget the bloodbath that had greeted her on that grim winter day. Three hours, a lot of laughs, and a couple of warm hugs later, she left by the back door.

"The front's for company," Rowan told her that night. "You're family now. Next time, come around back, and don't worry about knocking. Just come on in."

She always does. Always . . . until tonight.

For a brief, awful moment, standing on the steps, she imagines that something terrible has happened to them— all of them, the whole Mundy family.

"Rowan?" she calls, knocking. "Jake?"

Nothing from inside the house, but she hears a high-pitched cry somewhere behind and below her.

Just a cat, poking a curious head out from under the steps, offering an unblinking green glare.

The stray cat, the one who had kittens under the porch.

"It's okay," Sully tells her, bending to give her a pat.

The cat hisses.

Fierce maternal instinct—she's protecting her babies.

This morning at Valley Roasters, Rowan had offered Emerson a kitten. She said she was allergic.

Runs in the family . . .

What else does?

The door opens, and Jake is there. "Sully! Ro said she invited you, but she didn't think you were coming."

"I'm not here for dinner. Where did she go?"

"To the hospital to visit Ora Abrams. It's kind of been a . . . strange night."

Momentarily forgotten, the old woman's plight charges into Sully's brain with new implications.

"Can I come in, please, Jake?"

"Sure. Come on back to the kitchen. I can't leave Doofus alone with the food. I've got to go put it away."

Following him through the house, Sully is reassured to see the usual array of jackets and shoes, sports equipment and tote bags.

But in the fragrant kitchen, bowls, pans, and platters of food sit out untouched. Why is he alone, putting it away?

Sully's heart beats a little faster. "Jake . . . are the kids home?"

"Ours are here. I think Sean is at work."

"At the Windmill?"

"Yes."

"Isn't Emerson coming over for dinner?"

He opens a drawer and pulls out a long yellow cardboard box of plastic wrap, a blue one of foil. "She was already here."

"She left without eating?"

"Yes, she—"

"Do you know where she went? I haven't been able to reach her, and I'm supposed to take her to the morgue, and—"

"The morgue!" Jake gapes at her.

"She didn't tell you?"

"Tell us what?"

She explains about Roy, framing it as a suicide, not betraying her suspicions.

"Ro said Emerson was with Ora this afternoon when she collapsed. I couldn't believe she came over here for dinner like nothing happened—and now you tell me her fiancé committed suicide on top of it? No wonder she seemed so strange."

"Strange how?" Sully asks sharply.

"Jittery. Preoccupied."

"Anything else unusual?"

"She was anxious to find out about the family. We were in the front room, and I was showing her the family tree and some old pictures, when she just got up and left."

"Why did she leave? What did she say?"

"She didn't say anything at all," Jake says. "She spilled some wine, and I went to get something to clean it up, and when I came back, she was gone."

"She walked out of here without saying good-bye?"

"Yeah, and she took the picture she was so interested in."

"What was it?"

"One of the family reunion photos my grandfather took years ago, back in '79."

Seventy-nine. The year Deirdre Mundy disappeared.

"What did the photo show?"

"Just some random cousins. My grandfather wrote their names on the back. Jerry and Deirdre."

Struck by a frightful new possibility, Sully asks Jake if he's sure Emerson left the house.

"At first we thought she might have just gone into the bathroom or something, but then we saw that her car was gone. Why? Do you think something happened to her? Was she in some kind of danger?"

Sully shakes her head.

Emerson said she was afraid of Roy, but if he's dead . . .

Her mind's eye sees the bloated blue corpse hanging from the tree.

Definitely dead.

"What the hell is going on, Sully?"

Before she can answer, her cell phone rings.

Barnes.

Finally.

"I think I'm about to find out," she tells Jake, striding into the next room to take the call.

Driving through the night, bombarded by memories, Emerson needs a quiet place where she can process what she's learned.

Where do I go?

Not the inn. Sully will look for her there.

Not the hospital, either, though she'd intended to visit Ora later tonight.

That can wait. She needs to be alone, to figure out her next move, though she's pretty sure she knows what she has to do.

She's known ever since the truth came out last summer, as she sat beside her father's hospital bed.

He'd had a difficult night, and his breathing was labored. He needed heart surgery, but wasn't likely to survive the procedure. The doctor asked if he'd signed a DNR and whether his affairs were in order.

The answer to the first question was a solid yes. Jerry Mundy had made his wishes clear all along. He couldn't bear the thought of being helpless, incapacitated, a prisoner in his own body.

Ironic, Emerson thinks now, clenching the steering wheel harder as she slows the car at a fork in the road.

As for the second question . . .

Jerry Mundy asked for time alone with his daughter. The doctor and nurse left the room and she sat at the edge of his bed. As he spoke, she was forced to lean in close so that she could hear. Even when the words were coherent, she wasn't sure she grasped what he was telling her.

Her mother *hadn't* abandoned them all those years ago?

"Not you," he said. "Just . . . me. She wanted to leave me . . . take you with her."

Emerson sat listening to him telling her that her mother wanted her to have the perfect Christmas. How she spent money they didn't have on gifts for her little girl, running up debt for toys and a Cabbage Patch doll that had cost more than Jerry made in a month. They argued, he said, as he was outside in the yard assembling the rope swing Santa had left under the tree. Her mother said that she was leaving him, and taking Emerson—then called Emily— with her.

"I went crazy," he said. "I couldn't let you go. You were my world. You are my world. My everything."

Numb, Emerson listened as her father told her he'd flown into a rage and strangled her mother with the rope from the swing. Tears trickled from his eyes as he spoke of his horror when he realized what he'd done.

"I don't know how it happened . . . I just lost my mind. It was like some kind of crazy spell, as if I wasn't even there.

When I snapped out of it, and saw her . . ." His voice broke. "I loved her. I did. From the moment I saw her. I'd have married her right then, at first sight, if I could have, but . . ."

He didn't tell Emerson what he meant by that, but now she knows. A forty-year-old man and a fifteen-year-old girl—his cousin's daughter, no less.

No wonder.

He told her how he'd made up the story about her mother leaving, for Emerson and anyone else who happened to ask. There couldn't have been many inquiries. They kept to themselves . . .

Dear God, no wonder.

She slows to a stop at the fork in the road. A sign indicates that Schaapskill is to the right, off Highview Road. The road to the left leads into town.

She bears right, toward the sprawling oak tree with outstretched arms.

Many things—but not everything—fell into place that night last summer.

Her father swore he did it for her. That he hid the truth about her mother—hid her mother's body—for Emerson's sake. That he couldn't go away to prison and leave her alone. He had to be there for her.

"And I was," he reminded her. "I was there for you."

Yes. He was there.

Dammit, he was there. For her. With her. In the night. In her bed.

"But now you're grown up, and you don't need me anymore."

No, Dad. You don't need me anymore. Not that way. You haven't in so many years that I'd forgotten. Buried it.

But on that summer day at his bedside, the shameful brutality surfaced to roil and rot her brain, her gut.

"Thank you for listening," he whispered, closing his eyes. "Now, if I don't make it, I can rest in peace . . ."

"Or you can go to hell, you son of a bitch," she hissed, and fled to be sick in the bathroom down the hall.

Stepping into the Mundys' dining room to take her call from Barnes, Sully finds linen and china, crystal and silver—table set for seven—the family, Emerson, and Rowan's nephew.

Sean Chapman wasn't here the day his mother was attacked. But that doesn't mean he doesn't think of it, playing it over in his head, imagining himself the hero who rescues her and changes her fate.

Sully understands that. She's been there.

Some people whose lives are altered by violence do find their way back to normalcy. Others are forever tainted—some numb, some wracked with sorrow, some so angry that violence begets violence.

"Barnes?" she asks, pulling out her notepad and pen. "What do you have for me?"

"First, Roy Nowak. Well-liked, judging by his social media accounts. No blemishes on his academic reputation. No police record, unless you count a speeding ticket yesterday. He was doing ninety, eastbound on the Pennsylvania turnpike."

"No evidence of obsession, stalking, delusion . . ."

"None. But I'm sure he was concerned about Emerson."

A chill slips over her. "Why?"

"Did you know she had problems at work?"

"What kind of problems?"

"Erratic behavior. Absences. They gave her a short bereavement leave last winter and provided counseling services—looks like she was having trouble processing her grief."

Sully writes it all down. A parent's suicide is traumatic. This isn't surprising.

Then Barnes says, "She tried to finish the school year, but they let her go."

"Wait, they let her go? As in, fired?"

"She didn't tell you, either?"

"She said she was a teacher. She said she'd just come from a history teachers' convention in Washington."

"She'd scheduled that trip months ago. From there, she was flying to New York and then driving to Mundy's Landing. After she lost her job, she should have canceled the conference, but she didn't. She really was there, but she wasn't supposed to be."

"How do you know?"

"Group photos on a public social media page for the conference. She's in a few of them. I saw some snarky comments about her being a party crasher, that kind of thing. Hang on, I'll text you the link."

Sully's brain sprints back over what she knows about Roy Nowak.

Every negative detail, she realizes, was filtered through a single lens: Emerson Mundy's.

As Sean pulls up at the curb out front, Savannah is glad to see that the historical society is brightly lit.

"It looks like Miss Abrams is here after all," she says, having tried to reach her several more times. "I wonder why she didn't answer the phone."

"Maybe she didn't hear it ring from way downstairs. She lives on the top floor, and you said it was her personal line, right?"

She nods. That makes sense, although the elderly woman's hearing had seemed sharp when they met last night.

Sean tells her he'll come back here after he finds out what's going on over at the Windmill. She could tell he was concerned when the police detective summoned him, though he seemed to play it down—for her sake, or for his own.

He's been through so much. It can't have been easy to get a call from a cop, even though she assured him that it has nothing to do with his family.

"I bet another crate of booze went missing from the back room," he says now. "It happened a few weeks ago, and the owner questioned all of us. Or maybe Laura's lowlife husband violated his restraining order again."

"I really hope it's something minor." Something that doesn't directly involve Sean.

Twenty-four hours ago, she'd have had no problem envisioning him in trouble with the police, based on the way he looked, his attitude, and the direct comparison to his clean-cut cousin. First impressions are so misleading, she thinks as she gets out of the car with the fragile documents from Hadley's archives.

She watches Sean drive away, rounding the corner onto the town Common. Then she takes out her phone and looks at the text that came in as they were getting into the car.

It's from Braden.

Sorry about this afternoon. Hope Sean got you home OK. Will call later.

Maybe he will; maybe he won't.

Maybe she wants him to; maybe she doesn't.

Why, she wonders as she pockets her phone and walks up the mansion's front steps, does life have to be so messy?

Death, too.

She's haunted by what she found in the files today. All those terrified people watching helplessly as their loved ones starved to death, starving to death themselves, refusing to eat the human flesh that would have saved their mortal lives, but—in their Puritan eyes—doomed their immortality.

What set the Mundy family apart? Were they less pious? More educated? Suffering some diabolical DNA mutation?

It's long past the visiting hours that are posted alongside the door. Savannah knocks.

When Ora fails to answer, she rings the bell.

Still no response.

Deciding Sean might have been right about the elderly woman's hearing loss, Savannah turns the knob, expecting to find a locked door.

For the second time today, she does not. Ora must have gotten her message after all, and is expecting her.

"Ms. Abrams?" she calls, poised on the threshold. "Hello?"

No reply.

Savannah assures herself that it's perfectly fine to enter and close the door behind her. It is, after all, a public museum, and she's here to see the curator on official business.

She isn't convinced the old woman is hard of hearing, but she has mobility issues. It might be difficult for her to jump up and answer a landline, and certainly to descend several flights of stairs to greet a visitor. She's probably upstairs.

Savannah shouldn't feel as though she's trespassing, or—strangely—a sense of foreboding, as though someone is going to jump out at her, or something bad is about to happen.

For a moment, she stands motionless in the grand foyer, wondering if she should heed her instincts and get out of here.

But her instincts were wrong about Sean. Maybe about

Braden, too. And who wouldn't be feeling jittery, given the day she's had?

She crosses the grand foyer and starts up the sweeping staircase.

The house is quiet, except for the sound of the ticking clock and her own voice calling for Ora.

But then, reaching the second-floor hall, she hears a rustling sound in a windowed alcove behind her.

She turns to see a velvet drapery moving as though someone might be lurking behind it. Just a breeze, she assures herself.

Then she sees that the window is closed.

She bolts for the stairs, but someone—something—does, indeed, leap from the shadowy nook.

A large orange cat skids in front of her, nearly tripping her. She cries out as she grabs the banister, sparing herself a harrowing nosedive.

Steadying herself, and her nerves, she looks down to see the cat regarding her with feline disdain.

"You're right," she tells the creature. "I'm being ridiculous. Come on, let's go find our friend Ora."

Barnes is back on the line.

"I sent the link," he tells Sully. "Just take a quick look. Emerson was either acting as though she still had a job, or she was delusional and believed it. Either way, the behavior is bizarre."

"So Roy had a real reason to worry about her."

"And about himself, but maybe he didn't realize it. If she was unstable, and he followed her here, she could have snapped. She didn't tell him she'd been fired. He found out after she left California."

"How do you know?"

"I reached out to one of her teaching colleagues. Said

I was a landlord and that she'd listed the woman as a personal reference."

Sully nods—an old, favorite tactic they'd often used on the job together. "The woman told me Emerson had lost her job. Then she said Roy had called her Sunday, saying he couldn't reach Emerson and asking if she knew where she might be staying. The friend was shocked to hear Emerson had gone to the conference, and Roy was shocked to hear she'd been fired."

Sully's phone dings as she contemplates that.

"Wait, the text is here. Let me take a look."

She clicks the link he sent, and is taken to a site containing photos displayed beneath a purple and white conference logo and the headline WASHINGTON WHIRLWIND WEEKEND. A message at the top invites attendees to upload their personal photos to share with the group.

Leaving the screen open to that page, she presses the phone to her ear. "There are tons of photos, Barnes. Where am I looking?"

"About a quarter of the way down, look for the pictures from the scavenger hunt. She's posing with a bunch of people in front of a shuttle bus."

She looks for it, scanning captions and crowds of unfamiliar faces.

Scavenger hunt . . . scavenger hunt . . .

Some of the pictures are of famous locales—the Lincoln Memorial, Ford's Theater . . .

Some are of objects—a museum brochure, a MetroCard, a tote bag imprinted with the logo alongside an array of contents the contributor has labeled "goody bag."

Sully stares at that one in disbelief. Alongside typical convention freebies—a lanyard, a pack of pocket tissues, mints, a travel coffee mug—are two items that catch her eye.

Imprinted with the conference logo are a small spiral-bound notebook, about four inches by six, and a packet of purple-ink markers.

After what seems like an eternity, Emerson's headlights find the stone pillars marking the entrance to the nature preserve.

It will be deserted now. The old oak tree is there, waiting for her. So is the rope in the car trunk.

She can be alone in the dark, on the spot where her ancestors suffered their terrible fates.

She pulls over to the side of the road, turns off the car, and leaves the keys in the ignition.

Taking a deep breath, she opens the door—

"Ma'am?"

A voice in the darkness, accompanied by a bright, bobbing beam and footsteps crunching on the dirt road.

She isn't alone.

A uniformed park officer appears in the glow of his own flashlight, turning it away from the car so that it won't blind her.

"Sorry," he says, smiling. "The park is closed."

For a moment, she can only stare at him.

"Ma'am? Come on back tomorrow morning, all right?"

She nods, turns the keys, and heads back toward town.

"Emerson . . ."

"Yes," Ora hears Rowan's voice say. "Emerson Mundy told me that you can use some help around the house. She was concerned about you. You're so lucky she was there with you this afternoon. She saved your life."

"No!"

It takes every bit of her strength to utter the word. Depleted, she struggles to find another word, another breath, another glimmer of light here in the darkness, or Papa's voice . . .

Silence within, silence all around her.

Then Rowan speaks. "Ora, did she do this to you? Did she . . . hurt you?"

You must tell.

You must.

And then you can be with Papa.

She feels a hand close over her own, warm and strong, and for a moment she believes it's him. She sucks air into her lungs again, another precious breath.

"Ora, can you squeeze my hand? Squeeze it. Let me know you can hear me."

Somehow, she musters the power to squeeze Rowan's hand.

"Good. Good job. Oh, Ora. You must be exhausted, I know. And you just want to rest. I . . ." Her voice seems to choke, and then she recovers. "I promise you can rest. But I just need to know if Emerson hurt you. If she didn't, you can just . . . go to sleep. But if she did, squeeze my hand, so that I'll know."

Ora is tired, so very tired. She doesn't know if she can find the strength to take another breath, let alone move a muscle in her hand.

But then she remembers those eyes—one blue, one gray—the eyes of a madwoman, looming over her, right before the smothering darkness. She fought in that moment to free herself, to breathe, and she'll fight again in this one.

She squeezes Rowan's hand with all her might.

She hears a sob, and a whisper. "Thank you, Ora. You can rest now. You've been a dear friend to me . . . to all of us. I'll take care of everything for you. I'll feed Briar Rose, and I'll take care of your things, and I'll make sure your work continues on, and no one will ever forget what you've done for Mundy's Landing."

Mundy's Landing . . .

Those are the last words Ora Abrams hears before

Rowan's gentle touch is replaced by a firm, masculine, familiar grasp, and the darkness gives way to warm, bright light.

Papa.

Hand in hand, they walk home together at last.

July 10, 1979

Dear Didi:

    See? I told you I would write to you. I always keep my promises. I hope you will keep yours and come visit me. We can do all the things I told you about—go to Disneyland, see the movie stars' homes and the Hollywood sign, and stroll along the Walk of Fame. One day, I know your own star will be on that sidewalk. I'm sure you're the most talented young actress in Philadelphia. Out here, they will recognize your talent and see that you're something special.

    I've enclosed a SASE so that you can send me those pictures we talked about. My agent friends out here will go crazy for them. Just remember you want to look sexy, but not older than your years. You can even try to look younger, so that they'll consider you to play little girls.

    I'm also enclosing enough money for a bus ticket to LA when you're ready to come. That way, you don't even have to ask your parents to send you. Like you said, they'll get the wrong idea.

    In fact, you probably shouldn't tell them you heard from me. I love my cousin Artie, but I know how old-fashioned he can be. He treats you like a child. I will treat you like an adult when you visit.

    If you ever need anything at all, remember, I'm here for you. And if you ever want to talk to me, you can call me collect anytime from a phone booth. Hearing your sweet voice will be worth every penny.

    I hope to see you soon!

Love,

Jerry

"**W**here could she have gone? Any ideas?" Sully asks Barnes, still holding the phone as she gets behind the wheel of her car.

"She can't have gotten very far. What kind of car was she driving?"

"I don't know. I didn't see it. She said she rented it after she landed at JFK."

"I'll see what I can find out."

"Thanks. I have to let Nick know."

She disconnects the call to Barnes and dials the lieutenant as she drives away from the Mundy home. In the rearview mirror, she can see Jake still silhouetted in the doorway. She didn't take the time to pause and explain anything, but she could tell by the look on his face as she rushed toward the door that he knew.

"Colonomos."

"Nick, we need to find Emerson Mundy."

"Is she in danger?"

"She *is* the danger."

She explains, zipping along the road until she spots the sign at the fork.

Emerson would have seen the same sign.

"I don't know," Nick is saying in her ear as she brakes, wondering which way Emerson would have turned.

"You don't know? You don't know *what*?"

"I don't know if I understand why you're chasing her down. You don't have any solid evidence, Detective."

"I have the notes, and—"

"But Roy Nowak is already dead. Even if she killed him . . . she can't kill him again. What is it that you think she's going to do?"

"I don't know. But I'm the one who spent time with her, and my gut is telling me that something is off. We have to find her."

"Where do you suggest we look?"

"Forget it. I'm on it." Sully hangs up the call and veers to the right, toward Schaapskill Nature Preserve. A woman with an obsessive interest in her own ancestry would likely do the same.

The road narrows as it approaches the river, winding past the vast parcel of land where the Valley Cove Pleasure Park had stood a century ago. The spot had played a pivotal role in the Sleeping Beauty murders of 1916, and in last summer's tragedy.

Sully hasn't been out here in a while—not since the blustery March day when she came to watch workmen dismantle the last of the ruins and haul them away, including the abandoned icehouse.

It was there that she confronted the handiwork of a madman who called himself Holmes, along with ghosts of her own past. She couldn't save Manik Bhandari back in New York. Nor could she save every innocent life tainted by violence, not there, not here. But that time, at least, she wasn't too late.

Tonight as she drives past, she can see construction equipment parked in the field, now mown, that lies between the road and the wooded slope along the river. A developer is preparing to break ground on a new hotel on the spot. There's been talk of a riverfront boardwalk, an echo of the one at the old Pleasure Park that drew so many people—strangers—to Mundy's Landing.

They'll never learn, Sully finds herself thinking, before she remembers that she herself is an outsider here, lured by the quaint village and its friendly residents.

Up ahead, she can see the stone markers at the entrance to Schaapskill. She turns off her headlights as she rolls to a stop beside them. She opens the car door, one hand at her holster.

A bright light sways over the trees to glare in her eyes.

"Sully? That you?" a voice calls.

Herschel Milks, one of the park's security guards. Still wary, she asks if everything's all right out here.

"Busy tonight. What are you doing here? Is something going on?"

"Busy how?"

"Most nights, I don't see a soul. You're the second person to come by here after closing."

"Is someone in the park?"

"Nah, I told her to come back tomorrow."

"What did she look like?"

He does, indeed, describe Emerson, complete with a weird look in her weird-colored eyes.

"Weird how?" she asks Herschel.

"Weird like she was just . . . no good. Know what I mean? Is she up to something, you think?"

"Maybe. We're looking to question her. If you see her again, Herschel, you steer clear and let us know right away, okay?"

Sully gets back into the car. Her phone buzzes as she makes a U-turn, wondering where to go next.

Expecting Barnes, she sees that the caller is Rowan Mundy, and answers immediately.

"Sully?" Rowan sounds like she's crying. "Where are you?"

"I'm—where are *you*? What's wrong?"

"At the hospital. Ora Abrams passed away just now."

"Oh . . ." Sully exhales—not in relief, because she has great affection for the old woman. It's just that for a frightening moment, she was worried that this might have something to do with—

"Sully, do you know where Emerson Mundy is?"

"No, why?"

"Because she was with Ora at the historical society this afternoon when she fainted, and Ora told me that she hurt her—"

"*What?*"

"—and now Ora is dead, and I'm afraid that . . . I'm afraid."

Ora.

The historical society.

Sully thanks her and hangs up. About to call Nick back, she changes her mind.

She dials Barnes as she speeds toward town.

She's at least five minutes away from the historical society by car.

He's one, tops, on foot.

Barnes answers with a gruff "Yeah?"

"I know you're in some kind of trouble," she says in a rush, "but if you can take a risk and leave the apartment, I need you to do something for me."

She waits for him to tell her that he can't leave.

That he's in hiding.

That they don't work together anymore.

That she's chasing a crazy whim.

"Tell me where to go," he says, "and I'm there."

Emerson drives past the Dapplebrook Inn, where she, the spurned Oswald's great-granddaughter, could have locked herself away in Horace J. Mundy's sumptuous suite if things hadn't gone awry.

Instead, she pulls into the driveway alongside the historical society and parks around back beside Ora Abrams's sedan, and she wonders what other secrets the old woman might have shared, had she not collapsed at the sound of Nancy Vandergraaf's horrified screams.

Ah, irony.

Her whole damned life has been a series of ironic episodes from start to . . .

Not finish.

Not quite yet.

She wouldn't be here, in this situation, if not for the greatest irony of all.

Her father had made a stunning deathbed confession . . . and then lived.

After the surgery, the doctor told Emerson how lucky she was that he'd pulled through.

Yes . . . so lucky.

The patient was heavily sedated, intubated, recovering.

She sat dutifully at his bedside day after day, making friends with the nurses and orderlies who wheeled carts past his room, and sometimes into it. Carts filled with food, equipment, medication . . .

She knew what they had, and where they kept it, and how to use it.

When they were there, she spoke lovingly and sometimes teasingly about her father, and to him. She spoke about the strange concoctions he whipped up in the kitchen, and their nightly tradition of watching *Wheel of Fortune* together, and the arm-wrestling matches he never let her win. They said he could hear her, even when he appeared to be dozing.

She spoke to him, too, when no one else was around. In a low voice, she told him about the past—about what she remembered of their lives together.

Unable to answer, fat tubes clogging his throat, he could only stare at her, eyes wide, as she reminded herself—and him—what he'd done to her.

And to her mother.

With his sick, perverted fantasies.

With his lies.

With a rope . . .

A rope like the one that's coiled now in the trunk of her rental car. She stopped to buy it on the drive up from New York, just in case, just in case . . .

But it wasn't meant for Roy.

Damn him, following her here.

If only he'd stayed away when she'd told him she wanted to be alone. If only he wasn't always sniffing around, worrying, asking questions . . .

Maybe he sensed the truth about her father long before Emerson allowed herself to remember. Maybe Roy really was trying to help her. Maybe that was why he came to Mundy's Landing. To rescue her, save her life.

Instead . . .

But he didn't belong here.

She could have belonged. She'd finally found a place where she could make a fresh start. No one would have known about her strange, solitary childhood, or the emotional breakdowns that had plagued her this past year, after her father died . . .

No. No more lies.

After you killed him.

The idea came into her head that day at his hospital bedside, when he told her he'd murdered her mother.

The funny thing is, she'd already thought of it long ago, when they were talking about the historic execution of James and Elizabeth Mundy. He'd mentioned that there are worse ways to die.

"Worse than being strangled to death by a noose?"

"It's faster than you'd think. You fall, and your neck breaks, and it's over. Better than wasting away."

That, she knew, was what he feared more than anything else. The wasting. The helplessness.

She had promised she wouldn't let it happen to him. That if there ever came a day when he was suffering, she wouldn't blame him if he decided to end his own life. She agreed that she would do whatever she could to ease his way.

The day, when it came, didn't play out the way she'd first conceived it—with herself as the merciful angel releasing him from an agonizing plight.

By then, she knew what he'd done to her mother. By then, she'd remembered what he'd done to her.

She didn't want to end his suffering. She wanted to end her own.

She wanted him *gone*.

He was released from the hospital to "recuperate"—a synonym for waste away until you die, and they both knew it. He'd survived the surgery and the aftermath, never reaching a point when a DNR would come into play and someone—the doctors? God? Emerson?—could make a decision about whether he lived or died.

He lived, but the quality of living was negligible. He was wheelchair-bound. Couldn't stomach solid foods. His legs were covered in sores.

Insurance would pay for a home health aide for one hour a day.

"What the hell am I going to do the other twenty-three hours?" he'd blustered.

"Thank goodness you have your daughter," the hospital staffer said, handing him a clipboard full of papers to sign.

Yes, he would have his daughter.

She and her father returned to the house filled with secrets hidden behind closed doors and in dark, spidery nooks.

For several days, she did what was medically necessary to keep him comfortable, medicated, nourished, alive.

On the final day, she did what was necessary to kill him.

Perhaps he knew it was coming. Perhaps he welcomed it.

He was asleep when she injected him with the strongest sedative she'd managed to steal in her time at the hospital. She fixed the noose around his neck.

It was ordinary rope, purchased at a hardware store, though she'd have preferred the shiny plastic rope from a child's swing.

"You have to get stronger, Emerson . . ."

"How am I supposed to do that?"

"Lift some weights. Do some pull-ups."

She'd listened.

She's strong.

Strong enough to hang him and make it look like a suicide . . .

Just as she'd done with Roy.

When she called him back late last night, he said he was in Mundy's Landing, about to check into a hotel. He kept asking where she was.

She didn't tell him, but thanks to Sully, he guessed. She saw him drive by the Dapplebrook. He kept texting, late into the night, waking her from the nightmare about the gallows.

He wanted to see for himself that she was okay.

Finally, she told him to meet her outside. When he arrived, she was waiting, in a hood she'd hastily fashioned from a charcoal gray pillowcase, using the stolen steak knife to jab eyeholes. Waiting with a syringe filled with medication and the noose she'd planned to use on herself if she didn't find what she was looking for here in Mundy's Landing.

It happened so quickly.

I just lost my mind. It was like some kind of crazy spell, as if I wasn't even there. When I snapped out of it, and saw . . .

Perhaps she should understand, now, how her father could have done what he had to her mother.

How her great-great-uncle could have done what he had to his brother.

How Elizabeth Mundy could have killed—and eaten— the young servant girl who was carrying her grandchild.

That was the first of the many twisted ironies that had led her here, and the one that had sealed her own fate centuries before she was born. There must be something—in her brain, her chemistry, her blood—some violent compulsion, a trait passed from generation to generation along with the heterochromia.

We shall never tell . . .

Their terrible deeds may have gone undetected for the duration of their own lives, but Emerson had pieced it all together. She alone knew who they really were.

She'd come to Mundy's Landing bearing evidence of what had happened in 1666—that James and Elizabeth had *not* been executed for a crime they didn't commit. Their claims that they'd eaten only the flesh of fellow settlers who'd died naturally were supported by historical accounts. But no one had seen the letters Emerson had inherited.

They had murdered Anne Blake in cold blood.

Emerson had done the same to her own father.

And to Roy.

When she came to her senses in the shadows of the

Dapplebrook Inn last night, she found herself staring through tattered pillowcase holes at his lifeless body.

She panicked. Upstairs, in her suite, she deleted the telltale final text exchange from her cell phone and from his. Then she grabbed her suitcase to begin packing, knowing she had to flee.

But where could she go?

If she left, they'd suspect her. They'd find her. Punish her.

If only there was some way she could make Roy's death look like a suicide, as her father's had. If only she could link the two somehow to something else, someone else . . .

Staring into the bottom of her empty suitcase, she thought of the letter that lay beneath—the one Priscilla Mundy had written to Jeremiah. The one that mentioned the name of the pregnant girl he'd loved, the girl their parents had killed, only to face the hangman . . .

Anne . . .

Hangman.

In that moment, the idea came to her.

The local authorities are no stranger to serial killers leaving cryptic notes, or to copycat killers.

She wrote four notes, each containing a letter of the dead girl's name.

She crept downstairs and tacked one to the tree beside Roy's corpse.

She slipped the rest into the lining of her bag. If she offered one voluntarily, claiming to have found it with her father, she might be able to deflect suspicion.

She wasn't sure, at that time, what to do with the other two notes.

Then Ora Abrams collapsed at her feet after triggering the notion that her father was an imposter. Emerson instinctively did the right thing and called for help. But as the old woman drifted in and out of consciousness and she sat breathing the foul, familiar scent of age and squalor, she was back in her father's house, back to the lies, and the rage.

Only when she heard the paramedics at the door did Emerson realize that she'd taken the sofa pillow from beneath Ora's head and was pressing it against her face.

She threw it aside in horror as the rescuers burst into the room. Ora was still breathing when they took her away, but will she live? Does she know? Were her eyes open when the pillow came down? If she saw, and if she lives to tell someone that Emerson tried to kill her, will they believe her?

She's senile. And she's lived out her years.

No one would be surprised to see Emerson at the hospital, visiting Ora. She planned to go over there with the third hangman note in her pocket. This time, she really would be an angel of mercy, saving an old lady from the inevitable sad, slow decline.

As for the fourth hangman note . . .

In Mundy's Landing, she'd found everything she'd always wanted—roots, and the warmth of friends and family, and the sense of belonging somewhere at last. But the unexpected photo of her parents in the old family album had shattered everything. She can no longer live here—but she can die here.

The Schaapskill park officer unwittingly intercepted her fatal leap out at the hangman's tree.

Now, she parks the car in front of the historical society and presses the button to release the trunk with a satisfying pop. From it, she retrieves the hood and then a coil of rope, quickly, expertly, fashioning a noose at one end. She grabs the remaining length of rope and both hangman notes.

It hasn't worked out the way it was supposed to. For her, nothing ever does.

She finds the front door unlocked just as she'd left it.

Stepping into the foyer, she sees the staircase and balcony above.

It isn't the tree, but it will do.

She climbs the flight surefootedly and drops the noose over the rail, gauging the length. She looks around for a place where she can anchor the other end and sees a closed door behind her.

Stepping closer, she sees that the plaque on the door reads: Mundy's Landing 1665–66: Early Settlers Exhibit.

Ah, the final irony.

She finds herself smiling as she secures a length of rope to the doorknob and checks the noose again. It dangles about eight feet off the floor. If the fall doesn't break her neck, she'll strangle there.

Either way, it will be over.

The name of the first innocent will have been revealed.

The guilty will have been punished.

And—

She hears a creaking sound somewhere overhead. For a moment, she wonders if it might be the cat.

Then she realizes that it's footsteps and knows that Ora Abrams, like her father—like Emerson herself—has come home to die.

"Sean?" Savannah calls from the top of the steep flight leading to Ora's apartment.

As she waits for his answering voice, she looks nervously, guiltily, over her shoulder.

She should have left as soon as she found the door to Ora's private quarters ajar, and realized Ora wasn't here. But then she glanced out the window at the top of the stairs and saw the old woman's car parked in the driveway below.

What if something had happened to her? She could have fallen. She could be lying injured right now.

Savannah hurried into the apartment. She hasn't found Ora, but she's discovered something else.

Beneath a built-in bookshelf, a wide, shallow drawer is concealed behind a panel that matches the room's carved baseboard moldings. It's open, revealing an assortment of boxes in an array of shapes and sizes. Labels describe the contents of each, written in vintage penmanship—not as old-fashioned as the seventeenth-century script on the letters in her bag, but certainly not of this century, and maybe not the last, either.

Savannah was tempted to delve in, but that would be wrong. Instead, she was about to head back downstairs when she heard a noise below.

"Sean?" she calls again. "Miss Abrams? Hello?"

Poised at the top of the stairs, she listens for a reply, or movement.

All is still.

She must have been mistaken. She descends anyway, intending to check the rest of the house for an injured Ora Abrams. If she doesn't find her, she'll walk over to the Windmill and alert Detective Leary that the house is unlocked and Ora unaccounted for.

Or is that overstepping? she wonders as she reaches the second-floor hallway.

Maybe she should just—

She freezes, feeling a hand on her arm.

Turning, she sees . . .

Someone.

Someone whose face is covered by some kind of dark gray hood with ragged eyeholes.

Someone who, in one swift movement, puts a noose over her head and gives her a hard shove toward the balcony.

When the girl appeared before her eyes, Emerson was stunned.

Anne Blake.

Back from the dead, haunting the attic, come to avenge her cruel death at the hands of Emerson's ancestors.

The girl struggles, arched backward, the balcony banister against the small of her back. Her feet are crooked into the railing and her hands flail, trying to grab Emerson, grab the rope that tightens around her neck with every movement. Her abdomen is bared above the waistband of her jeans, muscles straining, no sign of Jeremiah's child growing in her womb.

Emerson shoves a piece of paper into her front pocket—the hangman puzzle and word diagram showing only the first of four letters, an A.

"No! Please!"

Straddling her body, Emerson sees that the knot is no longer on the left side of her neck, where she'd positioned it for optimum efficiency. It's shifted in the struggle, now at the back, not as likely to snap her neck and sever her spinal cord, making her death instantaneous.

It isn't Emerson's concern.

She pushes the girl's shoulders, feeling her wobble . . . wobble . . .

Then her pillowcase hood shifts sideways and she's blinded, eyeholes no longer aligned. She releases Anne to yank the hood from her head.

Gaining leverage, Anne struggles upright, again moving the knot, trying to loosen it with one hand as she reaches for the railing with the other. Emerson tosses the hood aside and lunges again.

Back, back, back Anne goes. As before, only her feet, wedged between the spindles, hold her on this side of the rail.

Emerson reaches down, grabs hold of one ankle, and yanks it free.

"No!"

Anne's leg swings forward, her body slips backward.

Emerson reaches for her other foot. The rubber sole rubs along the curved wood, coming loose inch by painstaking inch . . .

It's stuck, her shoe turned sideways, toe stuck behind one spindle, heel behind the other.

Time stands still, Anne poised in midair, dangling between life and death.

She screams shrilly.

"Help me! Please! Help m—"

Infuriated, Emerson gives her ankle another jarring tug—not toward her this time, but upward.

The shoe remains wedged between the rails, but Anne's foot is no longer in it. With a final thrust, Emerson sends her up, up, and over the edge.

She manages to grab on to a spindle, and it breaks her fall.

Then she goes down with a swoosh and a thrashing of limbs, the length of rope slithering after her. For a brief, terrible moment, Emerson wonders whether it will hold.

It does, lashed to the doorknob on the far wall. It grows taut as Anne's feet halt in midair two, maybe three feet above the polished hardwoods.

Emerson peers over the edge. She's still moving, clawing at the rope constricting her neck.

She shouldn't have moved the knot; shouldn't have grabbed at the railing. A hard, fast fall with the knot positioned to the left beneath her chin would have killed her instantly.

Now she'll strangle to death—a barbaric, painful way to die.

That's what her father said about her mother. He made it happen that way, watched it happen.

Emerson will not.

She grabs the other length of rope she'd taken from the

car—much shorter than the first, but long enough to do the trick. Her fingers tremble as she loops one end into a noose; as she pulls the other end once, twice, three times around the balcony railing before tying it in a firm double knot.

She stands facing the crystal chandelier suspended from a plaster medallion. Below, Anne Blake dangles, struggling, gasping.

Emerson fumbles for the pillowcase she'd tossed aside and pulls it over her head again, this time, with the eyeholes at the back of her head. She pulls the noose down over her shrouded head, and fixes the knot just below her jawline, on the left.

She swings one leg over the railing, sits, swivels to throw the other leg over.

From her pocket, she takes the yellowed pages that started it all, and the final hangman note that will end it.

Another gallows, and the remaining letter, an N.

Combined with the others, the name will be complete.
A-N-N-E

We shall never tell, Priscilla vowed to her brother.

But she broke the promise. She did tell—and paid a terrible price.

Now, so will I.

Clinging to the papers, Emerson heaves herself into a fast, forward dive.

The last sound she hears is the front door banging open below, a voice shouting a name . . .

Not her own.

Not Anne's.

"Savannah!"

Sully zooms back into town, replaying scenes as if she's trying to dissect a murky art house film with a cast of characters whose plotlines intersect, but whose motivations are unclear.

Emerson Mundy . . .

Roy Nowak . . .

Jerry Mundy . . .

Ora Abrams . . .

Barnes.

Barnes doesn't fit in anywhere, except . . .

He's here, and on his way to the historical society.

Please, she prays. *Please let him be all right, and please . . .*

Please let him be the person I thought he was.

"**S**avannah!"

The sound breaks through the frantic buzzing in her ears and desperate croaking in her throat as the rope compresses her windpipe.

Sean.

He's going to save her.

She isn't going to die.

She hears him shouting, moving around her. She feels his arms encircling her legs, pushing her weight up, up, trying in vain to loosen the tension around her neck.

He'd have to loosen the knot around her neck, or cut her free. But the noose is beyond his reach, and he can't see where the rope leads, trailing along the dim upstairs hallway.

There's no way, no way, he can do this singlehandedly or go for help. Not in the time she has left.

Her lungs are on fire, and she can't get any air, and her head is going to explode . . .

Cerebral anoxia.

Soon she'll be lying, cold, on a steel table beneath bright lights. Someone in a lab coat will peer and poke and probe, noting the signs of asphyxial death, thinking about what to have for dinner, whether the car needs gas, how to pack for the weekend away . . .

Savannah will be just another lump of flesh and bone. Tagged and embalmed, mourned and buried, remembered and, inevitably, forgotten . . .

Unless someone else comes along to help Sean save her. And no one is coming.

Rounding the corner onto Prospect Street, Sully sees an unfamiliar car parked at the curb in front of the historical society—driver's-side door open, lights on, engine running.

The front door of the mansion is also wide open.

Sully screeches to a stop, jumps from the car and springs toward the steps.

What if this—all of this—was an elaborate ploy to smoke Barnes out of hiding? What if—

But the first thing she sees when she bursts through the door, weapon drawn, is Barnes.

Alive.

Barnes . . . saving a life.

He's on his knees, performing CPR on a young woman, assisted by . . . Sean Chapman?

Sully takes it all in.

Rowan's nephew.

A cell phone on the floor beside him, connected to a call on speaker.

". . . on the way," a voice is saying—emergency dispatch. "Continue the compressions . . ."

A chair in the middle of the room.

Several serrated kitchen knives on the floor around it.

Papers scattered—old, yellow pages, crumbling at the edges.

A length of rope, frayed at one end, a noose at the other.

Sirens approaching.

Sully looks up . . .

And there, hanging from a second noose high overhead, is Emerson Mundy.

Her head is turned at an unnatural angle, neck broken.

"Come on, Savannah," Barnes says. "That's it. That's it, honey . . . come on . . ."

"Is she breathing?" Sean asks.

"She's breathing. You saved her, kid."

Sean bows his head with a sob, and Barnes looks up at Sully.

He'd risked his life for her.

If they know where I am, I'd already be dead. Or someone else would.

Yet he said it wasn't Sully.

"Who else is there?" she'd asked.

"In my life? Besides you?"

He never had answered that question, only told her—how many times?—that it's complicated.

There are always women, but for Barnes, those relationships aren't complicated. He hasn't been seriously involved with a woman since his divorce, unless his habits have changed since she last saw him. Maybe he's fallen in love. It's possible—anything is possible.

But—gut instinct again—Sully doesn't feel like this has anything to do with a romantic relationship. It's something else. Something with far higher stakes. Something connected to his past.

"You've been there," he said earlier, in her kitchen, as he ate the sandwich she'd brought him, and tried to explain why he'd taken money from Perry Wayland at his partner's urging. "You know how it is. Inner city cop. Us and them."

Yeah, she's been there. Young, new to the force, bonding with your fellow officers like soldiers in a war zone. You're in it together, protecting people who don't get what you do, don't care, don't respect or appreciate you. As cops, you're all fighting on the same side. You defend each other because you're the good guys.

And if the good guys make mistakes—hell, everyone makes mistakes—well, they're still not the bad guys. You've got their backs, and they've got yours. They're family.

"You okay, Gingersnap?"

Gingersnap.

There it is, at last.

He alone knows her well enough not to question her gut feeling about a case. He trusts her instincts, trusts *her.*

And she trusts him. Rookie or not, for Barnes, taking that money was out of character.

There's more to his story. When this is over, she's going to find out what it is. But for now . . .

"Yes," she whispers around a lump in her throat. "I'm okay."

25th December 1676

Dear Jeremiah:

It is with bitter tears and a heavy heart that I write to tell you that my husband Benjamin perished yesterday. He had gone before dawn to hunt a goose for Christmas dinner. When dusk came and he failed to return, several men went looking for him.

They found my beloved by the river, hanging from a noose in the very oak tree where our parents were executed. He surely did not die by his own hand. There were two sets of footsteps in the snow. Some unknown assailant came up from the river, took my husband's life, and went back the way he had come.

Benjamin will never know the sweet secret I was going to share with him on this Christmas morn. Instead, I shall reveal it to you. I have a babe in my womb, and I know in my heart that it will be a son. I shall name him after the two men I have loved most dearly. One is lost forever. I only pray that the other might return, filled with forgiveness, to greet Benjamin Jeremiah when he is born in the springtime.

Your sister,

Priscilla Mundy Ransom

Sitting across the kitchen table from Barnes, Sully sips a cup of hot tea. Full leaf, properly brewed for her by Barnes while she was swinging through the Dunkin' Donuts drive-through on her way home from the station.

The late night movie theater rush had come and gone. Twyla had long since gone home.

For Sully, for now, the investigation has concluded. The paperwork is completed. Savannah is stabilized in the hospital, Sean Chapman and Rowan keeping an anxious vigil.

Emerson Mundy lies in the morgue beside her dead fiancé.

They'll probably never know for certain whether Emerson's father killed her mother, whether he killed himself, or why—if he did not—Emerson would have.

They can only guess.

It wasn't difficult to uncover evidence of pedophilia in Jerry Mundy's past. Several incidents, throughout his twenties and thirties, involved inappropriate behavior around young girls. He was arrested in California, served time as a repeat offender, and was released a few months before he attended the family reunion in Mundy's Landing.

There were no incidents of molestation in the years after young Deirdre Mundy had moved in with him and given birth to a little girl.

Before leaving the station tonight, Sully made a difficult phone call to the recently widowed Arthur Mundy in Philadelphia. She informed him that his daughter had spent the final years of her life not on the streets, as had been presumed, but as a young mother.

"I have a granddaughter?" he asked incredulously.

A glimmer of connection to the daughter he'd lost, cruelly snuffed by Sully's somber reply, and the news that his own cousin was responsible for the torment the family had endured.

Sully didn't tell him the rest of Jerry Mundy's story—a fact that turned up in his California records. In 1996, the state passed a law that mandated chemical castration, upon parole, for repeat sex offenders.

By then, Jerry had been staying out of trouble for years, living quietly—with his teenage daughter.

He voluntarily sought and subjected himself to chemical, and then surgical, castration. Perhaps his dalliance with his young cousin wasn't the only incestuous relationship in his life. Perhaps he wanted to protect his daughter—from himself.

Perhaps Emerson was both victim and perpetrator, as so many are.

All victims of sexual abuse suffer guilt and shame.

A few also experience rage and suicidal tendencies.

There's no disputing the tragic ending to this case. Emerson Mundy took her own life, and at least two others. But where, how, did it all begin?

In her childhood?

In her parents' childhoods?

Or, as she might have believed, in 1666, when her ancestors James and Elizabeth Mundy murdered a servant girl?

It wasn't hard to piece together the hangman puzzle after Sully had gathered and read the pages of the letter strewn across the foyer floor.

A-N-N-E

According to Sean, Ora Abrams had given her remains to Savannah Ivers. She'd come to the historical society with evidence corroborating what Priscilla Mundy wrote in her letter. Ora hadn't lived to see the mystery solved.

Some mysteries never are.

Driving back through the quiet streets, Sully thought about what she wanted to say to Barnes. Knowing the words aren't going to come easily, no matter how well rehearsed, she clears her throat and begins.

"I want you to know that—"

"Wait," he cuts in. "Before you say anything, I need to tell you two things."

"Well, I need to tell you *three* things."

"Me first."

"What happened to ladies first?"

"Show me a lady, and she can go first."

She rolls her eyes, but is as relieved to hear the familiar quip now as she was earlier when he called her by her nickname.

"Go ahead, Barnes. Say it. What are your two things? I'm guessing one is 'I told you so.'"

"What do you mean?"

"You always told me not to get caught up in emotion when I'm on a case. This time, I did. I kept trying to talk myself out of suspecting Emerson. I bought every lie she told me."

"You weren't the only one. And you have a huge heart, Gingersnap. Always have, always will."

She smiles. "Is that one of the things you were going to tell me?"

"No. I was going to say thank you, and I'm sorry."

"Dammit! Those are two of *my* things."

He laughs. So does she.

Apologies and gratitude—mixed with a little attitude. All is right in the world.

"Before you tell me your third thing," he says, "I owe you an explanation."

"That's okay. It can wait till tomorrow. I'll make you some breakfast. Make that lunch," she amends, glancing at her watch and trying to swallow a deep yawn. Maybe her third thing can wait until tomorrow, too.

"No, see, that's the thing. I'm not sticking around. There's an early bus back to the city, and I'm going to be on it."

"I thought you were hiding."

"More like running scared."

"That doesn't sound like you."

"It didn't feel like me. But tonight, I remembered . . . I know who I am. I know what to do. I have to go back to New York."

"Is someone after you? Wayland? You don't have to tell me if you don't—"

"No, I do. Not the details—they can wait. Remember when I went to Cuba last fall?"

"With the reward money? What about it?"

"I ran into a familiar face down there."

Her eyes widen. "Perry Wayland?"

He nods.

"That makes sense. Back in '87, that's one of the few places in the world he wouldn't have expected to run into anyone he knew from back home."

"Exactly. Now that diplomatic relations are restored and American tourists are showing up . . ."

"*You* showed up. Lucky him. So he lost everything in the stock market crash, faked his death, and left the country?"

"Not that straightforward. I'll give you the short version. Back in college at Brown in the early seventies, Wayland got involved with a hippie chick. Well, not just a hippie chick. She was . . ."

Sully swallows another yawn. "Sorry."

It isn't that she's not interested in his story. But exhaustion is catching up to her.

"It's okay," Barnes says, "it doesn't matter about her. Key facts: She was mesmerizing. She was a doomsday conspiracist. Not marriage material for a blue-blooded kid from New York."

"But Kirstie Billington was."

"You remember her name."

"Even when I'm exhausted, I'm a brilliant detective, Barnes. So he graduates and he marries Kirstie. What happens to the hippie chick?"

"Off the grid. Probably went to live in a cabin somewhere."

"Or on an island?"

He nods. "She'd told Wayland to beware of certain signs that would mean the end was coming. Famine, plague, financial crisis . . ."

"Everything old is new again." Sully sips her tea.

"Right. Back in 1987, you had headlines about starvation in Ethiopia, about AIDS, and then the stock market crashed . . ."

"Doomsday."

"Wayland thought so. And he saw one way to salvation."

"Hippie Chick saves the world?"

"Hippie Chick saves Wayland. To hell with the world, including his wife and kids. When Stef and I found him, he was waiting to meet up with her. Apparently, he did.

They left the country, and that was the last anyone saw of them."

"Until you spotted him in Cuba. And now he's after you because you know about him?"

"It's deeper than that. And it isn't him. It's her."

"Hippie Chick?"

"Not just her. This is big, Sully. She's powerful. It's . . . a cult."

Wide-eyed, she asks again, "They're after you?"

"Not just me."

"Not just you, not just her—I might be brilliant, but you're losing me. What are we talking about, Barnes?"

"I told you there was a good reason I took the money that day." He looks her in the eye. "It wasn't for me. It wasn't what you think."

"I don't even know what I think. Why did you take the money? What—*who*—was it for? Who are they after?"

"I have the one answer for all of those questions," Barnes says. "My daughter."

Sully gasps.

He nods. "Yeah. I never told you. I never told my ex. I never told anyone, except Stef."

"You have a daughter?"

"Yes."

"And they're after her?

"Yes. She doesn't know I exist. But they know she does."

Sully reaches out and touches his hand. "What are you going to do?"

"Save her," he says simply.

Sully nods. "I'll help you."

"I know where you are if I need you."

"What about me? Will I know where *you* are?"

He swallows the last of his coffee without answering her question.

Sully watches him in silence.

He pushes back his chair, tosses his empty cup into the garbage, and looks back at her. "I never had time to change your sheets for you."

"It's okay. You can sleep in my bed again if this is your last night."

"No way, Gingersnap. I'm not letting you sleep on the couch again."

She walks over to him. Takes his hand. "Who said anything about the couch?"

Warily, wearily, they leave behind all the reasons they shouldn't make their way to her bedroom together, accompanied only by the reason they should.

Sully's third thing.

The one that comes after *Thank you*, and *I'm sorry.*

I love you.

Maybe she'll never get to say it, or hear it back from him. But at least she knows.

For now, that's enough.

5008

NEW YORK TIMES BESTSELLING AUTHOR

WENDY CORSI STAUB

The Mundy's Landing Novels

BLOOD RED

978-0-06-234973-6

Mundy's Landing is famous for its picturesque setting in New York's Hudson Valley—and for a century-old string of gruesome unsolved murders. Rowan returned to her hometown years ago, fleeing a momentary mistake that could have destroyed her family. Now, an anonymous gift brings her fears to life again. Soon everyone in town will know the past cannot be forgotten or forgiven—not until every sin has been paid for, in blood.

BLUE MOON

978-0-06-234975-0

Annabelle Bingham, living in one of the three houses where the infamous Sleeping Beauty Murders took place a hundred years ago, can't escape the feeling that her family is being watched. Having unearthed the startling truth behind the horrific crimes, a copycat killer is about to reenact them—beneath the roof of Annabelle's dream home . . .

BONE WHITE

978-0-06-234977-4

Emerson Mundy travels to her ancestral hometown to trace her past. In the year since the historic Sleeping Beauty Murders were solved, she and the village have made a fresh start. But someone has unearthed blood-drenched secrets in a disembodied skull, and is hacking away at the Mundy family tree, branch by branch . . .

WCS3 0417